TIM SHO...

EVEN IN DARKNESS

A HIGH WATER NOVEL

FOCUS
ON
THE FAMILY.

A Focus on the Family resource
published by Tyndale House Publishers

To those who feel trapped in darkness right now
. . . seeing no light, and no way out.
I've been there, my friend. There is always hope—
even when there's none in sight.

Even in DARKNESS

light dawns for the upright,

for those who are gracious and

compassionate and righteous.

PSALM 112:4

CHAPTER 1

Rockport Harbor, Massachusetts
Spring Break—Monday, April 17, 11:00 a.m.

Jumping into the ocean wasn't like leaping into a pool—except for getting wet. A pool held no nasty surprises. The ocean was full of them.

Even here, standing in full wet suit on the floating dock in the South Basin of Rockport Harbor, Parker Buckman felt that moment of hesitation from the place deep in his brain where survival instinct is king. That part that fired messages and questions at him. *Diving alone isn't smart. Is this safe?*

Parker knew that cleaning boat bottoms paid a lot better than mowing lawns. And he loved his new little business. Except the part about going underwater without a dive buddy.

Parker eyed the water around his client's sailboat. Whenever his imagination started with creepy images of what might be lurking below the surface, he herded them into a vault and locked the door tight. But those images always seemed to escape right at the no-turning-back moment when he stepped off a pier or a boat and let gravity do its thing. For three long seconds after he plunged underwater, temporarily blinded by the bubbles, all kinds of creepy images flashed in his head. This had prompted a new routine. Just before dropping into the water, he'd slip his dive knife from its sheath and have it at the ready.

His own boat was tied just three slips away. The twenty-five-foot Boston Whaler had once belonged to his employer Mr. Steadman. *Ex*-employer now, and still a fugitive at large.

Steadman's boat had been auctioned off ridiculously cheap, and it was Parker's now. The boat had never been named—until Parker became the owner. *Wings*. Right about now he'd rather fire up the 400-horsepower Mercury motor on the transom and take flight.

Parker glanced at the dark waterline on the rocks along the shore. The tide would still be going out for a couple more hours. If he didn't get to work soon, the water would be too shallow, and his tank might hit bottom as he scooted under the keel.

Stop thinking and do this, Parker. He shuffled to the edge of the dock until the tips of his fins hung over the dark water. He stood there staring, unable to see the bottom.

"Hey, Parks!" Parker's friend Harley Lotitto jogged along the granite-block wall of T-wharf, holding a leash. A chocolate lab trotted alongside him. The dog was dripping wet, and so was Harley.

Parker raised his mask. "You starting your own side business now? Walking dogs?"

Harley grinned and took the ramp down to the floating network of boat slips. The dog led the way to where Parker stood—like it knew exactly where Harley was headed. The dog jumped up—its paws resting on Parker's waist, tail swinging like crazy.

"Hi, pup." Parker guessed the thing was six or eight months old. Definitely under a year. "Whose dog?"

"No idea. Found her paddling in a circle just off Tuna Wharf. Trapped—with the leash stuck between some rocks. Can you imagine what would've happened when the tide came back in? I had to swim out to free her. She's been sticking to me like a tick ever since."

Had the pup fallen off a fishing boat? The dog shook, spraying saltwater in a three-foot radius. A short length of green garden hose circled the dog's neck. Both ends were connected with brass couplings like on a full-length hose. An eye loop had been welded to one of the fittings, and a metal Harley-Davidson logo dangled below it. Probably a keychain fob originally, but it made a tough-looking dog tag. A carabiner was clipped onto the custom collar—with the leash attached. "Crazy collar," Parker said.

"Right? Not some foo-foo thing. Pretty creative owner, I guess."

"The owner's name on that tag?"

Harley shook his head. "Not the dog's name either. Just a phone number—which I already called. Voicemail is full."

"So, what now?"

"I'll ask the harbormaster's office if anyone reported a missing dog." Harley knelt on the dock next to the dog and tapped the motorcycle-emblem tag. "Your owner has a motorcycle? I used to have a Harley-Davidson. Its name was Kemosabe. And I'm saving to get a new one." The dog fanned its tail like it understood everything Harley said.

The dog turned her attention to Parker. She nuzzled Parker's gloved hand, then dropped onto her belly. She hung her head over the edge of the dock, sniffing the air above the water. Her ears went straight back; she whined like she intended to jump in.

"Don't even think about it." Harley coiled up the slack in the leash. "I'm not going in for you again, pup."

A man wearing an expensive-looking suit stood on T-wharf, looking their way. He had shoulder-length hair and was shielding his eyes from the sun with a manila envelope. "Harley Lotitto?"

The moment Harley turned, the man headed for the ramp leading down to the docks.

"How does that guy know my name? And how did he know where to find me?" Harley rolled his shoulders like he was psyching himself up to play football. "You don't think he's from social services, do you? What if there's a problem?"

"Not a chance," Parker said. Victoria Lopez, the owner of BayView

Brew Coffee and Donut Shop, had legally become Harley's foster mom. It seemed to be going well. Pez was more cheerful than ever these days, and Parker had never seen Harley happier than after he'd moved in.

"What if he's been assigned to my case?" Harley stood. Brushed off the knees of his jeans. Coiled the leash tighter. "They can't take me away from Miss Lopez, right?"

By the look on his face, Harley was already imagining worst-case scenarios. Parker set his mask on the dock and tugged off his hood so he could hear better. Something about the guy in the fancy suit walking toward them didn't sit right.

The man's hard-soled shoes thudded noisily on the dock boards. The dog tugged at the leash like she intended to find out if the man were friend or foe. Harley held her tight, and the man stopped just beyond the dog's reach. "Harley, I'm Sebastian Kilbro, your uncle's lawyer. He gave me something to give you." He tapped the manila envelope.

Harley took a step back, like he didn't want to get near anything that had been in his uncle's hands.

"Maybe he's sending you a birthday card," Parker said. "A week early."

"He doesn't even know when my birthday is."

Kilbro pointed to the envelope. "Your uncle needs you to do something for him."

Harley stared at the guy. "Is he delirious?"

"He's completely lucid. And, I might add, trying to do something *good*. But he needs your help—and your friend's here. I presume this is Parker Buckman?"

Now Parker was pretty sure his face must have looked as stunned as Harley's.

"Your uncle says he has hard evidence—enough to put a very bad man in jail."

"Quinn Lochran." Harley spit the name out. "That loan shark who wanted me dead."

Kilbro nodded. "The district attorney is eager to work out a deal, but only if we can actually produce the evidence."

A deal? The DA could get Harley's Uncle Ray released from prison? That didn't sound like good news to Parker.

"I don't know anything about any proof," Harley said. "So there's nothing I can do to help even if I wanted to—which I don't."

Kilbro smiled like he'd expected that. "He *hid* the evidence and seems to think only you and your friend can find it." He waved the envelope. "It's all here in a letter from him, and it includes a special incentive for you. I'll be back tomorrow for your answer. When you accept, I'll give you the clue sheet from Ray." The man held out the envelope and shook it as if he expected Harley to take it.

But Harley stuffed his hands in his back pockets, still holding the leash. The lawyer stared at him for a long moment, then handed the envelope to Parker instead.

"I got no time for Uncle Ray's little treasure hunt," Harley said. "I'm trying to help my foster mom out. She owns a coffee shop, and there've been all these burglaries around town."

Every store owner in town was on edge. Harley was too—though he'd never actually said it. Parker knew that Harley kept a baseball bat beside his bed at night. That said it all, right?

"I suggest"—Kilbro smiled the way some do when they think they're a lot smarter than those they're talking to—"you boys *find* time. This is important."

"I'm not playing my uncle's game, Mr. Kilbro. Take that message back to him. I'm doing what I can to be sure the coffee shop isn't hit— and *that's* important," Harley said. "And Parker is going to help me."

That last part was news to Parker.

"You're not seeing the full picture here, Harley. This may well be a matter of life and death."

"Uncle Ray can rot in prison for all I care. This doesn't involve me— or Parker."

Kilbro chuckled. "That's where you're wrong, son. Every bit of correspondence that leaves the prison is read. Mr. Lochran seems to have eyes everywhere. I fully expect he has your name—and Parker's, too—even now, as we speak. He's now going to believe you know about some evidence that can put him in prison. You think he's going to sit back and do nothing?" He locked eyes with Harley, then Parker. "Here's a little free advice from a lawyer: Don't be stupid, boys. Just read the letter. Carefully. I'll see you tomorrow for your answer. But no pressure."

"Right," Harley said. "No pressure at all."

Parker stared at the envelope in his hand. Whatever this was about, he was pretty sure there wasn't much of a decision to be made. If what the lawyer said was true about Lochran, Harley had already been sucked up in this—and Parker, too. Right up to their necks.

The lawyer strode back to the ramp and up onto T-wharf.

"Do you believe that guy?" Harley took the envelope. "I say we look at this later. *Much* later." He folded it in thirds and stuffed it in the back pocket of his still-wet jeans. "You got work to do, anyway."

But they had to talk about it before tomorrow, right? This thing wasn't going to just disappear.

"So"—Harley pointed at Parker's tank—"you going to actually go *in* the water, or have you found a way to clean the barnacles and crud off the bottom of the boat from the dock?"

Parker stuffed a hull scraper and scrub pads into the mesh bag. Pulled the hood back over his head and tucked the ends inside his wet suit collar. Slipped his knife from the sheath. "I'm going, I'm going."

"I can see that." Harley inspected the twenty-eight-foot sailboat in the slip. "You keep telling me how great this hull-cleaning business of yours is, but it sure looks like there's a lot of stalling involved."

Shake it off, Parker. His friend was right. He'd never convince Harley to work alongside him this way. "I'm savoring the moment."

Harley read the name on the transom. "*Flight Risk.* Interesting name. How long will this one take?"

He'd done *Flight Risk* before. "Forty-five, fifty minutes." As long as there were no glitches and his arm injury didn't flare up. "Less if you suit up and join me. Think about it. A hundred and fifty bucks. We'd split it fifty-fifty."

"I got a job."

Working for Pez at BayView Brew was more than just a job. Parker's friend was totally invested in it, especially since the burglaries had started. "Think how much faster you'll get that motorcycle if you do hull cleaning too. Not to mention the fun—no . . . the total *bliss* this job brings."

Harley laughed like he saw right through Parker. "Maybe I'll stick around for a bit. I'd like to see what total bliss looks like. I'll time you— starting now."

Going in alone wouldn't be quite as bad knowing Harley was on the dock. Instead of jumping in, Parker sat on the edge and eased himself off the floating dock into the narrow space between the pier and the sailboat.

Immediately the water found his wet suit seams—and stole its way in. If going in alone was the number one downside to this job, the cold harbor was the second. Even with the seven-millimeter-thick neoprene wet suit, he sucked in his breath against the water—as frigid as the fingers of a corpse chilling in the morgue.

Harley knelt low and grinned. "Water a bit *icy*, Parks?"

"Just hold on to that leash." The pup looked way too eager to go swimming. "I don't want a dog jumping on my head." Parker reseated his mask and dipped his head below the surface to get a quick look at the job ahead of him. The growth on the hull didn't look bad. The keel dropped down a good three feet from the center of the boat, adding stability when the boat was under sail. Even with the tide dropping like it was, there was still room between the keel tip and the bottom for Parker to pass under it without his tank scraping. That's when he saw the wallet—just lying there on the bottom, almost directly under the keel.

Parker slid his knife back in the sheath at his calf. He let the air out of his BCD and eased below the surface feetfirst. He held his fins still as he descended to the ocean floor to keep from stirring up silt. He snatched the wallet. Brown leather with some kind of rubber band double wrapped around it, like the wallet was too stuffed to stay folded without it. Not a bit of silt or growth on the wallet either—like it had been dropped recently. He ascended slowly and spit out his regulator the moment he broke the surface. The dog's tail wagged like crazy.

"That was quick," Harley said. "Maybe I *should* join your crew."

Parker raised his mask. "Check this out. More perks of the job." He tossed him the wallet.

Harley stretched off the rubber band, holding the wallet low to the dock so Parker could see. "Holy moly!" he exclaimed.

The thing was filled with cash. Harley lifted out a soggy stack of bills and picked at the corners. "They're all hundreds. There's gotta be nearly *thirty* of them!"

Who'd carry that kind of money around on them? "Somebody's probably frantic right now, wondering where they lost this thing."

The dog sniffed the wallet, her tail slowing to a stop.

Harley tucked the cash back inside and slid out the driver's license. "Mike Ironwing." He angled it to show Parker the guy's picture.

The guy in the ID photo looked as tough as his name. "So what do we do?" Not that Parker didn't already know. But it was a little game they played sometimes. Ever since Harley had accepted Jesus back in November, he'd been as serious as Parker about doing what was right.

"I say we split the money down the middle and drop the wallet back in the harbor." The teasing in Harley's voice was obvious. "Finders keepers, right?"

Parker laughed.

"Or," Harley said, "I'll call the police while you're cleaning. I'll knock on the hull when they pull up."

Parker reseated his mask and flashed Harley the okay sign. "I'll get busy." The water in his wet suit had warmed somewhat now. He ducked back below the surface and pulled the scraper from the bag. A glint of light caught his eye. He spotted a couple of coins seesawing their way to the bottom from the other side of the keel. They kicked up a tiny plume of silt within inches of where the wallet had been. *What?*

Nobody was on the boat. So it had to be Harley, messing with him.

He'd climbed aboard *Flight Risk* and was dropping coins over the edge. Maybe Parker should surface on that side of the boat and douse him with water.

Parker dove deeper and grabbed the bottom of the huge, finlike keel. He pulled himself around it—keeping his belly tight to the keel so his tank wouldn't scrape the bottom. He looked up—and screamed into the regulator.

Mike Ironwing hovered above him, his back against the bottom of the boat by the base of the keel. Arms outstretched like he was waiting to embrace Parker. Eyes open—but as dead looking as a great white shark's. Black hoodie framing his face like Ironwing was the grim reaper himself. Except the reaper's face wasn't blue.

Parker gripped the keel, fighting to control his breathing. Ironwing's mouth hung open like he had been just as terrified as Parker. But no bubbles escaped. A few more coins trickled out of Ironwing's pocket and writhed to the bottom.

Maybe it was the moving tide. A wave Parker couldn't see. Or maybe there was a current Parker hadn't noticed. But slowly one of Ironwing's arms moved . . . like he was motioning Parker closer.

Parker totally locked up. Arms. Legs. Every part of him seemed welded in place. Only his brain was capable of movement at this moment—and it was racing at Mach 5.

His instincts—or whatever had warned him against going into the water before Harley had arrived—had been absolutely right. It was wrong to squelch that internal warning system.

Parker also knew he'd been wrong about what the worst part of his job was. It definitely wasn't diving underwater alone. It was what might be waiting for him when he did.

CHAPTER 2

HARLEY POCKETED HIS PHONE and stared into the water. His call to Detective Greenwood had been *interesting*. Maybe he'd tap on the boat to signal Parker back to the surface. His friend would want to hear about this conversation. Harley hesitated, reviewing the quick phone conversation in his head.

"No missing wallet calls, Harley. Hang on to it for now. I'll pick it up from you later today." Greenwood wasn't rushing right over, and Harley wasn't surprised. The cop had bigger fish to fry.

Greenwood had been laser-focused the last few weeks on all the break-ins on Bearskin Neck—the Rockport Harbor peninsula that was filled with shops and restaurants—and along Main Street. One or two businesses were broken into every night. Greenwood had been meeting with lots of owners, including Miss Lopez, who'd been open to every tip Greenwood offered to make sure the coffee shop wasn't hit by the "Bearskin Neck Bogeyman."

But Harley didn't love the idea of carrying around that kind of cash. "It's just that there's a *lot* of money inside."

"Tell you what," Greenwood said. "I'll move some things around. I'll meet you in an hour. How's that?"

"Better." Harley pocketed the soggy wallet. "The driver's license was inside. Want the guy's name in case he calls?"

When Harley mentioned Ironwing's name, Greenwood's tone changed. "I'm in Gloucester, but I'm leaving now. Stay put. I'll be there, twelve minutes max. Don't talk to anyone about this."

So what was *that* all about? Harley sat next to the dog he'd pulled from the harbor and scanned the parking spaces along T-wharf. He half expected Greenwood to roar up in his cop SUV at any instant.

Parker burst to the surface, eyes wild. He clawed at the pier and kicked hard, boosting himself out of the water.

Harley jumped to his feet and helped pull Parker onto the dock. He scanned the water. "Shark?" What was one doing in the harbor?

Parker shook his head. Spit out his regulator—breathing heavy. Was Parks shaking? Parker raised his mask and stared into the water—like whatever he'd seen down there might come after him. Even the dog looked skittish.

"You're *so* not selling me on this hull-cleaning business," Harley said. "It looks like you've seen a ghost."

Parker's eyes actually looked haunted. "I kind of did."

CHAPTER 3

ANGELICA MALNATTI—"JELLY" TO HER FRIENDS—stared at the heavy brass plaque that her friend Ella held. *Clutched* would be a better word.

"We *have* to buy it." Ella kept her volume low, like she feared one of the locals wandering the farmer's market might rip the thing from her hands.

Jelly had never seen this vendor here before, and plenty of people in Harley Park gravitated to the booth. Weathered boards, rusting anchors, and dozens of salvaged pieces from sunken boats dominated the space. A handmade sign claimed every artifact had been pulled from wrecks that littered the bottom somewhere off the snaking shoreline of Cape Ann.

"Seriously, Jelly. You think he'll love it?"

"Or hate it."

"I know, right?" Ella held it out at arm's length. The actual nameplate from his uncle's lobster boat. "This was screwed right there in the pilothouse. I remember it."

Deep Trouble. The name was engraved deep in the weathered brass. Small barnacles had started to attach themselves to the face of the sign in the eight months since the boat had sunk, making the thing look older than it was.

"Harley can hang it on his bedroom wall," Ella said. "Like a trophy. How he triumphed over his uncle."

"Or a daily reminder of a really, really bad chapter in his life," Jelly said. The sign was about as long as her forearm and as wide as she could stretch her hand—pinky to thumb. With all the license plates and street signs Harley liked to decorate with, the plaque would fit in perfectly. "What if it triggers some kind of PTSD reaction? His uncle tried killing Harley with that boat. The thing may give him nightmares."

"Or . . . the nameplate might help him sleep *better.*"

"Okay," Angelica said. "You might have to explain that one."

"Harley says God rescued him from his uncle. The sign will be a constant reminder of that." Ella raised her eyebrows in a hopeful expression. "We've been looking for the perfect birthday gift for him—and I say this is it. It's way more than we wanted to spend, but if I put this thing down, somebody will snag it pronto."

Angelica wasn't so sure. "*Eighty* bucks? You won't be buying art supplies for a while." It would use up every bit of Angelica's tip stash too.

"It's worth it. And we'll go in together. Fifty-fifty."

"That would be forty-forty, by my math."

Ella laughed. "Whatever. Barely a week until his sixteenth birthday. We haven't come up with a decent gift idea yet."

"We still haven't, if you ask me."

A man stepped up—maybe mid-forties. Work boots. Jeans. Pullover sweatshirt that had seen better days. An old Rockport Dive Company baseball cap with a red-and-white diver's flag and *Don't Drink and Dive* emblazoned across the crown. Weathered face with lots of stubble. "I'm Danny Miller. Diving instructor, salvage diver, and owner of the booth. You two young ladies fighting over the plaque? There's not another like it."

Ella hugged the sign. "It's for a friend. Any chance you can drop the price? We know the man who owned the boat, if that helps."

His eyes narrowed. "Ray Lotitto? The price just doubled. Actually," he held out his hand for the sign. "It's not for sale."

Ella held the thing tighter. "The original price is fine. We'll take it."

Danny shook his head. "He was no friend of mine. I don't wear this hat because I liked the guy. It's my *justice* hat. Every time I slap it on my head, I smile. It reminds me that what goes around comes around." He leaned in close, his face suddenly looking sunburned. "Ray was a python. A snake. As low as they get. He had a 'rule' for everything—but paying back his debts wasn't one of them. The nameplate ain't for sale at twice the price. No-siree-Bob." He reached for the plaque with both hands, like he'd pry Ella's fingers free if he had to.

Angelica had to do something. "Mr. Miller, please. Ray was no friend of ours." She stepped between Ella and the guy. "We're buying this for his nephew, Harley. Ray hated him. Tried to kill him with the very boat you salvaged this from. It will be Harley's *justice plaque* . . . a reminder that God saved him from his Uncle Ray—and all his cockeyed rules."

Something about Miller's face changed. Softened. "The kid who filled the tanks at the dive shop? Ray called him *barista* or *dead weight* or something like that?"

"Yes, that's Harley," Ella said. "And he's nothing like his uncle. He's quiet. Kind. He'd do anything for a friend, even if it would cost him big. But don't ever tell him I told you that."

The salvage diver gave a half smile. "He always topped my tanks off real good. Never shorted me. Helped me carry them to my van, too. He was a good kid."

"He's even better since his uncle went to prison," Ella said. "He works at BayView Brew now. You should stop in. He'll top off your coffee just fine too."

The man pointed at the oversize Navajo cross necklace around Ella's neck. "Care to trade? The necklace for the plaque."

"Family heirloom," Ella said. "Can't do it."

"Sounds like that plaque is a family heirloom too." He moved to one side so they got a better view of his display of barnacle-encrusted finds. "How about the steering wheel from the very same boat? I'll sell that cheap."

It was just a steering wheel from an old junker car adapted for use on the boat. A Chevy logo was inset at the very center.

Miller walked over to a row of anchors. "One of these is from *Deep Trouble*. Twenty bucks."

"Mr. Miller," Ella said. "Please."

Danny eyed the plaque in Ella's hands. "Eighty bucks still sounds way too cheap. I sucked up half an air tank unbolting that crazy thing."

"Eighty dollars will buy lots of air fills," Angelica said. "Think of all the treasures you'll salvage."

"And we'll even toss in coffee and a donut if you stop by the shop." Ella raised her eyebrows. "They'll fuel you to find soooo many things on the bottom of Sandy Bay. You'll need *two* tables next time you set up at the farmer's market."

The man growled, but there was no malice in it. "Eighty bucks. One cup of coffee. And *two* donuts."

Ella beamed. "You drive a hard bargain, Mr. Miller."

Minutes later the plaque was mummified in bubble wrap. Even if they ran into Harley on the short walk home, he'd never guess what was inside.

Grams shuddered when they revealed their find. She refused to touch it. "That boat should've been left alone," she said. "It sure put our Harley in some deep trouble. I sense it still holds some kind of evil for our boy."

"C'mon, Grams. Sounds like your superstitions are running a *teensy* bit wild." Ella leaned over and kissed her forehead. "Uncle Ray is in prison. *Deep Trouble* is on the bottom of Sandy Bay. Neither of them can hurt Harley anymore."

"I'd still feel a whole lot better if you walked that wicked relic straight to the Headlands and pitched it into the bay."

That wasn't going to happen—especially after they'd shelled out eighty bucks for the thing.

"We'll keep that in mind, Grams." Ella rewrapped the plaque tight and secured it with lengths of packing tape. She ran it up to her bedroom while Angelica did her best to get Grams thinking about something else, like joining them the next time the farmer's market came to the park.

Ella returned with her roll-aboard suitcase she used for art supplies. "I'm off to paint something gorgeous. I'll be back by dinner, Grams!"

Grams gave both girls a hug before they stepped out the door.

Angelica tied her sweatshirt around her waist. With spring break stretching out before her, she wasn't going to waste one minute of it. Ella would split off at Bearskin Neck to set up her easel out on the breakwater someplace. Angelica would walk to Back Beach and work her way along the rocks to where El was painting.

Angelica did her best thinking while on the move. Especially where she could talk things out aloud without risk of anyone listening in. Only the waves would hear . . . and the gulls . . . but they'd always been good at keeping her secrets.

Angelica's phone and Ella's chimed at the same instant.

Ella grabbed Angelica's arm to keep her from checking the screen. "What's your guess—who's texting? Harley or Parker?"

It had to be one of the boys. Who else would text them both on the same thread? "Harley," Jelly said. "Parker's probably still scraping the scum off some boat bottom."

"Agreed," Ella said. "But birthday boy will just have to wait. What could he possibly have to say that would be more important than enjoying this beautiful day?"

CHAPTER 4

THERE WAS NO WAY PARKER WAS GOING BACK in the water today. Not after what he'd just seen. Parker had tucked his gear in his dive bag, peeled off his wet suit, and stowed it all aboard *Wings* before Detective Greenwood arrived. He'd rinse the equipment later. He tugged on a pair of jeans and a sweatshirt, but he still couldn't stop shivering.

The moment Parker told Greenwood about the body, the detective led Harley, Parker, and the dog away from the North Basin boat slips and down onto the floating dock at the far tip of T-wharf. It felt more isolated here. Probably exactly what Greenwood wanted.

"After I call this in, T-wharf will turn into a circus," Greenwood said. "For now, I want to keep you boys out of this."

He asked Parker question after question. Did he see anything else suspicious? Besides the wallet and coins, had he noticed anything else in the water that looked out of place? Had he gotten a good look at the man's face? Greenwood picked the driver's license from Ironwing's wallet. "You sure this is the guy you saw?"

The guy's face was burned into Parker's memory. "Unless he has a twin, it's him."

Greenwood squeezed his eyes shut and nodded. "Okay. Give me a minute, will you guys?" He pulled out his phone and stepped away from Harley and Parker, but the floating dock wasn't big enough to go far.

Parker wasn't *trying* to eavesdrop, but he did find himself straining to hear.

"I think we lost a key witness," Greenwood said. "Ironwing." For a few moments he said nothing, but based on the way Greenwood nodded, the person on the other end of the phone was saying plenty. "Agreed. Definitely a convenient accident—or our boy is cleaning house."

Harley locked eyes with Parker for a moment and mouthed, *Cleaning house?*

"I don't think we were supposed to hear that," Parker whispered. Up until that moment, Parker figured Mike Ironwing had slipped off the dock or a boat, maybe hitting his head as he fell into the water. A victim of a tragic accident. But what if it was more than that?

Greenwood ended his call and hustled back. "Police. Ambulance. Search-and-rescue team. Coroner. All of them are on the way. I need to be there to meet them, but I want you boys to stay down here for a good five minutes or more—then leave like you know nothing. Got it? You're just taking this dog for a walk. And don't go back to your boat."

"What's going on?" Harley asked the question that burned in Parker's mind too.

Greenwood hesitated. "Okay, I'm going to level with you. Ironwing was a very bad dude who worked for someone even worse. The kind of people you shouldn't *ever* get mixed up with."

"Hold on," Parker said. "Are we in trouble? Some kind of danger?"

"Look, if the wrong person hears that you found the body, they're going to wonder if you saw something else. So I'd rather keep your names out of the news. I don't want you tangled in this."

Spring break was supposed to be about having a great time with his friends—and it felt like Parker's week was vaporizing in front of his eyes. Greenwood feared them finding the body could cause them trouble. And then there was that whole situation with Ray Lotitto's lawyer. *Terrific.* Two unexpected ways to ruin a vacation.

"Sometimes we see things we wish we hadn't. It happens to cops a lot," Greenwood said. "A counselor can help sort all that out. I'll give your dad the name of a good one."

Parker just wanted to forget everything he'd seen. "The last thing I want is to talk about it to a counselor. Or anyone."

"Tell your parents. And, Harley, bring your foster mom into the loop. But other than them?" Greenwood locked his lips with an invisible key and tossed it over his shoulder. "Tell nobody the victim's name until I get an official ID."

Greenwood patted the dog on the head. "That means you, too. Not a word."

"Now, both of you, give me your phones—one at a time." He held his palm out. "Unlock them first."

Harley gave Parker a questioning look but handed Greenwood his phone.

Greenwood's fingers flew over the keys. "There." He did the same with Parker's phone. "Now you both have a second number for me, and I just sent myself texts from your phones so I have your numbers. If you remember *any* detail, no matter how small it may seem to you, call me. And if you see something suspicious—something that makes your antenna go up even a quarter inch—you call."

Parker looked at the new contact. "Race Bannon. The bodyguard from the Jonny Quest series? I used to watch that show with my grandpa."

Greenwood smiled. "He kept Hadji and Jonny safe—and took down the bad guys too. I'm going to do the same."

It felt good to see Greenwood's confidence. Suddenly Parker wanted to tell him about the lawyer . . . and the fact that Harley's uncle had hidden evidence somewhere about another very bad man. He glanced at Harley—and pointed at the envelope in his back pocket.

Harley shook his head. That made sense, in a way. The note from Harley's uncle was a different problem, and Greenwood had his hands full.

Sirens wailed, coming their way. Greenwood started up the ramp. "Wait here like I said. Then disappear. I'll be in touch."

"What about Ella and Jelly?" Harley looked genuinely concerned.

"I texted them before you got here. I didn't tell them about the body— just told them to get here. They already know something's up."

"Keep it low key. Parker saw a drowning victim and got out of the water. You called the police. End of story."

To Parker, this felt more like the beginning of a story than the end. The kind of story he wouldn't want to be reading alone at night.

A very dark story.

CHAPTER 5

A POLICE CAR—NO, MAKE THAT TWO—flew down Broadway, sirens blaring. Ella Houston watched as they dashed past the farmer's market, crossed Mt. Pleasant Street, and whipped out of sight onto T-wharf. "What's *that* all about?"

Jelly smiled. "Maybe they got a tip that America's Most Wanted was spotted on the docks."

An ambulance zipped onto T-wharf. Jelly's smile faded. She got a look on her face that Ella hadn't seen in months—since she'd learned that Parker's nemesis Clayton Kingman had escaped from prison during that hurricane last fall. "Let's find out what's going on."

Exactly Ella's thoughts. "Parker was cleaning a boat in the harbor." *Just a coincidence, right?* Her stomach tightened.

They looked at each other. A message passed silently between them, and they both reached for their phones.

Ella read Harley's text aloud. "We got trouble. T-wharf. Get here."

They broke into a run. Why hadn't she checked the text immediately when it came in?

T-wharf was a madhouse. Cops everywhere. But it was the yellow *CRIME SCENE DO NOT CROSS* police tape that spooked Ella most. A sailboat tied in a slip was taped off, along with the ramp down to the docks and a huge section of the parking spaces along the granite edge.

"Well, they're not on *Wings*." Jelly's voice sounded tense. "I should have asked the name of the boat he was cleaning."

They slowed at the edge of a growing crowd of gawkers.

"Jelly." Ella pointed at the far end of T-wharf. Parker and Harley stepped off the ramp leading up from the floating platform—with a dog on a leash?

"Thank God the boys aren't involved," Jelly said. "What's with the dog?"

The boys stayed wide of the police tape. Like *way* wide. Any farther, and they'd drop off the edge into the North Basin. Normally the boys would be running to see what was up with the police. "Something seems off."

"For sure. *Wings* is down there," Jelly said. "But Parker isn't checking to make sure it's okay?"

Ella waved at the boys, and they jogged over.

"You had us scared for a minute," Jelly said. "Your text, and now all the police. What's going on?"

Ella couldn't keep her eyes off the dog. It wagged its tail like it was happy to be noticed. "Who's your new friend?"

"Not here." Parker steered the group off T-wharf to the park across the street. He stopped at the edge of the farmer's market. In less than a minute, he'd recapped the grisly discovery under the sailboat.

"Parker." Jelly looked as if she'd seen the body too. "Are you okay? Strike that. Of *course* you aren't. What can we do?"

"Nothing. I just want to forget it happened."

"Good luck with that," Harley said. "I'd be having nightmares for a week if I'd seen a dead body in the water."

"Harley," Ella said. "We're trying to *help* Parker."

"Is it . . . anybody we know?" Jelly squeezed her eyes shut, like she dreaded the answer.

Parker shook his head. "But don't ask us his name. Detective Greenwood asked us to keep a lid on that for now."

Ella could understand that. "They probably have to notify the family, right? But you've never seen his face before, right?"

"His face was *blue*," Parker said. "I'd remember seeing a guy with a blue face."

Normally that kind of wise-guy crack would've earned him a slug in the arm from Jelly. Not this time, Ella noticed.

"Tell them the rest," Harley said. "Technically, Greenwood didn't say we couldn't."

Parker seemed to be wrestling with that. "I'm not sure . . ."

"Hey," Ella said. "It sounds like you need the expert insights of a couple of *really* smart girls."

"Agreed," Parker said. "And if we ever meet a couple of really smart girls, we'll—"

Jelly didn't hold back this time. She gave Parker a punch in the arm, which seemed to loosen everybody up a bit. She snagged his cap and slapped it on her head. "Come on, let us help, Parker."

"Let me think this through, okay?" Parker looked like he wanted to say more, but clearly Detective Greenwood had told him to only reveal what was necessary.

"Take your time." Ella turned her attention back to Harley. "How does the dog fit into all this?"

"She doesn't." Harley told them the whole story—including his plan to drop the dog at the harbormaster office until he'd gotten sidetracked with Parker at the dock. "But obviously Eric and Maggie are busy with more important things now. I'll keep calling the number on her tag to find the owner. Strange that there's no name on her tag."

Ella knelt and caressed the soft folds behind the dog's ears. The dog had warm brown eyes that turned dreamy with Ella's touch. "You're a good puppy, aren't you? Somebody's missing you something fierce right about now, aren't they?" The dog, still wet, leaned into Ella, leaving a damp spot on her jeans.

The garden hose collar was unique, and the Harley-Davidson tag only had a phone number, just like Harley said. "Maybe there's no name on the tag because the tag *is* the name." Ella pointed to the motorcycle logo. "What if the dog's name is *Harley*?"

Jelly groaned. "Who'd do that to the poor pup? One Harley is enough."

Ella read Harley the phone number aloud—just to be sure he hadn't misdialed. He tried calling again, but no luck. "Losses come in threes, you know. It wouldn't hurt for you two to be extra cautious for a few days."

"Wait, what?" Parker shook his head. "You're getting way too superstitious, Ella. I love Grams, but she's definitely rubbing off on you."

"You boys could learn a thing or two from Grams," Jelly said.

"Absolutely true," Ella said. "Never discount the *code of threes*. First, a lost wallet. Second, a lost dog. A third loss *is* coming. What's next? Or . . . the bigger question?" She waited until Parker and Harley looked her way. "*Who* is next?"

"Well, some guy did lose his life," Parker said. He looked like he was about to say something else, but Harley held up his hand to stop him.

"They're right, Parks. But I'm thinking about something else." That haunted look shadowed Harley's face again. "One of us lost something— and it's big."

Now they were getting somewhere. "What is it, Harley? You can talk to us."

Parker seemed to be just as much in the dark as Ella.

But Harley just shrugged.

"Harley." Ella stepped closer, trying to get Harley to look into her eyes. "One of us lost something? Tell us so we can help look for it."

He finally looked up, a pained look on his face. And in that instant, she knew. "Is it me? *I* lost something?"

Harley toed the ground for a moment. "Yeah, El. It's you. You've lost

. . . your *mind*. If you really believe all that superstitious mumbo jumbo, your brain is—"

"You're *so* going to wish you didn't say that," Jelly said.

Actually, Ella was kind of impressed. Harley had set her up perfectly. She grinned. "Yeah, you're definitely going to regret that."

Parker slung his arm around Harley's shoulders. "I'm in total agreement with him."

No surprise there. A siren gave a single whoop as the coroner's van approached T-wharf. Parker's face clouded over. Harley's, too. The heaviness of the tragedy was back.

Jelly stood looking at T-wharf. "A drowning is a big deal—don't get me wrong. But doesn't it seem strange just how many police are there? I mean, if this was a car accident, even with a fatality, there wouldn't be half this many cops on the scene, right?"

"What if it *wasn't* an accident?" Ella looked from Jelly to the boys. "Either of you think of that?"

Harley's eyes darted toward Parker for an instant. *So . . . they had thought of that?*

"Okay." Parker glanced over his shoulder. "There's more to our story." He quickly relayed what they'd overheard of Greenwood's phone conversation. "So, yeah . . . we both got the feeling this was no accident. And the victim sounds like one nasty character. That's why Greenwood wants to keep our names out of this. To *protect* us."

Jelly groaned. "That does *not* sound good."

Clearly the boys had told them what they knew, except for the victim's name. Ella wanted to say everything was going to be okay. But she wasn't so sure she believed that. She needed to talk to Jelly. Together they'd figure out some way to help.

"I should get back." Harley bent down to talk to the dog. "You want to meet Miss Lopez?"

Seeing Harley talk to a dog? That was a first.

"She's your foster mom now," Jelly said. "Are you ever going to call her anything other than Miss Lopez?"

Harley shrugged. "She's okay with it."

Pez was more than okay with it. After Harley's former foster dad, Mr. Gunderson, had kicked him out back in October, Pez had secretly started checking into becoming a foster parent. The state approved her—and only then did the social worker propose the idea to Harley. Ella thought both Harley and Pez seemed so happy these days after the third-floor Crow's Nest above BayView Brew had become his.

"You'll like her," Harley said, still talking to the dog. "She's alone in the shop right now. How about we check in on her?"

To say Harley was merely protective of Pez would be underpainting the canvas. Since the burglaries, he'd stepped it up even more.

Parker shivered for an instant, as if back in the icy water. "I'm going home for a warm shower. And to tell my parents what happened."

They made quick plans to all meet after dinner. Parker took off at a jog toward his house. Harley headed the opposite way.

The dog didn't need any kind of coaxing to follow him. Not even a little tug on the leash. Ella thought you could tell plenty about people by watching how dogs reacted to them. Dogs weren't fooled by smiles. They could sniff out a mean streak—or a rat. A dog could sense something about the heart.

The dog trotted alongside Harley, looking up at him every few seconds. A large manila envelope rode in Harley's back pocket. It looked dry, so he must have gotten it after rescuing the dog. What was that about?

Harley bent down at the corner and spoke to the dog. He pointed up the street one way, then the other. Was he teaching the dog how to watch for traffic? "Are you seeing this?"

"I had no idea Harley was such a dog lover," Jelly said.

"I don't think Harley knew it either." Even as he walked, Harley grinned at the dog as often as the dog looked at him.

"El?"

Something about Jelly's tone was enough to make Ella look directly at her friend.

"Do you have a bad feeling about this—or I am the only one?"

Ella glanced back at T-wharf. The yellow police tape fluttered in the breeze, blocking the crowd from the crime scene. But somehow, the boys had already been across that line, hadn't they? "Yeah. I'm sensing it. So, now what?"

She was quiet for a long moment. "We find a way to help them— although I have no idea how."

Ella gave her a sideways glance.

"Don't worry." Jelly raised both hands. "I'm not trying to be their *protector*. I just want to be . . . a good friend."

CHAPTER 6

PARKER'S MOM HAD BEEN WORKING out of her home office all day. He tried to act normal that afternoon, but it wasn't long before she could tell something was wrong. Moms could be like that. It was their sixth sense.

"What happened?"

He took a deep breath, then started in. He began with the strange conversation with Ray Lotitto's lawyer as kind of a ramp up into the real news. She listened, wide-eyed, as he told her what he'd seen. When he got to the part about discovering the body, she'd stopped him and called Dad. He was in Boston for work—at the National Park rangers' offices near the USS *Constitution*. Mom put him on speakerphone and had Parker rewind the story.

When Parker mentioned what he'd overheard Detective Greenwood saying on the phone, his mom gasped. "Vaughn . . . could Parker be in danger?"

Parker wasn't so sure he wanted to hear the answer. And the fact that Dad took a few moments to think before saying anything wasn't helping.

"Parker, did you see anybody suspicious hanging around?"

"Not a soul."

"And you didn't pick anything up that might be evidence—other than the wallet?"

"Nothing. And the wallet went right to Detective Greenwood. Anybody watching would've seen that." *Anybody watching?* Parker couldn't believe he was even considering the possibility.

"And the blue face indicates the body was in the water for some time. Could've happened last night."

Right. If it was a murder, whoever did it was long gone before Parker showed up. And who knew where it actually happened anyway? "With the tide changes, the guy might have been outside the harbor when he hit the water."

Dad agreed. "I don't think we are in any danger."

We. As in the whole family. What happened to one impacted them all.

Dad asked a bunch of questions about how Parker was doing. And other than the fact that there was no way he wanted to go back in the water to clean boat hulls, Parker was pretty sure he was doing okay.

"I'll leave work a little early anyway. I'll see you both at dinner."

Parker and his mom kept talking even after they hung up. Obviously, she wanted to be certain he was doing as good as he reported. The longer they talked, the calmer she looked. Finally, she took a deep breath, smiled, and hugged him tight. She prayed.

"Harley's uncle is a horrible man, if you ask me," Mom said. "This letter to Harley . . . you don't know what it is he's asking of you?"

"Just that Harley will need my help to find some evidence he hid. But I wonder if helping Harley would just enable some scheme of Uncle Ray's."

Mom looked at him for a long moment. "It sounds like what you're really asking is how far do you go to help a friend."

Maybe that was it.

"We'll talk about it—with Dad, okay? And it might be an interesting question for Grandpa in your next M101 session."

Something new he'd been doing with Grandpa. Manhood 101—a weekly call with Grandpa where they'd talk about what it meant to be a man. Usually, he'd take *Wings* out into the harbor, cut the motor, and drift while they talked. He hadn't missed a single session since they'd started. "I'll do that."

A text dinged in from Harley. Parker read it, then held it out for his mom to see.

This letter from my uncle is driving me nuts. Haven't read it yet. Want to check it out together, since you're part of this? Meet at Wings in an hour?

"Ray Lotitto is a self-serving pig of a man who has no conscience," his mom said. "I don't want either one of you trusting a thing that snake says."

"First he's a pig . . . then he's a snake?" Parker smiled. "Make up your mind, Mom."

She gave him a swat on his seater. "Don't let Harley get manipulated by his uncle either, or it'll mean trouble for him. And be back by six."

Back by six? Easy. Keeping Harley out of trouble? Not so easy. Parker feared he was already in it.

CHAPTER 7

LIFE WAS WAR. And since war was good, life was good. Vinny Torino stood at the boat ramp waterline in the North Basin of Rockport Harbor. Across the basin, T-wharf was still buzzing with activity. People leaning into the yellow *CRIME SCENE, DO NOT CROSS* tape like that extra couple of feet would give them a better view. Vinny saw everything that really mattered from a hundred yards away.

Wars of any kind were fought for only two reasons. To stop someone from taking something you didn't want to lose or to take something away that belonged to someone else. One politician wants to keep his cushy job—and some young buck enters the race, intent on taking it for himself. War. One national chain fighting to keep its market share— while another strategizes to take it. War. Even one church determined to grow its numbers—by wooing members from other churches. Even that was a kind of war. Maybe a sort of holy war, but it was war.

Many believed war was only real when bombs and bullets were

flying. But those who didn't see *life* itself as war would eventually learn how wrong they were—but by then it could be too late.

Vinny slid a hand in his pocket and pulled out three smooth stones. Black river rock—the kind pet stores sell for aquariums. Each of them flat and rounded perfectly. He chose one and sidearmed it into the harbor toward the Motif Number 1 fishing shack. The thing skipped five times, easily passing the halfway point before disappearing below the surface.

Mike Ironwing had made two mistakes. Actually, three. The first time they'd met, Ironwing had threatened Vinny. Ironwing had basically said the two would meet again—and that Vinny would wish they hadn't. Declaring himself to be Vinny's enemy was a strategic error.

Even after Ray Lotitto went to prison, there'd been no truce. No peace treaty. No attempt on Ironwing's part to reverse his unofficial declaration of war. Ironwing thought he was the biggest, meanest guy on the block, and he obviously hadn't liked seeing that Vinny wasn't scared of him. Guys like Ironwing expected people to fear him. Given the chance, he'd have bushwhacked Vinny some dark night just to prove how afraid Vinny should have been.

Which led to Ironwing's second mistake. He'd underestimated Vinny. He'd assumed his little threat would ensure that Vinny would steer clear of him. He'd never guessed Vinny would make a preemptive strike. Ironwing had failed to put himself in his enemy's shoes, to anticipate what his enemy might be thinking. Or planning. Vinny had started planning the very day he'd first met Ironwing. Soon after, he came up with *Operation Clipped Wings*.

If Ironwing had been a little less cocky—and a lot more cautious— he would've seen how things were really coming together for Vinny. How he'd worked hard to cover his tracks while still planning for the future. And he would have recognized that Vinny was too close to the goal to let Ironwing's threat mess everything up. Vinny was a soldier on a mission—a soldier who'd learned to identify and neutralize threats plenty of times in the past.

Vinny's new business was going to bring in a whole lot of cash. If Ironwing had done a little digging, he might've had second thoughts about crossing swords with Vinny. He would've known the threat he'd made hadn't been taken lightly—or forgotten. He would have discovered that Vinny was the kind of man who'd plan to eliminate that threat. Ironwing would have known that he needed to either initiate a truce—or strike first.

Vinny winged another stone low over the water. It kissed the surface, took flight, and touched down again. The stone reminded him of the ways he preferred to wage war. Stay below the radar. Come in fast, strike, and disappear. His fights were often over before his adversary realized they'd even been facing each other on the battlefield.

Water had to be one of the most popular places to dump a body. In certain circles, there were all sorts of terms used to refer to a watery grave. If a person had *retired to southern Florida*, it meant a killer dumped their body in the Everglades. But up here, where the water was cold enough to turn a body blue, Vinny had his own terminology: *singing the blues*.

The coroner's van sat inside the yellow tape, the back doors wide open. Two men wheeled a stainless-steel gurney toward the van. People stood on tiptoes for a better look at the body bag. Rubberneckers held their phones high to get a clear shot, as if the gurney was a float in some parade. The coroner loaded the body and slammed the back doors of his van.

Ironwing's third mistake? He'd grown careless. Sloppy. Slid into a routine of going out for a walk at night before hitting the hay. He took the same route, at the same time, and didn't look over his shoulder nearly as much as he should have.

The night he took his final swim, Ironwing had looked happy when he saw Vinny approach him. Like he thought their meeting was random. Honestly, it looked like the guy was ready to break out singing some happy showtune. But Ironwing was singing the blues now. Vinny had eliminated the threat. And now there was nothing to stop his plans.

Vinny always liked to reflect on things a bit after a battle was over. Could he have done anything better? Had *he* gotten sloppy anywhere? Had he missed anything?

He skimmed the last stone across the water. Hit, hit, hit, hit, hit—and gone. Just like Vinny. Come out of nowhere. Hit your target. Disappear. He didn't think he'd made any mistakes when he'd neutralized Ironwing. And if by some chance he *had* missed something, he'd know soon enough. And he'd fix it. He'd come out of nowhere. Hit hard and fast. And disappear. With Ironwing gone, Vinny could focus all his efforts on his new venture, and anything—or anybody—that got in his way.

Cops still crawled around T-wharf like they expected to find some kind of lead. Not any more likely than for somebody to dive down and retrieve Vinny's skipping stones. Anyway, the police weren't anywhere near the spot where he'd actually dealt with Ironwing—or where Vinny had dumped his body. Vinny had been careful . . . and he was going to be okay. The two boys who'd found the body? They'd be worth watching. The detective seemed awfully interested in them. Which meant Vinny was interested in them too. Oddly enough, he knew one of the boys—Ray Lotitto's nephew. Ray had missed his chance to eliminate that kid last summer—and now look where it got him.

Strangely, the image of Victoria Lopez popped into his mind. The owner of BayView Brew Coffee and Donut Shop. For some reason, she had pinged his sonar—that part of him that sensed when someone could be a monkey wrench to him. She set off a warning alarm deep inside—but not in the way Ironwing had. It wasn't like she'd threatened him. He'd never even talked to her. There was just something about her. A strength. A *resolve*. And she was making noise about the burglaries. Actually, she was doing more than just raising a ruckus. She was organizing shop owners in ways that could spell trouble. So he'd watch her. Rank her in his little risk-assessment model. If she climbed into the red zone, he'd deal with her.

Life was good. Life was war. And war was truly good. He'd successfully pulled off *Operation Clipped Wings*. Would there be more battles? Vinny didn't doubt it, especially with Miss Lopez in mind.

Before this war was over, Vinny was pretty sure Mike Ironwing wasn't the only one who'd be singing the blues.

CHAPTER 8

WHEN SOMETHING GNAWED AT HARLEY, it took something physical to get his mind off it. He scanned the coffee shop dining area. He'd wiped down all the tables and chairs. He'd swept the floor. Locked the front door. Hung the *See You in the Morning, Sunshine* sign in place. But still, he couldn't shake the jittery thoughts in his head. The dog sat at his side like she was waiting for a work assignment too.

He eyed the manila envelope on the table, wishing Uncle Ray's lawyer had never given it to him. He didn't want to know what was inside, but he couldn't exactly avoid it, either.

He had to bounce this off someone, and he wished it could be Miss Lopez. He'd told her the bare minimum—that it was a letter from Ray—but not that his uncle wanted Harley and Parker's help and how that was eating at him. She had enough on her shoulders with the burglaries. She didn't need to carry Harley's baggage too. He didn't want Miss Lopez thinking he was more trouble than he was worth.

And if he wasn't going to tell Miss Lopez more, he'd have to keep this from the girls, too, wouldn't he? What if one of them slipped—or talked about it at the coffee shop when Miss Lopez was around? And honestly, he wanted Ella to forget he had a felon for an uncle.

Miss Lopez knelt down and held the dog's face between her hands. "What a gorgeous puppy you are." She dropped into some kind of baby talk, or was that the way everyone talked to a puppy? "Yes, you're such a good girl. Such a *good* girl."

The dog's tail wagged like crazy. "Miss Lopez would love having you around all the time. Would you like that, girl? Huh? Would you like that?"

The dog squirmed and barked.

"No bogeyman would dare break into our shop if you were here, would he?"

And he wouldn't with Harley around, either. That was one thing he could do for her. One small way Harley could pay her back for taking him in.

"You could be our very own guard dog." She still had that baby talk thing going on, which energized the dog even more. "And you'd be the best-looking guard doggy in town. Wouldn't you, girl?"

The dog yipped again.

She laughed and ruffled the dog's ears. "When your owners come for you, we'll give them gift certificates for coffee and donuts." She kissed the dog on its forehead. "Then you'll visit us—and we can talk more."

The dog seemed about as happy about that idea as Harley.

"A wonderful dog—and a dead body. You two boys couldn't have made more different discoveries today." Miss Lopez shuddered. "I can't imagine how awful that must've been for Parker. I'm glad you were close."

Harley was too—except for the fact that he'd been so easy for that lawyer to find. He stared at the envelope. Everything about it fired off warnings in his head.

"Want us to open that together, Harley?" Miss Lopez must have followed his gaze. She had that you-know-you-can-talk-to-me look going on.

"I'll open it when I'm with Parker—if that's okay." He had to downplay it a bit. "You've got enough to worry about. This is probably no big deal."

She eyed the envelope. "I don't trust that man."

"Me neither."

That seemed to satisfy her. A text dinged in, and Miss Lopez stared at the screen for a long moment. "Seems the girls are worried about you two."

"I didn't even tell them about the lawyer's visit."

Miss Lopez watched his face, like Ella did sometimes. Did she guess he wasn't telling her everything? It killed him to hide things from her, but he had to, right?

He'd learned to keep secrets from Uncle Ray. Where he kept the title for his motorcycle. Where he hid his money or the key to the shed. What he didn't keep secret, he lost. And somehow, he just knew that if he told Miss Lopez too much, he'd lose her, too. She'd discover the truth: He wasn't worth the trouble.

"Ella is asking if I can think of a way they can help." Miss Lopez looked at him. "Any ideas?"

"How about they don't talk about the drowning when we get together after dinner? Tell them to pretend it never happened."

Miss Lopez smiled. "I can do better than that." She tapped out a message and sent it off.

"What did you say?"

"I suggested that they pray about this whole situation."

No surprise there.

Miss Lopez's phone dinged almost immediately. "Sounds like they're coming over, hoping to cheer you up."

Normally, he would've loved that idea. But he wasn't ready for them to know about the letter. "I think I'd rather open this with Parks. Get it over with." Maybe after he read it, he could shred it.

"Well, you'd better hurry. They'll be here in minutes." Miss Lopez pulled him into a hug. "I worry about your safety too. You know that, right?"

He knew. Which is why he'd felt it was best not to tell her about what Kilbro said was in the letter. He picked the envelope off the table. He folded the flap over and creased it hard. "I'll be okay."

She motioned him upstairs. "Go. Grab your stuff and slip out the back. See you for dinner." Miss Lopez emptied the tip jar and put the bills in his hands. "All this came in this morning when you were working. Add this to the fund."

The fund. His motorcycle stash. At this rate he'd be saving for years to replace the one he'd lost. But he was making progress. He gave her a tight hug, wishing she could fathom how much he meant it. "Thank you, Miss Lopez."

She kissed him on the forehead. "Oh, Harley." She let him go and turned away, probably hoping he hadn't seen her tears. "Get going."

He bounded up the stairs to the Crow's Nest, the dog following right behind him. When Harley's dad was still alive and they were rebuilding the 1999 XL Sportster—the motorcycle later known as *Kemosabe*—Harley had a piggy bank in his room. Not a ceramic, for-real bank. Just something Dad made for him out of an empty gallon milk jug. Dad painted eyes on either side of the handle. The cap made a perfect snout, and Harley unscrewed it whenever making a deposit. Dad had written the letters *HOG* on the side—the acronym for Harley Owners Group. Dad said that the money was Harley's motorcycle-rebuild fund, and Dad was always slipping a little extra cash through the snout.

And Harley was going to be a motorcycle owner again. Same model. Same year as the one that Uncle Ray had stolen from him. That would take a whole lot more money than would fit in a milk jug. Harley had modified an old aluminum scuba tank to do the job. It had failed the regulation inspection, even though it looked like it was in great shape. Instead of it going to the dumpster, Harley kept it. The bottom had been cut off, and the rubber boot replaced. Nobody would know the tank had no bottom. It stood upright in the corner of his room—by the window overlooking Sandy Bay. He'd painted pig eyes on it and the letters *HOG*. The valve on top was only screwed on hand-tight.

Harley unscrewed the valve, rolled the bills, and stuffed the cash inside. Not exactly a piggy bank . . . more of a piggy *tank*. He smiled.

When he'd lived with Uncle Ray, he'd grown to become really smart with how he hid the cash he saved. Before he learned that little lesson, Uncle Ray would sniff out wherever Harley stashed the money and find ways to justify skimming it too. Since Miss Lopez had taken him in, he'd never worried once about money going missing.

When Miss Lopez had said the Crow's Nest would be his room, she really meant it. She let him hang his road signs. License plates. Every one of Ella's watercolor scenes. It wasn't like the Gundersons', where he could only hang what he could tack on the corkboard.

The Crow's Nest felt like home. And home was something a guy protected—especially when it belonged to someone as terrific as Miss Lopez. If the place was burglarized, there was nothing of real value in the Crow's Nest—unless they figured out the secret of his piggy tank—which they wouldn't.

Miss Lopez was the one he needed to protect. So far, nobody had been hurt in the burglaries. But then again, no shop or business owner had been around when their place was hit. Miss Lopez lived right above the coffee shop. Harley's room was one floor above hers. What if Miss Lopez was in the kitchen when the burglar broke in? What if she needed help and Harley didn't hear her? Harley had been thinking about that a lot lately, and a plan was forming in his mind.

Harley dropped the envelope from the lawyer on the bedspread. The dog did a sniff-explore around Harley's room, then curled up on the rug alongside the bed. Laid her head down flat on the floor.

"Don't get too comfy, girl. Your real owner is going to answer the phone one of these times."

She raised her eyes and eyebrows to look up at him, but not her head. Like she was determined to stay.

"Harley?" Miss Lopez called up the stairs. "I see the girls coming up the street."

Harley grabbed the envelope and his hoodie. "Let's go, girl." He bounded down the stairs as the chocolate lab shouldered past him.

Miss Lopez stood by the front window—motioning him to hurry. The girls would be knocking in seconds.

"Thank you," he said. He grabbed the dog's leash and lunged for the back door.

She smiled, but her eyes darted to the envelope in his hands, a slight worry line creasing her forehead.

He wanted to tell her she had nothing to be concerned about. That everything would be okay. But that would be difficult.

He wasn't sure he believed it.

CHAPTER 9

PEZ OPENED THE DOOR BEFORE ELLA KNOCKED. "Sorry, girls . . . you just missed him. He slipped out the back."

"Did he say where?" Maybe they could catch up to him.

"To meet Parker. He needed some guy time."

Jelly nodded. "Did he tell you what happened?"

"Plenty," Pez said. "Rescuing the dog. Parker finding the body. And everything Detective Greenwood told them."

"Did he say anything about some paperwork?" Ella pictured the envelope in Harley's back pocket.

Pez looked from Jelly to Ella. "He didn't tell you about that, did he?"

"Not a word. Soooo," Ella said, "what is it about?"

"Some papers from his uncle's lawyer. He hasn't looked at them yet. Stalling it off, I'd guess. I'm *really* new at this parenting thing, but I figure he'll look at it and tell me when he's ready. Right now, I've got to be okay with that."

Was she hinting that the girls should give the boys some space? Probably.

"He took the dog—which I thought was adorable. But don't tell him I said that."

"Well, he kind of was," Ella said. "Just watching him with that dog . . . I saw a side of Harley I didn't know existed."

"And it's probably best you didn't tell Harley I mentioned the papers, either," Pez said.

"So, now what?" Leave it to Jelly to get them back on track. "Both El and I have the uneasy sense that this is bigger than we even realize."

Pez nodded like she understood.

"This is so hard," Jelly said. "I hate doing nothing."

"Harley may just need some time," Pez said. "But that doesn't mean I'm going to sit back and do nothing while I wait for him to open up."

Jelly angled her head slightly. "You're going to pray."

Pez smiled. "Way ahead of you on that one, girl. I already started."

CHAPTER 10

PARKER WAS A BIT SURPRISED THAT the floating docks in the South Basin of Rockport Harbor had cleared out already. No police. No paramedics. No recovery dive team. And no coroner.

He jogged to the slip where *Wings* was tied and hopped aboard. He still needed to rinse the saltwater off his gear, but that would have to wait. Harley's text sounded way too urgent. He checked his texts again, hoping there'd be a note from "Race Bannon." Something like . . . *Confirmed . . . it was a drowning accident. Not murder. Nobody will be looking to question you on this. Enjoy the rest of your spring break!*

Yellow tape stretched from bow to stern on *Flight Risk*. Parker had no desire to get aboard that boat. And he was in no hurry to get back *under* that boat, either. He'd wait until the police removed the tape. Hopefully, not for another week. Or three.

"Parks!" Harley tore down T-wharf, the dog trotting happily alongside him. "Fire her up." He checked over his shoulder like he was being chased.

Parker turned the key, and the 400-horsepower Mercury outboard motor rumbled to life. He released the dock lines, keeping a watch behind Harley as he did. Still nobody on his tail.

Harley sprinted down the sections of floating dock. "Go, go, go!"

Parker threw *Wings* into reverse even as Harley leaped aboard. The dog kept pace with him, like this was all some kind of game.

Harley hunkered down to one side of the steering console, shadowed by the hardtop overhead. "The girls showed up. I barely got out in time."

"You *ditched* them?"

"They were coming to see how I was." He stopped to catch his breath. "If I hadn't ditched them, they'd figure something was wrong and start asking questions." He pulled the envelope out from under his sweatshirt.

Parker swung the boat around the docks and past the yacht club—right into the Outer Basin. He didn't cut the engine until he'd nearly reached the breakwater. He walked around the console and plopped down in the seat directly in front of it. "So you haven't even *peeked* at the letter?"

Harley shook his head and sprawled out on the bow seat. "I don't want to see anything Uncle Ray sends." He pitched the envelope to Parker. "Read it aloud."

The note was handwritten—like Ray had been in a big hurry too.

"'Harley, this is Uncle Ray. This letter is about life and death stuff. Stay focused.'"

Parker glanced up. Harley stared at the breakwater at the end of Bearskin Neck, working one hand under the dog's garden hose collar as he did. He must have hit the right spot, because the dog leaned against Harley's leg like she didn't want him to stop.

"'You probably thought I'd lost it, going to a loan shark like Lochran. But your uncle ain't stupid. Ray's Rules *number four*: *If you think someone might cross you, do your homework and build the perfect double cross.*'"

"See?" Harley grabbed his own hair like he wanted to rip it out. "He *says* he's not stupid. But if he really thought Lochran might hurt him?

The smart move is simple: forget the loan." He gave a frustrated growl. "Sorry for the rant . . . keep reading."

"'We needed the boat. So I borrowed the cash, but I was careful. I recorded *every*thing with a second phone. Every meeting. Every threat. Even the time he thought he had me cornered—and forced me to stage the little accident when you and the Buckman kid were out on his boat. The phone picked up every word. Lochran was the stupid one, thinking I wouldn't dare record him.'"

Parker stopped. "So even though your dear Uncle Ray tried to kill us, it wasn't his fault . . . is that what he's saying?"

"Can you believe this guy?"

Parker went back to the letter. "'I figured if Quinn Lochran tried blackmailing me after it was all over, I'd shut him down with those recordings—or turn the tables on him. Your Uncle Ray played it smart all the way. Thank God you survived. But if you hadn't, and if Lochran wanted to waste me so I'd never rat him out, all I had to do was let him know about the recordings—they'd be my secret Kevlar vest to keep me alive.'"

Parker flipped the letter over and continued reading. "'I wanted to use those recordings at my trial. But I learned real fast that the judge was in Lochran's back pocket. I clammed up about the recordings and figured I'd give it some time. And here's another brilliant move on my part—I sent a letter straight to the DA. He came to talk to me a couple of days ago about the evidence I have. They are *very* interested in what I have to trade. The guy was drooling when he heard what I'd captured on those recordings. I brought my lawyer into the loop to broker the deal. To the DA, I'm just a little "catch and release" fish. Lochran's the prize-winning tuna. I already have the hook set deep in him with those recordings. When I produce the goods against Lochran, the DA will get me out of this joint, guaranteed. Those recordings are more than a Kevlar vest. They're my get-out-of-jail-free tickets.'"

Harley snorted. "The guy should never be let out. Sorry." He waved at Parker to keep reading.

"'Once the DA gets the recordings, all they have to do is reel Lochran in. Ray's Rules *number two*: *I always land on my feet*. Ray's Rules *number twelve*: *If somebody hurts me, I hurt them back—worse*.'"

Parker frowned at the next line, but he kept reading. "'Harley, you have a lot to learn about what it means to be a real man. Pay attention to Uncle Ray's rules, and you'll be on your way.'"

Harley put his hands over his ears. "Rules, rules. He's got so many rules. And if I wanted to learn about being a man, I'd be talking to your dad. Or your grandpa."

"There's more. Want me to keep going?"

Harley nodded.

"'Ray's Rules *number five*—I don't think I ever gave you this one . . . but it's worth memorizing: *When someone puts you in a corner, you put them in a box*. Lochran backed me into a corner, and now I'll put Lochran in a box, so to speak. A cell, anyway. I just need your help.'"

Parker looked up to make sure they weren't drifting too close to a moored sailboat or the rocky shoreline. "He always needs your help to make his plans work. Did you ever notice that? What makes him think you will?"

Harley shook his head. "He manipulates. Threatens. I learned never to let him know what I really wanted—or cared about deep down inside. If he figured it out . . . he'd use it against me."

Parker couldn't imagine that. "He's been gone for months. How would he know what you really care about?"

"I hope you're right. But he's got that gift. Keep reading."

Parker leaned closer to Harley and lowered his reading voice to be sure it didn't carry across the water. "'Here's where things get dicey, Harley boy. Lochran has ears everywhere. And the DA's office has a leak. Lochran knows I got something big on him. He just don't know where I stashed it. That's where you come in. I need you to get the recordings to my lawyer, Sebastian Kilbro. He'll take it from there. Do not give them to the police. *Do not*. Those recordings are my bargaining chips. The DA gets them after they make the deal with my lawyer.

"'Somebody has already attacked me in this joint, and I don't need three guesses to know who was behind it. I won't be safe until I'm out—and Lochran's in my cell instead. Tomorrow you'll tell the lawyer you're all in for this task. He'll give you the clue sheet I'm working on right now. This will lead you to the recordings.'"

Parker looked at Harley. "You're not doing this. This is insane. If Lochran thinks you have the evidence—or that you know where to find it—what do you think he'll do?"

"Nothing good." He looked at the letter in Parker's hands. "Is that it?"

"There's a second page."

Harley motioned for him to keep reading.

Parker continued. "'If you decide not to help your Uncle Ray, I have two reasons that will change your mind in a big fat hurry.'"

"Here we go." Harley took a deep breath, like he was bracing himself. "This is where we see Uncle Ray at his finest."

"'One: You get me the recordings—and I give you the latitude and longitude of where your motorcycle was dumped in Sandy Bay. I talked to my third man. Got the coordinates right here in my head. Think about it. You hoist it off the bottom, and you got your bike back. Lots will be salvageable. More than you think. The frame. Some engine parts. Give it a light sanding and scraping, some new paint. Kemosabe is just waiting for you to save him. Your dad would be so proud.'"

It was just like Harley said. Uncle Ray knew what mattered to Harley. He'd use it to manipulate Harley into doing his dirty work. "Are you buying this?"

"All those months on the bottom? The bike would be in way worse shape than he says. It'd have more barnacles and growth on it than any hull you've ever cleaned. Rust would be blistering everywhere." Harley shook his head. "The bike is beyond salvaging now. The frame—maybe. And that's a *big* maybe. It could have easily gotten bent when the thing hit the bottom. Kemosabe's gone. Period."

But Ray had created a shadow of doubt in Harley's mind, hadn't he? Would he really be okay walking away from a chance to find his bike?

"I'll never see Kemosabe again. I've known that for months." Harley was quiet for a long moment. "I'm not biting, Parks. He doesn't know me as well as he thinks." Harley took a deep breath and blew it out. Smiled. "Maybe I really am free of him."

That made Parker smile too. "Want me to read his second reason—or should we just shred this thing?"

Harley pressed one fist into his palm, working each knuckle until it cracked. Switched hands. "We just rip the bandage off fast, right? Read it."

The handwriting was worse now. "'Reason Two: It's not just my life on the line, buddy-boy. You can bet cash money Lochran knows about the letter in your hands. What do you think he'll do when he finds out you know how to find the evidence—with the help of my clue sheet?'"

Parker stopped reading. "Harley, we have to take this to the police. We'll go right to Detective Greenwood. Even if you say no to your uncle, Lochran will think you know where to find the evidence. He'll come after you."

Harley nodded. "I say bring it on, Lochran. Do your worst. I'm not afraid of his hired muscle." Harley's smile was back. "Uncle Ray thinks he knows me soooo well. But I beat him. *Finally.*" Harley thumped his chest.

Park pointed at the letter. "Still a half page. Read it or rip it?"

He was still grinning. "Go ahead. But I've made my decision—and it feels *good*."

Parker continued reading. "'Ray's Rules *number eleven*: *Keep life exciting. Cheat death every day.* I've been cheating death for years. And I'll keep doing it because I'm a pro. But you're exposed. So pay attention to what I'm going to tell you now. Tell nobody about what I wrote you. No police. Not your foster mom. And definitely not those yappy girls. Nobody except the Buckman kid, because you'll need him.'"

Harley locked eyes with Parker for a moment. "I'm not pulling you into this, Parker. No way. I'll tell that Sebastian Kilbro dude that my uncle can rot in jail—or he can find someone else to follow his clue sheet." He brushed off his hands. "I want nothing to do with the man."

"Okay," Parker said. "Let's not even finish reading the letter." Harley's uncle was a manipulator . . . but the only way he could control people was if they listened to him, right? "Maybe we just rip it up, stuff it in the envelope, and drop it at the lawyer's office. He'll get the message."

"How much is left?"

"One paragraph."

Harley growled. "The man makes me crazy. Just finish reading it. Then we'll rip it up."

Parker cleared his throat. "'Lochran will be coming for you. Your only hope to keep safe? Stay ahead of him. Move fast. Get those recordings. You think you can protect yourself? Maybe. But can you protect the Buckman boy and your girlfriends? You willing to bet their lives on it? Lochran's boys know how to get you to do what they want. I bet they'll go for that pretty foster mom of yours first. Unless you get that evidence to the lawyer—fast.'"

"What?" Harley stood—both fists clenched. "Anybody gets *near* Miss Lopez, and I'll rip him apart."

Obviously, the master manipulator knew what buttons to push—even from prison.

Harley dropped back on the seat, knit his fingers behind his neck, and pulled his head down to his knees. "This is so messed up. Uncle Ray always gets what he wants. Why'd he drag her into this?"

And in that moment, it was clear Harley had reversed his earlier decision. Parker could back away. He could say absolutely, positively, no way would he get involved. But wasn't he already in this? Harley and Parker wore matching lanyards. A gator tooth—with a key to a lost motorcycle too. They were brothers. And Parker's brother was in trouble.

Harley sat slump-shouldered, like all the fight had drained out of him. "When I was a kid, my dad bought me a birthday cake. Chocolate with white frosting. There were eight candles—which he told me to blow out. And I did—but they kept relighting themselves. Trick candles, you know? We had a good laugh over it."

Parker just listened.

"My uncle is like those trick candles. You think he's gone—you're totally *sure* he's snuffed out of your life—and then *whoosh*, he's back and ready to burn you."

He looked at Parker for a long moment. "I feel like we're back in the water out by Little Salvages that night—and he's behind the wheel of *Deep Trouble*, bearing down on us. Only this time, it's way worse, Parks. Because he's got Miss Lopez in the water with us."

Uncle Ray seemed to have found Harley's Achilles' heel. And seeing the pain on Harley's face? Maybe Ray had found Parker's, too.

CHAPTER 11

HARLEY TOOK THE LETTER AND JAMMED IT BACK in the envelope. He wanted to rip it up, burn the scraps. The dog stared at him with an apologetic look, like even *she* knew it was too late for that. "Prison officials have to read letters before inmates send them out, right? The envelope wasn't even sealed. We have to assume Lochran knows. Now Miss Lopez is in danger—and it's my fault."

"No. Your uncle is to blame. And Lochran."

"But if I wasn't living with her—"

"Then you'd be living with someone else, and they'd be in the same danger. So what are we going to do?"

"For starters, we can't tell anybody."

"Do you really think Miss Lopez or my parents have a connection to Lochran?"

"Definitely not." Harley stood and paced the length of the boat. The dog walked with him, constantly looking up at Harley as if asking what to do next. "But they'll take it to the police. To Detective Greenwood."

"You don't trust Greenwood?"

"Him I trust. But he'll have to tell his commander about the evidence, right? Word will get out. The wrong person hears we've got evidence to deliver—and we won't live long enough to deliver a pizza."

"But you said it yourself—Lochran probably knows already. He's got ears everywhere. So what's the harm in talking to Pez? Or the police?"

Parker had put his finger on it, hadn't he? "What if Miss Lopez tells me I simply can't help Uncle Ray? I could see her doing that—thinking she's protecting me. And then what if Miss Lopez gets hurt?"

"Then we need to warn Pez, right? Maybe Detective Greenwood can patrol the area more."

Harley shook his head. "Don't you see? The only way to keep Miss Lopez safe is to find the evidence—*fast*—and hand it over to the lawyer. Once we do, we're in the clear. There'll be no reason to target us *or* Miss Lopez, right? We get the clue sheet and find the recordings—and Lochran gets arrested before he makes a move."

"This is too big," Parks said. "We need help."

"Only if we can't figure out the clues by ourselves. If we have to pull others in, then we pull them in."

Parks didn't look so sure. "Anybody who asks you to keep a secret from your parents isn't trying to help you. My mom knows you got a letter. Pez does too, right? And if anyone needs to know, parents should, don't you think?"

It felt like a test question—and honestly . . . the answer was obvious. "Look . . . we can tell them Uncle Ray has evidence he wants us to give to the lawyer. But let's not talk about the threats."

"Telling only *part* of the story is still telling a lie."

Parks was right. And Harley wanted to do the right thing. He really did. "Okay. Okay. Tell your mom and dad. And I'll tell Miss Lopez." He thought he could just downplay the potential danger a bit. "We'll hope they let us find this evidence and get it done with. There's no harm in looking for it, right?"

"And we'll tell Ella and Jelly?"

Harley shook his head. "Miss Lopez and your parents may need to know. But if we tell the girls, all they'll talk about at the coffee shop is the danger—and Miss Lopez will pull the plug on our search. That could put *her* in more danger, right? I say we don't tell the girls a thing about the letter."

That made Parker smile. "*I* won't. But I'm not so sure *you* can keep that a secret."

"I didn't tell them Mike Ironwing's name, did I?"

A trio of gulls dipped low over the boat. Circling like they expected a handout—or were trying to listen in. Maybe they worked for Lochran too. Harley found himself scanning the shoreline again. Looking for anyone who might be watching them. "The girls won't get anything out of me—even if they try."

"Looks like you'll have a chance to prove that." Parks nodded toward the floating dock off the end of T-wharf. Ella and Jelly stood there, waving them over.

"How about we make a run for it? Go out into the bay for a while."

Parker laughed. "Yeah, and they'll never guess we're hiding something if we do that."

He was right. "Okay. I'm officially putting the letter in my steel safe." Harley tapped his head. "And I won't give them a chance to pick the lock."

"Easier said." Parker didn't have to finish the statement. He swung *Wings* around to pick up the girls.

Harley took a couple of deep breaths—like he was about to run the ball to the end zone. "I'm Fort Knox."

"Totally."

"I've outmaneuvered lots bigger players on the field."

"Absolutely."

Ella waved and smiled like she held the combination for the safe.

"All I have to do is keep them out of the vault. I can do that." Harley pulled the dog closer. "You and me, right, girl? We won't say a word."

The dog yipped. Wagged its tail. Like this was all a game. Maybe it was. A game Harley had to win.

CHAPTER 12

ANGELICA STOOD ALONGSIDE ELLA on the floating dock. Parker motored *Wings* their way. "What do you think that lawyer wanted with Harley?"

"I'm hoping he'll tell us."

"We can't let him know Pez said anything, or we'd be throwing her under the bus. Maybe he'll open up. Or *slip* up. Harley can't keep secrets from you."

Ella smiled apologetically. "I can't do that to him."

"But if that letter is *really* important, he'll need help from two very smart girls. You'd be doing him a favor."

El laughed. "Poor Harley. I'll go easy on him."

Parker eased back on the throttle. Shifted into reverse and goosed the gas. The boat glided to the float.

Harley tossed the bow line. Angelica caught it and pulled *Wings* tight to the floating dock.

"We're heading to the slip," Parker said. "Want a ride—for a whopping hundred and fifty yards?"

The dog jumped from the boat—and beelined to El. Harley called the dog back, but she pulled the deaf act.

Ella dropped to her knees, loving on the dog like she'd been waiting all day for this moment.

Angelica stepped aboard *Wings*. "I think the dog is done riding the boat, Harley. I'll help Parker dock." There was a better chance of one of the boys mentioning the lawyer letter if they weren't together anyway. More importantly, maybe Parker would open up about how he was really doing after seeing that body.

Harley swung out of the boat, grinning.

Angelica pushed the boat away from the floating dock and sat in the bow seat. She leaned over the side just enough to let her fingertips trail in the water as Parker headed for his slip.

"How are you doing, Parker? Honestly."

The look he gave her . . . definitely guarded.

"Hey, I don't need to know anything Greenwood asked you to keep quiet. But if I saw a body like that? I'd still be freaking out."

Parker focused on the water in front of them, rounding the east end of the yacht club and turning into the South Basin. He avoided her eyes and kept a white-knuckled grip on the wheel. Not exactly good signs.

"I want to help—but I don't know how."

"I'd rather talk about something else."

Was he afraid she'd drop into her old *protector* ways? "Like?"

"Anything other than how I'm doing." His jaw muscles clenched and unclenched.

Actually, he'd just revealed *exactly* how he was doing . . . hadn't he? *Let me help you, Parker. Please . . . let me do something.*

His face . . . The only word that came to her mind? *Clouded.* Like a squall had swept in—deep inside him somewhere. And in that moment, she got the definite feeling that the storm would sweep over all of them before this was over.

CHAPTER 13

HARLEY SET THE MANILA ENVELOPE on the floating dock and watched Ella petting the dog. He knelt beside her.

"I think somebody loves me," El said. "Am I right?"

Harley froze. "What?"

"Do you love me, girl?" El dropped into that baby-talk voice that moms did. "Tell me, girl. C'mon . . . tell me. You can do it."

The dog yipped. It seemed Ella had some supernatural ability to get into the head of man *or* beast—and get them talking, too.

"When Harley pulled you from the water, it was his lucky day, right, girl?"

Lucky? He'd found a dog that he couldn't keep. He'd gotten zero yardage finding the owner. His best friend found a wallet loaded with money—not a dollar of which either of them could keep—just before discovering a dead body. Not to mention Uncle Ray's letter. "There was nothing even remotely lucky about today."

"What's this?" Ella held up the manila envelope.

He reached for it, but she pulled back. "Ooohhh. Something important, I see."

"I need it." A totally lame comment.

"I'm getting that vibe." She held it up to the light as if she could see through the heavy paper. "Are you going to tell me what's inside—or do I have to guess?"

Keep your mouth shut, Harley. You're a vault. Ella would get nothing out of him. *Stay in control.* She'd never actually take the letter out without him saying she could. This was just her way of having fun.

"So you want me to guess." Ella held the envelope to her forehead. "You got it yesterday."

He'd play her game to show her just how tight-lipped he could be—and to get her thinking the letter wasn't as big a deal as it was. "This morning."

"So before this whole thing . . ." She pointed toward South Basin.

Harley nodded. There was no harm in giving her that.

"And this contains a letter congratulating you on winning a poetry contest you secretly entered."

That made him smile. "Nice try. Just a letter."

"And it's from"—she closed her eyes and tapped the envelope against her forehead—"the coach, begging you to go to football camp this summer."

"You're really losing your touch, El."

She scanned the envelope, then flipped to the front. "You're right. Definitely sloppy on my part. The return address would say Rockport High School, not Kilbro, Hutchins, and Wiley, Attorneys at Law."

He hadn't thought about the firm's name on the envelope. But it still gave her nothing.

"So . . . a lawyer visited BayView Brew last week—and sent a letter thanking you for making the best cup of coffee he's ever had. Am I right?"

Harley was enjoying this. "I wish. The letter wasn't even from a lawyer, technically. He was just my uncle's delivery boy."

She stared at him for a moment. "Your uncle sent you a letter? What does he want?"

Instantly the warning not to tell those "yappy girls" echoed through his head. Cold fear knifed through his body. Would this put his friends in danger? What if something happened to Miss Lopez? He had to do something. Get in front of this somehow. *Dear God, you have to help me. Parker and I need to find that evidence.*

"Harley?" Clearly, she wasn't playing a game anymore. The teasing was gone from her eyes now. "Something is scaring you, and that's scaring me."

Sheesh. Harley should've never played her game. He lunged for the envelope and snatched it from her hands. He tucked it in tight, like he'd just gotten a handoff from the QB. "Let's find out what's holding up Parks and Jelly." He patted his thigh, and the dog turned his way. "C'mon, pup."

Harley felt Ella watching him as he hustled up the ramp, the dog trotting alongside him.

"Talk to me, Harley."

There was no way. Not that he didn't trust her. He didn't trust himself. She'd gotten into the vault. Just a tiny bit . . . but still way too much.

"You act like the envelope holds your death warrant."

Maybe it did. And not just his. He felt like anybody close to him was also in danger. Parker. Ella. Jelly. And if he didn't find that evidence in time? Even Miss Lopez.

CHAPTER 14

EVERYBODY HID THINGS—even from their closest friends. That's what Angelica believed, anyway. Secrets. Stories—good and bad. Failures. Dreams. Fears. People locked things inside their heart and set up their own security system, an internal motion detector. Somebody getting too close to their secrets triggered a warning.

But Ella always told her there were ways around such systems. It was like everyone had a keypad allowing access to even their most guarded secrets. You just had to figure out the right combination.

As a kid, Angelica would play a "beat the burglar alarm" game at her grandma's home. A motion detector was mounted near the ceiling just outside Grandma's upstairs bedroom. The trick was to move slow enough—and stay low enough to the ground—to avoid triggering it. After too many attempts to count, Angelica had finally mastered it. And she thought she could get past Parker's security system too. *Go slow. Stay low.* She'd figure out what he was hiding.

Why are you doing this, Angelica? You aren't his protector, remember? It took a bullet in her leg to teach her that lesson. She didn't want to go back to her old self . . . not ever. But how could she help Parker if he didn't open up? If she didn't know what he really needed, what were the chances she'd guess right? And if she guessed wrong, it might even hurt him.

If you're going to get sneaky to figure him out, you'd better do it for the right reasons. And she would. She promised herself that.

When people hid something, there were usually little signs. When Ella was holding something back, she cried. The smallest thing could bring tears to her eyes. Angelica's dad talked when he had something to hide. About anything and everything—as long as it wasn't what was really on his mind. It was like he tried filling every second of dead air, thinking Angelica wouldn't have a chance to get suspicious—and ask questions.

Parker went quiet when he had a secret—and he kept busy with a nervous energy. He'd get distant. Distracted. She was already seeing that. He hadn't said a word while he docked *Wings*. He fell into his little routine. Tying the boat securely to the dock cleats. Neatly coiling the line that remained. He hosed off his dive equipment while he was at it. *Busy, busy, busy.*

Angelica wiped down the seat cushions. But she was multitasking. She'd learned to watch his body language. His actions practically shouted that something was wrong—and that he needed help.

He looked over his shoulder. A lot. But not toward the end of T-wharf—where Harley and Ella were. Every time, it was the start of T-wharf he checked . . . like he expected somebody to show up— someone he didn't want to see.

It was when he dried and sheathed his dive knife that Angelica's heart rate really picked up. He didn't stow the knife in his dive bag. He left it on the console—like he wanted to keep it within easy reach.

Oh, yeah. Parker was hiding something big, for sure. But why not tell her? Did he think whatever he was hiding might push her back to her old ways?

The best way to find out what was on his mind? Stay close. Stay quiet.

Let him open up in his time. Sometimes he'd just start talking about whatever was on his mind—like he was processing aloud. But if whatever he was hiding was causing him to keep a knife close, maybe there wasn't time to wait him out. Throwing out a question to get him talking was risky, but it had worked before—as long as she did it just right.

Angelica didn't know much about fishing, but she knew this much: Reeling in a fish too fast or hard usually meant snapping the line. Reeling info out of Parker wasn't much different. She had to play this smart—and get him talking without him *knowing* she was fishing.

"Did you and Harley have a nice run out in the bay?"

Parker dried his dive mask and snapped it in its case. "We just stayed in the harbor."

She glanced his way. He was eying the shoreline again. "I love your boat—and how God provided it, you know?"

"It's a real beaut."

Normally he'd talk her ear off about the motor. How well it handled the swells. How quickly it leveled off when he throttled forward hard. He could talk for an hour about how he saw it as a gift from God.

Sheesh, Parker . . . you're scaring me now. Whatever he was holding back was eating him up, and that had to mean trouble. All the more reason to encourage him to open up.

"Parks!" Harley trotted along the granite-block edge of T-wharf. He held the dog's leash, and Ella followed two steps behind.

Ella shook her head and shrugged. Okay . . . she hadn't had any more luck than Angelica had.

"Thanks, Jelly," Parker said. "Nice talk."

It took all the self-control she possessed not to laugh. "*So* good."

He gave *Wings* a visual once-over, then climbed onto the dock. "I think we're done here."

She smiled. "For now." But that didn't mean she was finished. Not by a long shot. Parker needed her help. But she couldn't do a thing for him until she found out what was going on. She'd get to the bottom of this one way or another . . . and she'd do it tonight.

CHAPTER 15

PARKER FINISHED DINNER FAST and helped wash dishes. He gave Mom a hug and kiss before running out. He was back to the boat thirty minutes before he was to meet the others for the walk to the Headlands. Mom and Dad had been terrific listeners—totally dialed in. Detective Greenwood had given a counselor's name to Dad . . . and Mom had already scheduled an appointment for tomorrow. Not exactly how Parker wanted to spend an hour of his spring break—but his parents weren't giving him any leash on that one.

Wings sat at the dock like it was itching to make a run out into Sandy Bay. When Steadman had narrowly avoided capture by the police last June, the twenty-five-foot Boston Whaler had been one of the things he'd left behind. Parker had taken the boat under *his* wing, so to speak. He kept it clean and running. And when the yacht club had a quiet little auction, Parker bought the boat for the amount Steadman had been behind on the boat slip rent. It was a gift—and Parker knew it.

Somehow the auction hadn't been publicized well. As in horribly. Parker, his parents, the auctioneer, and harbormasters Eric and Maggie were the only people there. And Parker was the only bidder. He totally suspected a setup, but the harbormasters never admitted a thing. The boat was *definitely* a gift from God.

Steadman had outfitted the boat well. Ten times the power of the motor that had propelled the *Boy's Bomb*.

Steadman had never named the boat—which was just plain wrong, the way Parker saw it. But then again, it was a good thing. Parker probably would've changed the name anyway.

Parker sat in the driver's seat and looked at the name plaque he'd screwed onto the console. *Wings of the Dawn*. He'd pulled the name directly out of the Bible—from a couple of verses in Psalms that held truth Parker never wanted to forget.

If I rise on the wings of the dawn,
*   if I settle on the far side of the sea,*
even there your hand will guide me,
*   your right hand will hold me fast.*

He was never out of God's reach, right?

Flight Risk was exactly the way he'd left it this morning—except for the yellow police tape. He stared at the boat's waterline . . . picturing Mike Ironwing surfacing and waving him over.

Shake it off, Parker.

He forced himself not to look at the sailboat, but he didn't turn his back to it either. His parents were both concerned about the letter from Uncle Ray. The two of them were going to talk about it—and Parker absolutely knew he hadn't heard the end of it.

Flight Risk rocked, its mast swinging port to starboard like a giant hand had grabbed the keel. Parker stared at the sailboat for a moment. "You don't scare me. I'll finish scraping you." He sounded way more confident than he felt. He had zero interest in getting in the water again. "Maybe tomorrow." He climbed out of *Wings* and onto the dock. He'd wait for the others on T-wharf.

He spotted Harley first—and he still had the dog. He took the route closest to the water—just like Parker would've. El and Jelly had taken the window-shopping route. They rounded the corner from Pleasant Street onto Broadway, entering at T-wharf's mouth.

Harley was coming from a totally different direction than the girls— which pretty well summed up what was going on right now. All of them friends but coming from different directions. Harley and Parker had secrets to keep. Jelly and Ella clearly wanted to know what they were hiding. And every one of them was playing a game to keep the others from figuring out what they were really doing. The only real question? How hard would the girls press to win?

CHAPTER 16

ELLA FOUND A GREAT SPOT FOR THE FOUR of them to kick back on the rocky shore of the Headlands. Parker had a fire going from driftwood they'd found above the high-tide line. She tugged off her cowgirl boots and stood them beside her, toes looking out to sea. The swells rose in a mesmerizing dance as if briefly introducing themselves before crashing against the rocks.

Harley pocketed his phone. "That must've been my eighth call. The owner has to pick up one of these times."

The dog circled the group before choosing the girl's side of the fire. Smart doggy.

"The owner is probably worried sick—and out looking for her right now," Jelly said. "You should bring the dog right back where you found her."

"In the water—with its leash caught between the rocks?" Harley patted his thigh. The dog stood and trotted over. "Don't worry, pup. I won't dump you in the harbor, no matter what Jelly says."

Ella threw her boot at Harley, which put a grin on his face for the first time that night. The smile faded quick, and he went back to staring out to sea. Parker was doing the same. Both of them looking lost in thought . . . or maybe just lost.

Jelly locked eyes with her and exchanged a what's-up-with-the-boys look.

It was one thing to keep a secret about a gift—like the plaque they'd bought for Harley's birthday party Saturday night. Nothing wrong with that. But whatever was hounding the boys definitely wasn't good. Which probably meant there was danger. An uneasy knot tightened in Ella's stomach. She reached for the cross around her neck. If she got the boys talking . . . maybe they'd let down their guard.

"Hearing about the drowning really rattled Grams," Ella said. "You know what she wanted me to ask?"

Parker raised an eyebrow. "His name?"

"Nope. How was he dressed?" Ella raised one hand. "Honest. Her exact words."

Parker looked out over the water again. "Dark hoodie. Jeans. T-shirt. Same as half the men in town. Why would that matter?"

"Everything means something—especially because the body came in with the tide." Ella shrugged. "Shoes?"

"No idea. I didn't really see past the face."

"Which was higher—his head or his feet?"

Parker stared at her. "What? Seriously?"

"If the head was lower, it means the man was looking for something— and never found it. He'll keep searching, even if he's dead."

"Of course." Harley smacked his forehead with the heel of his hand. "His wallet."

"Don't you dare make fun of Grams, me—or the dead, Mr. Lotitto. Grams says the world is full of spirits."

"Parker doesn't believe in ghosts," Harley said. "And neither do I."

"I didn't say I believed."

Harley laughed. "Of course you do."

"Look," Ella said, "I know Grams's beliefs can be out there sometimes—"

"*Sometimes?*" Parker looked at her like he thought Ella was crazy. "I love Grams, but she'll quote a Bible verse one minute and believe in superstitious signs and omens the next."

Okay, Parker wasn't far off.

"So you really believe this dead guy's spirit may be doggy-paddling around Rockport Harbor . . . looking for his wallet?" Harley grinned. "Or will he come ashore and search down Bearskin Neck, too?"

"Make fun of Ella all you like," Jelly said. "But there are mysterious forces at work in the universe. And I, for one, don't want to discount anything."

Harley stood and stretched his arms out in front of him like he was imitating Frankenstein's monster. He took a couple of stiff-legged zombie steps. "Must . . . find . . . wallet." Harley sat on the rocks again. "If I see the dead guy walking down Bearskin Neck tonight, I'll send him right to Detective Greenwood. He's got Ironwing's wallet now." Immediately, he clamped his hand over his mouth.

"Ironwing?" Ella flashed a triumphant smile. "Thank you, Harley."

"I'm an idiot." Harley talked through his fingers. "Idiot!"

"Don't be so hard on yourself," Ella said. "We love that you don't keep secrets from us."

Harley groaned. "Forget that name, okay? Detective Greenwood was counting on us. Sorry, Parks."

Parker shrugged like it was no big deal. "I'm sure the word will be out tomorrow anyway. How long can they keep a lid on that? And honestly, I have no idea how knowing the name will matter. We probably could have mentioned that already."

Harley was still shaking his head. "I'm an idiot."

But Ella felt better, for sure. Now that she knew the victim's name, she'd do a little searching online later tonight. Maybe she'd find something that would give her a feel for whether this was a drowning accident—or something more sinister.

The boys changed the topic—and Ella was okay with that. They had the victim's name—a step in the right direction. But Harley and Parker were still holding back on the big secret—whatever was in that manila envelope. She wanted to reel in more info from the boys, but pushing it now wouldn't be smart.

"Found you!"

Ella would have jumped out of her boots if she'd been wearing them. She whirled to see Bryce Scorza sauntering toward them out of the dark.

The dog howled and tore across the rock right to him.

Football jersey over his hoodie. Holding the ball like he was ready to throw. The football team's quarterback stepped back, smiling. "Didn't mean to *scare* everyone."

"You can't help it," Jelly said. "You're a terrifying human being."

Scorza grinned. "I was running pass patterns on Front Beach with some of the boys. After dark a couple of us sat out on the breakwater— and I saw the fire. Figured it was you four."

Ella had once heard that cockroaches could withstand a nuclear blast. She had no idea if that was true, but it seemed believable. Especially when she thought of Bryce Scorza. The guy was always crawling out of some hole.

The dog sniffed at the cuffs of Scorza's jeans—probably trying to figure out if he was a good guy or bad. When her ears went back flat, Ella smiled. She was liking that dog more and more.

"Just wanted to *pass* along a personal invitation." Scorza got in his QB stance like he was going to throw the ball to Harley. "Every day during spring break we're meeting after dinner. You should join us. It'd be fun."

Apparently Ella's idea of fun and Scorza's were worlds apart.

Jelly didn't look impressed. "You're inviting all of us?"

"Absolutely. You and BB here could be our cheerleaders."

Ella wasn't sure she liked BB any better than Black Beauty—which he'd stopped calling her months ago. "*So* tempting."

"Think about it." Scorza looked directly at Harley. "You don't want to get rusty."

Would Harley even go to team tryouts next season? Ella wasn't so sure.

"You heard about the drowning?" Scorza pointed the football toward Rockport Harbor.

"We've just been talking about that," Jelly said.

"Yeah, well, my dad knew the guy, and he was a *really* bad dude." Scorza nodded like he had the inside scoop. "My dad said it was Mike Ironwing. Also said this was no accident."

"You're saying . . . murder?" All of Jelly's annoyance disappeared.

Scorza smiled as if he'd noticed Jelly was hanging on everything he said. "Ironwing hated the water. Wouldn't go on a boat unless you paid him. And you know what else my dad said?"

Jelly shook her head.

"Maybe I shouldn't say. You're all pretty jumpy . . . and I don't want to make it worse."

Jelly gave him her warning face. "Come on, just *tell* us."

Scorza raised both hands. "Okay, okay." He glanced over his shoulder, like he really thought someone might be hiding in the shadows. "Here are his exact words: 'Anybody able to take out Mike Ironwing is definitely not someone you'd want to tangle with.'"

For a moment, nobody said a word.

"He could be out here. The guy who took out Ironwing." Scorza swept the ball side to side. "You better not be out alone with a killer on the loose."

Harley didn't look fazed. "Need us to walk you home, Scorza?"

The QB laughed and turned to Jelly. "Want me to find out more about this guy, Everglades Girl?"

"Whatever." But that's not what her face said. She looked way too eager to hear more.

"I'll see what I can do."

Ella was pretty sure he'd make that a priority.

Scorza backed away from the fire. "You all be careful out here. I'm dead serious. And, Lotitto . . . stay sharp." He fired the football at Harley.

Actually, it sailed right at Ella. She ducked—and heard the sharp smack of flesh against football. Harley was standing, holding the ball in a solid grip—practically in front of Ella's face.

"And Scorza completes another wild pass," Parker said.

Or was it?

Harley tossed the ball back.

"You still got it, Lotitto. Join us. Tomorrow night," Scorza said. "He focused on Jelly for a moment. "Meantime, how about you give me your phone number? I'll text you with more intel on Ironwing."

"Nice try," Jelly said. "I'm sure you'll find me."

"Of course! You want to see me in person. Even better." He turned and strode into the shadows.

For the next ten minutes it seemed all they could talk about was Mike Ironwing.

The boys stepped away from the fire and wandered close to where the rocks were wet with spray. They threw sticks out into the bay.

Harley looked antsy. Full of pent-up energy but with no place to direct it. His restlessness went way beyond letting the victim's name slip out like he had.

Ella left her boots by the fire and walked to a higher spot on the Headlands. She phoned Grams, updating her with Parker's description of the body—and Scorza's intel. Honestly, she wanted to hear Grams assure her that everything was going to be okay. If Grams could rest easy on this, maybe Ella could too. And maybe she could make Harley feel a little better at the same time.

By the time Ella returned, the boys had come back to the fire too. Parker looked just as troubled as Harley. Ella's eyes met Jelly's for a moment . . . and it was as if she knew Jelly's thoughts. If they were going to help the boys, they needed to know what was wrong.

"I told Grams everything," Ella said. "Except the guy's name, of course. She says there's nothing to worry about as long as the man's eyes were closed. That means it's over . . . and we can all rest easy."

Parker stared at the fire, like his mind was someplace else. Someplace dark.

Jelly watched him for a few long moments. "Parker?"

The guy was still in a fog.

Jelly walked over and waved her hand in front of his face. "Ironwing's peepers. Closed, right?"

He locked eyes with her for a moment. "Wide open." He looked out at the dark waters of Sandy Bay. His face looked spooked, like maybe he was underwater again. Reliving the scene. "Dead eyes. And I had this sense . . ."

Jelly plopped down on a rock next to Parker, like his answer drained the strength from her legs. Only the sound of the waves gurgling in the miniature canyons between the rocks broke the silence.

"Parker," Jelly said, finally, "what did you sense?"

Ella moved closer, wishing Grams was with them to hear Parker firsthand. She sat next to Harley and leaned forward so she could watch Parker's face. Read his body movements.

The wind blew the hair away from his forehead. He shook his head like he'd had a change of mind. "It was stupid."

"Tell us anyway." Ella gave Jelly a do-something look.

"Parker." Jelly spoke slowly. Carefully. "You can talk. It's only us here."

Parker nodded like her words got through. "I had this weird feeling that the guy had been waiting for me. Like he knew I'd be coming."

The fire popped, and Ella practically jumped off the rock. Even the dog looked skittish. When a dog got spooked, people should pay attention. Ella didn't know how she knew that, but it was true.

"What was it . . ." Jelly did a great job of keeping her voice calm. "What gave you the impression he'd been watching for you?"

"His arm. It . . . moved." Parker seemed mesmerized, staring at the fire.

"Whoa, partner." Harley cringed. "I thought we weren't going to tell them that."

Ella stomped on his foot—afraid he'd break the spell of the moment. "Let him talk, Harley. He needs to get this out."

"So," Jelly said. "He moved his arm. Do you think maybe he was still alive when you saw him?"

The firelight flickered against Parker's face. "Not alive. No bubbles coming out of his mouth or nose. But . . . it didn't seem like he was dead yet, either."

Ella definitely wished Grams was hearing this so she could tell them what it all meant. "He was *un*dead—like a zombie or something?"

"Here we go," Harley said. "Welcome to Superstition City."

Maybe Ella had been looking at the fire more than she'd thought, because everything outside the glowing ring of light looked incredibly dark now. She tossed another chunk of driftwood onto the fire.

"His arm," Jelly said. "You said you imagined it moved . . . is that it?"

Parker raised his arm and swept it in a wide, slow arc, like he was motioning for someone to join him. "It. Moved. A full circle. It wasn't my imagination. Waving me closer—like he desperately needed to tell me something."

"Sheesh, Parker." Ella rubbed down goosebumps rising on her arms. No wonder he'd looked like he was in some other world. "Do you think he *did* have something to say?"

"Parks." Harley shook his head. "Let's change topics."

Jelly knelt directly in front of Parker, shadowing his face from the fire. "So you felt he wanted to tell you something?"

"Definitely." He paused for some long seconds. "He had a secret."

Ella tugged her phone from her pocket. Swiped on a recording app. She should have done this five minutes ago so she could play it back for Grams.

"You're doing good, Parker." Jelly's voice was gentle. Mesmerizing in her own way. "What made you think he had a secret?"

Parker shook his head. "No idea. I just . . . knew. His mouth . . . gaping open. Like he was in mid-sentence—but something scared the living daylights out of him before he got the words out."

Ella held the phone closer to Parker. She found herself holding the cross around her neck with the other hand. "Any sense of what the secret was about?"

"It was important. That's all I know. And that it wasn't about him."

Ella stared at him a moment. "If it wasn't about him . . . *who*?"

He looked almost embarrassed. "Me. I felt like he wanted to warn me about something. Stupid, right?"

Ella felt like she was shaking inside. "Not at all."

A fresh breeze rose off the waves, and Parker turned to face it. And just like that, the spell was broken.

"Whatever secrets that man had," Parker said, "he carried them to the grave. Dead men tell no tales, right?"

Jelly hugged herself. "You're creeping me out, Parker. I thought Ella was the one who told the scary stories."

Ella stopped the recording. Took a shaky breath.

"We've heard way more than enough about real-life scary stuff," Harley said. "What we need is a creepy ghost story to get our minds off this. How about it, El? We're still waiting to hear that tale about the Masterson place."

"The Masterson account is just as real as Parker's story." The cool ocean air seemed to pass right through Ella's sweatshirt. She pulled on her boots, warm from the fire. "When I'm sure you can handle it, Mr. Lotitto, I'll tell you the story. I may need you to get a permission note from Pez first."

"Funny." Harley stood. "I should get back. Miss Lopez is really worried about all the burglaries. She doesn't let on much, but I can tell."

It was bad; Ella wouldn't argue with that. And the situation seemed to be getting worse. Couldn't the police do anything?

"Grams said that Parker seeing the body was a really bad omen." Ella looked genuinely concerned. "Stay away from the water, Parker. Okay? Just for a couple days."

"Believe me, I have zero desire to put my wet suit back on. Not until the police tape is gone from *Flight Risk*, anyway."

"Good. I don't know how I know this, but this thing with the drowning victim isn't over."

"Super-duper superstitious, Ella," Harley said.

"Discount what you don't understand, is that it, Harley?" Jelly nodded at Ella. "This is way beyond superstitions. More like women's intuition, wouldn't you say?"

"Totally."

"And that's another thing," Harley said. "Women's intuition. If you ask me, it's something moms made up to keep their kiddos in line." He put one hand on his hip and shook his finger at the girls. "If you don't obey, Mommy will know."

"Keep telling yourself that, Harley." Ella touched her temples with her fingertips. "We girls have a wavelength—a sixth sense that you boys can't even imagine."

Parker cracked a smile. "Maybe I'll check in with you two before I go back under to clean a boat." He poked his pointer fingers up on each side of his head like antennae. "If one of you gets a bad vibration, or however it works, I guarantee I'll listen."

"So you're saying you'll actually *trust* our instincts for once?" Jelly feigned amazement. "We'll have to celebrate. Maybe we'll commandeer the Rockport High marching band. We'll start a parade."

Parker laughed, and it was soooo good to see him loosen up a bit. "What gave you the idea we don't trust you two?"

"Seriously? How about the mystery envelope that Harley is protecting." Ella blurted it out, instantly wishing she'd kept to the plan of being more subtle. But the boys were being ridiculous, right? How could they possibly help these two if they didn't open up? "It's eating at you, Harley. I can tell. Why all the secrecy—or did Detective Greenwood tell you not to talk about that, either?"

Had the fire gone down, or had Harley's face gotten darker? "It has nothing to do with Greenwood. Uncle Ray told me not to tell anyone."

"And since when has your Uncle Ray done what was best for you?"
Harley didn't answer.

"So you can't tell any of us?" Jelly said. "Or does Parker know?"

Parker stamped out the edges of the fire—like suddenly there was some huge rush to leave. Okay . . . Parker knew.

"Harley." Ella had pushed too hard—and if Harley stayed tight-lipped about this, how could that be good for him? "I'm sorry. Let us help. That's all we want to do."

Harley grabbed the dog's leash. Stood with hands in his back pockets. Looked like he had no idea where to go—but was absolutely determined to get there quick.

"Looks like the man under the boat isn't the only one with a secret," Jelly said.

"Harley," Ella practically whispered his name. "Let it go. Confession is good for the soul. Maybe that's what Mike Ironwing wanted to do. He was trying to say something, remember?"

"Yeah," Harley said. "And look where it got him."

CHAPTER 17

HARLEY TOOK THE STAIRS TO the Crow's Nest two at a time. The dog bounded ahead, like she thought this was a race. Harley flopped back on his bed. The dog did a couple of quick circles on the rug and curled up right next to the bedside.

Football games were won or lost based on how well each player executed their role—play after play. A player who didn't focus on their job was a whole lot more likely to make a mistake or miss something. And right now, Harley couldn't afford either.

The problem was, there were too many things to focus on. The burglaries were weighing heavy on Miss Lopez—even though she was careful not to say much. That was one problem.

He pulled the manila envelope out from where he had stashed it earlier—under his pillow. The letter from Uncle Ray was another problem—and could be even bigger than the burglaries if he didn't get it off his back *fast*. Miss Lopez did not need one more thing to worry about.

How was he supposed to find Uncle Ray's evidence—especially when that meant being away from BayView Brew? Parker's head was a little scrambled after finding the body this morning. And Parker hadn't actually said he was all in on this, had he? Which meant Harley might need to do most of this on his own.

Miss Lopez tapped lightly on his bedroom door. "Harley?" He smiled. Since the first night he'd lived here, she'd come up to say goodnight. Not one miss.

She sat on the edge of his bed and sighed. "Well, I did it. Sent an email to every business in Rockport—with a little help from the Chamber of Commerce. We're organizing. We'll compare notes. See what we can do to protect ourselves from the burglaries."

"Building a team. I like it."

"First meeting is tomorrow night. I wish I'd thought of this a week ago." Miss Lopez leaned over and stroked the dog's head. "If you hear anybody trying to get in, you let Harley and me know, okay? You give the most ferocious bark you can and scare that mean Bogeyman away. Can you do that, girl?"

The dog thumped the rug with her tail.

Her eyes rested on the envelope. "You've had a big day yourself. Anything you want to talk about?"

Harley couldn't stand keeping secrets from her. He didn't pull out the letter, but he gave her the basics. He found himself opening up to her in more ways than even he would have expected—stopping just short of telling her how his failure could mean danger for her.

She listened. Nodded. Didn't interrupt. When Harley asked her advice, she gave it. And when Harley was all talked out, she hugged him tight and prayed with him. The only other person he'd seen do that was Parker's mom.

"I'll find it. Turn it in to the lawyer. Maybe it will get a bad man off the streets." *And keep Miss Lopez safe.*

"I'll help any way I can. You know that, right?"

Yeah. He did. He wasn't so sure why she kept giving, though.

"I'm hitting the sack. You sleep good, Harley." She kissed her fingertip and touched his forehead. "I'll make sure the doors are locked."

Harley had already checked the doors. Windows, too. But she didn't need to know that. Miss Lopez would probably sleep better if she checked them herself. She slipped out his bedroom door, leaving him alone with his thoughts.

The dog sat up and nuzzled Harley, whimpering softly.

"Missing Miss Lopez already? Yeah, she's pretty fantastic. Or are you missing your *real* owner?" He worked his fingers under her garden hose collar and scratched. She raised her snout and closed her eyes.

"You like that?" The dog's back foot thumped like crazy, like she was telegraphing a message with her leg. Harley laughed out loud. "I guess you *do* like that. You're going to miss us when your owner picks you up. But Miss Lopez and I will definitely make sure you visit, okay?"

Harley cracked open his window facing Sandy Bay. If the Bearskin Neck Bogeyman came slinking around the coffee shop, Harley wanted to hear him *before* he got inside. And now it wasn't just the Bogeyman he had to think about. Uncle Ray's loan shark could also be on the prowl. What if Lochran sent some goon to Miss Lopez's place to look for Ray's evidence, thinking Harley already had it? What if she walked in while the guy was ripping the Crow's Nest apart looking for it?

He really had no choice. He had to make the deal with Uncle Ray. He took the dog's head in both hands. "I'll talk to that lawyer and get this over with. How's that sound to you?"

The dog's ears went back. She actually looked worried. What was up with that?

"I'll be careful. It's the only way to keep Miss Lopez safe."

The dog whined softly, like she wasn't buying it.

And the truth? Deep down, he wasn't so sure himself.

CHAPTER 18

Parker woke early Tuesday, the second day of spring break. Sleeping in wasn't an option, even if he wanted to. He was meeting with the counselor at ten o'clock, but first he had to grab a quick breakfast, dash to the harbor, and finish cleaning the hull of *Flight Risk*. He still wasn't ready to get in the water again, but he'd decided in the middle of the night that the job needed to be done. And what better way to prove he was totally okay and didn't need counseling at all?

Dad seemed proud of him after hearing Parker's plans. But then, he was pretty fortunate that way. Dad always seemed proud of him, didn't he?

T-shirt. Swimsuit. Hoodie. Running shoes. Towel. The rest of the gear was already stowed in *Wings*. By the time he got to the harbor, he wasn't feeling nearly as confident. He stood on the dock alongside *Flight Risk*. Forced himself to look into the water despite fearing it would trigger images of Mike Ironwing's ghostly blue face, dead eyes, and gaping mouth. The water looked dark, and he imagined Ironwing's hand appearing . . . motioning him into the water.

Scanning the sailboat deck didn't help. A short length of yellow crime scene tape still clung to the rail. A nice reminder that everything he'd seen yesterday was real. He stepped out of his shoes and just stood there. Did he really want to do this? Absolutely not. He wasn't even so sure he could.

His phone vibrated with an incoming text. He whipped it out. Maybe Mom needed help with something. Hey, he'd clean his room, wash the car, or scrub toilets. Anything for an excuse to stall off going underwater.

But the text came from Harley.

I think the Bearskin Neck Bogeyman struck again. Lots of flashing lights on the Neck. Taking the dog for a little look-see. Join me?

He wriggled his feet back into his shoes and took off at a run—tossing his towel into *Wings* as he passed. Not two minutes later he spotted Harley and the dog. They jogged up the Neck together.

It was The Fudgery this time. Police had already formed a yellow-tape perimeter, but not so far away that Parker and Harley couldn't see display cases had been shattered—which meant glass fragments everywhere. All the fudge would have to go to the dumpster now.

"Wasting good fudge? That alone should make it a felony."

Harley wasn't laughing. "This place is lit up really well at night. And it's right here on Tuna Wharf. Easy to see."

If the Bogeyman could pull off a successful hit here, no shop was safe. "Pez won't like this."

"We gotta do something. You and me, Parks. For Miss Lopez."

"Like what?"

"We'll have to figure that out." Harley did his best to smile. "Together, right?"

Parker reached inside his shirt and pulled out Kemosabe's ignition key. "Oh yeah. I'm not letting you do this alone." But what could they really do?

"I got to get Uncle Ray off my back. I already texted that lawyer."

Which meant Parker was in on this one too.

"We'll get Uncle Ray's note—and find out where he stashed the evidence. All we've got to do is grab it and hand it off to the lawyer. Boom—we're done. Then we'll focus on the burglaries."

"Definitely," Parker said. "Unless . . ."

Harley gave a little smile, like he was tracking. "Unless there's something my uncle isn't telling us. But what are the chances, right?"

CHAPTER 19

SOMEDAY ELLA WOULD OWN A COFFEE SHOP just like BayView Brew. Or maybe Pez would realize how badly she needed a hardworking partner.

Ella repositioned the life-size replica human skeleton holding the daily specials chalkboard. He was compliments of the coffee bean company Pez had started featuring, and so they dubbed him Mr. Bones. The skeleton wore a Bones Coffee apron and cap. So far, the coffee had been a huge hit.

Ella set Mr. Bones in a chair and crossed his legs. She liked changing his position throughout the day—and customers seemed to appreciate her effort. She slipped a pair of lobsterman boots on his feet and stepped back to admire her work.

Harley barged through the back door—along with his new friend. Harley took the dog's face between his hands and spoke quietly to her. The dog's tail fanned air the entire time. He smiled and roughed up her ears in a playful way. He grabbed his apron and hung the leash in its place. Maybe Harley wasn't trying all that hard to find the dog's owner.

Pez breezed in from the kitchen. "How bad—and who?"

"Not good." Harley boosted himself onto the counter but didn't take his eyes off Pez's face. "The Fudgery."

"No! They did not need one more thing." Her face looked pained. "Damage?"

"Display cases mostly. Glass everywhere." He kept watching her. Ella had seen him like that before. Miss Lopez may have been Harley's foster parent, but he definitely wanted to look out for her too. It was one of his best qualities . . . unless he took things too far.

"I'll phone them," Pez said. "See if they can use help cleaning up. This has got to stop. We're not a day too early with the business owners' meeting tonight. I'm guessing we'll have a packed room." She disappeared into the back, the dog trotting right behind her.

Harley checked the time—which wasn't like him at all.

"Did you sleep good last night, Harley?"

He wiped his hands on his BayView Brew apron. "I did okay." He grabbed a rag and rubbed hard at an invisible stain on the counter.

Ella smiled. Harley was more likely to talk when he got nervous. "Getting that secret off your chest did you good."

He gave her a suspicious look. "Secret?"

"The name of the man who drowned."

Harley actually looked relieved. "With Scorza blabbing away, I guess keeping the name secret didn't matter anyway." He hustled from table to table, straightening chairs like it was the most important thing in the world.

"I think it's bad to keep secrets from good friends. What do you think?" Okay, maybe that was a little too obvious.

He grinned. "Sometimes I *like* seeing friends squirm. To see them wondering what's so important that you can't tell them."

"Well, I don't like it that you're keeping a secret from me."

"Just *one?*"

She studied him for a moment. He was getting annoyingly better at this. "One big one, anyway. Aren't you going to tell me what was in that manila envelope?"

"Would you believe my uncle sent a letter encouraging me to enter a drawing contest?" He smiled and grabbed a stick of chalk from the daily specials board and drew a stick figure riding a motorcycle.

"Doubtful. *Cave* drawings are more detailed than your artwork."

"Right," Harley said. "It was a coloring contest."

"You'd have to stay inside the lines, Harley. Probably not in your skill set. No . . . whatever was in that envelope scared you."

"And you're so sure because . . . ?"

She wasn't about to reveal the telltale signs. "Let's call it women's intuition. And I kept wondering why you won't tell me about it."

"So, what did your women's intuition tell you?"

He didn't even look rattled. Was she losing her touch? "Seems like you're protecting someone."

Harley glanced back at her, and for the tiniest fraction of a second, she saw something in his eyes that she hadn't seen since he'd nearly gone off the deep end last summer. Whatever he was hiding was bad enough to spook him good.

The bell on the front door jangled, and Detective Greenwood entered the coffee shop.

BayView customers had habits, and Ella found it weirdly interesting to observe them. Maybe it was the artist in her, but she liked noticing what others missed. Many women stopped within three feet after stepping inside. They'd get something from their purse or brush some piece of nothing off their clothes, giving them a chance to scan the room. They wanted to know *who* was there—friend or foe. Ella could tell immediately if they recognized another customer. If a friend, their face would light up, and they'd breeze over to that table. If it was somebody they didn't want to see, they'd march to the counter like they were late for an appointment.

Most men didn't seem to care about who was there. Their focus was all about how long the line was—and whether Pez still had their favorite donuts. The moment they stepped inside, they didn't stop or slow until they were at the counter.

Not Detective Greenwood, though. He scanned the room like he was on a mission. A hunt . . . but not for coffee and donuts. He looked at her and stopped. Detective Greenwood wanted to talk to her?

Actually, he was looking *past* her. At Harley . . . and Greenwood strode their way.

"Uh-oh." Harley's voice was barely there. If Ella hadn't been so close, she would've never heard it.

"Morning, Ella." Detective Greenwood gave her a nod. "Harley."

Pez stepped out of the back room, drying her hands on her apron, the dog trotting beside her.

Greenwood smiled politely. "Morning, Pez. Mind if I have a word with young Mr. Lotitto here?"

Pez hesitated, like she was still figuring out her foster parent role. "The three of us, or . . . ?"

"Just Harley for now." Greenwood motioned toward the back door. "We'll step outside so we don't get in your way."

Get in your way? It sounded like a super-polite way of making sure nobody would overhear. Did this have something to do with Harley's mystery envelope? Greenwood walked Harley a good twenty feet away from the back of the building. The dog tore out after them and stood at Harley's side. Harley's face looked as pale as the towel in his hands.

Pez stepped up beside Ella, a puzzled look on her face.

So Ella wasn't the only one Harley kept secrets from. "Detective Greenwood—in a top-secret conversation with Harley? What's up with *that*?"

"No idea." Pez watched Harley and Greenwood. "But I intend to find out."

Ella flashed her a smile. "That makes two of us."

CHAPTER 20

HARLEY JAMMED THE CLEANING RAG in his apron pocket. The dog batted Harley's leg with the side of her snout, like she wanted to remind him she was with him all the way. He reached down and stroked her head.

"Mind if I see your phone again, Harley?" Greenwood asked.

"Twice . . . in twenty-four hours?" He reached in his apron pocket.

"And I'm going to ask you to unlock it. Strictly voluntary—you can say no."

Harley tried reading Greenwood's face, but the detective wasn't giving anything away. "I've got nothing to hide."

"So you're giving me permission to look through it?"

"Sure. I guess. But what if I said no?"

Detective Greenwood shrugged. "We'd take a little trip to the station, and we'd bring your foster mom with."

What? He did not want to drag Miss Lopez into this . . . whatever this was. He tapped in his 9-9-9-1 security code and handed Greenwood the phone.

Greenwood scrolled fast, like he knew exactly where he wanted to check. Suddenly he stopped and stared at the screen. "I'm in the middle of an investigation." He locked eyes with Harley, like he wanted to see his reaction. "There's a number you phoned. And I need to know why."

"You're monitoring my calls?"

"My interest is the person on the other end." The detective still had the gazer beams on Harley. "Your name comes up on his phone records—and I need to know why."

Uncle Ray's lawyer. Who else had Harley talked to recently? It figured that his uncle hired some slimeball of an attorney who was being investigated himself. "Show me the number."

Greenwood turned the screen. Harley recognized it immediately—and it definitely wasn't Uncle Ray's lawyer. "Yeah, I called it. Probably nine times. The dog I rescued. Check her tag."

The detective dropped down on one knee and checked. He whistled softly. "Well, how about that."

So whoever owned the dog was under some serious investigation? No wonder they hadn't called back.

Greenwood actually looked relieved. "Sorry to bother you, Harley. We're all done here."

"What do I do about the dog? I keep trying to call the owner. You saw that for yourself."

Greenwood thought for a moment. "Can you keep the dog awhile?"

Harley loved the idea—but then again maybe not. "What if the owner sees me walking his dog down Bearskin Neck? He'll think I stole her."

"Won't happen."

"But what if it does?"

"Then call Race Bannon." Greenwood smiled. "You like the dog?"

As if on cue, the dog nudged Harley's hand like she was reminding him to pet her. "She's great."

"What about Miss Lopez?"

Harley nodded. "Especially with the burglaries going on."

"Perfect. Keep the dog. If you want her."

Wait . . . what? "Like . . . finders keepers?"

"Exactly. The owner is in no position to care for a pet. So either you keep her or I bring her to a shelter." Detective Greenwood hesitated, like he wanted to say more.

Suddenly Harley understood why there'd been no return calls. "The owner is in jail, is that it?"

Greenwood shook his head. "No, he's in the morgue."

CHAPTER 21

PARKER AVOIDED BAYVIEW BREW ALL AFTERNOON. He would've liked hanging out there, but Jelly and Ella would be watching him a little too closely—playing junior shrink to see if he really was okay. One appointment with a therapist was enough for the day, thanks very much.

Talking with the guy had been okay, but he'd told Parker that they should meet again. So much for Parker's one-and-done hopes.

How was he supposed to convince everyone he was fine when he really didn't believe it himself? Parker sat in the captain's chair on *Wings* and stared at the sailboat three slips away. Just the thought of cleaning the hull of *Flight Risk* gave him chills.

Harley phoned to tell him about the dog belonging to Mike Ironwing. So Parker found the owner, and Harley found his dog. Somehow, both had ended up in the water. Absolutely bizarre—and creepy.

Harley had told the girls the dog was his to keep—but nothing more.

He'd promised Parker he'd tell the girls the whole story, but he wanted to update Pez first. And get her permission to keep the dog.

The way Harley told it, both Jelly and Ella screamed when they heard the dog was his. Immediately they started a list of potential names for the pup.

"I'm *not* letting them name my dog," Harley said. "The girls say we're naming her tonight. Right before Miss Lopez's business owners' meeting. So you and I have to come up with ideas—or they will."

Not fifteen minutes after Parker pocketed his phone, a text dinged in from Harley.

Uncle Ray's lawyer is on the way. Get here, okay? You're in this too.

Parker pocketed the boat keys and hustled to BayView Brew.

Jelly ambushed him the moment he stepped inside. "A sleazy-looking guy walked Harley outside two minutes ago—asking to see you, too." She pointed out the back window. "What's going on?"

"I'd better get out there." Parker walked out the back door without answering. Today the lawyer was dressed in black jeans, a blue-striped shirt, and a vest. Cowboy boots. Inked forearms peeking out from under his rolled-up sleeves. A worn leather satchel over one shoulder.

Harley looked relieved the moment he saw Parker and motioned him to hurry over. The lawyer handed each of them an orange business card. The thing was a total knockoff of a Monopoly *Get Out of Jail Free* card. It pictured the Monopoly guy wearing striped prison pj's, getting booted out of jail. The name Sebastian Kilbro was printed in all caps above a phone number. No address. No email.

Harley looked at the card. "You're springing my uncle from jail for *free*?"

Kilbro laughed. "Actually, it should say *Get Out of Jail OR It's Free*." The guy's voice . . . whispery. Raspy. "Your uncle will pay plenty—when I get him out."

"You really think you can?"

"With the evidence he has? Definitely." Kilbro handed Harley a manila folder from inside the satchel.

Harley pulled out a handwritten letter and held it so Parker could read it too.

Harley—you're going for it. Smart choice, for once. Maybe there's hope for you yet.

I had the goods on him—tucked away safe. But I hit a little obstacle—and couldn't bail quick enough, if you know what I mean.

The evidence is on a phone. I can't spell out exactly where I hid it. Too many eyes will see this before it gets to you—and Lochran and his goons would snatch the evidence long before you got there.

It's up to you and the Buckman kid to salvage this situation. Figure out the clues together. If you're totally stuck, get your tail back here for visiting hours Saturday, and I'll feed you hints.

Tell nobody about this. NOBODY. It's too risky. Every person in the circle of information potentially enters a ring of death.

Your life is in danger now. Only after the evidence is in Kilbro's hands will you be safe. And remember, he has the coordinates showing where my third man dumped your motorcycle. The instant you give him the recordings, he'll give you the location. Now go get that recording, and make me proud, boys!

Uncle Ray

Parker's stomach knotted. Harley pulled out the clue sheet.

Here's where to find the killer evidence that'll put Lochran away for good.

Within earshot of the old bell,
but only if you're feeling swell.
Watch your time, 'cause there's not a heap,
Soon you'll both be in trouble deep.
Below the place where some might crash,
in a bag never meant for trash.
You'll find it's all there, nice and dry,
Enough to make Quinn Lochran fry.
The place is dark, when it's not night.
So use your head, and bring a light.
Watch for Lochran, and Mr. White,
both have a nasty appetite.
They'll take your life, they'll take your soul,
They swallow careless dummies whole.

Parker looked from Harley to the lawyer. "What does this even *mean*?"

Sebastian Kilbro shook his head. "No idea. Believe me, I've been working on it. He says you two will figure it out—easy. And you'd better do it quick. Time isn't on our side."

Harley scanned the cryptic poem again. "How do I watch out for Lochran? I wouldn't know him if he walked into the coffee shop. I could be making him a latte and *blam-blam-blam* . . . he puts a trio of 9mm's in my back."

"Lochran won't order anything but coffee. Black. I'll text you his photo," Kilbro said. "If you see him? Hit the bricks. Run."

Harley nodded. "Who's Mr. White?"

"No idea. Maybe he works for Lochran—or Lochran works for him. Just keep your eyes open."

The lawyer insisted they put his number in their phones and got theirs in return. "When you figure this out, call. Day or night. I'll get the evidence out of your hands—and into the DA's. I've never lost a client yet, but your uncle is going up against a shark—and I don't just mean a *loan* shark."

Sheesh. Parker stared at Harley. What did they just get themselves into?

CHAPTER 22

THE ONLY CUSTOMER IN THE COFFEE SHOP headed for the front door. Angelica pulled El down behind the ordering counter. She didn't want the boys to see her at the window spying on them and the sleazy lawyer they were talking to.

"I don't like the looks of that guy," Angelica knelt behind the counter and kept her voice down.

"Maybe if we find out more about this lawyer dude, we can figure the rest of this out." Ella hesitated. "Think it has something to do with the body they found?"

Angelica was sure of it. "I hate it when the boys keep secrets from us."

"Which is why you need a new friend." Bryce Scorza's voice was unmistakable, and as annoying as ever. "Somebody who won't hide things from you. Speaking of hiding. . . ."

He leaned over the counter, grinning down at both of them. How did he slip in without the bell ringing?

Angelica stood. "Mr. Scorza. What can I get you?"

"It's what I can get *you*." He stood there in his football jersey, the number eight emblazoned on the front. "First, I'll give you a promise."

"Wonderful. Promise you'll never sneak up on me again." Angelica held out her hand to shake his.

Scorza grinned like he thought she was joking. "I'll promise not to keep secrets from you. How's that? Go ahead. Test me. Ask me a question."

He was a coward. A truth-twister. An egotistical, self-centered moron. "I already know more about you than I want to know."

"Not the important stuff. C'mon. Shoot me a question."

El pointed at the door. "How fast can you leave the shop?"

Scorza laughed. "You *want* a guy like me around. One who won't keep secrets from you. So . . . how about I get things rolling by telling you something you don't already know. Secrets . . . secrets." Like he had so many he couldn't figure out where to start. "How much can I bench press? A hundred and ninety-five pounds—and that's with free weights, which are harder than just lifting on a machine. And I can run a hundred yards—that's an entire football field—in eleven seconds flat. Easy. That puts me in the top 5 percent of high school males."

"Why would I want to know—?"

"I can come and go at home whenever I want. My stepmom doesn't care. You need me in the middle of the night, I'm your man."

"I will *never* need you in the middle—or any other time—of the night," Angelica said, "and you definitely aren't my man."

"I can fold my eyelids back if I really want to freak someone out." He reached for his eye.

Angelica lunged forward and grabbed his arm. "Do *not* demonstrate. I believe you."

"See there?" Scorza smiled. "You're hanging on me already."

Angelica dropped his arm like it was a dead rat.

"Okay, Mr. I've-Got-No-Secrets." El pointed at the door again. "Unless you want to buy something, we've got to get to work."

"Are you worried about the burglaries?"

Where did *that* come from? "It's on Miss Lopez's mind, for sure."

"It's on *every*body's mind. See, that's where I can help. Why don't you give me your number, and I'll send you my contact info. The nights you're closing the shop, I can walk you home until this burglar is caught. I'll keep you safe."

Angelica was *not* giving him her number. "I feel a lot safer when you're not around."

He laughed. "You're a terrible liar, you know that? There isn't a girl at Rockport High School who wouldn't love to get my number."

"Except me," Angelica said.

"And me." El pointed at the door again. "Why don't you go find all those girls who want your number so badly."

"I'm going." Scorza raised both hands and backed toward the door. "But I talked with my dad this morning. About Mike Ironwing? Thought you might want to hear what I found out."

So *that's* what this was all about. "Get back here."

Scorza smiled—and took his time strolling over. "There's a rumor that Ironwing ran into the burglar. Wrong place, wrong time, you know?"

"You're saying Mr. Ironwing was killed because he saw the Bearskin Neck Bogeyman?" Angelica tried not to act as interested as she was.

"They're not calling him the Bogeyman anymore. Not after what he did to Ironwing."

He was baiting her—and she knew it. But Angelica really wanted to know. "What's his new name?"

Scorza gave a half smile. "The Bearskin Neck *Strangler*."

Angelica's stomach did a couple of somersaults. What if the guy broke into BayView Brew, and Harley—or Pez—tried to stop him? What if Parker was working late at the yacht club and ran into him on his walk home?

Scorza seemed to notice Mr. Bones for the first time. "So you hired a security guard—or has Miss Lopez cut back to a *skeleton* crew?"

His lame joke wasn't worthy of a response.

He tugged a napkin from the dispenser and wrote his number on it. "Take this. You'll need it someday."

"I'm not the one who needs protection." She wouldn't be caught dead on Bearskin Neck after dark. The chances she'd run into the Bogeyman—or the Strangler—were too small to measure. She instinctively looked Parker's way.

The lawyer looked like he was finishing up with the boys. He shook their hands. And now Harley had a new manila envelope. By the looks on their faces, whatever was inside was no prize.

"What's *he* doing here?" Apparently, Scorza had followed her gaze.

"You know him?"

"Sebastian Kilbro. Criminal lawyer. He represented my dad back when he got tangled up with Steadman."

That was the lawyer who got Mr. Scorza off the hook?

"He's good," Scorza said. "*Really* good."

Angelica disagreed. "If he got your dad off, I'd say he's really *bad*."

"No arguments from me." Scorza laughed. "He could get the devil a 'not guilty' verdict. But why is he talking to Harley—and Gatorade?" Scorza's eyes narrowed. "What did they get themselves into this time?"

"Exactly what I'd like to know," Angelica said.

Scorza looked at her for a long moment and smiled. "Admit it, ladies. They look like a couple of freshman asked to play the varsity team. Totally out of their league."

Ella frowned. Parker stood staring at the ground with hands in his back pockets. Harley ran his hands through his hair, face turned toward the clouds.

The lawyer stepped back inside and strode directly to the front door. He didn't even glance toward the counter. Maybe he wasn't a coffee lover, but men never walked by without at least a glance at the donuts.

"How about I see what else I can learn?" Scorza kept a bead on the lawyer. "You've got my number if you need it."

And just like that Scorza tucked his football under one arm and trotted for the front door.

Pez came out from the kitchen like she'd been watching for the lawyer to leave. Without a word, she slipped out the back door and listened intently as Harley pointed to the envelope and talked. Hands clasped together, she pressed them against her lips and shook her head.

"Look at him," El said. "I've *never* seen Harley talk that fast."

Harley slid a paper out of the envelope and held it up while Parker took a picture of it.

"C'mon, boys," El whispered. "Tell us what you're up to."

Angelica wished it were that easy.

Pez put one hand on Harley's shoulder. The other on Parker's. Her eyes . . . squeezed shut.

"Praying?" El whispered.

No doubt. Some people bowed their head when praying. Pez did that sometimes. But with more urgent situations, Pez often faced the sky. Maybe she wanted her prayers to have the clearest shot—a direct line.

"I've got a really bad feeling about this, Jelly. They need help. We've got to find out what that lawyer told them."

Angelica agreed. "And what's in that envelope."

CHAPTER 23

Wings TUGGED AT THE DOCK LINES like she just couldn't get comfortable in the slip. Parker sat staring at the poem from Harley's uncle. Harley held a pen to jot down the answers as they deciphered the thing, but he hadn't written anything yet. The dog sniffed its way around the boat—as if the boat were telling her all its secrets.

Harley tossed the pen onto the deck. "Bell. Bell. What bell is he talking about? We're never going to figure this out."

It was definitely harder than Parker had expected. "It says we don't have a heap of time. That's easy enough to understand. And the part about Lochran is clear enough—and Mr. White being his boss or hired muscle."

But none of that was helping them find the hidden evidence. "We need help." Parker tried to sound casual about the suggestion.

"If you're talking about Jelly and Ella, they'll spend more time trying to talk us out of finding this evidence than they will solving the mystery.

Miss Lopez is letting me run with this for now—but what if the girls change her mind?"

Harley had told Pez what Ray wanted but didn't let her read the letter—or the poem. She couldn't possibly have a full picture of the threat to her.

"It was tricky enough getting out of the shop without answering questions from the girls. You know they'll use this dog-naming party to worm some info out of us." Harley groaned. "They'll be here any minute. I thought we'd have this figured out by now."

Parker reread the poem. "What if we get the girls to help—without telling them what it's about? Maybe only give them part of this. If we could figure out what bell he's talking about, maybe the rest will fall into place."

Harley shrugged. Nodded.

"Harley! Parker!" Finn Bilba . . . the drummer they knew from school. They'd been seeing more of him lately—and he probably texted Wilson as much as they did. Finn shouted from the edge of T-Wharf. He held up a bag of Oreos and gave them a shake.

Parker waved him over. "What if Finn sticks around—even after the girls get here? They can't grill us with him around."

Harley smiled. "I like it." He put Ray's note back in the envelope, then tucked it out of sight inside his hoodie.

Finn was sitting on the boat's port gunwale when the girls arrived. Jelly looked from Finn to Parker, her eyes narrowing just a bit, like she suspected his strategy. She climbed into the boat and sat on the bow seat.

"So, what are we naming this beautiful doggy?" El climbed aboard and knelt on the deck. She stroked the dog's head. "Got something yet?"

"Plenty." Harley shrugged. "Trying to narrow them down, in fact. Skeeter. Scooter. Bowzer."

El gave a totally exasperated sigh. "This is a *she*. How about a name with a little less testosterone?"

"What about Davidson?" Harley smiled. "Clever, right?"

El stared at Harley. "So when you're walking her down the street, people say, 'Hi, Harley Davidson,' or something equally lame?"

"It's good. It's got a ring to it."

"So do toilets in public restrooms—and that doesn't make them good," El said. "You will *not* give this doggy any such name. You'd have a constant reminder of the motorcycle you lost. Bad idea."

"How about Oreo?" Finn smiled. "The dog is a chocolate lab, right?"

"Lame, lame, lame," Jelly said. "What else do you boys have?"

"Fudge?" Parker raised his eyebrows, hoping to see a little affirmation from the others.

"The chocolate theme works," Jelly said, "but Fudge has been used before—in one of my favorite books, as a matter of fact."

Ella walked right up to Harley and rested her fingertips on his temples. "Close your eyes. Concentrate. Her name is in your head, but it's having a hard time finding its way out."

Harley looked at her like she was crazy.

"I said close your eyes, Mr. Lotitto."

Harley obeyed, a slight smile on his face like he'd forgotten all about his uncle and the evidence he needed to find.

"Think of a name you liked as a kid. Maybe a friend. Or a character in a book." She rubbed his temples in a slow, lazy circle. The dog leaned in, like she hoped to be next.

Harley's smile stretched just a bit.

"There. What name just streaked through your brain?"

"Zippy."

"What?" Ella stopped the temple treatment.

Jelly didn't look thrilled. "Not exactly a girl's name, though, is it?"

Ella took a seat and patted her thighs. The dog trotted over. "How about Precious? Would you like that for a name, girl?"

Finn hunched over, trying to imitate Gollum from *Lord of the Rings*. "My Precious."

"Ah, *no*." Harley shook his head. "Absolutely not."

"Princess."

Harley covered his ears.

"Or maybe the name *of* a princess." Ella angled her head, like she was watching the dog for a reaction. "Aurora? Belle? Jasmine?"

"You're killing me," Harley said.

"Ariel," Jelly said. "Our doggy came from the sea . . . and wanted to be part of your world, right?"

"Oh, my goodness." Ella looked way too excited. "I think I *love* that!"

Harley crossed his eyes. "Guys, help me out here."

"I say we go back to something chocolate," Parker said. "A favorite candy?"

"I love Tootsie Rolls," Finn said.

"Tootsie." El raised her eyebrows. "That's got potential, right?"

"Here, Tootsie. Sit, Toots." Harley shook his head. "What else?"

"Snickers. Baby Ruth. Reese's. Oh Henry." Finn looked at Harley. "One of them work for you?"

Harley looked more confused than ever.

"Three Musketeers? Twix?" Finn looked determined. "Clark. Goobers."

"Finn," Jelly said. "We're not naming this girl Clark, Henry, Goobers—or any of your other ridiculous suggestions."

"I got it," Finn did a drumroll on the gunwale. "*Hershey.* King of chocolate—and a hundred-percent girly. *Her. She.*"

"I love it!" Ella clapped. "Harley and Hershey. Cute, right?"

"Cute?" Harley groaned. "Okay, her name is *not* Hershey."

"Milky Way," Finn said. "KitKat."

"KitKat." Harley stared at him. "That was my dad's favorite." He motioned for the dog. "Hey, KitKat. Come, KitKat."

The dog bounded over and sat next to him. Harley grinned. "Okay, everybody, I'd like you to meet my dog, KitKat." He lifted KitKat's front paw and waved to the group.

"I actually like that." El raised her eyebrows like she was surprised.

Nobody looked happier than Finn. He passed the bag of Oreos around the boat to celebrate.

"Okay, everybody. I need help with something else." Harley looked at Parker like he suddenly wasn't so sure this was a good idea. "I'm looking for something hidden near a bell in the area. I have no idea *what* bell."

All eyes were on Harley.

"That's it?" Finn shrugged. "You want us to list every kind of bell we can think of?"

Harley nodded.

"Maybe if you told us what you're looking for," Ella said, "that'd help."

Harley glanced at Parker, and he took that as his cue to join in. "Let's just say Harley is on a scavenger hunt—and he's already told you all he can. Bells . . . bells. Let's make a list."

Over the next five minutes they got plenty of ideas for bells. Nothing that jumped out at Parker—but he jotted down every suggestion, no matter how ridiculous it seemed. Church bells. Sleigh bells. Bicycle bells. The bell at Rockport High School. Alarm clock bells. Barbells. Parker felt Jelly watching him.

"What about those bells mounted on shop doors in town," Finn said. "You know, the ones that ring when customers come in—like at BayView Brew?"

Harley's eyebrows rose slightly. "We had one at the dive shop. That's *good*."

"Wind chimes." Ella pointed toward Bearskin Neck. "Some would call them bells—and they're all over the Neck."

Harley checked to make sure Parker wrote it down. "Circle that one. Anything else?"

The bell brainstorming stalled out, and the boat got quiet.

KitKat did more exploring and sniffed at the bag of Oreos in Finn's hand.

"Smart doggy." Finn moved the bag from left to right, watching KitKat follow with her nose. "So the cop is just letting you keep the dog? That's great—but seems weird, right?"

"Exactly my thoughts," Jelly said.

"I found her in the water. Call it salvage rights."

"Right." Jelly angled her head slightly. "I see you've removed the Harley-Davidson tag. So you're just going to stop trying to find the real owner?"

"*I'm* the owner now," Harley said. "Kit is mine."

"That feels dishonest, Mr. Lotitto." Ella shook her head. "Which doesn't sound like you—*or* Detective Greenwood."

Harley hesitated. "Greenwood said the owner is in no position to care for a dog anymore." He nodded his head toward *Flight Risk*, the sailboat where Parker had found the body.

There was a moment where the only sound was seagulls screeching overhead. Ella's eyes grew wide. "The dog belonged to . . . *him?*"

Jelly gasped. "KitKat . . . come." The dog trotted right to her. She held Kit's face between her hands. "You poor orphan doggy. Your daddy drowned and left you all alone!"

For an instant Harley looked stunned, like he hadn't thought of it quite that way. "Guess we've got that in common, Kit." The dog ran to him, like she knew who she belonged to now. "He couldn't help it. He didn't *leave* you. Somebody hurt him."

Parker wasn't sure if he was still talking about Mike Ironwing—or his own dad.

"I am soooo sorry," Jelly said. "I wasn't thinking."

Harley waved her off. "Forget it. That was a long time ago."

Almost four years now . . . when he was twelve.

Kit nuzzled Harley's hand, like she understood what they'd been talking about. The bond forming between her and Harley seemed to vulcanize at that moment.

"So the guy who drowned didn't go in the water alone," Finn said. "Kit was there when he died. Creepy, right?"

Ella seemed to be thinking that through. "Parker finds a body, and Harley rescues the dead guy's dog? That *must* mean something. I've got to ask Grams about that."

"Here we go," Harley said. "All it means is they both ended up in the water, and only Kit made it. Maybe the guy tipped in one of those two-seater kayaks. With her fur, Kit would survive a lot longer than a human."

Ella shook her head. "I feel like this whole thing is some kind of omen."

"This wasn't just a drowning," Jelly said. "And every one of us knows that. Too much police attention for that. And Bryce Scorza pretty well confirmed that." She quickly relayed what they'd learned while Parker and Harley were talking to the lawyer.

"How would Scorza know?" Parker couldn't believe she'd buy anything Scorza said. "The guy wears his football jersey all year round. Scorza doesn't know what he's talking about."

"Says the one who doesn't talk about what he knows." Jelly locked eyes with him. "Scorza said the man you two were talking to is a criminal lawyer. Is that right?"

Parker didn't answer.

"I'll take that as a yes. And Mr. Scorza said his name is Sebastian something. Kimbro?"

"Kilbro."

"So, he was right again." Jelly sighed. "Maybe he's right about the rumors, too. What if we're dealing with more than the Bearskin Neck Bogeyman? What if there really is a Bearskin Neck Strangler . . . and Mr. Ironwing ran into him?"

Actually, the theory made sense.

"Strange things have been happening here for weeks and weeks now," Ella said. "Burglaries like crazy all around this harbor . . . and now a man ends up dead in it? It's a sign."

"Of *what*?" Finn popped an Oreo in his mouth and worked it to one cheek. "People shouldn't swim in nasty-cold water?"

"Look," Jelly said, "arguing about this doesn't change the facts. Mike Ironwing owned KitKat. Now he's dead. Whatever happened to him . . . KitKat knows."

Finn raised his eyebrows in mock horror. "Better get that doggy in the witness protection program."

"Do *not* make fun of me, Mr. Bilba. Something big is happening here. And in a way, we're connected."

Harley gave Jelly a questioning look.

"Kit and the dead man were connected . . . and now she's connected to you . . . to all of us."

Parker had to dial this back a bit. "Look . . . Jelly makes a good point. That drowning may not have been accidental. We shouldn't overreact, but it won't hurt if we all are more careful—especially at night."

Jelly gave him a little bow. "Thank you. At least one of you understands."

"And I'm still talking to Grams about all this," Ella said. "I don't like it."

"You don't think I should keep Kit?"

Ella shook her head. "That's not it. KitKat is yours now. I just have this sense it means something."

"The important thing? Kit is mine—and nobody can take her away."

"Just watch yourself. Okay, Harley?" Ella looked serious. "The last person who owned KitKat ended up dead."

CHAPTER 24

VINNY TORINO PARKED HIS RAM 1500 LARAMIE PICKUP on the strip of Beach Street that separated Front Beach from the Old Parish Burial Ground. It'd been a favorite spot for as long as he could remember. Sandy Bay . . . teeming with life. The cemetery . . . filled with the dead. It was how he lived life—parked somewhere between life and death.

He arrived early for the meeting. He'd done his prep work. After his little speech, shop owners would line up to give him their money.

Advertising people often created ads that promised happiness. They hired perfect models for photo shoots who'd laugh and smile like life was good—just because they were using whatever gimmick the ad designers were selling.

But there was another motivator that worked soooo much better than the promise of a better life. *Fear.* Most people hated feeling afraid—unless they were watching a movie. Promise people a way to save them from their darkest fears, and sales go through the roof. Insurance companies made ridiculous profits by preying on the fears of decent people—and Vinny would do the same.

Vinny knew a thing or two about including raw fear in his marketing plan. He'd been careful to spread a growing uneasiness on the Neck for weeks now. Nobody wanted to pay for extra security. Vinny got that. But the shopkeepers would throw their money at him if they were scared enough. The Bearskin Neck Bogeyman continued to strike—and hadn't been close to getting caught . . . not once. Now he'd start phase two of his business plan. This was where things really got fun.

Vinny was the ringmaster, controlling a two-ring circus. One ring was the new business he'd introduce tonight: Cape Ann Angels Security. That's where he'd keep the spotlight: his angels of light. But there was one *other* team of angels he employed: his angels of darkness. This team was all about the burglaries and extractions, getting the team safely out before the cops arrived. Vinny's business plan was simple. Slick. And if anyone got in his way . . . deadly.

He grabbed his over-the-shoulder bag and slid out of the truck. He straightened the new magnetic sign on the door. *Cape Ann Angels Security* in a Harley-Davidson-type shield logo. He especially liked the slogan printed directly below it: *Little Wings. Big Guns.* The graphic of an angel packing a Glock in a shoulder holster set things off just right.

Vinny had finished a light workout at the gym before coming. His new Cape Ann Angels T-shirt bulged in all the right places. It would send a message. If Vinny couldn't keep their businesses safe, nobody could.

He'd always liked wearing short sleeves—to show off his tattoos. It added to his intimidation factor as a bouncer, which gave him an edge when things got dicey. He'd always paid top dollar for his tats. Nothing that looked like he'd spent time in prison with a wannabe tattoo artist. His tats would work their magic on the business owners tonight too.

People entered BayView Brew like the place was giving out free bagels. A couple of girls wearing coffee shop aprons stood outside the door, smiling and greeting them. A redhead and a black girl. Both likely in high school. He'd seen them around the boys who'd found poor Mikey . . . the park ranger's son and Ray Lotitto's nephew, Harley, who was now Victoria Lopez's charity project.

Speak of the devils. The boys rounded the corner of the building—with a dog on a leash. *The* dog. That might make things interesting.

He sized up the boys quick. Harley wore a coffee shop apron and looked like a football player, but without the swagger. Vinny respected that. But he needed to watch the dog right now.

Suddenly the dog's ears pricked up—and the thing looked right at him. *Here we go.* It had Vinny's scent. The animal strained at the leash, barking its fool head off. Vinny didn't slow his pace.

The dog pulled Mr. Football until the kid put some muscle into the job. "Whoa, Kit. What's the matter?" Even the ranger's kid took a grip on the leash.

Vinny had given the dog a chance to swim to shore when he'd dumped Ironwing. And this was the way the animal repaid him?

The thing tugged hard—its collar digging deep, making every bark and breath raspy. Rabid-sounding. The girls left their post at the door and got their hands on the leash. It was a regular tug-of-war. Mr. Football, the ranger's kid, and two girls against the dog, but somehow the thing held its ground—even on the sidewalk.

Never appear afraid. Not of anyone—or anything. Vinny dropped onto one knee and held his hand out toward the dog. "Sign this pup up for that big dog-sled race. The Iditarod. Quite a puller you've got here."

"Sorry." The football guy choked way up on the leash—keeping the dog just out of reach. Its fur stood up like it had some massive static charge going. "I just got the dog. I don't know what's eating her."

"Looks like she wants to eat *me*." Vinny smiled. "Hey, pup. Do you smell my cat or something?" Okay, he was fibbing a little. The only cat he owned was his 9mm Springfield Hellcat—neatly concealed in the holster above his back hip pocket.

"Hey, KitKat." The black girl was on her knees, smoothing down the animal's fur. "It's okay. Nothing to be scared about."

That made Vinny smile. If dogs could talk, this one would have a story to tell that'd scare the cowgirl boots off the girl.

The girl had a calming effect on the dog, but there was something about the uneasy glance she gave Vinny that was disturbing. Almost as if she understood something of what the dog was trying to tell her—and wondered if it were true.

Vinny introduced himself and didn't let on that he knew who Harley was. He got their names in return. Parker. Ella. Angelica—who the others called Jelly. He instantly wrote their names on the walls of his memory. The boys backed the dog around the corner of the building, even though the thing put up an impressive fight. With fresh apologies, Ella and Angelica got the door for Vinny, and he stepped inside.

The coffee shop was packed tighter than the donut racks in the morning. Small business owners—and most looking spooked. Others had the tough talk going. Mostly about what they'd do if the Bogeyman broke into their place. But they'd be singing a different tune when they were all alone—and the Bogeyman came calling.

He could smell the fear in this place. The whole thing gave Vinny a sense that he was truly invincible. A rush like he'd get when passing a car on a two-lane country road. A windows-down, ninety-miles-an-hour-in-the-oncoming-lane kind of exhilaration.

Victoria Lopez had been decent enough to give him a spot on the program to pitch the new business. While he waited, he gave the place a quick once-over. Front door. Back. Doorway into the kitchen. Stairs leading up to what? Likely living quarters. A replica skeleton sat at a table set up with a checkers game. Its hand was on a checker, like it was ready to make its move. Somebody was creative.

He sat in the back and watched Lopez corral the crowd. She announced that she'd like to open the meeting by praying to "Almighty God" for help. She was going straight to the top—which proved just how scared they really were, right?

He expected some desperate, pleading kind of prayer. Something weak and pathetic:

*Mighty God, we hope you can
save us from the Bogeyman.
But if you can't, then be our guide,
and help us find a place to hide.*

Instead, the woman prayed with confidence. Like God had come through for her before. She almost sounded excited to see what he'd do this time. It was bunk. It had to be.

But it felt . . . *powerful.*

Vinny scanned the room as she prayed. Shop owners seemed totally dialed in. Clearly this woman was not someone to underestimate. He sensed that she could prove dangerous if she put her mind to working against him. So he wouldn't let that happen.

Victoria Lopez followed with a rousing "rally the troops" speech. She was good, he had to hand it to her. Miss Lopez had a way of uniting and calming the crowd. Clearly, she had too much influence over them. He'd have to do something about that.

Detective Greenwood was there too. He gave a good talk about the need to install security cameras—and leave lights burning inside after closing. He urged them to keep outside lights on behind their stores at night. He painted a picture of cooperation between the police and the business owners. For the police's part, they'd be stepping up cruiser patrols all night—every night. And without going into details, he promised he had some surprises planned for the Bearskin Neck Bogeyman. "We'll get him. You have my word on that."

Don't bet on it.

Only a handful of shopkeepers clapped when he finished. The rest didn't look convinced. Another week of burglaries, and this entire crowd would be ready to lynch him.

Working at the bar taught Vinny a lot. People complained about their problems—but usually wanted someone else to fix them. People in the bar tossed their money down just to make their problems go away for a couple of hours.

The people in this room were no different. They didn't want self-help, leave-your-lights-on-and-buy-security-cameras solutions. They wanted the police to make the Bogeyman go bye-bye. And if the cops didn't? Shopkeepers would definitely be willing to lay down money for Vinny to do it.

Lucius Scorza stood. Vinny had never worked directly with him, but Ray Lotitto had. How he got in tonight without owning a business, Vinny had no idea.

"I'd like the detective to tell us," Scorza bellowed, "if the South Basin drowning of Mike Ironwing was an accident—or not. There are rumors he ran into the Bogeyman . . . and was murdered as a result."

The place went up for grabs. Greenwood tried quieting the crowd with both hands above his head. "I don't know where you get your information, but it's too early for me to—"

"This isn't the Bearskin Neck Bogeyman we're dealing with any-more," Lucius thundered. "This is the Bearskin Neck *Strangler*. I say if the police can't do their job, let's hire new ones!" Lucius Scorza had some history with Greenwood . . . and apparently he'd come for a little payback.

Greenwood wouldn't confirm or deny anything—which fueled the frenzy. It was a lob pitch. They were making Vinny's job easier and easier.

By the time Miss Lopez motioned Vinny to the front, the crowd was ready to follow anyone who promised relief from their fears.

Vinny hustled up. He locked eyes with Detective Greenwood for a moment. He'd never had a love for cops. And he'd learned how to get things done without showing up on their radar. Right now, he was going to school the cop on how to get a crowd eating out of his hand. *Take notes, detective.*

"I'm Vinny Torino. I grew up in the part of Boston where you got tough quick, or you learned to hide. I worked my way through college as a bouncer. My job was simple. When somebody got out of line, I got them out of the bar. The owner didn't want nasty drunks tearing up the place—or intimidating customers. Turns out I was kind of a natural for the job." He made a fist and kissed his knuckles. "But keeping the bar from getting busted up wasn't my big motivator."

He paused and scanned the room for effect. A woman looked at him like she was ready to sign up right now. A man sitting at the cop's table nodded—like he was already liking where this was going. Harley and Parker stood in the back. They must have tied the dog somewhere. Harley was smiling, his arms folded across his broad chest like he was imagining himself in Vinny's shoes—and liking it. Parker was a little harder to read.

"I wanted to protect the property, for sure. But what I really wanted to protect? The people who came there. The way I saw it, plenty of them were in the bar because life was giving them a rough go of it. People came in to escape something hard. In my own way, I made sure the bar was a safe place to forget their problems. And if someone hassled them for whatever reason, I'd quietly step in and suggest they change their tune, leave the bar, or put on a flight suit." He pantomimed giving some guy an uppercut with his right—and he zoomed his left hand into the air like he was sending someone to the moon.

The crowd clapped and cheered. Harley gave a whistle that would carry across any football field. Miss Lopez didn't look all that impressed. Or maybe it was Vinny's imagination. Ella and Angelica stood with her, and they definitely reflected her vibe.

"After college I moved to Gloucester. Up until recently, I've still worked nights at bars—and doing deliveries or anything else I could to bring in a few extra bucks by day."

Detective Greenwood watched him. *Analyzed* him was more like it. Not just listening to what was being said, but Vinny sensed the cop was taking in everything. How Vinny moved. Listening for what Vinny wasn't saying. Okay, so maybe there was a reason the cop carried a detective's shield. He was like Vinny that way. Smart. The cop was another one he'd have to watch.

"When I heard about the Bearskin Neck Bogeyman—or Strangler, as it seems we're calling him now—something about it just kind of stuck in my craw. I love Cape Ann. This is my home. And somebody's messing with people who just wanted to make an honest living here? I decided to do something about it." Vinny held up both hands to quiet the applause this time.

He told about setting up his company and how it worked. How any shop that signed up with him would get Cape Ann Angels Security stickers for their doors and front window. "Here's my guarantee: Any business that signs up and still gets burglarized? I'll reimburse your security service fee for the entire month. No . . . I'll pay you two months. How's that?"

If there'd been any donuts left on the shelves, they'd have been bouncing with the thundering reaction. "My prices aren't cheap, but I'm not going about this in a half-baked way, either. I'm not afraid of Mr. Strangler; he'd better think long and hard before he messes with the Cape Ann Angels—or one of the businesses we're watching over. Like I said, growing up I learned to get tough—or hide. Well, we've been hiding too long here . . . and we won't hide anymore. The Strangler better hide—because I'm coming for him."

Vinny had never gotten a standing ovation before. Usually when he did his job well, there were more people on the floor than on their feet. But desperate shop owners stood and cheered now. Shop owners mobbed him for business cards like he held Willy Wonka golden tickets.

This was almost too easy. His business plan had been simple. Give a legit reason for people to be afraid. Feed that fear. Then offer a way to save them from the very fear he'd created.

Harley was talking like crazy to Parker. Both of them looked downright inspired by Vinny's speech. Good.

The only two in the room who weren't acting like they'd just won the Super Bowl were that detective and Miss Victoria Lopez. But that was okay. He'd keep his ear to the ground when it came to Detective Greenwood. And Miss Lopez? She'd be scrambling for one of his business cards yet. Vinny could make that happen. All she needed was a little visit from the Strangler.

CHAPTER 25

HARLEY CLIPPED THE LEASH ONTO KIT'S COLLAR and slipped out the back door. Miss Lopez was still talking to a couple of shop owners who'd hung around after the meeting.

He'd placed a note for Miss Lopez on his bed saying he'd left to walk the dog and he'd be home by ten. He added a PS that he'd be careful so she wouldn't worry. How long had it been since anyone worried about him being out? With any luck, he'd be back before she knew he'd ever left.

Parker had left with his parents to drop off the girls at their homes. He'd promised to work on Uncle Ray's crazy clue sheet the moment he got to his room. Taking the dog for a walk made for a perfect opportunity for Harley to do a little patrolling down Bearskin Neck himself.

He turned off the main street and instead walked Bradley Wharf— the road running between the rear of some of the shops and the North Basin of Rockport Harbor. The way he'd walked thousands of times when he'd lived above the Rockport Dive Company.

There were enough lights on poles to light the way. But there were plenty of shadows, too. He stopped at the spot where his shed once stood. Where Kemosabe had been parked before it'd been stolen.

Kit sniffed the ground like she knew something important had happened there.

He walked to the back of what was once his uncle's dive shop. Could the recordings be hidden inside? That didn't seem likely. Wouldn't the new owners have found it?

But the recordings could be hidden within earshot of the front door bell, right? Obviously, Uncle Ray didn't want the evidence to get into the wrong hands—and he'd made the clues incredibly cryptic just in case. But how was Harley supposed to figure it out? Maybe he'd come back with Parks tomorrow and give the area a good going over.

A set of headlights swept onto Bradley, cruising slow. *Really* slow. A low growl rose up from somewhere inside Kit. He took a fresh grip on the leash. "Easy, girl. What is it?"

Kit zeroed in on the approaching truck—and Harley did too. "We're okay. The burglar won't drive up with headlights on."

Sure enough, the Cape Ann Angels Security logo covered the driver's door. The window was down, and Mr. Torino's elbow rested there. The truck stopped. Torino swung out, leaned against the truck door, and folded his arms across his chest. "Harley? What are you doing?"

Mr. Torino recognized him? That actually felt pretty good. A rumble grew from somewhere deep inside Kit. "It's okay, girl," Harley said. "He's on our side." He jogged to the truck with Kit trotting alongside.

A tattoo of a triangle dinner bell filled the side of Torino's upper arm. The words *COME and GET IT* were tattooed across his forearm. "Taking the pup for a walk—or doing a little patrolling yourself?"

Busted. "Both."

"This isn't the safest place to walk at night—you know that, right?"

Harley shrugged. He had Kit. And who'd want to take on both of them?

"Why do I get the idea you'll keep walking this dog down here no matter what I say?" Torino smiled. "I'd have done the same at your age."

Kit started that rumbling thing again.

Torino nodded his chin toward Harley. "You play football?"

"Running back."

The head of Cape Ann Angels smiled. "Seventeen?"

"Sixteen. This week."

"Happy birthday. You're built like I was."

Obviously the guy must have never stopped working out. Torino looked like he could still play the game—and keep up.

"When you turn eighteen, you let me know if you want a job as a bouncer in Gloucester. It pays well."

"My dad was killed by a DUI driver four years ago. I'm probably not the guy to take a job protecting drunks."

Torino shook his head. "That makes you *exactly* the right guy for the job. You get paid to keep drunks in line—and *off* the road. You take their keys—and dare them to take them back. And if one tries?" He made a fist. A letter was tattooed above each knuckle: *BANG.* "I treat them to a knuckle sandwich. Everything they eat for the next few days will come through a straw, believe me.

"If one punch doesn't do it—and they come back for seconds?" Torino showed the word tattooed above the knuckles of his other fist: *ZOOM.* The word *LAUNCHPAD* was tattooed across the other forearm. "*Bang. Zoom.* I send them to the moon until they sober up."

Harley smiled. He'd broken dozens of random bottles of liquor in the last couple of years . . . his small way of keeping drunks off the road. The idea of doing that in a more aggressive way sounded kinda nice.

"Do me two favors, okay?" Torino grabbed a business card from the dashboard. "Put my number in your contacts. And you be careful out here, okay? You don't know what this Bogeyman—or Strangler—is like. And if you do see someone—or something—that doesn't quite feel right?" He handed Harley the card. "You call me. Don't go playing the hero alone. Got it?"

Harley nodded.

"I signed up over a dozen shop owners at tonight's meeting." Again, Torino smiled. "A good start. But your foster mom wasn't one of them. I'd like to get her on my patrol circuit."

Definitely something Harley wanted to see too. "I'll talk to her."

"Do that. And stay safe."

"It's not me I'm worried about."

Torino angled his head slightly like he was weighing what Harley had just said. "Your foster mom?"

Harley gave a single nod.

"I respect that. Well, you keep *her* safe, then. How's that?"

"Exactly what I intend to do." With everything he had. And right now, he had the feeling it was high time he got back to her.

CHAPTER 26

PARKER RAISED HIS BEDROOM WINDOW, filling his lungs with the cool, salty air. The sound of waves pummeling the Headlands pulsed through his room. He pulled out his phone and studied the photo of Ray Lotitto's cryptic message. The thing made no sense.

If they didn't figure it out, Uncle Ray would stay in prison. Was that so bad? Wouldn't it be worse for Harley if his uncle were free? The bigger question? Was Harley really in danger—or had his uncle played up the risks to get Harley to do what he wanted? If finding this evidence was so important, why not make the clues easier?

They needed help. Parker wanted the girls to know more, but Harley was still pushing back on that one. And Parker definitely wanted to pull his mom and dad in the loop. The more eyes on this, the more likely they'd figure it out, right?

A message dinged in from Harley.

`Just heard from the lawyer-asking if we found it. Told him`
`I don't think we ever will.`

Parker whipped off a text making the case to let more people in on the mystery. Harley wasted no time answering.

`Let's sleep on this, Parks. If we've got nothing in`
`24 hours, we take it up a level. For now, loop Wilson in. And`
`maybe your grandpa?`

Harley picked people far enough away not to spill the beans? Smart. But at least it was something. Parker texted back, `I'm on it. Stay safe.`

Harley sent back a smiley face emoji. `I keep hearing that. But`
`I'm not alone now, remember?`

Parker thought about that for a moment. `Miss Lopez? KitKat?`

`Ha. I was thinking of the one who made both of them.`

`Good job, Harley.`

Harley was right. God would never leave them. Like the Bible verse that had inspired the name for his boat . . . God was with them no matter what—or where. A chill swept through him, strong enough to raise goosebumps on his arms.

What was that all about? He got the creepy sense that danger was stalking someone in their group. Harley? Jelly? Ella? Wilson?

Harley's face was the one he kept seeing. Maybe it was the dark room. The lonely sound of the waves. But he had the feeling that whatever was going on with the poem was somehow bigger—and more deadly—than any of them imagined.

He sent the picture of the cryptic poem to Grandpa and Wilson, with an explanation nearly as mysterious as the rhyming clues themselves. Again, his mind drifted to Harley. Could he really be heading for some kind of trouble?

"God . . . I don't know if I'm imagining this . . . or if this is from you. But I'm thinking I need to take this even more seriously. Is that what you want me to see?"

He waited, but no answer came. Just a sense that he wasn't wrong. And that they'd need to do a whole lot more praying before this was over.

CHAPTER 27

IT SEEMED TOO EARLY TO GO TO BED on spring break, but Ella lay her head on the pillow anyway. She needed to think. Grams smoothed the covers over her—like she'd been doing since Ella was little. But back then, Grandpa had been there too. Sitting beside her. Telling her stories—but not about unicorns or princesses. It was the stories that made her want to pull the covers over her head that she liked best. There was something kind of delicious about getting a little bit scared—but deep down knowing she wasn't in real danger. Grandpa's story time would always end the same way.

"But you're safe here, cupcake. Grandpa's on patrol." He'd salute. "I'll check back in a little bit." He'd give her a kiss goodnight and tuck her cowgirl boots under his arm as he left the room.

When she'd wake late in the night, she'd see those boots at attention by her door. She'd smell the fresh polish. And she'd know he'd kept his word. He'd come back . . . and made sure his girl was safe.

Some nights she'd tried staying awake. Just to whisper goodnight one more time. Get one more kiss on the forehead. But Grandpa was like the elusive sandman. He slipped in and out undetected. In the morning, she'd inspect her boots to find them buffed to a rich luster, with every scuff gone.

Now she was the one who kept her own boots shiny. But she'd give anything to see her boots magically polished and buffed in the morning again.

Grams raised the window an inch. Lowered it half that amount. Readjusted again.

"What is it, Grams?"

Her face glowed with soft moonlight. "I can't stop thinking about bells, Ella-girl."

"Well, Harley didn't make it sound like it was a very big clue. If it was so important, don't you think he would have given me more?"

"Not if he thought it might put you in danger—or make you stop him from doing what he believed he needed to do."

Okay . . . Ella had *not* thought of it that way.

"I keep picturing a church bell. Five words keep slow dancing through my mind: *For whom the bell tolls.*"

Ella raised herself on both elbows. "What does that even mean?"

"It's from an old poem—or maybe it was a story. But it had to do with church bells ringing at a funeral. One hearing those bells wasn't to ask who died . . . but rather to know that the bell was tolling for them. Death's fingers snatch at all of us, not just the latest person in the casket."

Ella found herself feeling for the familiar edges of the cross around her neck.

"Perhaps there's more to this than simply a bell. It's a warning. An omen. I feel this business of a bell is about announcing another death. They come in threes you know."

Something Grams had taught her since she was a little girl. "The man under the boat?"

Grams nodded. "He's the first. I fear the Reaper has two more appointments before he leaves town. I don't like that our boys were the ones who found the one cut down by the dark scythe, Ella-girl."

Okay, this was creeping her out way more than any of Grandpa's stories.

"I've said too much." Grams adjusted the window a brushstroke lower. "You just tell those boys not to get reckless—especially out on the Neck . . . or around the harbor."

Right. Would they even listen? They'd see it as more superstitious talk.

Grams kissed her forehead just like Grandpa used to do. She slipped out the door, then leaned in from the hallway. "I'll check on you later."

Instinctively Ella looked for the boots, but they were still on the floor where Ella had set them.

Grams blew her a kiss and closed the door a bit, but not all the way. "You sleep tight, Ella-girl."

After all that? Sleep would be a whole lot more likely if Grandpa were on patrol. Ella pulled the covers up instead . . . right over her head.

CHAPTER 28

VINNY TORINO PARKED HIS TRUCK and stood at the far side of the circle turnaround at the end of Bearskin Neck. He liked the talk of a Bearskin Neck *Strangler* on the loose. Way more effective than *Bogeyman*. The shops were locked up tight—although it wouldn't do much good. The Strangler would strike again tonight. But with a bit more force this time.

He stood on the curb, balanced on the balls of his feet. The moon winked off Sandy Bay in a million spots. It was just one of the things he loved about the night.

A car approached, and Vinny judged the distance without turning. Likely a tourist driving up the Neck. Or maybe a nervous shop owner who hadn't bought his protection plan. They had good reason to climb out of bed and give their store a drive-by.

Still, Vinny paid attention to anybody approaching at night. Vinny was pulling in dollars instead of pushing up daisies because he was careful. He stepped off the curb and onto the granite blocks making up the massive breakwater that separated Rockport Harbor from the potential fury of Sandy Bay.

Only after he'd put a good thirty yards between him and the curb did he turn to reassess. A Hummer entered the circle but didn't follow the stay-to-the-right driving rule. Instead, the Hummer took the turn-around in a clockwise direction, and stopped at the halfway point.

There weren't many Hummers on this part of Cape Ann, and Vinny had a pretty good idea who was inside.

Vinny reached for his concealed carry in the waistband holster. His Springfield Hellcat fit neatly in his hand. He slipped it into the gut pocket of his hoodie and kept his hand inside, waiting. The metal felt warm from being tucked away against his body. It'd get lots warmer if whoever was inside the Hummer had less-than-honorable intentions.

He ran through several quick what-if scenarios. If someone swung open the door and rushed him, Vinny could retie his laces before needing to react.

What if there were two men? He'd hunker down between the rocks and pick them off one by one.

The door swung open, but no interior lights blinked on. A moment later, a dark figure stepped out of the shadows and onto the rocks. "Mr. Torino. Quinn Lochran here." He stopped and made no quick movements. "May I approach for a word?" The man kept his hands away from his body like he was making a point of proving he wasn't carrying a weapon.

"No bodyguard tonight?"

Lochran chuckled. "I'm in the market for a new one. But somehow, I think you know that. Care to join me for a drive?"

"I'd rather we talk right here." Vinny motioned him closer.

Lochran moved easily across the uneven rocks—but kept his hands in sight the entire time.

"I know you've got a busy night ahead of you," Lochran said, "so I'll get right down to business."

How had Lochran known where to find him? Vinny gave a quick shoulder check—just to make sure nobody was sneaking up from behind.

"I assure you, I'm alone," Lochran said. "Something I'd like to change. But first, I owe you a debt of gratitude."

This was beginning to sound interesting.

"I'm a businessman, Mr. Torino. I have interests from Boston to Newport. But Cape Ann is home turf to me. Some call me King of the Cape. A man in my position makes enemies, and there's always someone who thinks they can take my crown."

"I'm more of a baseball cap guy myself," Vinny said.

Lochran's face looked friendly enough in the moonlight. "I lost my wingman. It turns out he has a nephew in Boston who's gotten himself in quite a mess with the police. Mr. Ironwing began having troubling conversations with the authorities . . . offering some very damaging evidence about his boss in exchange for a plea bargain."

How could Ironwing be that stupid? "You think he offered police evidence on you—for a promise that his nephew would go free?"

"Oh, I *know* so. My source said he'd collected enough evidence to put me away for good. Which comes to my business of coming to thank you."

He was guessing. There was no way Lochran could know he'd rolled Ironwing's body into the bay.

"Mr. Ironwing was going to be permanently retired from my employment. You've saved me the trouble. Which allows me to concentrate on dealing with another burr under my saddle."

For just an instant Vinny wondered if the man was wearing a wire. Was this a trap to get him to confess? But that made no sense. There was no way he'd have said what he did. He'd be putting the noose around his own neck.

"I want you to work for me."

"I've got a business."

"And you can still operate it," Lochran said. "You've done a commendable job. But surely you know this can't last. The burglaries increase—you sign up more accounts. The burglaries go down—you lose accounts." Lochran shrugged. "Eventually you'll need to take more and more risks—and that can only put you under suspicion."

He wasn't going to get caught, but even Torino knew his little scheme would only pay out well for a year or so.

"You've got a clean record. I like that. You bested my man—and he was *good*. That impresses me. I want you as a bodyguard to accompany me to meetings. Sometimes to help collect debts. To be an extra set of eyes and ears. You'll still have all the time you need to keep your business humming along."

Tempting. "That hard evidence your man collected. He didn't turn it in?"

"He took a swim before he was able to." Lochran hesitated. "Actually, I'm on the hunt for it myself. We've searched his house good. But we'll keep looking."

Is that what this was really about? Was he fishing to find out if the evidence was on Ironwing when he ran into Vinny? "A wallet—stacked with Benjamins. Driver's license. Two credit cards. Set of keys. Buck knife with a five-inch blade. Handful of change. Glock 19, Gen5. Full clip. Dog leash—and a dog. But no little black book, if that's what you want to know."

Lochran held his gaze. "Exactly the inventory reported by our man in the evidence room. Phone?"

"Not on him when he went swimming."

Lochran nodded real slow, like he'd been afraid of that bit of news. "You didn't take the money? Why?"

"Bad luck."

"How so?"

"I prefer it when people *hand* me money. I don't take it out of their pocket."

"Admirable quality."

A lobster boat entered the channel and chugged into Outer Harbor. There was no reason to suspect Lochran had someone on board with a rifle, aiming to take Vinny out. But still, he kept the boat in his peripheral. If the boat slowed at the wrong moment, he'd give it his full attention.

"Think about that job, Mr. Torino. You're a straight shooter. I can tell. I won't keep you in the dark on things, either."

"I like the dark."

Lochran chuckled. "Another admirable quality. You'll be working close with me. You'll see things. Hear things. It requires a mutual trust."

"Doesn't sound like that whole trust thing was working so well for you, though."

Lochran laughed again. "No indeed. I should have trusted my gut when I first began to have doubts about Mr. Ironwing. But it all worked out in the end—thanks again to you."

"Except for that tiny little detail about the incriminating evidence."

Lochran sighed. "We'll find it. In the meantime, think about that job."

Vinny glanced behind him, more for show than anything. "You know this is Vinny Torino you're talking to. You realize I played for the other team—not even a year ago."

"You're speaking of Ray Lotitto. A frequent flyer in the bar you worked at as a bouncer. He needed your help, and you were there for him. Unfortunately, he ended up getting stupid and stiffed me."

"And you still want me working for you?"

"*You* didn't stiff me. You tried to bail your friend out of a jam. I respect that. But Mr. Lotitto is the kind of guy who needs a bib. He's always making messes, and he's made himself a big one now. Turns out he's been talking to the same investigator—and the DA. Trying to work out a deal to get himself off the hook—in exchange for evidence he claims to have."

"What?" That was news to Vinny. "What evidence could he possibly have to trade?"

"Ray Lotitto had an extra phone. He recorded everything."

It didn't quite add up. "Do you believe him?"

"I have a *very* reliable source. And Ray had the foresight to hide the phone before he was taken into custody. He's given his nephew clues to find it. Ironically, Ray is trusting his life with the very boy he tried to kill, right out there in Sandy Bay."

"I had no part in that."

"Truly spoken. I suspect if you'd been on Ray's boat, the job wouldn't have been bungled."

How did this guy *know* this stuff?

"You were given the job of making the motorcycle disappear. And obviously you did that right. It was never found."

"And it never will be." Vinny was sure of that. The coordinates he'd given Ray were bogus.

Lochran smiled. "I need a man who can make things happen." He paused for a moment. "Anything else you can tell me about Ray? Where he'd hide something valuable?"

Vinny shook his head. "No idea. And even if I did, I don't rat on friends."

"Another reason I want you for my friend," Lochran said.

"For whatever it's worth, about the only thing Ray had left in the end was his pickup. And I think the repo guy got that."

"We found it. Went over it real good. It's not there."

A car started into the circle turnaround, found the Hummer too wide to pass, and backed away.

"If Ray is a witness—and has evidence to put you away—isn't it a bit optimistic to be offering me a job?"

Lochran laughed. "The offer is good. I'll not be going to prison. The witness is on death row, so to speak."

Vinny nodded. That was clear enough. And so was the fact that Quinn Lochran had just trusted him with some insider information. Was it a test to see if he'd somehow get word to Ray? Whether Ray actually had incriminating evidence, or was pretending he did, he had to know his life was in danger. Vinny couldn't tell him anything he shouldn't already know.

"You'll find an envelope in your glove box with a handsome sum inside."

Lochran had been in his truck? When?

"If you join me, consider the envelope your signing bonus."

"And if I don't—how do I get it back to you?" There was no way he was going to hold on to this loan shark's money if he didn't take the job.

"You don't." Lochran smiled. "You took care of a very big problem of mine. Consider that my thank-you card."

Classy. Maybe it was time for Vinny to toss Lochran a bone. "You think that evidence Ironwing collected may be hidden in his phone somewhere?"

Lochran shrugged. "That thought occurred to me."

"You check his truck?"

"Bumper to bumper. No phone."

There would be no harm telling him, would there? He'd stripped the phone from Ironwing after tasing him. As much as Torino would've liked tossing it directly in the bay, he didn't want it in his own pocket for as long as it would take to get there. "I'd look inside the gas cap door."

Lochran stared at him for a long moment. "Mr. Torino, I am in your debt." The King of the Cape looked thrilled. "Now I'll leave you to get back to your business. Consider my offer. And either way, know that I thoroughly enjoyed our conversation tonight."

Vinny did too. "What about Ray's nephew? What if the kid finds that evidence?"

"I want him to. We've had no luck deciphering a clue sheet his uncle left him. So I'm hoping the boy leads us to it. I need to make those recordings disappear for good. I could use some help with that, quite honestly."

Lochran was dangerous—but only to those who crossed him or got in his way, right? "What happens to the kid?"

Lochran stopped, hands still in plain sight. "Suppose you're my bodyguard. What would you advise?"

It was a test. "If my job is to protect you, there's only one answer."

"And that would be?"

Vinny found himself gripping the Hellcat. If Harley found the evidence, how could they be sure he didn't make a copy and turn it in to the police? "He needs to disappear too."

"Oh, Mr. Torino . . . I really do want you as a bodyguard."

CHAPTER 29

ANGELICA GOT THE GROUP TEXT FROM PEZ just after 10:30 p.m. Her coffee shop keys were missing. She'd left them in the door lock during the meeting so people could let themselves out when it ended. She guessed someone accidently pocketed the keys. But still, she'd wanted to check with Angelica and Ella.

Neither one of them had taken the keys. Pez thanked them for their quick answer and was convinced somebody would return the keys tomorrow when they realized their mistake. She wasn't worried.

But clearly Harley was. He started a new text thread—but only to Angelica and Ella. His texts fired in minutes after they'd answered Pez.

You sure neither of you saw the keys?

Did you see who was first out the door after the meeting?

Do either of you think this might not have been an accident?

She stared at that last question for what seemed like twenty seconds

before answering. Honestly, she wasn't sure what to think. Only that she felt uneasy—and she had some questions of her own for Harley.

What will Pez do tonight? Any extra security?

He answered immediately.

Not officially . . . she thinks we're fine—but I'd bet she'll pray a little more than usual.

Okay, Angelica got it. She really did. But come on, Pez needed to be realistic too. She had to take some extra precautions, right? She texted Harley back.

She needs extra protection.

His reply came back fast.

She's got it.

What?

She signed up with Cape Ann Angels???

No. She's got me. And KitKat.

Angelica groaned. Of *course*. Once again, he was doing that guy thing . . . and it sounded reckless.

What are you going to do . . . sleep downstairs? She added a smiley face emoji to let him know she was kidding.

He fired back a picture. His mattress was actually on the floor of the coffee shop, halfway between the front and back doors. KitKat sat beside it, like this was some kind of adventure. Was he crazy?

Does Pez know?

I asked Kit to tell her.

She stared at his text. Should she send Pez a message herself? She wouldn't exactly rat on Harley, but she could ask Pez to check the front locks one more time. She'd see Harley and send him upstairs to bed. What if the Strangler broke in—and Harley caught him off guard? The intruder might attack rather than run out of the shop. Her thumbs hovered over the screen for a moment. *Make a decision, Angelica!*

A text came in from Harley.

Miss Lopez could use some good sleep. Let's let her have

that. If keys don't turn up tomorrow, we'll change locks. Problem solved.

Like he knew exactly what she might be planning to do. *Let it go, Angelica. Let it go.* She wasn't going to fall into the old trap of being overprotective.

Harley sent another text.

Relax, Jelly. It's just one night. What could go wrong?

Angelica wished she'd never read his text. How was she supposed to sleep now? *What could go wrong?* She sent back her one-word answer.

Everything.

CHAPTER 30

ELLA COULDN'T GET COMFORTABLE. Couldn't stop her legs from moving—even with a bar of soap in her bed. Grams insisted it calmed jittery legs—but apparently not tonight. She swung out of bed, pulled Grandpa's shoe polishing kit from the closet, and set it on her lap. She slid back the lid and bent low, inhaling the memories. Black. Brown. Natural. Hockey puck–sized tins of each, along with leather conditioner and a genuine horsehair buffing brush.

She had every set of boots Grandpa had ever bought her. Each pair was polished, buffed, and stored for her own little girl someday—if she were lucky enough to have one. She'd tell her daughter about her great-grandpa and the prince of a man he was.

She opened a tin and worked the polish into the leather, rubbing in tight little circles. Grandpa had done more than buy her every set of boots she'd ever owned. He'd planned ahead, too. Maybe there'd been some crazy good sale years ago . . . or maybe he just knew he would die before she was all grown up. But Grams said he'd bought enough pairs of boots, moving up one size at a time, to keep Ella's feet in fine leather for years. Actually, if she took care of them like he did, they'd last and last and last. Whenever a set of boots grew tight, Grams would pull out another box. Each pair had been better than the last. Grandpa loved his girl, and he'd known she loved her boots.

Grams ducked her head inside the room. "Looks like I'm not the only one who can't sleep."

She shuffled over and sat beside her. "That grandpa of yours never missed a night. No matter how tired he was, he polished those boots and gave you a kiss on your forehead."

Sometimes she imagined that he still did. She set the boots right where he'd always put them. There was something comforting about that.

She told Grams about the lost keys.

"You text that boy and tell him to be careful. Whatever is going on in Rockport isn't over. It may be barely beginning. I don't like it."

And she wasn't making Ella feel any too comfortable either. Ella wanted to ask Grams if she had any premonition—a sense of what might be coming.

"Sometimes I don't like being right," Grams said. "You know I don't. And I'm sure of one thing." She stopped like she'd suddenly been distracted. "Is there a fog coming in?"

Ella leaned close to the glass and looked toward the streetlight. "Clear night skies, Grams."

"But it's building. Maybe farther out to sea. It will come."

More superstitions. "What was that one thing you were sure of?"

Grams shook her head. "You sleep now. There's no good that will come of this talk. Not tonight." Grams ushered her back to bed. She pulled the blankets to Ella's chin and smoothed them for the second time that night. She slipped out without another word.

Even long after Grams went to bed, sleep eluded Ella. The house seemed just as restless as she was. It creaked. Shifted. Yawned. She didn't dare look at the clock. That would only make it worse.

The dim light from the hall filtered in, illuminating her boots. She closed her eyes and wished that somehow Grandpa would be on patrol again. Everything would be okay, just like it used to be.

Were the Cape Ann Angels cruising the Neck? Or maybe Detective Greenwood? She wanted to think so. But right now, it seemed that she was the only one in Rockport who was still awake. Actually, maybe that wasn't true. She could think of one other who was likely *wide* awake: the Bearskin Neck Strangler.

CHAPTER 31

HARLEY WOKE TO THE LOW RUMBLE OF KIT'S GROWL. For a moment he had no idea where he was. But seeing coffee shop tables around his mattress oriented him pretty stinkin' quick. He'd worked on Uncle Ray's stupid poem upstairs until he got himself more confused than anything. The thing was impossible. After he was sure Miss Lopez was asleep, he'd grabbed his mattress and tiptoed downstairs.

Kit growled again, her ears alert. Eyes fixed on the rear door.

"What is it, girl?" He focused on the doorknob. Did it turn? It was too dark to tell for sure. He silently kicked off the covers and stood. Kit sprang to her feet, eyes laser-focused on the door. Harley grabbed the Louisville Slugger. He held his breath, listening.

The hair at the base of Kit's neck rose, and she bolted for the door. Kit dropped her nose to the ground. Sniffed along the threshold.

Should he call the police? He pictured the Race Bannon contact Detective Greenwood added to his phone. But what would he say to the detective? Kit was acting funny? To make a call would mean setting down the bat—and right now that wasn't an option.

Harley took a step toward the door. Then another. Barely twenty feet away now. His imagination raced as fast as his heart.

Kit started that growl thing again.

"Easy, girl." Or maybe it was good that she made some noise. If someone really was out there, wouldn't the growling make him run the other way?

Harley stepped up beside Kit and pressed his toe against the base of the door, just in case. Still holding the bat, he peered out the peephole mounted on the door. The clamp light hanging out the Crow's Nest window lit the area outside well enough to read a football playbook. But nothing was there. No stray animal. And no Strangler.

He stood there for probably a full minute, just watching. Whatever had been outside—if there'd even been something—was gone.

Harley held his breath. Tried not to blink. "Everything's okay." He wrapped his hand around the garden hose collar and gave it a gentle tug to back her away from the door. "What do you say we do a quick patrol around the rest of the shop?" The way Harley's heart was beating, he'd need the walk to calm the jitters before he'd be able to sleep.

He walked Kit to the front window. Main Street sat quiet. Still. Had anyone even been out back at all? Maybe Kit was just as jumpy as Harley and had imagined the whole thing.

Kit batted Harley's leg with her nose. "What is it, girl?" With the Louisville Slugger over one shoulder, Harley let go of her collar and checked the front door lock. "Easy now, Kit. *Easy.* Let's just dial it back a little. We got ourselves worked up, that's all. False alarm."

Harley flipped on the lights. The shadows in the room weren't the only ones that disappeared. It seemed to calm him, too. Maybe he'd leave the lights on for a while.

A dull thud came from the back, followed by a splintering noise. The back door eased open. A gloved hand appeared just inside the door.

Kit tore for the back—barking her head off.

Harley raced after her. "Kit!"

The hand disappeared—leaving the door slightly ajar.

"Kit—no!"

The dog used its nose to slap the door open enough to squeeze through. An instant later, she was gone.

Harley fresh-gripped the bat—and sprinted out the door after her. Where was she? He slowed, glancing both ways. "Kit!"

She barked—somewhere beyond the shallow backyard. Out on the boulders? He bolted into the shadows.

"Kit! Come!"

His eyes were barely adjusting to the night when he got to the rocks. Kit was at the water's edge, barking like crazy . . . at *nothing*.

Harley ran to her side. "You okay, girl? Huh? You all right?" He held the bat like a club, reaching for her collar with his free hand. He swept the shoreline in both directions.

Unless the burglar was crouching behind a rock somewhere, he was already out of sight. Which seemed impossible. The moon reflected on the surface of the water like it was playing a game of hide-and-seek. And maybe the burglar was too. But there was no skiff in sight. And if the guy had jumped into the bay to get away from Kit—as cold as the water was? He'd have realized his mistake instantly and would be pulling himself back up on the rocks by now.

Harley dropped onto one knee and set the bat beside him, his head still on a swivel. He scratched behind Kit's ears. "You did good, girl. Real good. But you could've gotten hurt bad. So you wait for me next time, deal? I'll step it up too." He wasn't sure exactly what he'd do . . . but he'd think of something—or Parks would. He was pretty sure Parks would suggest they both pray, too. Maybe Harley would get a jump on that and start now. He definitely wasn't going to be sleeping anytime soon anyway.

"Harley?" Miss Lopez's voice. But the pitch was higher. Desperate. "Are you okay?"

He signaled back with a wave and bent low to look KitKat in the face. "We got some explaining to do. Any ideas how we're going to do that?"

Her ears dropped back flat against her head.

"Yeah, that's what I thought."

CHAPTER 32

Parker was up early. His dad hadn't left for work yet—which seemed odd.

The Bearskin Neck Strangler had been busy last night, or maybe it was early this morning. Just as Parker finished his second bowl of Cocoa Puffs—with chocolate milk—he got a string of texts from Harley:

Bogeyman hit next door.

Police crawling all over the place.

He tried here, too. Meet me out back.

Parker took a last bite, then guzzled the milk in the bowl. He gave a quick explanation to his parents.

"Go," Dad said. "I arranged for a late start today. . . . I wanted to talk to you about something. But it can wait. Meet you at *Wings* in an hour?"

He had no idea what his dad wanted to talk about, but right now all he could think about was the burglaries. He hopped on his bike and tore through town to the back side of the coffee shop. Harley was waiting—with Kit on a leash. The dog's nose was to the ground, sniffing with nearly enough force to suck gravel into her snout.

Harley caught him up to speed and pointed at the back door. The doorjamb was splintered like somebody had used a crowbar for a key.

"Detective Greenwood says I probably gave my guardian angel a good scare—and that I shouldn't have gone outside."

"How's Pez?"

"Quiet," Harley said. "Like way, way too quiet. She's thinking about something—and whatever it is, it ain't good."

"She's got to be worried the coffee shop is next."

"Maybe." Harley looked pretty keyed up himself. "Or maybe she's thinking being a foster mom is more trouble than it's worth."

There was no way. "If you hadn't been sleeping downstairs, whoever tried to get in would've trashed the coffee shop."

"Yeah, well, I'm not so sure she'll let me sleep downstairs again. I'm hoping she doesn't bring it up. I sure won't."

Pez walked out the back door of the neighbor's shop at that moment, spotted them, and strode over. "Four places hit last night. It's a new record—even for the Strangler. Cape Ann Angels are going to be *real* busy signing up new clients all morning—or refunding payments."

Parker had seen the truck parked on the street out front. "What about you, Pez? You signing BayView up?"

"Absolutely, positively *no*." She pointed to a lobster boat in the bay. "There's a better chance of that thing sprouting wings and flying away."

"I could've told you that," Harley said. "She was mumbling in nautical terms after last night's meeting. You didn't like the cut of his jib, right, Miss Lopez?"

Pez laughed. "Something about him bothered me, that's all."

"Miss Lopez says she's got a built-in lie detector up here." Harley tapped his head.

"Not a lie detector." Pez smiled. "An EKG machine."

"Right. She says she can read somebody's heart just as if the guy was wired up to some electrocardiogram gizmo."

"Mr. Vinny Torino won't get a penny from me." Pez looked downright annoyed. "Business is hard enough in the offseason. I don't like him waltzing in like he's the angel of Cape Ann—when he's really just making a fast buck off the misfortune of others. Nobody can afford this."

The owner of Cape Ann Angels Security rounded the corner of the building with Brian Stephens, the manager of the shop next door.

Immediately KitKat started a low growl. Pez knelt in front of her, blocking the dog's view. "I *so* understand." She smoothed the fur on Kit's head—and the growl drained back to wherever it had come from. "Let's just not even look at him, okay, girl?"

Torino was listening intently to whatever the manager was saying. He put one hand on the guy's shoulder and said something that made Stephens pump Torino's other hand.

Apparently, Pez couldn't resist looking over her shoulder. "Looks like he signed up another one."

Torino put a sticker dead center on the back door of the building next door. The thing was the size of a medium pizza. He used his tattooed forearm to rub out all the bubbles. If the objective was to be sure a burglar didn't miss who was protecting the store, Torino accomplished it. Parker could read most of it from thirty feet away.

Protected by Cape Ann Angels Security
Little Wings. Big Guns.

A head-and-shoulders likeness of Vinny Torino dominated the circle below it. Tiny angel wings sprouted off his shoulders. His arms crossed his chest . . . definitely the big guns part. A couple more lines were written along the bottom, but Parker couldn't make them out from here.

"Kit and I are going back inside." Pez was still watching Torino. "We've seen enough. We'll come up with our own plan to be sure the Strangler doesn't try our place again."

"He won't." Harley motioned toward the door. "I'll get that fixed up before closing today. And I'll put in a stockade bar on the inside—just like I used to have inside my shed. Nobody will get through that."

"Oh, Harley." Pez pulled him into a hug. "Put two bars up if that will keep you inside next time." Pez and Kit disappeared inside the coffee shop.

Torino stepped back, admiring his work. He motioned the boys over. "What do you think?"

Parker read aloud the personal message at the bottom of the sticker. "If you know me, you'll turn around now and pick a shop without this sticker. If you don't know me, know this: I'm an avenging angel. You touch this shop, and I'll find you. Guaranteed. Now, smile. You're being photographed. Time to walk away while you still can. Vinny Torino."

"Sheesh," Harley said. "Not the typical thing a security company would say, I'm guessing."

Mr. Torino laughed. "Nothing about my business plan is typical. That's what makes it work."

"The other shops that were hit last night," Harley said. "Any of them yours?"

Torino went through the motion of wiping off his forehead. "Not one." He turned his attention to the store manager.

Parker led the way back to the coffee shop. "Did you get anywhere on your Uncle Ray's clue-poem?"

Harley shook his head. "I was kinda busy. You?"

"Nothing. Wilson and Grandpa aren't doing any better. We need help. I say we give the girls the whole clue sheet."

Harley still wasn't on board with that. "I'm just going to tell the lawyer I need to talk to Uncle Ray—or get a new clue sheet. That'll buy us time, anyway."

Parker was sure that of the two threats—the Strangler or Lochran—finding that evidence was the more urgent need. "We can't stall this off, Harley. It's too dangerous."

The two of them walked around to the street at the front of the building. Police cars were still parked at the entrance to Bearskin Neck. Detective Greenwood strode out the front door of BayView Brew. He seemed as busy as Vinny Torino, but he wasn't handing out any door stickers.

"You did the right thing by calling me, Harley. But no more chasing this perp into the dark. You hear something, you call. If you gotta walk the dog at night, go out the front. Don't go alone, and don't go far."

Harley didn't argue with him, but he didn't promise to follow all Greenwood's instructions, either.

"If you'd caught up to the burglar last night—what would've happened?"

"He'd be handcuffed to a hospital bed."

The detective eyed him for a moment. "How does one perp hit four places spread out over three blocks—in one night—even with all the police we had patrolling?"

That got Harley's attention. "You're saying he's some kind of super-human?"

"I'm saying what he did was impossible . . . *unless* . . ."

Parker got it. "There's more than one. This is a gang!"

"That's my theory." Greenwood shrugged. "What if you ran into more than one Strangler?"

"I had Kit. And my bat."

"Look, guys. Something was *different* last night." He paused like he was deciding how much he should say. "The guy heard the dog—yet still broke in? Either the Strangler is getting sloppy, he wasn't alone, or hitting the coffee shop wasn't random."

Any one of those made the Strangler even more dangerous.

Maybe Harley sensed it too. His tough-guy act disappeared. "What do you mean . . . not random?"

"What if the Strangler was sending a personal message? Maybe he doesn't like how your foster mom is organizing the other shop owners. Maybe . . ."

Harley looked at him for a long moment. "Maybe *what*?"

"Forget it," Greenwood said. He pointed at his own phone. "You call Race Bannon. Let *him* do the chasing—especially at night. Got it?"

That look on Harley's face—one Parker had seen before. Determined. Reckless. "You started to say something before—but stopped. You think the Strangler *wanted* to hurt Miss Lopez?"

The letter said Pez could be Lochran's target. What if the Strangler was taking aim at her now too?

"I really can't speak to his motives."

"There's something you're not saying," Harley said.

Greenwood's face was impossible to read. "No more heroics. That's all." He looked from Harley to Parker. "You both heard what I said, right?"

Oh yeah. They heard. But it was what he didn't say that had Parker worried.

CHAPTER 33

ANGELICA SLID HER BAYVIEW BREW APRON over her head and watched the front window. The shop had been quiet this morning. Like the robberies kept people away.

Ella had decked Mr. Bones out in foul weather gear. She'd wired a fishing pole in his hands as the finishing touch. Her daily specials board was propped next to him with apple cinnamon donuts listed as the catch of the day.

She joined Pez and Angelica near the front of the store. KitKat sat at the front window too, still as a statue, watching the boys.

Parker and Harley stood out front on the walk, talking. No laughing. No smiles. Totally unlike them. Parker looked like he was selling something. Trying, anyway. Harley's hands were jammed in his back pockets. Head down, staring at the sidewalk. Clearly not buying.

Pez kept glancing out the window. "He took a big risk going outside last night. I know I'm new at this foster parenting thing, but I feel like I should've been one step ahead of him."

"You can't guess what Harley will do—or Parker," Angelica said. "They're *guys*. They act first—and think later."

"Later? Aren't you being a teensy bit generous?" Ella grinned. "I'm not so sure they *ever* think. If you ask me, Harley ran on pure instincts." She moved her arms like a robot. "Must protect store!"

"Maybe." Pez leaned on the counter, still studying Harley. "But I fear it's more than that."

"Harley's all *about* protecting the store." Ella raised her fists. "Why else would he have slept down here?"

"I think he was protecting *me*." Pez looked dead serious. "But that feels upside down. As his foster mom, I'm supposed to look out for him, right?"

"Good luck stopping him," Angelica said. "When Harley gets something in his head, he's got to finish it." Even if it might finish *him* in the process. And that meant Parker would likely be beside him all the way too. How many times had she seen the boys do something completely reckless like that?

"I love that boy," Pez whispered. "Lord Almighty . . . protect my boy."

Her boy? If Angelica hadn't been standing as close to Pez as she was, she would've never heard the prayer.

"I can't have him risking his neck for me." There was a determination in her voice. "It's my job to protect *him*—and the store."

Ella exchanged a look with Angelica. "So you're signing up with the security company now?"

Pez shook her head. "I have something a bit less predictable in mind."

The front door opened at that moment. Rosie. A regular who worked in the office at the Rockport PD. Pez smoothed her apron. Waved.

Angelica wanted to keep Pez talking. "You have a plan?"

Pez nodded. "To keep me, Harley, and the store safe. But it means doing something I *really* don't want to do."

What? Was Pez thinking of buying a gun? "Sounds kind of scary."

"There's only one thing that scares me more."

"Which is?"

"Doing nothing."

CHAPTER 34

PARKER BIKED TO T-WHARF, dreading the idea of going back in the water. It was as if he was a bronc rider. He'd been thrown good—but he had to get back on that horse. All the yellow police tape was gone. Everything looked normal—except for the images of Mike Ironwing in his head.

Dad was already aboard *Wings*—wearing a wet suit. So *that's* what he was up to. Tank. BCD. Weights. Mask. Fins. All Dad's gear was out. Parker's, too. Even the brushes and scrapers.

Parker hustled down to the Boston Whaler.

"Thought you could use a hand finishing up *Flight Risk*. What do you think?"

Had Mom and Dad known he'd been stalling the job off? Probably. But the idea of his dad there with him? "That sounds *really* good."

"I've only got about an hour. Maybe less. Can we do it?"

"Easy." He grabbed the swimsuit he stowed aboard *Wings*, changed at the yacht club, and was back in five minutes.

"Okay, show me how it's done," Dad said.

And Parker did exactly that. They scraped and brushed. Scum fogged the water. Barnacles got knocked free and seesawed away. And Dad stuck right beside him. With his gimpy arm, Parker barely kept up with his dad's pace.

At just over the halfway point, Parker's scraper tangled with Dad's—the thing slipped from his grip. For a moment he stared at the thing spiraling to the bottom, seeing coins dropping instead. Dad handed off his own scraper and went down for Parker's.

Parker watched. When Dad reached the bottom, he motioned for Parker to join him. Parker hesitated just a moment, then pushed off the hull. Dad pointed at a tiny crab that had already climbed aboard the scraper like he was claiming possession of it. Parker knew exactly what Dad was up to. He'd gotten Parker in the water. Got him cleaning the boat. Even coaxed him all the way to the bottom. Dad was getting Parker back on the horse, one step at a time. Parker shooed the crab away, claimed the scraper, and headed back to finish the job.

The entire hull was clean and they were back on *Wings* with their gear off in less than forty minutes.

"I hate sticking you with rinsing everything," Dad said. "But I've got to hit the shower before I leave."

Parker didn't care if he had to rinse the gear for a whole boatload of divers after what his dad did for him. "I got this. Take my bike. It'll be faster."

Dad grinned. "I'll do that." Without another word, he was on the dock, trotting for the ramp. He didn't give Parker a speech about the need to conquer fears or remind him how Dad was always there for him. He just was.

"Dad!" Parker shouted after his dad. "You have no idea . . ."

His dad swung a leg over the bike. "I bet I do." And with that, he was off.

Parker hauled his gear to the hose and carefully rinsed both wet suits and all the gear. He took his time. Dad had met Parker right where he was at. Helped him move forward. Such a man thing. Parker wanted that. To do that for others.

Loud footsteps banged down the pier—heading his way. Ray Lotitto's lawyer, Sebastian Kilbro. Back in a suit this time. Different suit, though. And different shoes. Still an absolute mismatch to see someone dressed this way on the docks.

"Harley isn't here." Parker pointed toward BayView Brew. "He's working."

"I just talked to him," Kilbro said. "It's you I want to see now."

What?

"Young Harley says there's been no progress finding the evidence." He shook his head. "Not good."

"Those clues make no sense," Parker said. "You've seen the thing, right? I mean, the evidence could be anywhere."

"Look, Harley doesn't grasp the full importance or urgency of this. I'm hoping you will."

A chill knifed through Parker.

"I heard about the break-in."

"They didn't get—"

"*This* time." Kilbro leaned in close. "Until we have that evidence, Ray isn't getting a transfer, and he sure as shooting isn't getting out. Lochran wants that evidence even more than Ray. Do you think he'll sit back and wait for you to find it?"

Parker's stomach swirled. "We need help."

"And you'll need a lot more if you don't find the evidence. Fast." Kilbro looked away for a moment, then turned back. "Look, Ray Lotitto made a very dangerous man his enemy—one who has a very powerful organization behind him. He'll use every resource he has to destroy that evidence."

"But if we can't find—"

"Find it." Kilbro squeezed his eyes shut tight like he wished he'd never taken on Ray as a client. "Until I get that evidence on the DA's desk, you . . . Harley . . . and anybody you might've brought in the loop—against my advice—are in danger."

The lawyer actually looked spooked, and it wasn't helping Parker stay calm.

"You boys keep this thing secret. Nobody who has a *clue* as to where that evidence is hidden is safe. Including me."

Parker's stomach did a slow twist. "Did Harley ask about meeting with his uncle Saturday?"

"I told Harley we need to expedite. He has to see his uncle tomorrow afternoon. Saturday is too late. Please tell me you understand why."

Parker was pretty sure he did. Sebastian Kilbro didn't think Uncle Ray—or Harley and Parker—had that long.

CHAPTER 35

HARLEY RAN KIT TO THE HEADLANDS just after dinner. He'd promised Miss Lopez he'd be back before dark—which didn't give him a ton of time. The original plan had been to meet out on the breakwater, but El and Jelly absolutely refused. Until the Strangler was captured, they wouldn't be out on the jetty or Bearskin Neck anywhere near dark.

Parks had convinced Harley to fast-lane the step of bringing others into the loop—no matter how hard the lawyer stressed the need to keep it secret. "When someone asks you to keep something secret, think through if that's really wise—or if it's all about benefitting them."

What if Harley kept the secret and didn't find the evidence? Wouldn't Miss Lopez be in more danger than ever? He couldn't risk it. Not after last night.

They needed help, and that meant sharing the complete clue sheet with Miss Lopez. Ella. Jelly. Parker's parents. Grams. Even Finn. Maybe together they'd figure the poem out—and Harley wouldn't have to see his uncle tomorrow after all.

Miss Lopez had been first. After Harley had finished, he wished he'd done it way sooner. She didn't insist he stop looking for the evidence like he'd feared. In fact, she was going to help. She'd hugged him tight. "No more secrets, Harley. We're in this together. And we're stronger together, don't you think?"

No more secrets. It was the right thing to do. And now that he'd made the decision, he couldn't spill his story to the others soon enough.

Harley unclipped Kit's leash. Together they climbed the rocks and took in the view for a few moments. The breeze, steady enough to keep a kite in the air without running. The waves pounding against the rocks with relentless energy. He was pretty sure he'd never get tired of this place. Even Kit raised her nose, sniffing the sea air.

Parker, Ella, Jelly, and Finn. All of them were already there. Ella wore the dress that reminded Harley of spring, for some reason. Pale yellow, with some kind of checked pattern in it. White sweater. Her cowgirl boots were already off. She looked Harley's way and smiled. "Kit!" She patted her thigh, and the dog bounded to her.

Harley gave them the full story about the hidden evidence and the promise of getting Kemosabe's location. "Anyway, I don't want secrets between us anymore."

Jelly lightly slapped her cheek—then pinched her arm. "Am I awake? I'm dreaming this, right?"

"It's about time you wised up, Harley," Ella said. "Grams always says, 'Hang around smart people, and you'll get smarter yourself.' This proves she was right."

"So," Harley said, "you think you're smarter—because of hanging around *me*?"

Ella took Kit's face between her hands and leaned in close. "Oh, girl, what are we going to do with that guy?"

The laughing probably did them all good. But Harley absolutely knew it helped him.

Parker told the group about the surprise visit from Uncle Ray's lawyer—and how the guy stressed the urgency . . . and the danger. The mood changed, and they got really quiet.

Harley handed each of them a copy of the poem, once again stressing the absolute need for them to treat it like the football team's playbook. Top secret.

Jelly gave a shoulder check—like she was worried Lochran might've somehow appeared. Satisfied, she read it aloud.

> Within earshot of the old bell,
> but only if you're feeling swell.
> Watch your time, 'cause there's not a heap,
> Soon you'll both be in trouble deep.
> Below the place where some might crash,
> in a bag never meant for trash.
> You'll find it's all there, nice and dry,
> Enough to make Quinn Lochran fry.
> The place is dark, when it's not night.
> So use your head, and bring a light.
> Watch for Lochran, and Mr. White,
> both have a nasty appetite.
> They'll take your life, they'll take your soul,
> They swallow careless dummies whole.

When Jelly finished, each of them seemed to be focused on the paper in their hand. Rereading it, no doubt. Finn passed around a bag of Oreos for a little brain food.

"We have to keep the poem within the family," Harley said. "Parker will show his parents. El—you can show Grams."

The girls made a case for giving a copy to Detective Greenwood, too. No surprise there. But what if the police found the evidence? There'd be no deal for Uncle Ray. Actually, that didn't bother Harley. It was the fact that the lawyer insisted it go to him first. He was the one who knew how to keep Lochran from going after them. He needed that lawyer to keep Miss Lopez safe, right?

"I'll tell Detective Greenwood when the time is right, okay?" Thankfully, the girls cut him some slack on that one. For the moment, anyway.

Together, they made a list of the things they all agreed on.

There wasn't much time. That one was easy enough to decipher.

There were two enemies to stay on the lookout for—and both were deadly. Lochran. And Mr. White—and likely one worked for the other. That bit about taking their soul was a mystery, but likely Uncle Ray only had it there because it rhymed with *whole*.

"Okay," Harley said. "The bell. Any new ideas?"

Finn studied the sheet. "It's tied in with feeling swell. As in feeling well? Healthy? What kind of bell would you hear only if you were feeling good?"

They kicked that around for a few minutes, but it felt like another dead end.

"What about the place where some might crash? As in a car accident?" Parker looked around the circle. "Ideas?"

"The intersection of Broadway, Main, and T-wharf," Finn said. "Lots of crashes there."

Ella didn't seem too impressed. "But where's the bell?"

"Maybe we go there and we'll hear it."

"But Ray says it's hidden below that. As in below the street?" Jelly shook her head. "So he hid the recordings in the sewer or something? I don't think so."

"Hold on," Parks said. "Let's run with this a little. Finn is right. We've all seen accidents there. If you're looking at a map, *below* that spot would be in the park where the farmer's market sets up."

That actually made sense. "In a bag not meant for trash. There's a trash can in the park."

Finn jumped to his feet. "And what if there was a bag hidden at the bottom of the trash can. Below the trash bag?"

It was the best idea they'd had yet. "And we'd have to move fast—or we'd be in trouble, right? It's a public place. We could get spotted by Lochran—or Mr. White. This all fits with the clue sheet."

"Let's go . . . right now," Parker said. "Before dark."

Harley patted his thigh and KitKat trotted over. "I'm with Parker—and Finn."

"Of course you are," Jelly said. "Because they're guys. But there's another way to interpret this."

All eyes were on her now. Even Kit.

"If we aren't looking at that intersection on a map, you don't have to go into the sewers to get below that spot." Jelly raised her eyebrows like the answer was obvious. "The harbor?"

"Think about it," Ella said. "You have to climb down below T-wharf to get down to the harbor. I think he hid it below the buildings. Maybe it's strapped to one of the supporting beams . . . the stilts."

"And," Jelly said, "*and* you have to watch the time because the tide is coming in. This is working perfectly."

Maybe. Hopefully. It was a lot more than they'd had to go on before.

"Or it could be in your boat, Parker." Finn gave a half shrug. "It's below the intersection, right?"

"But it wasn't my boat until after Harley's uncle went to jail. It was Steadman's then. Would he have stashed the evidence in someone else's boat?"

"What better place?" Ella was on her feet now. "It was nobody's boat. It was close enough for Uncle Ray to stash it there—and keep an eye on it. He had no worries about somebody finding it there, though. That's why he wanted Parker involved. He was already maintaining the boat. That was a clue."

An exceptionally big wave hit the rocky shore at that instant, like God was adding his own exclamation mark to Ella's statement.

"The bag—not meant for trash. I just had a thought." Harley could hardly contain his excitement. "A *dry* bag."

"Meant to keep keys and phones and valuable stuff dry—even out in a boat." Ella pointed to the poem. "And here . . . it says we'll find the evidence *nice and dry*. It's in a dry bag for sure."

"I've got a couple of dry bags in the storage compartments," Parker said. "Or maybe there's a dry bag strapped to one of the beams below the buildings along the shore. Everything fits."

Except the bell part—and the thing about "feeling swell." But that didn't matter. Maybe they'd figure that out when they got there. They divided into three teams. Finn would check the park—especially the trash cans. Parker and Harley would check every inch of *Wings*. Ella and Jelly would check every beam underneath the buildings at the start of T-wharf. But even now, the incoming tide might make some of that impossible.

"If you find something, don't be shouting it out or waving the rest of us over," Harley said. "We'll start a group text and keep in contact. We have to act casual . . . in case Lochran is watching. Or Mr. White."

The five of them and Kit headed for town.

"We got this." Ella walked alongside Harley. "You should have gotten us girls involved sooner."

Hey, if they found the evidence tonight, Harley wasn't going to deny the girls their bragging rights. "I hope you're right." Actually, he had to do more than cling to hope. "I *pray* you're right."

CHAPTER 36

PARKER CHECKED EVERY INCH OF *WINGS*. Below every seat. Under the steering console. Nothing.

Harley emptied both dry bags stored on board. No mystery phone or key to a safe deposit box . . . not a thing that looked out of place. They emptied Parker's dive gear bag, too. They even removed the engine cowling in case Ray had duct-taped a waterproof bag inside.

The tide had already crept in too much for the girls to check some of the poles. But every time Parker looked their way, the two of them were searching hard. Sometimes kneeling at the base of the poles and digging in the sand a bit, just in case the dry bag had been covered.

Finn hopped into the boat. "The park is clean. No second bag under the garbage bag. Nothing in the bushes. Nothing out of place anywhere."

The tide may have been coming in, but the tide of hope inside Parker was seeping out pretty stinkin' fast. Were they really in as much danger as the lawyer implied?

Harley stood near the bow, scanning Rockport Harbor. A fresh breeze came from the North Basin. "Listen. Hear that?"

A bell. Faint, but definitely nearby. Parker pinpointed it seconds later. A wind chime hanging from the boom of *Flight Risk* itself. "Okay, that's creepy, right? Coming from *that* boat?"

"So the evidence *has* to be within earshot of that wind chime."

Jelly and Ella walked up together. Ella cradled her cowgirl boots in her arms. Jelly's pants were rolled up to her knees. "We'll be back at it tomorrow. And we'll check under the buildings on the other side of T-wharf. We'll find it."

"It's got to be right here in Rockport Harbor somewhere," Ella said. "Too much of the poem fits too well."

Could the wind chime be heard all the way over at the building that used to be the dive shop? If so, she was right. Anywhere in the South or North Basin of Rockport Harbor was fair game. Ray was a diver. Maybe Parker would gear up and check under all the docks.

Harley's phone rang on the console. The name *Miss Lopez* came on the screen along with a smiling picture of her looking through the hole of a donut. Ella snagged the phone before Harley could grab it. She tapped on the speaker.

"I was just noticing," Pez sounded almost apologetic. "It's almost dark."

Harley motioned for them to sit on the floor of the Boston Whaler. He hunkered low over the phone and spoke quietly. "Voices carry over the water."

The rest of them gathered around the phone, and Harley lowered the volume way down. He quickly gave her the status on the search for the evidence.

"I've got more bad news," Pez said. "A customer of ours called. The one who works in the police department."

Ella leaned closer. "Rosie?"

"She asked me to keep her name out of it." Pez hesitated long enough that Parker glanced at the screen to see if they'd lost connection. "It's official. That man in the harbor didn't drown. No seawater in his lungs. And there was bruising. On his neck."

Scorza had been right.

"She wanted to warn me to be extra careful—which is why I'm calling. I know we've talked about it . . . but all of you . . . you've got to stay off the Neck after dark."

Jelly locked fearful eyes with Parker.

"We'll walk Harley back now, Pez," Jelly said. "Then Parker and Finn will make sure Ella and I get home okay." Immediately she stepped out of the boat and onto the dock, like that's all it would take to get everyone to follow.

"I don't need an escort," Harley said. "I'll be home in ten."

"I'm so sorry," Pez said. "I'm thinking it doesn't hurt to err on the side of caution, right?"

But going into hiding would be like giving up. If everybody did that, the Strangler would never get caught. Parker met eyes with Harley. Likely Harley's mind was swirling all over the place, just like Parker's. But he was pretty sure that whatever Harley was thinking, it had nothing to do with being cautious. Only one thing was clear. Harley's eyes were asking Parker a question. It was one of those are-you-with-me looks.

It was one of those moments when Parker didn't have to think anything through—even though he probably should have. His response was instinctive. Parker reached up and tapped the motorcycle key hanging from the lanyard around his neck. Harley gave the slightest smile—and a single nod.

CHAPTER 37

ELLA WALKED BESIDE HARLEY AND KIT toward the coffee shop. Parker, Jelly, and Finn set the pace ahead of them. Ella eyed every stranger they passed. Harley didn't look at anyone—like he wasn't one bit worried about meeting the Strangler. His reaction unnerved her a little. What was going on in his head right now?

She knew the boys better than they knew themselves. Harley, the guy who'd announced he didn't want to keep secrets from the group, was definitely holding on to something right now. She had to get him talking.

"What are you thinking, motorcycle boy?"

He gave her a sideways glance. "I'm trying to figure out what Miss Lopez is thinking. You're a girl. What's your guess?"

Not what Ella was expecting. "Pez? You're worried about what's going on in Pez's head?"

"She's planning something. It has to do with the coffee shop;

protecting it—all of us, really—from the Strangler. I just can't figure out what."

"Any idea at all?"

He shook his head. "And then there's all this stuff with Uncle Ray. I've brought his madness into her home."

"Harley, that isn't on you."

He gave her that sideways glance again. "Isn't it? And I even had a chance to stop the Bogeyman—right there at BayView—and I missed the catch."

"The *Strangler* now. Remember that. This guy is a killer."

"Which makes it even worse that I didn't stop him."

Ella was ready to strangle him herself. He was missing the point. "Do you have some kind of a plan?"

He stopped and stared through the window of the silversmith shop. "Still sorting that out, I guess."

She looked at his reflection in the glass. "How about thinking out loud?"

"Probably best I didn't."

Sheesh. He *did* have a plan. Only a half block before the coffee shop . . . definitely not enough time to get it out of him. "Hey—you said no more secrets, remember?"

He walked faster, like he wanted to catch up to the others. But she knew exactly what he was doing.

"You'll stay off the Neck at night, right?"

"Kit doesn't know how to use a toilet yet." He gave her a half smile. "She'll still need a little potty walk now and then."

She groaned inside. So that was it. "Harley. You think just because you're some kind of football star that you can handle yourself no matter what happens—right?"

"I won't be alone. I'll have Kit."

Like it was as simple as that. "Harley . . . Mike Ironwing was probably walking Kit when he ran into the Strangler, remember? And look where it got him."

CHAPTER 38

PARKER CAUGHT HIS MOM AND DAD UP with everything. Now he sat alone at the kitchen table with a glass of milk and a plate of his mom's chocolate chip cookies. A feeling of helplessness crept in. Maybe he'd talk to Grandpa about it in the morning during their M101 time.

Jelly and Ella had double-teamed him on the walk home from the coffee shop. How they all had to work together to keep Harley from doing something stupid. They knew he wasn't telling them his plans and insisted that Harley would have to meet them halfway on this.

Mom breezed in and gave him a kiss on the head. "How has Wilson taken this last bit of news?"

Actually, he hadn't told Wilson yet. "I'll find out." The moment she left, he pecked out a text with a quick review of the new facts. He admitted that he felt things were unravelling and he really didn't know what to do next.

Wilson answered immediately.

Hold on. Already working on it. I'll come up with a plan.

That was it. No other response from Wilson at all. Maybe he had the same problem Parker had at this moment. The more he thought about the situation, the less clear the next step became.

CHAPTER 39

HARLEY CHECKED THE LOCKS FOR THE UMPTEENTH TIME. He'd had a good talk with Miss Lopez about him sleeping downstairs in the coffee shop. In the end, she gave him the green light. He was pretty sure she knew she couldn't change his mind on that one.

She actually helped him carry his mattress down. She made him a cup of hot cocoa with real milk instead of just water—and it was fabulous.

They talked for a long time about his dad. "He would've liked you, Miss Lopez."

"Enough to take me for a ride on the back of his motorcycle?"

Harley laughed. "You wouldn't have had to ask him twice."

They talked about Uncle Ray like they'd done so many times before. Each time he seemed to remember something more. He cupped his mug with both hands, and Miss Lopez placed her hands on his. "When I drive you to the prison tomorrow . . . mind if I go in with you?"

He shook his head. Ray had a way of hurting people. "He's poison. I don't want him anywhere near you."

She thought about that for a moment. "Maybe that's best. Not because I'm afraid of him. But I'm liable to do something that'll land me in prison myself. He had no right dragging you into this. It was selfish."

"I'm sorry for all the trouble this is causing you."

She squeezed his hands. "I'm not. I've got *you*. The stuff from your uncle doesn't even register on my Richter scale. He's barely a blip on my radar."

But *still*. Harley had to do something to help her. Actually, a few things were taking shape in his mind.

"I do need to be realistic, though," Miss Lopez said. "I won't pay protection money to Mr. Torino—which is how I see his operation. You did a great job fortifying our back door, but I want to guard ourselves even more against a visit from the Strangler."

"What are you thinking?"

She smiled. "We'll talk about it tomorrow. Deal?"

Which said whatever she'd planned was a big step, right? And no matter what anybody said, it was all pretty much because he'd missed his chance to catch the guy. Between that and the threat of Lochran . . . Miss Lopez didn't sign up for any of that, right? She didn't deserve it. Was she thinking of throwing in the towel on the foster parent thing?

Miss Lopez knelt in front of Kit. "Okay, girl. I'm counting on you. You keep one ear to the ground, okay?"

Kit wagged her tail.

Harley waited until Miss Lopez had gone upstairs before leaving the table. He took his empty mug to the kitchen and rinsed it out. Kit padded beside him, tail swinging wide.

"So I have some ideas, Kit." He kept his voice low. "Whenever we go for a walk, I'm bringing the Louisville Slugger. Or Parker's machete." It had been in his room ever since Wilson had visited last fall. "Maybe we get lucky and I get another swing at the guy. Starting tonight."

Kit looked up at him, her tail still wagging, like she was good with his plan.

Harley gave her a hug around the neck. "That makes two of us."

CHAPTER 40

Parker steered *Wings* wide of the docks and past *Alert 1*. Eric was on board the harbormaster boat, standing at the console and making notes. Parker waved as he passed.

The harbormaster held up his phone. "Say hi to your grandpa."

Was Parker that predictable—or was Eric that observant? Then again, pretty much anytime he was alone on the boat early, it involved a phone call to Grandpa. Some days he sat in the boat and didn't leave the slip. Today he needed to feel disconnected from land entirely.

The back side of the shops along the Neck looked quiet from here. He found himself checking the tide line on the rocks and the supports under the yacht club. Anyplace Harley's uncle could've stashed a dry bag. He passed the Motif and the Tuna Wharf. There were a million places Uncle Ray could have hidden that bag. When the tide dropped later today, they'd all be searching again.

Parker cut the motor just shy of the breakwater. There was no wind, and he could just let the tidewaters ease him around a bit.

He was early, but he hit Grandpa's number and propped the phone on the console anyway. His grandpa answered the FaceTime call immediately—like he'd been just as anxious as Parker to start their time together. Grandpa listened while Parker caught him up on the latest Strangler and Lochran details.

Sometimes Parker brought a question about being a man to their M101 calls. Other times Grandpa had a principle to share. Today Parker just needed advice. "So how far do I go to help Harley out? I mean, I'm going to keep searching, for sure. I'll spend the whole spring break looking for that evidence, if that's what it takes. But should I be doing something more—if I were a man, that is."

"Manhood is about character," Grandpa said. "About your heart, not your age. You're already a man, Parker. The question always is, What kind of man do you want to be?"

"One who does the right things." Like his dad. His grandpa.

"I like that answer. So, what are the right things you should do for Harley?"

"That's just it. I don't know. I'd have him bunk at our house until things cool down, but there's no way he'd leave Pez there alone."

"Okay. So Harley could be in danger if the coffee shop has another break-in—while he's sleeping downstairs by himself."

"Right." Parker sat back and watched the gulls diving and wheeling overhead. "Maybe I should ask Mom and Dad if I can sleep over at Harley's place."

"Is that what Harley wants?"

"He's never asked. And he wouldn't, you know?"

"And you don't think it sounds a bit dangerous . . . you going over there?"

He wanted to say it wouldn't be dangerous at all. Not with the two of them together. But that wouldn't be entirely realistic, would it? "Okay, sure. More than being in my own bed, I guess. But we'll be together, Grandpa. That means it'll be a lot safer for Harley. I can talk him out of doing something stupid. And if someone breaks in—and sees the

TIM SHOEMAKER

two of us there, *and* the dog? One of us would be phoning the police immediately. The burglar would run, don't you think?"

"I certainly would." Grandpa laughed. "Sounds like you're ready to float the idea past your parents."

"But what do you think, Grandpa? Sleeping over. Giving up spring break to search for the evidence. Am I going overboard here a bit?"

Grandpa thought about that for a moment. "How far should a man go for his friend—is that the question?"

That about summed it up. Parker nodded.

"All right. Sometimes with big what-do-I-do questions, I run them through a grid to see if that helps me sort it out. I ask myself, *What does the Word say?* In this case I might search for Scripture that deals with how far to go to help another person. Make sense?"

Wings drifted close to a sailboat. Parker fired up the engine and moved to a clear spot. "Yeah, I can see that. Can you think of someplace in the Bible that deals with that?"

"Yep . . . and I'll bet you can too. Think about it. Do a little digging."

"Grandpa . . . help me out here. I'm not sure how much time I've got to do some big search."

"Fair enough," Grandpa said. "Here's a head start. Once Jesus explained how far a guy should go for his adversary. And you'd probably do more than that for a friend, right?"

"That makes sense."

"Okay, so check a concordance, or just Google the words *Jesus extra mile* and see what the Bible says."

Parker made a mental note.

"Next, when making a decision, ask yourself what Wisdom would say."

Parker studied his grandpa's face on the screen. "Wisdom. I'm not sure I've got his number in my contacts."

Grandpa laughed. "Sure you do. To get in touch with wisdom, you simply talk to people who are wise. Not just your friends, but those who have been around the block a few more times than you. People who know you. Care about you. Anybody come to mind?"

Parker's dad. Mom. Grandpa. "Yeah, I guess."

"Good. And if you're still having trouble knowing what to do, there's always the World test."

"World test?"

"Think about someone who isn't a follower of Jesus. Like your old friend Mr. Scorza . . . what would he advise?"

"First, he was never my friend—and I'd never take his advice."

"Bingo. Imagine what a person like him might suggest, and most of the time it's the wrong answer. You know what *not* to do."

Check what the Word says. What Wisdom says. Do the opposite of what the World says. "That helps. But what about friends? Where are they on this decision grid?"

"They know you, so that's something. But chances are, they lack experience—which means they may not have quite the level of wisdom that you need."

"Jelly would tell me I'm going too far. She'd say I need to find some middle ground. Find something Harley and I can live with."

"The Halfway Principle. Great tool for negotiating, but lousy in any kind of relationship—like with friends. Meet each other halfway, and neither of you are in a great spot, you know?"

"I guess that makes sense."

"Take your time and think it all through," Grandpa said. "I know you have to get going. So one little story—and maybe an assignment before our time is up."

No surprise there.

"There was a song that came out in the early eighties, when your dad was taking his first steps. Your grandma liked the song—and not just because her name was the title. It was something the song said. Your grandma and I had a million-dollar marriage, and that song revealed one of the secrets we both practiced to keep it that way. It works for close friends, too."

Parker waited for a couple of seconds. "So . . . what was it?"

Grandpa laughed. "Oh, no. You're going to have to work for it.

When it comes to sleeping over at Harley's, you don't need the answer until tonight, right? Find the song. Figure it out. Let me know when you do. Now get that gorgeous boat back in the slip and help your friend find that evidence."

He was right. It was almost time to meet Harley. He started the engine, throttled forward, and spun the wheel. He'd have to check out the song and the Bible passage later. But right now, Harley needed him . . . and he wasn't going to be late.

CHAPTER 41

THE EARLY MORNING RUSH WAS OVER, and Angelica wiped down the working counter during the nine o'clock lull. The break relaxed her.

But Harley was a completely different story. He seemed at his best when the line was five deep and some customer spilled their entire to-go order in the middle of the seating area. When there was no time to think. When the workload eased, the weight on Harley's shoulders seemed to build.

And he had plenty on his mind, right? No wonder the guy liked to stay busy. And right now, he looked just a little bit lost. He grabbed a rag and wiped down the tables—ones he'd already cleaned minutes ago. Was he dreading the visit with his uncle this afternoon? For sure.

Maybe Pez sensed Harley's tension too. It was the way she kept checking him. Just quick glances when he wasn't looking, but Angelica noticed.

"Well, what do you say we take a little break?" Pez swung a chair from under a table and straddled it backward. "It's been a busy morning."

And not just in the coffee shop. The Strangler had hit another four shops last night—and they weren't all in a row. How the guy moved from one business to the others without being spotted by the extra police on patrol was a mystery. Normally, they'd all be talking about the burglaries, but today was different. Everyone avoided the topic. Maybe it was hitting too close to home now.

Clearly Harley wasn't slowing down. He'd keep busy right up until he met Parker to do more searching for the evidence. Even now he wiped down the chairs and set them back in place. KitKat tagged along, sniffing under the tables for donut crumbs.

"What can we tease Harley about, ladies?" Angelica was pretty sure a little verbal sparring would get his mind in a better place. "How about the fact that he wore his apron inside out this morning?"

Harley checked—and for just an instant there was a look of disbelief. "And you waited until *now* to tell me?" He untied it and pulled it over his head, then ducked back in it the other way. "Customers probably thought I was an idiot."

"Probably?"

Pez and Ella laughed. Even Harley seemed to loosen up.

The front door chimed, and Detective Greenwood stepped inside. He smiled politely, but he was all business.

"Can I get you something?" Pez stood. "Donut?"

He shook his head. "Two things."

Angelica found herself wringing the rag in her hands.

Harley dropped the rag he was holding. He stepped closer—with Kit at his side.

"There was an injury last night," Greenwood said. "Nothing too serious, but the Strangler isn't just staying in the shadows anymore. He's stepping up his game. We're passing the word quietly to all the shops."

Pez let out a soft cry. "We keep a light on all night out back—and front. We've got Kit—and Harley slept on the first floor again last night."

"You're doing all the right things. We'll get him. We've got an army scheduled for tonight." Greenwood looked distracted. Like he still hadn't done what he'd really come to do. "Harley. Got a minute?"

Angelica's stomach dropped.

Pez took a step forward—like she wasn't sure if she should join them. Greenwood glanced her way. Whatever look passed between them, it was enough to make Pez stop.

The detective weaved his way past the tables to the back door. This was beginning to be a regular thing with Harley. Private conversations with lawyers. Cops. What was it *this* time?

The detective stepped outside, with Harley and Kit following. The moment the door closed behind them, Angelica was on the move. She twisted the rag around one hand now.

All three of them filtered to the back, where they had a good window view of both Harley and Greenwood outside.

Greenwood walked Harley all the way to the granite blocks between them and Sandy Bay. The cop put both hands on Harley's shoulders. Talked to him.

Harley drove his hands in his back pockets. Head down. He nodded. He looked up and asked a question—and honestly, it looked like he was ten years old instead of two days shy of sixteen. Again, his head was down. Shoulders slumped. He nodded again and again. But didn't look up a second time. He reached for Kit. Moved his fingertips in a slow circle on top of her head.

"This is *so* not good," Ella whispered. "Pez . . . what could it be now? Do you think he's taking KitKat away?"

But Pez wasn't watching anymore. Her head was down. Eyes squeezed shut tight. Lips moving. Obviously, she was just as concerned as Angelica and Ella. But she wasn't standing there wringing a cleaning rag. She was doing something about it. She was taking it to the top.

CHAPTER 42

HARLEY SHOULD'VE FELT SOMETHING. Maybe it was the shock of it all. Maybe news like this came with some kind of anesthesia—numbing the part of the brain that should make you cry, or at least feel *some* emotion.

"He's absolutely . . . positively *gone*?" Instantly Uncle Ray's voice was in Harley's head. Ray's Rules *number two*: *I land on my feet. I always do.* "You're sure?"

"I'm sorry, son," Greenwood said. "Early this morning."

Ray's Rules *number three*: *Be the survivor.* Which hadn't exactly worked for Uncle Ray this time, had it? "How?"

Greenwood shook his head. "I can't go into that. You know I can't."

Ray's Rules *number seven*: *Make your own luck.* Right. "Murdered?"

The detective's grip on Harley's shoulders tightened. Like he was trying to transfer some of his own strength to Harley in the only way he knew how. "I can't say."

"I think you just did." If his uncle had died accidentally or naturally, Greenwood could have told him.

"All I can say . . ." Greenwood hesitated like he wasn't sure he should be saying anything. "He didn't choke on his breakfast."

That was all Harley needed to know. "It was Lochran. He got to him, didn't he? This is about the evidence Uncle Ray had on him."

Greenwood bent over just a bit to look Harley in the eyes. "What do you know of Lochran—and evidence?"

There was no point keeping Uncle Ray's secret anymore, was there? Harley gave a quick replay of the visit from Sebastian Kilbro—and the letter that along with the clues had proved hopeless. "Miss Lopez was taking me there to visit him after closing today. See if he could give us a better idea of where to look. Guess it doesn't matter anymore."

"Oh, Harley." Greenwood squeezed his shoulders again. "You shouldn't have been put in the middle of that. It was dangerous."

"He said he'd tell me where the bike had been dumped if I got the evidence for him. But that's not why I was doing it. My motorcycle is gone. I know that. But he said Miss Lopez would be in danger if I didn't find those recordings."

The cop looked downright ticked now. "Kilbro is slimy. He should've never gotten you involved. I'm sorry, Harley. I really am."

Greenwood was the real deal. Harley knew that. And he knew the detective would need Ray's clue sheet—but probably hated to ask. He reached in his back pocket and pulled out the folded piece of paper. He wouldn't be needing it anymore. "You probably want this." Lochran was still dangerous, and maybe his uncle's evidence could help put that animal away for good.

The detective gave it a quick scan. "Thanks, Harley. I'll work on this."

Harley had dreaded going to see Uncle Ray ever since Kilbro set it up. He would've gladly taken any excuse he could find to get out of going. But this?

Harley watched a lobster boat scoop a trap buoy out of the water. The lobsterman never had to worry about somebody showing up at his door with bad news. Right now, that's where Harley wanted to be. In a boat. The farther from shore, the better.

"You going to be okay?"

Harley had no idea. He nodded.

"Don't keep all this bottled up. Talk to Miss Lopez."

But how much should he say? "That'll make her whole day."

Greenwood nodded like maybe he understood. "God created moms to do a whole lot more than keep their boys in line. They'll keep them out of a lineup, too. But you have to open up . . . and listen, too. That's how a family works."

Harley wasn't so sure foster families worked that way.

"Want me to talk to Pez—just to get things rolling?"

When would Miss Lopez realize Harley was more trouble than he was worth? When would she throw her hands up and say, "I didn't sign up for this!"? Part of him wanted to tell her himself. But he couldn't bear to see the regret in her eyes. That one instant when she admitted—even silently—that she'd made a mistake becoming his foster mom. "Maybe that's best." That way she'd have time to get her game face back on before he saw her. And maybe he could go on pretending she never regretted taking him in.

CHAPTER 43

PARKER GOT THE FRANTIC talking-over-each-other update from Jelly and Ella the moment he walked into the coffee shop. Pez sat on a stool at the counter, hands clasped—with her knuckles pressed against her lips. He walked over to her. Hated to interrupt whatever thoughts she was turning over in her head. "Uncle Ray is *dead*? For sure?"

She nodded. "Detective Greenwood told me everything."

"Harley in the Crow's Nest?" Parker eyed the stairs.

Pez held up her phone. "He texted. He and KitKat took a walk. I told him to take his time. We've got things here."

"He sat on the rocks for a few minutes, holding KitKat close. Then the two of them took off down the shoreline." Ella looked genuinely worried. "Don't you wonder what God was thinking? I mean, how much can one guy take?"

Jelly stared out the window, like she expected Harley to reappear. "Pez . . . do you think Harley's okay?"

"No," Pez said. "But he will be."

Parker had to find him. At that instant a text dinged in—from Harley.

Kit and I could use some Wing-time in the bay. Meet at dock in 30?

Parker held the phone so Pez could read it—despite the tears glossing her eyes. She nodded. "That's a really good sign. He needs you, Parker. Go."

Grandpa's voice was in his head. *What does Harley really need?* Parker fired a quick text back.

On my way.

Ella pointed to herself and Jelly. "Does he say anything about us joining you?"

Was she serious?

Pez stepped between the girls and put an arm around each of them. "Let's give Harley some space, girls. And I need you here."

"It's getting rough in the bay." Jelly pointed toward the back windows. "You'll both get soaked."

"Our men have different ways of processing things," Pez said.

Actually, Parker liked the way she referred to them as men.

"When hard things happen, a man needs to feel like he's doing something . . . like he's fighting back somehow." Pez spoke so quietly . . . almost reverently. "But Harley only has shadows and ghosts to fight. Doing battle with the wind and the waves might do him good."

Parker slipped out the door and jogged all the way to *Wings*. Maybe he needed to feel like he was doing something too. The search for the evidence was likely over now. He had no idea what was next. But he wanted to be at the boat plenty early in case Harley showed up sooner.

He checked the fuel level. Gave the motor a test start. Scanned T-wharf. And waited. He pulled out his phone, tapped the YouTube app. He typed in his grandma's name. Seconds later the 1982 Grammy Award–winning "Rosanna" echoed from his phone.

He hadn't gotten halfway through the song before he had a pretty good idea of what Grandpa wanted him to discover. "Meet you all the way." The line repeated over and over. No halfway principle here. No meeting in the middle. No finding common ground. A true friend figured out what the other needed—and met them all the way.

"That makes sense, Grandpa." If Grandma and Grandpa had each tried meeting the other all the way—whenever they could? No wonder they'd had a million-dollar marriage.

He scanned the docks and T-wharf for any sign of Harley and Kit. It was still early.

Back to his phone. He Googled *Jesus extra mile* like Grandpa had said. Matthew 5:42 popped up: "If anyone forces you to go one mile, go with them two miles."

And that was written in context about an enemy, right? How much more should Parker be doing for a friend like Harley? It all came together.

He texted Grandpa.

Find out what they need. Meet them all the way. Do even more than they expect. I got it . . . right?

Immediately Grandpa texted back a clapping hands emoji. Parker would update him later about Uncle Ray. Right now, he needed to talk to his dad. He made the call and gave him the news. Dad prayed for Harley at the end of the call. "Praying for you, too, Parker. We'll talk more later."

Still no sign of Harley. Parker took the opportunity to catch Wilson up to speed with what happened to Uncle Ray. He was able to sum the whole thing up in a three-line text.

Uncle Ray murdered in prison. The search for the evidence to get him out of jail is over. Meeting up with Harley now to blow off some steam on Wings.

Wilson's response was just as short.

What he really needs is an airboat ride. And don't think this is over. There's still the Strangler—and a bad guy who thinks Harley has evidence on him. I'm still coming up with a plan.

Hopefully the police would nab the Strangler and this whole thing would be over long before Wilson figured out what to do. Parker prayed it would be.

Harley showed up right on time, hustling down the ramp and onto the docks to the slip. Kit stayed glued to Harley's side. She kept glancing up—like she was making sure she stayed on pace. Maybe Mike Ironwing had hired a private trainer or had enrolled that dog in obedience school. Kit must have graduated at the top of her class.

Harley leaped into the boat, and Kit jumped from the dock, over the gunwale, and dropped onto the deck beside him in one smooth move. Harley untied the ropes even as Parker fired *Wings* up. Minutes later they were heading out the channel into Sandy Bay. The swells were bigger than Parker had figured, but *Wings* didn't seem to mind.

Harley hadn't said a word about his uncle, and Parker hadn't asked. Likely that would come later. When Harley was ready. But right now, Parker had a pretty good idea of what Harley needed. And Parker intended to meet him all the way.

"We're gonna get wet," Parker said.

Harley moved to the bow. He knelt down by Kit for a sec. "You hear that, girl? You wanna get wet? Huh? Do you?"

Kit's tail slapped back and forth like windshield wipers at full speed. She gave a happy-sounding yip.

"You heard her, Parks. Let's take *Wings* for a flight."

Parker cut a wide arc out of the channel and charged north, pretty much into the waves. The Boston Whaler was made for this. And so was Parker. Umbrellas of spray burst over the bow, pelting him across the face. Within minutes, the front of his hoodie hung a couple of inches lower with the weight of the water it'd absorbed.

Harley kneeled on the front seat—facing forward. He held the port and starboard bow lines, one in each hand, like he was holding the reins to a team of horses. Kit kept her front paws on the seat next to him, ears flapping. Every time Parker hit a wave just right, Harley tumbled into Kit—and buried his head in her neck.

"Yee-haw, Parks!"

"Enjoy it while you can!" Parker shouted over the roar of the wind and the engine. "Can't do this with the girls."

"Why not?" Harley grinned over his shoulder. "We absolutely should."

"Not without ear protection."

"Right." Harley was still smiling. "Their screams would damage our hearing forever."

They pounded their way past Granite Pier and on to Pigeon Cove. The water seemed rougher. Whoever said swimming was the best universal exercise had never piloted a boat at this speed—in these kinds of waters. Holding the wheel and keeping the Boston Whaler's nose from burying in the troughs worked every muscle in his body.

He backed off the throttle and let the waves turn their bow toward home. Harley rolled onto the deck. Stayed on his back—arms spread wide. Soaking wet. Laughing. Kit gave a full-body shake, spraying him while he was down. He reached for Kit and pulled her in close.

Parker let go of the wheel and leaned back against the captain's chair. He flexed his hands, trying to get the numbing prickles out of his fingers. He stretched his gimpy arm. Licked salty lips.

"That's what I call a *ride*." Harley's face got serious. "You heard, right?"

Parker nodded. "What can I do?"

"You just did it." He smiled. "Maybe we'll talk later. I just need to catch my breath—and then I'm ready for another flight."

Parker had a million questions. But for now, it was just good to see his friend smile again and know the only weight Harley was feeling on his shoulders was his soaked sweatshirt. He revved the engine a couple of times. "Stow your tray table, put your seatbacks in an upright position, and fasten your seatbelts."

Harley grabbed the bow lines and gave him a thumbs-up.

"Prepare for takeoff." Parker slid the throttle forward—and charged ahead. Maybe he needed this ride as much as Harley did. Uncle Ray's death changed everything . . . and maybe nothing all at the same time. Wilson was right. The Strangler was still out there. And then there was Lochran, who'd still be looking for that evidence—not to mention the mysterious Mr. White.

Their nose caught a wave and dragged for just an instant. It seemed like twenty gallons came over the bow. Nothing the bilge pumps couldn't handle—unless he took on much more. Harley rocked backward and tumbled into the console, laughing hysterically. "Careful, or you'll get us all killed!"

He wasn't wrong. And somehow those words felt more like a warning. A foreshadowing. Like there was something coming . . . and Parker would need to keep his focus long after the boat was safely back in its slip. He eased back on the throttle just a bit . . . and prayed.

CHAPTER 44

ELLA GOT PERMISSION FOR JELLY to spend the night—and Grams was thrilled. They set a square game table on the wraparound porch for dinner. Grams added a simple cotton tablecloth and candles. The soup was hot, but Ella couldn't seem to get rid of the chill deep inside. The entire dinner conversation revolved around Uncle Ray's death.

"Death comes in threes." Grams spoke like it was an absolute truth. A scientific fact, as real as gravity and the speed of light. "And now . . . we've had two."

"But they've got to be connected," Ella said. "And these deaths aren't."

"Mr. Ironwing was found dead barely a hundred yards from where Mr. Lotitto lived—until he went to prison."

Jelly shook her head. "Isn't that more of a coincidence than a connection?"

"*Coincidence* is just a word some use to explain away a connection."

Grams raised her eyebrows like she wanted the significance of her statement to sink in. "Threes."

Ella sat with her back to the house, looking toward the Headlands. There was no fog tonight. If there was, Grams would've never risked sitting outside. Not with the sea vapors rolling in.

"Those violent deaths have spread their toxic tentacles to our boys," Grams said. "There are too many connections."

"Okay," Jelly said, "Harley is connected to his Uncle Ray—but Parker isn't. And not one of them has a connection to Mike Ironwing."

"Child," Grams said, "young Parker found Mr. Ironwing's body— and Harley, his best friend, was with him when he did. Harley found the deceased soul's dog—and now calls Kit his own. Harley shares his uncle's blood, and those two boys are blood brothers, are they not?"

Ella immediately pictured the shared motorcycle keys and gator tooth lanyard. "That's what they call themselves—blood brothers."

"Connections." Grams nodded. "For sure."

"You're scaring me," Jelly whispered.

"I mean to." Grams leaned closer to the candles. "The boys must be careful. There are powerful forces at work. We dare not forget that our boys both have connections to the first two deaths."

Right now, Ella would much rather be hearing a spooky story. Some tall tale that would make them keep a light on in their room tonight. But this felt too . . . real.

Her eyes met Jelly's for a moment. Her friend's wheels were turning, and she had to be thinking of a way to keep a closer tab on the boys until this blew over—without relapsing into full protector mode.

"There's a verse in the Holy Book that says this," Grams said. "A man who strays from the path of understanding comes to rest in the company of the dead."

Ella stared at her for a moment. "*That's* in the Bible?"

"In the book of wisdom itself. Proverbs 21:16."

Jelly pointed at the goosebumps rising on her arms. "Kinda creepy truth."

"But truth just the same," Grams said. "Raymond Lotitto made bad choices. He knew better but strayed from the good paths."

Nobody would argue with Grams on that one.

"Death comes in many forms," Grams said. "Death of dreams. Death of respect. And ultimately—physical death. When that happens, it comes in multiples. Three. Six. Nine. And Death hasn't finished its Rockport harvest. I feel it." Grams hugged herself. "Harley and Parker are good boys, but Raymond Lotitto has thrust them down a dark path of his own design . . . to find that evidence. We must pray our boys don't do something foolish."

Okay, now the bumps were rising on Ella's arms. "Like what, Grams?"

"I surely don't know," she said. "But they best not leave the path of understanding, or I fear that wicked uncle will reach right up from the grave and pull Harley—and Parker—in with him."

CHAPTER 45

PARKER HAD LEARNED A LONG TIME AGO that his parents gave him a longer leash when he didn't break trust. That meant being honest with them . . . and telling them *every*thing. And the thing was, telling the whole truth was part of being a man of integrity—something he wanted more than anything.

Parker told them all he knew. Including what he'd come to understand after his M101 time—and how he felt meeting Harley all the way meant sleeping overnight at BayView Brew.

That's where things really got sticky. But they agreed that Ray's death likely marked the end of the evidence search. If Ray hid it as well as it seemed, it would never be found. Which meant Lochran had no reason to go after Harley. The Strangler was another issue. But with the reinforced security on the back door and the fact that they'd have Kit, the chances of the Strangler coming back seemed remote. He had never hit any other shop twice. Parker had the hardest time convincing Mom, but after Dad went over the ground rules, she finally agreed.

With no other living family member, Harley needed a friend to meet him where he was at. And with the burglar still at large, they totally understood why Harley couldn't leave Pez, and Pez couldn't leave her home.

From the texts he'd exchanged with Harley, his friend was still talking to Pez. But the minute he was done, he'd let Parker know. Dad would drive him over—and personally check that back door.

Dad prayed with him and reminded him about using his head.

"Get packed." Mom hugged him tight and whispered close to his ear. "You be careful—or you won't be doing sleepovers for a *long* time."

He squeezed her right back and bounded up to his room. He pulled out the big duffel bag. Stuffed his sleeping bag and a pillow inside. Clothes for tomorrow. His Bible. He hustled to the bathroom to get his toothbrush, towel, and all the other essentials.

"Slow it down, Speedy," Mom called up from the base of the stairs, "or you'll forget something."

Good reminder. He added three more things to the duffel. Flashlight. Jimbo, the survival knife. Eddie Machete.

Dad poked his head in the door. "Got everything?"

Parker whipped the zipper shut. "I do now."

CHAPTER 46

HARLEY BELIEVED MISS LOPEZ was the most amazing foster mom God ever created. Was his bio mom anything like her? Harley would probably never know.

Here, up in *his* room, he belonged. And where he belonged, he felt safe. Ella's watercolors on the walls. The street signs, license plates, and traffic signs he'd collected with his dad. Things that were his. Things that tied him to friends—and his family.

Miss Lopez had a way of listening that made him want to share. She sat on the floor beside his bed and stroked Kit's head. Miss Lopez listened with her eyes. Her heart. And he told her more than he'd ever told any adult in his life. Mostly what it had been like before his dad died. And what he was feeling right now.

Still . . . he didn't tell her everything. Like how he worried he was more burden than benefit. He'd come with too much baggage. Probably way more than she'd expected. She didn't say that, of course. Didn't even hint at it. But she had to be thinking that, right?

When he was pretty much all talked out, it turned out she had some news too.

"I've made a decision." Miss Lopez took a deep breath. Took his hands in hers. "I'm closing the coffee shop."

"What?" She couldn't do that. It made no sense.

"Temporarily, anyway."

"Why?"

She was quiet for a few long moments, like she needed to get the words just right. "The Bearskin Neck Strangler doesn't break into shops that aren't open for the season. So if we're closed for business . . . there's no reason to break in."

"But Cape Ann Security . . . Mr. Torino . . . we could hire him. I'm pretty sure nobody has robbed one of his accounts."

"See? Right there," Miss Lopez said. "That bothers me. I just don't trust the man. And I don't like being put in a corner—which is exactly what I feel he's doing."

But with the shop closed, how would she make it?

"Besides, he's expensive."

So money *was* an issue. "How long?"

She shrugged. "A week? Two? Hopefully long enough for the Strangler to get caught—or move on. Between the police and Vinny Torino . . . his job is going to get really tough—and riskier than ever."

Harley could definitely see that.

"I want you safe, Harley."

"You're closing the coffee shop . . . to protect *me*? You don't have to do that." He was supposed to protect her.

"That came out wrong," Miss Lopez said. "I think it's best for *both* of us."

Harley wasn't so sure. "If you think Lochran may come after me, maybe it's best to call the social worker. Have her place me in another home for a couple weeks." Maybe with him gone, she'd worry less. And way more importantly, Lochran would have no reason to visit either.

She looked at him like he was insane. "I'd worry more if you were someplace else. I don't want you to leave. Not ever. We're family now. When are you going to get that through your head?"

Uncle Ray was family—and he'd wanted Harley dead. Mr. Gunderson said they were family, but he tossed him out anyway. Family was kind of a loosey-goosey term when the word *foster* was tied to it. But clearly this was a hot button for Miss Lopez, and he had to keep some of his fears to himself.

"Maybe if other businesses close for a bit, the town will do even more than they are now. This has to end."

And soon. Somehow Harley had to help. "Do the girls know?"

She shook her head. "You're the first. I'll tell them tomorrow. We'll put signs up. Maybe our customers will put a little pressure on the town too."

Miss Lopez got quiet. "Nice of Parker to come spend the night. He's a good friend."

The best. "I'm going to get a couple things ready before I text him to come over."

She stood and gave him a kiss on the top of his head. "Good talking with you, Harley." She looked like she was about to say more, but caught herself. "I've got a couple things to do downstairs. Need help with the mattress?"

He shook his head. "Parks and I will get it."

The moment she left the room, Kit came over and nuzzled his hand, like she wanted him to take over where Miss Lopez left off. Kit looked at Harley like he was everything. Like there'd been no Mike Ironwing before him. Like she was all Harley's and always would be.

Somehow Kit had adapted. She didn't mope. She accepted the change. Leaned into it. She didn't see Harley as a foster owner. Harley *was* her owner.

KitKat looked into his eyes with an unblinking gaze.

"You challenging me to a staring contest, girl?" Harley leaned closer, practically nose to nose with her. Her eyes showed no fear that Harley might send her to a shelter. She'd been at his side ever since he'd rescued her. Clearly, Kit trusted him. Completely. "So why can't I be a little more like you, Kit?"

Maybe he didn't have enough faith in Miss Lopez. More likely he didn't have enough faith in himself—that he was worthy of her kindness.

Kit nuzzled his hand again, like she wanted to remind him she wasn't going anywhere. "Okay, girl, okay." He worked his fingers under her collar and scratched until she arched her head high and her rear leg tap-tap-tapped the floor.

"And I'll work on trusting more. Trusting Miss Lopez. And me." And there was someone else he hadn't considered. The one who orchestrated Miss Lopez being his foster mom in the first place. "And I guess maybe I need to work at trusting God a little more too."

CHAPTER 47

VINNY TORINO SKIPPED A STONE ACROSS the still waters surrounding Cape Ann Marina. Eight skips. Anybody could get four or five. But Vinny never settled for what everybody else could do. He took things farther. Mike Ironwing would testify to that—if he could speak from the morgue. Vinny wished he'd snapped a picture of the shocked look on the guy's face. He'd tape a ribbon to it and hang it from his Christmas tree.

It was going to be another busy night. But this one would be different. It would require a higher level of skill . . . and he was up for it. He'd have to be in two places at once. Or nearly. Not a problem, really, with the hand-picked team he had working for him.

His crew was busy on *Sea Monster*, readying the lobster boat for tonight's little circus. The boat was on loan from a buddy who spent more time in Florida these days than he did in Massachusetts. All it was costing Vinny was the diesel fuel—and he'd covered that expense when the first shopkeeper signed up for his security services.

Sal Rosario skippered the boat. The guy knew the shoreline like nobody else. Over the years since Vinny had known him, he'd proved to be a cool thinker when things heated up. A good man to have around. His job was to get the burglary team to the Neck—and get them safely away again. Police hadn't come close to catching his crew yet. They'd forgotten their local history, and the famous poem about Paul Revere putting signal lanterns in the Old North Church. *One if by land, and two if by sea.* Revere was smart enough to consider the British had more than one way to attack.

For some reason, the police only saw a land strategy when it came to the burglaries. They'd roadblocked the entrance to Bearskin Neck. Did lots of background checks on tenants renting on the Neck. *One if by land.* But they hadn't considered that the burglary crew came in by sea. Sal never got close to shore . . . and apparently no suspicions were raised. It was a really sweet setup.

Vinny's three-man burglary team was as dependable as the tides. All of them ex-military. Young. Fitness freaks. And each of them with a creepy dark side that was so real Vinny could feel it. He referred to them as the Tres Diablos . . . and for good reason. Eddie Salinas did bouncer work, just like Vinny. The guy was fearless. Jake Wickum worked a part-time shift at the fish-packaging plant. He wasn't afraid to get his hands dirty—and was always ready to make a little easy cash. Rocko Spinelli led scuba diving charters. He had a longtime history of breaking and entering—without once getting caught. Vinny had taught him the ropes, and he'd been a quick learner.

Sal. Eddie. Jake. Rocko. All of them working for Cape Ann Angels . . . but they were a whole lot more like angels of darkness. They'd worked plenty of jobs with Vinny before.

Three paddleboards—all painted flat black—sat stacked on *Sea Monster*'s deck. Rocko spread a tarp over them and tied the bundle down. They'd look like a crew of fishermen as they passed the operator at Blynman Canal Bridge.

Thanks to the coffee lady, more and more cameras had been mounted behind shops along the Neck. The job was getting tougher, but there was something really satisfying about pulling it off again even with the extra cameras—and cops.

Right now, he was glad he'd accepted Lochran's offer. The man was right: The security business on the Neck was short-term—although it beat working as a bouncer every night. The burglaries would stop, and he'd start losing accounts. Lochran had bigger plans—a vision Vinny wanted to be part of. If he did his job right—and he would—Lochran would depend on him more and more.

Even now, Lochran asked him to handle something that went way beyond personal bodyguard work. Was it a test? Probably. And when the time was right, Vinny would ace it. He'd done worse things in his life, and look where it got him. To a pretty good place.

He'd help Parker and Harley understand that just because Ray was dead, their hunt for the evidence wasn't over. Maybe he'd convince them to give *him* the evidence once they found it. And between himself and the crew, he'd watch the boys close to make sure they did. Sunday night. That's what Lochran said. They'd wait until Sunday night. No longer. If the boys found the evidence, Vinny's boss would rest easier. But that didn't mean it was over.

Lochran expected Vinny to deal with Ray's nephew whether he found the evidence or not. Letting him live would be a risk. What if he made a copy of the evidence before turning it over? He'd be a loose end. But Vinny would have to do the deed in a way that could never be traced back to him—or Lochran. He'd figure something out. He always did. Vinny sent another stone skimming across the surface. Counted the times it touched down and lifted off again. Smiled.

He went over tonight's final details with the gang. They'd hit three stores. And hopefully this time no shopkeeper would get in the way. Vinny hustled back to his truck. He wanted to be seen patrolling the Neck long before his team did their thing. He pulled out of the lot and took the coastal route toward Rockport.

The thing was, anybody could take *one* kid out. Vinny would go that extra mile. Deliver more than expected. Put more skips on the toss than anybody else would. Ray had believed the park ranger's kid could figure out where he'd stashed the evidence. That meant that moving forward, he was just as much of a threat as Harley. What if he figured out the clues a month later and turned in the evidence? Lochran would go to jail. And Vinny would lose a very steady and generous income stream.

It had to be this way. Maybe he'd write a note . . . leave it in the kid's room. If that didn't get him moving on finding Ray's little stash, he'd send one of the Tres Diablos to talk to the boys tomorrow night. Get them jacked up to find Ray's get-out-of-jail-free card. And if they didn't find the evidence by Sunday, no worries. They never would. Vinny would make sure of that.

CHAPTER 48

"GRAB THE OTHER END OF THIS, WOULD YA, PARKS?" Harley stood over the scuba tank standing in the corner. Silver, with a black boot. He tipped it on its side and gripped the rubber boot at the bottom.

Parks wrapped both hands around the valve and pulled.

Harley wiggled the rubber boot off the tank, and a ton of money spilled onto the Crow's Nest floor.

"Counting the motorcycle stash, are we?"

"I count it when it goes in. I know how much is here. Stack the bills. And we put the coins in a bag. I'm bringing it to the bank tomorrow."

Parks gave him a long look. "You think the Strangler will come up here . . . and steal *this*? The tank bank is brilliant. He'd walk right by and never guess you had money inside."

Harley didn't answer, kept stacking the cash.

"Okay. You're not worried about the money being stolen—yet you want to put it in the bank? Do you even have an account there?"

Parks wasn't going to let up. "It's not going into *my* account, idiot. Miss Lopez's. And keep your voice down."

He caught Parker up to speed about Miss Lopez's decision to close the coffee shop. "She's going to need the extra cash. And you've got to help me get it into the bank tomorrow—without her finding out."

He went over his plan, and together they fine-tuned it a bit.

"But she'll know," Parks said. "There's got to be over a thousand bucks here."

Actually, $1,253 and some change. Except for the money he'd dropped in the offering plate at church, the Christmas present for Miss Lopez, and a small weekly allowance he gave himself, he'd stashed every dollar he'd earned in his piggy tank.

"She won't know. Not if we do it right. Miss Lopez is great in the kitchen—and with the whole business. But she hates doing the books. She depends on the bank to keep track of her deposits and stuff."

"Okay," Parks said. "What about your motorcycle fund?"

"I'll rebuild it." He tried to make it sound like it was no big deal. But deep down he feared there'd always be something that would keep his fund from growing big enough to buy a 1999 Harley-Davidson Sportster. Not in half as good a shape as the one he'd lost, anyway. This was the right thing to do. Period. He needed to keep his focus there—not on what he'd miss by doing a good thing.

"You really think she needs money?"

"With no cash coming in—and two more mouths to feed?" He pointed at himself, then at Kit. "I have to do my part—without her knowing. She won't let me help otherwise." Harley stuffed the money in a bag and hid it back in the false-bottomed tank.

Parker told him about the M101 time with his grandpa that morning. Which was great. It saved Harley from asking.

"Grandpa would love what you're doing. You're meeting her all the way."

"Maybe sometime I can join your Manhood 101 sessions." Harley didn't dare look Parks in the eyes, or he'd know how much he really wanted that.

Harley set up his mattress downstairs. Parker unrolled his sleeping bag. Harley spread a rag rug for Kit between them. Harley's phone rang with a FaceTime call. Ella's picture was on the screen, but when he connected, Jelly was there too.

"Checking to make sure we're not doing something stupid?" Harley knew he was right.

"Us?" Ella smiled. "Never crossed our minds."

Harley tried to stay in the conversation. But all he could think about was Uncle Ray. The guy who was so full of hot air was now cooling in the morgue. The guy who'd messed with Harley's head for years . . . controlling . . . manipulating. Gone. All his looking out for number one got him exactly where?

A restless, antsy energy surged through him. The feeling he'd get on game day—just wanting to hit someone. He had the urge to run the rocks out to the end of the breakwater. And if he met the Strangler, he'd plow into him with enough force to make the guy wish he hadn't shown his face on the Neck tonight.

"What do you think, Harley?" Ella's question tore him from his thoughts.

How was he supposed to tell her he hadn't heard a word she'd said?

KitKat whined at the back door. She looked at him with pleading eyes.

"Gotta go, girls," Harley said. "Kit needs a little leash time before she can sleep."

There was a moment . . . a hesitation on the other end. Enough to show their true colors. "But it's late. Does Pez know you're going out?"

"So you *were* checking up on us."

"I'll be with him," Parks said. "And Jimbo. And Eddie. With Kit, that makes five of us."

"Six. You forgot Louis." Harley held his Louisville Slugger in front of the phone.

"You think this Strangler thing is a *joke*?" Jelly did *not* sound happy.

Okay, he'd had his fun with them. "I'll tell Miss Lopez we're going out. And we'll call you when we get back. Satisfied?"

"If you don't call in fifteen minutes," Ella said, "I'll call Detective Greenwood. I have his personal number, you know."

"So do we—but we'll probably see him out there," Parks said. "When my dad drove me over, seriously, like every cop in Rockport was patrolling the Neck. And the Cape Ann Angels pickup was cruising too. There's nothing to worry about."

"And don't forget," Harley said. "We're armed and dangerous."

"Right," Ella said. "But so is the Strangler."

CHAPTER 49

THEY LEFT THROUGH THE FRONT DOOR, and Parker walked alongside Harley down Main Street toward Bearskin Neck. Not the direction the girls probably wished the boys would go, but if they went inland, exactly where would Kit do her business? The Old Parish Burial Ground? He was pretty sure Ella would say it was risky or dangerous or bad luck—while insisting she wasn't superstitious.

KitKat had a spot along the Old Harbor, out by White Wharf, that had become her favorite go-to. And there was a back route to get there—which they'd need tonight. It was a pretty safe bet the police wouldn't want Parker and Harley walking Kit past their Bearskin Neck entrance blockade.

"The Strangler wouldn't be stupid enough to hit tonight," Parker said.

"Unless he's *that* good—and wants to prove it. Can you imagine if he put points on the scoreboard—with all these cops?"

"Nobody is *that* good." Parker hoped that was true. But nothing had stopped the Strangler yet. Not even when he'd gone up against Ironwing and Kit, right?

"The police are in for a long, quiet night," Harley said. "The Neck is probably the safest place in town right now."

Parker laughed. "I hope you're right." They cut north down Pier Avenue and seconds later were working themselves behind the shops and buildings along Old Harbor. White Wharf blocked the little harbor from the swells of Sandy Bay. A long aluminum ramp led down to a dock bristling with floating slips that rose and fell with the tides. Enough lights were mounted on old telephone poles to keep the place from looking as out-of-the-way as it was. How many times had he seen kids crab-fishing off those docks—having the time of their lives? The place had always felt safe. Even at night.

Harley unclipped Kit's leash. "I'm trusting you, girl. Don't make me regret this."

Kit wagged her tail and bounded for a patch of grass along the east wall of the harbor. She lowered her nose—and followed it on an unmarked trail.

Harley sat on the granite lip and let his feet hang over the water. *"Keep life exciting. Cheat death every day.* Ray's Rules *number eleven.* So stupid, right? I can't believe he's gone. And unless I see his body—which I won't—I'm not sure I ever will."

Parker hadn't even thought of a funeral. Did the prison have their own cemetery?

Kit froze. Ears on full alert. Nose in the breeze. She stared into the shadow zone between the back side of Bearskin Neck and the rocky shoreline of Sandy Bay. Hair on her neck rising.

Harley must have seen it too. "Kit. Come."

Kit erupted in a vicious barking rant—and bolted for the darkness.

Parker and Harley sprinted after her, but she was already out of sight. If not for her constant barking, they'd have lost her. The boys vaulted over a granite wall. Raced through a backyard. Still no visual on the dog.

Kit's tone changed. Like she'd cornered the Strangler. And then—a yip. High. Surprised.

"Kit!" Harley hurdled the next wall—holding the bat like a club.

Parker tugged Eddie Machete from its sheath on the run.

Another desperate yelp. She yipped again—but it was clipped short.

"You leave my dog alone!" Harley's voice roared over the pounding surf.

Parker scanned—but there was nothing on two legs in sight. Nothing on four legs, either. But there was a dark heap in the shadows—and he knew.

Harley slid to his knees beside Kit. "Where are you hurt, girl, huh? Talk to me. You okay?"

Parker couldn't bear to watch—and didn't dare. Machete out. Raised. He stood guard over them, searching for movement among the rocks. For an instant he thought he saw a dark figure hunkered low near the water's edge. Was it him? He strained to see.

"Parks—look." Harley had his flashlight app on Kit. Blood matted the fur on her head. "We gotta get her help."

Parker glanced back where he thought he'd seen someone, but there was nothing. Maybe he'd imagined the whole thing.

Harley scooped Kit in his arms. No resistance from Kit at all. Her tongue lolled out the side of her mouth. Parker sheathed Eddie and grabbed the bat and leash. They hustled toward the heart of the Neck down Doyle's Cove Road. Almost immediately he spotted the Cape Ann Angels Security truck cruising slow. Parker waved him over.

Vinny Torino took one look at the dog and pointed at the truck bed. "Hop in." He pointed at Harley. "Call your foster mom. Tell her I'm driving you to the animal hospital in Gloucester. We'll meet her there."

CHAPTER 50

PARKER RODE SHOTGUN. Harley insisted on riding in the bed with Kit. Vinny Torino barreled down the Neck and stopped at the entrance to flag a policeman. "Somebody clocked the dog good off Doyle's Cove Road."

The cop got on his radio immediately—and Torino mashed the gas. Parker glanced back at the pickup's bed every couple of blocks—and every time he did, Harley was holding Kit tight. Talking to her. The chocolate lab didn't seem to be aware of anything.

"God, please," Parker whispered. "*Please.*"

The tires on Torino's pickup squealed as he whipped into the Cape Ann Animal Hospital parking lot and braked to a stop. Pez pulled up seconds later, fear all over her face.

Torino dropped the tailgate and Harley scooted out, Kit's blood all over his T-shirt, his cheek and neck—except for spots where tears had cut a trail. He grabbed his baseball bat and tossed it onto the ground.

Kit was awake and thrashing around, like she wanted to get back on all fours. Harley set her down on the grass—and immediately the dog went into some kind of stomach convulsion. She gagged and upchucked something dark—maybe half the size of Parker's palm—then stood in a wide stance like she was trying to get her sea legs back.

"Are you hurt, Harley?" Pez ran her hands up his arms—probably trying to figure out if the blood was his.

"Just Kit." Harley scooped his dog up again and trotted for the front doors.

"I've got to make a call," Torino said. "Then I'll be in to make sure everything is okay."

Parker called his dad and updated him. He texted Jelly and Ella.

Dad showed up about the same time the doctor came out to update Harley and Pez. Kit had gotten clocked good, but other than needing stitches, seemed fine. To be safe, they wanted the dog to stay overnight for observation.

Harley looked torn. Like he wanted to stay with Kit but didn't like the idea of Pez at the coffee shop without both him and Parker on guard downstairs.

"Let's go home. They'll take good care of her." Pez took Harley's arm and walked him to the entrance, with Parker and Vinny Torino following.

Despite Pez's determination not to sign with Vinny Torino's security company, she held nothing back when it came to thanking him. She stood at the back of his pickup. "I'm in your debt." She gave him a hug. "Coffee and donuts on me anytime—once we reopen."

"I'll take you up on that." He smiled and headed back to Rockport.

Uncle Sammy roared up in his F150—with Ella and Jelly inside. Ella ran to Harley the instant they'd parked, her eyes searching for the source of the blood.

"I'm okay," Harley growled. "But I didn't get there in time to help Kit."

Jelly shook her head, her face looking spooked. "When will this *end*?"

Harley wiped Kit's blood off the grip of his Louisville Slugger—but left plenty on the taper and barrel. "Soon."

CHAPTER 51

ANGELICA DIDN'T HAVE TO DO MUCH PERSUADING to get her dad to stop at the coffee shop on the way home. Uncle Vaughn did the same.

The street out front of BayView Brew was empty. Angelica stuck right behind Pez, hoping maybe she could talk her into asking Dad to stay awhile. She had her own reasons for wanting that—but mostly so she and Ella could talk to the boys. They needed to cool Harley down before he did something incredibly stupid. Honestly? She could see him shouldering that bat and going out looking for the Strangler. And Parker would join him.

Pez slid her key into the lock on the front door, took two steps inside, and froze. "No! No, no, *no!*"

Tables upended. Chairs on their backs and sides. Donut glass shelves smashed. Mr. Bones had been propped on a stool at the donut counter. Even he looked horrified at what had happened. His mouth was tied wide open—like he'd seen a ghost.

Harley stalked into the dining area, eyes on fire. Bat in hand, he bolted into the kitchen like he thought the Strangler might still be inside.

"Harley!" Pez shouted—but it was like he didn't even hear her.

Dad, Uncle Vaughn, and Parker ran after Harley.

Pez reached for Ella and Angelica and pulled them close. "Touch nothing. We've got to get Detective Greenwood here." She grabbed her phone and tapped his contact.

Apparently, the kitchen was clear. Dad stayed on the first floor, checking the back door. Uncle Vaughn and the boys pounded up the stairs to check Pez's room—and the Crow's Nest.

Greenwood walked through the front door just as the guys came back downstairs. Harley had changed T-shirts, but his arms still had dried blood on them.

It was clear from Parker's face the Strangler had been upstairs. "The Crow's Nest has been turned upside down. The bed is about the only thing he didn't touch."

"This is a new twist." Greenwood focused on the stairway. "The guy has never messed with anyone's living quarters yet."

Clearly, it was going to be a long night. Uncle Vaughn and Dad were deep in conversation with Detective Greenwood. Parker and Harley didn't say a word to Angelica—or Ella.

Instead, the boys worked their way to the far side of the dining area like they were on a mission. Once out of earshot, they had plenty to talk about. They talked close. Quiet. Parker pulled his lanyard out from under his sweatshirt and closed his fist around the motorcycle key. Harley did the same with his. Ella exchanged a look with Angelica.

"Sheesh . . . what is this, some kind of brotherhood moment?"

"They just made a pact," Ella said. "But to do what?"

Only one thing Angelica was certain about. "Nothing good."

CHAPTER 52

HARLEY HAD NEVER SEEN MISS LOPEZ look more whipped. Not a sleepy kind of thing, though. It was a different kind of strength that had been drained from her.

The Strangler had gotten inside by breaking a back window. Before they left, the men screwed plywood in place to secure it.

Parks helped set the tables and chairs upright. Together, they swept up the broken glass shelves—but there were still bits of glass hiding in the corners.

"That's enough for now," Miss Lopez said. "We'll be closed tomorrow. We'll finish the rest then."

She convinced Harley and Parker to sleep in the Crow's Nest. The chances of the Strangler coming back tonight were deep in the negative numbers. Harley would keep his door open—and his ears—all night. He'd have felt a whole lot better if Kit was on the job too. Actually, he would've been happy just to see her sleeping at the foot of his bed.

Harley and Parker straightened the room. They checked the piggy tank. The money was still there—although his dive mask had gone missing.

"No matter what happens," Parks said, "we stick with our promise, right?"

"We shook on it—while holding Kemosabe's keys," Harley said. It was a rock-solid pact.

"Neither of us goes rogue on this," Parks said. "After dark, we walk Kit together."

Was Kit scared right now? In a strange place—without Harley? Did she feel she'd been abandoned? "Do you think Kit knows I'm coming back for her?"

"Absolutely."

"How can you be sure?"

For a moment Parks didn't say a thing. "Okay, this may sound weird . . . but I think she understands what you're saying. Or your tone. I've seen it in her eyes when you talk to her. You told her you were coming back, so yeah . . . she knows you will."

Okay, that made Harley feel a little better. "Kit has had two run-ins with the guy."

"Three."

Harley whistled softly. Parks was right. "When she was with Ironwing. Cats may have nine lives, but I have no idea how many dogs get. I have to stop the Strangler before he does something worse."

Parker held up his lanyard and gave the key a shake. "We."

"Right. *We* have to stop this guy." They'd have to start playing offense. But there was no playbook on this. Exactly how would they catch the Strangler and stop him for good?

Parks set up his sleeping bag on the floor of the Crow's Nest. Harley looked out the back window once, checking not just the circle of light but the shadows surrounding it. He shuffled back to his bed and lay back—and whacked something solid when his head hit the pillow. He found his dive mask under his pillow . . . with a note.

He held it closer to the lamp. "Parks . . . check this out. This is bad." The note was typed in a text style that could have been described as "ransom note." The letters and words looked like they'd been ripped from a newspaper. "Really, really bad."

Parker grabbed the note and read aloud:

FInD raMs EVIDEncE! YOU aNd ThE rANger kID HaVE 72 hOuRS or theRE'LL be ANOthEr bODy IN thE hARBOR. thinKINg AbOut lEaving tOwN? I never SAD WHOsE BODy did I? yOu got niCE frIENds. tHAt bLacK gIrL? IS SHE a gOOD swIMMer?! nOW AbOut tHAt reDhead wITh thE traIl-GUIDe shiRt. SHE cOULd gO mISSINg. OR mAybE thE cOffEE shOp Lady. lOtS OF OptIOns. beTteR hopE yOu fiNd thE EVIDEncE BEfoRe thE POlICe DO! kEeP thE COps oUT oF thIs. TEll NObODy. I'LL kNOW If yOu dO. I'lL BE IN tOuCH. DEad serIOuS, DEARSKIn Neck stRANGLEr PS. kEeP yOUr dOg on a LEash. NEXt tIme I'Ll fiNIsh HEr!

Parks stared at the note for a long moment. "Do you realize what this means? Who broke into the coffee shop?"

"The Strangler. The mess downstairs—totally his MO. And the note was signed by him."

"Right." Parks looked excited now. "But this note is all about the evidence. Which means it came from one of Lochran's guys, right?"

Harley got it. "The Strangler . . . and Lochran's gang . . . they're connected."

This meant they had a way worse field position than Harley had figured. The coffee shop was no random hit. It had been targeted—*because* of the missing evidence. Lochran's gang had eluded the police night after night. They were that good. And if Harley didn't deliver the evidence by Sunday night, that same gang promised to take Harley out for a swim

. . . or Parks . . . or Miss Lopez or Ella or Jelly. Parks looked exactly how Harley felt. Absolutely spooked. "What do we do?"

"This is too big." Parks shook his head, still staring at the note. "We need help."

"You read what it said. We can't tell *anybody*. Nobody." With Uncle Ray gone, Harley had truly believed the pressure was off to find the evidence. Wasn't that the whole point of somebody putting a hit on his uncle? He couldn't testify against Lochran if he was in the grave. The threat to Lochran was gone. Why did he need them to find the evidence? "How are we going to find it? All we know is that it's in Rockport Harbor—in a dry bag."

"You've got to show Pez this note."

Harley shook his head. "She'll tell the police—and someone's going to end up in the harbor." Or maybe she'd send Harley away . . . "for his own good." But if Miss Lopez did that, who'd protect *her*? Harley had to stay—and he had to sort this out.

"Okay," Parks said. "We tell my dad, then."

Parks just didn't get it. "No," Harley said. "We just have to find the evidence, that's all."

"And what if we don't?"

Harley didn't even want to think of that possibility. "We'll find it. We give the search a day. Two at most. If we don't find the evidence by Saturday night, we can tell whoever you want. I want to do this Lochran's way, if we can. We do what they say and nobody gets hurt, right?"

Parker shook his head. "Somebody *always* gets hurt."

"Parks, *please*. We'll look hard. And we'll have the girls looking too. We can have anybody look that we want . . . but we just don't mention this." He held up the note and shook it. "Not unless we absolutely have to."

Honestly, it didn't look like Parks was on board. Not completely. But he was close. "These people mean business."

"Exactly why we need help. I say we call Race Bannon." Parker waggled his phone. "We tell him not to come back here in case Lochran has someone watching. We'll text him a picture of the note."

"Look, Mike Ironwing was in the wrong place at the wrong time. Boom. He's dead. My uncle crossed the wrong guy—and he's gone." Harley still couldn't get his head wrapped around that one. "Kit was in the wrong place at the wrong time. If we hadn't scared the guy away, she'd be dead too. And now the Strangler has threatened to kill again . . . but this time it'll be Ella or Jelly or Miss Lopez."

"That's why we can't risk this on our own."

"Or," Harley said, "It's exactly why we need to do what the Strangler tells us to do—and figure this out. Look, I'm not saying we don't tell anyone. Just not *yet*. Not until we're sure we can't do it ourselves."

Parks was quiet for what seemed like a long minute.

"Look," Harley said. "Tomorrow I'll get that money in the bank. The coffee shop will be closed. We can spend all day searching—the girls, too."

"One person," Parker said. "Just let me tell one person so I don't feel we're all alone on this."

Harley smiled. "Wilson."

That actually made Parks smile too. "Wilson probably only counts as a half. I was thinking somebody a little older."

The solution hit Harley instantly. "Okay, there is somebody we can talk to about this. Somebody you trust with your life—and I do too. If I agree that we tell him—and only him—will you leave it at that?" He held the motorcycle key in one hand—and held his other hand out to lock in their agreement.

Parker looked relieved. "Okay." He held his own lanyard and shook Harley's hand. "So we're telling my dad?"

Harley shrugged. "Sort of. I was thinking your *Father*."

Parker squeezed his eyes shut. "Oh, that was slick."

"We're taking it right to the top," Harley said. "I hate secrets, Parks. I kept too many of them with Uncle Ray. Just help me keep this last stinkin' one . . . and I promise, then I'm done with secrets for good."

Parks thought for a long moment. "Okay. We tell Wilson. And we pray. We keep this note secret until Saturday night. Twenty-four hours before the deadline on the note. Not a minute longer."

CHAPTER 53

ELLA PULLED HER COVERS TIGHT AROUND HERSELF, but it didn't make her feel more secure. Jelly lay back on the other bed, her bare feet placed perfectly on a pair of painted footprints on the wall above the headboard.

Grams still looked shaken by the news of Kit being beaten by the Strangler—and the coffee shop break-in. "It's a sign. A warning. Our boys need to understand that this message is for them."

"Why would the Strangler give Harley and Parker a sign? I mean, what's the point?" She meant no disrespect, but Grams was just getting herself spooked. Ella didn't need it rubbing off on herself any more than it already was.

"The *Strangler* isn't giving the sign," Grams said. "Something bigger. Maybe fate. Maybe God Almighty himself. But some supernatural force is warning those boys that the Angel of Death himself is walking the Neck at night. They've *got* to stay away."

Jelly locked eyes with her, and even in the dim light Ella was pretty sure she was just as skeptical of Grams's superstitions as Ella was.

"You've heard of the circle of life." Grams looked at Jelly, then Ella. "It's a real thing, no?"

"For sure," Jelly said. "There's even a song about it."

Ella smiled.

"Just as real as the circle of life . . . is the triangle of death." Grams let that sink in a moment. "That poor man in the harbor. Young Harley's uncle. Both of them violent deaths. And this beating of Kit . . . it's a warning that there's still one corner of that triangle to go yet. But it's coming. Soon."

The look on Jelly's face had changed. She didn't look so leery of Grams's superstitions now. "Maybe there's another explanation." But there was no conviction in her voice.

"The dog was halfway out on the Neck when it got beat," Grams said. "How did the Strangler get past the police—and make it all the way to the coffee shop unseen?" She paused for a long moment. "It's just not humanly possible. Which is my point. Spirits. Ghosts. Something supernatural is happening here. Something beyond our understanding."

"What can we do?"

Grams shook her head. "You can't change the triangle of death. All we can hope to do is divert it someplace else.

"You mean to *someone* else," Jelly said.

"Nasty business, all of it," Grams said. "We must keep the boys off the Neck at night." She stood. "No need dwelling on tomorrow's evil. It's late. You young ladies sleep now." She left the room, but left the door open a crack.

"Sleep?" Jelly shook her head. "About as impossible as keeping the boys off the Neck."

Ella agreed. "Let's put our nervous energy to use—and make a plan." That would be the easy part. The tougher job? Figure out how to make the boys go along with it.

CHAPTER 54

Parker practically sleepwalked to the harbor with Harley Friday morning. But the sun was up, and the tide was down . . . so this was the time to search for the dry bag.

He sent a text to Jelly and Ella—and even Finn—inviting them to join the search. Finn showed up, smiling, before seven. The girls didn't make it until after eight.

The guys stayed in the South Basin. The girls focused on the North. Every support post was checked—right down to the sand. Every boulder on the shoreline was inspected along its base. Any rock that was movable was lifted to see if the bag was underneath. They even crawled deep into the low, shadowy pockets where overhead buildings met the rocks.

By eleven, the tide had reclaimed much of its territory. The five of them regrouped on the floating dock off the deep end of T-wharf and compared notes.

"I was sure we'd find it." Harley looked distracted.

"Harley," Ella said. "Don't take this wrong, okay?"

Exactly the kind of thing people said just before dropping a bomb on someone. But Ella's tone wasn't harsh. Even her eyes showed nothing but care and kindness.

"Why are we doing this? Help me understand. Your uncle is . . . gone. What's the point of finding the evidence that would've freed him?"

"I need to finish this."

"So it's a guy thing?"

Harley shrugged but didn't explain.

"So," Ella asked, "how long do we keep looking for this needle in a haystack?"

The tide was too high to do more searching now. Parker checked the app. "High tide is at 1 p.m. Low at 7 p.m. What do you say we all meet back at five o'clock . . . and check the north and south shorelines of the harbor?"

Clearly the girls were going through the motions. Putting up a good front until Harley gave up the search for good. But if they'd been allowed to see the note, they would've put on waders and kept checking—even with the tide in.

A text dinged in on Harley's phone. His face lit up the moment he read it. "Kit can be picked up after one." He headed up the ramp onto T-wharf.

Parker and the rest followed. They'd barely reached the top when another text chimed on Harley's phone.

"Look at Mr. Popular here," Ella said. "Who is it this time?"

Harley's expression was unreadable. "Miss Lopez." He paused, like he was rereading the short text over and over. "Detective Greenwood is there . . . looking for me. Wonders if I'm okay or if she sends him here." He thumbed off a quick answer.

It was one of those moments where everybody wished somebody would say something, but nobody seemed to know what to say.

"Maybe he's switching things up," Finn said. "I'll bet he's bringing good news."

"I doubt it." Harley kept his eyes on the spot where T-wharf butted into Main Street. "But I have no idea what else can go wrong."

"You want us to leave?" Ella didn't sound like she wanted to, but at least she offered.

Harley shook his head. Folded his arms across his chest. "You're my friends. Anything he needs to tell me—he can tell you."

At that moment, Detective Greenwood pulled onto T-wharf. He parked and swung out of the car with a manila envelope in his hand.

"It's *got* to be something good," Ella said. "You're due for a break."

But Detective Greenwood wasn't smiling, and Parker was pretty sure there was no break coming for Harley today.

CHAPTER 55

ANGELICA WAS STUNNED Harley invited them to stay. Was it some kind of I-don't-have-anything-to-hide act? Probably. But something still didn't add up. The boys were way too serious about finding the evidence. Maybe the conversation with the detective would shed some light on it.

Harley told the detective that whatever he had to say, he could do it in front of his friends. Greenwood hesitated . . . like he wasn't sure that was a good idea.

Angelica held her breath, hoping Harley wouldn't change his mind.

Greenwood gave the manila envelope a little shake. "These were released to us this morning. Your uncle's personal effects when he was brought to prison."

Harley took the envelope. Peered inside—then squatted down and poured the contents on the pavement. A ring of keys with a Rockport Dive Company key fob. A wallet. That was it. No ring, watch, or anything else of real value.

Harley looped his finger through the ring of keys. He held them up. Inspected them. "Keys to a store he lost—full of inventory that all had to be returned to pay bills. Keys to a truck that got repossessed. Key to a boat that's lying on the bottom of Sandy Bay somewhere."

Oh, Harley.

He closed his fist around the ring of keys. Flipped open the wallet. "A driver's license, and a stack of long-canceled credit cards." He looked in the pocket. "And under twenty bucks in cash. Ray's Rules *number eight*: *You see something you want . . . take it.* Well, Uncle Ray . . . I guess we can all see how well *that* worked out."

Angelica wanted to encourage him—but she had no words. Parker put a hand on Harley's shoulder. Maybe he didn't have the words either.

Harley stood but kept his eyes on the ground. "Thanks, detective. You sure you don't need these anymore?"

"No, sir."

Harley nodded. "Guess I don't either." He hauled back and heaved the ring of keys farther into Outer Basin than Angelica would've thought humanly possible. They hit the water with a distant slapping noise— like a startled fish had broken the surface. The wallet followed—cash included. "What I wanted from Uncle Ray was never in his wallet."

Ella hugged Angelica. Tears in her eyes. Angelica was ready to lose it herself.

Greenwood shifted his weight from one foot to the other. The kind of thing people do when they'd really rather be someplace else. Why was he sticking around?

And then Angelica knew. There was something more Greenwood had come to say. The envelope was just the warmup. Now he had to deliver the really bad news.

CHAPTER 56

HARLEY AVOIDED ELLA'S EYES. After throwing his uncle's only possessions into the harbor? What would she think of him? The truth was, none of Ray's keys would ever hang from Harley's lanyard. He wanted no ties to his uncle—even after he was gone. The stupid choices his uncle made before he'd died continued to haunt Harley. In fact, they just might get Harley killed—or Miss Lopez, or Ella, or Parker, or Jelly.

No, Harley didn't want souvenirs from his uncle, thanks very much. And he definitely didn't want reminders for Miss Lopez—or any of his friends—that he was related to him either. Would they fear that since he'd come from the same gene pool as Uncle Ray, somehow he might become like him? Harley wanted them to forget Uncle Ray . . . and hoped, somehow, he could too.

"Harley," Greenwood said, "there's one more thing. There's going to be a viewing for your uncle at the funeral parlor in town."

What? "I figured he'd be buried at the prison or something."

Greenwood shook his head. "A private citizen is footing the bill."

Why didn't she tell him? He'd have talked her out of it. "Miss Lopez can't afford it—and honestly . . . I don't want her to do it."

"Not Miss Lopez." Greenwood looked apologetic. "That's all I can tell you for now. I just thought you should know."

Greenwood gave the funeral details, where and when . . . but even then, Harley had a hard time focusing. Who would foot the funeral bill . . . for Uncle Ray?

"Come or don't come, your choice. Nobody will judge you if you don't," Greenwood said. "I'll stop in, and if you come while I'm there and you need anything? Just motion me over—or just lock eyes with me. Got it?"

That was a strange thing to say. But Harley nodded. "I'll be there." He had to. It's what a man should do.

"You'll be in and out," Greenwood said. "Just pay your last respects and leave."

Harley didn't answer. The last shred of respect he'd held for Uncle Ray was gone long ago.

"Tough day. Tough news. Sorry, Harley." Greenwood made a motion like he was holding a phone. "You've got my number. You can call me. Anytime. Day or night."

"Don't hold your breath," Harley said. "Not until you start bringing me some good news for a change."

CHAPTER 57

WITH THE TIDE TOO HIGH to search the harbor, Parker talked everyone into grabbing lunch at Rockport House of Pizza before Harley picked up Kit.

"We'll find the bag after the tide drops," Finn said. "Then we'll break out a fresh package of Oreos and celebrate."

Harley worked on his pizza but didn't answer.

Parker sketched the harbor on a napkin and divided it into boxes with a grid pattern. Each of them initialed the zones they'd check until it got too dark to see.

"Harley . . . you lost your uncle—and almost your dog," Ella said. "BayView Brew needs repairs after the break-in. You have sooo much on your plate. Let this hunt for the evidence go. It's history—like, really *bad* history. Unless there's something you're not telling us."

Harley glanced up at Parker, then focused on his plate of pizza again. It was just an instant. But Parker was sure Ella saw it. *Terrific.*

The front-door bell jangled, and Bryce Scorza sauntered in. He brightened immediately when he saw them. "I just came from the coffee shop looking for you all. Can't believe the place is closed."

"Temporarily," Jelly said.

He nodded in a mocking sort of way. "Right. *Closed for Remodeling. Opening Soon.* Businesses put those signs in their windows all the time. But most never reopen. Once you lock the door? The business goes bye-bye."

"Not helpful," Finn said.

Scorza seemed to notice him for the first time. "What's cookie-man doing here?"

"Ba-dum-bum-CHING." Finn drum-rolled on the table and hit an invisible cymbal. "Cookie-man. So clever."

Scorza slid onto the bench across the table from Parker and Harley. "Sorry about your uncle, Harley." But he didn't sound one bit busted up. "I don't know how you keep your friends. You're toxic. Your uncle's business closed. Now your foster mom's. Your uncle got whacked. Your dog almost did. You're a dangerous friend to have."

Harley's face had gotten a couple of shades darker.

"I'd worry if I was your foster mom. Seems like the people you live with end up dead—going back to your d—"

Ella backhanded her glass of cherry coke. The fizzing soda waterfalled off the table—and onto Scorza's lap. "Oops."

Scorza jumped to his feet, airing out his lungs with some choice words. He attacked a napkin dispenser from a nearby table.

Ella caught Parker's eye. *Go.* She mouthed the word and nodded toward Harley.

She was right. Parker nudged his friend. "Let's roll. Right now."

"We'll keep Mr. Scorza busy." Jelly shooed them out. "Hurry."

To his credit, Harley let Parker usher him out while Scorza mopped himself up. Finn stood between them and the door, ready to block Scorza if he tried to follow.

Seconds later Parker and Harley were across the street, jogging side by side for the coffee shop.

"Good thing you got me out of there," Harley said. "I was close to doing something very unchristian."

Too close.

Harley looked over his shoulder, like he thought Scorza might be following. "What's his problem?"

"Forget Scorza. Focus on what you need to do. There's still time to do that bank run before you pick up Kit."

They hammered out a quick plan. Harley would grab the cash, run two blocks to the bank. Parker would keep Pez distracted.

Parker's job turned out to be easier than he'd expected. Pez led Parker into the kitchen the moment Harley ran upstairs. From there, she'd never see Harley slip out the back door.

Worry lines creased her forehead. "How is he, Parker?"

It was a good question. "Angry. Embarrassed. Ready to pull the trigger—and looking for a target, I think." He wanted to tell her about the note left in the Crow's Nest, and how scared Harley was that something would happen to her.

She held up her phone. "Jelly texted. Said something happened at lunch."

"Scorza happened. Said some dumb stuff, but some of it stuck, you know?"

"Ahhh." She growled. "Scorza is a scourge to that boy! Why can't he just leave Harley alone?"

"He's jealous." Honestly, Parker didn't know where that came from, but he was pretty sure it was true. Maybe the root problem itself.

"I want to help Harley." She glanced at the door leading into the kitchen like she was afraid he might step through. "Tell me what Scorza said."

"*That* I can do."

Pez gave him a funny look, like she'd picked up on something Parker didn't actually say. "And then tell me everything *else* that's going on with our Harley."

The trick was not betraying Harley's confidence. "I'll tell you what I can."

CHAPTER 58

HARLEY SLID THE BAG OF CASH TO THE TELLER, along with a blank deposit slip he'd snagged from Miss Lopez's checkbook. He watched her pour the coins into the change counter. How long would it take to rebuild the motorcycle fund back to where he'd had it? It didn't matter. It would still take him years to get enough for the bike, anyway. What was another six months?

Scorza's words looped through his mind. *You're toxic. You're toxic.* Was he? All those other things Scorza said were true.

"God?" Harley cupped his hand over his mouth and whispered into it. "I almost blew it. I wanted to rip Scorza apart. Help me. And help Miss Lopez. Turn this money into rubber. Make it stretch until she opens the shop again."

He prayed they'd find the evidence. Prayed for protection for his friends. Thanked God that Kit was okay. Prayed for Miss Lopez some more. "Don't let her get hurt because of me, God. I don't want to be . . . toxic."

Was Miss Lopez better off in *any* way since she'd become Harley's foster mom? She'd had to close her business. Displays had been destroyed. And Kit's hospital stay . . . that would cost her plenty. Then there was the note the Strangler had left for him. Miss Lopez, Ella, Jelly, Parker—weren't they all in danger . . . because of him? He'd gotten every person he cared about dragged into this mess, hadn't he?

"Oh, God," Harley whispered. "Scorza was right."

"All set." The teller smiled and handed him a receipt for $1,573.25. He read it again. "Should be more like twelve hundred, not fifteen."

"The deposit slip is right." The teller smiled. "A good deposit is good medicine."

He hoped so. But Miss Lopez needed more than good medicine. She'd need an antidote . . . because Harley definitely was toxic.

CHAPTER 59

ANGELICA WATCHED OUT THE FRONT WINDOW of BayView Brew Coffee Shop. Another disappointed customer stood reading the sign about them closing until further notice—or the Strangler was caught.

Pez stepped in from the kitchen with Parker alongside her. "It's nice to know we're appreciated. I hope they come back when we reopen."

If they reopened. Right now, the police were no closer to finding the Strangler than they were a week ago. How long could Pez hold out without money coming in?

"We have to do something special for Harley," Pez said. "The funeral is scheduled on his birthday? That's just cruel. We've got to do this party up right." She scanned the room. "Where is he, anyway?"

"I'll find him," Parker said. "And keep him busy while you make plans." He disappeared out the back door.

Ella and Finn pulled up chairs and joined Angelica and Pez. In a way, it seemed ridiculous to still have the party Saturday night—now that the funeral would cast a dark shadow over it. But they all agreed it might be the best way to end—and hopefully salvage—the day.

"Harley needs a break from all this," Ella said. "And from whatever else he isn't telling us."

Pez looked at her. "You've sensed that too?"

Actually, Angelica was kind of glad that little fact came out in the open. Maybe they could brainstorm about it later. "Whatever it is, Parker knows. I can tell when he's holding something back."

Pez seemed to be thinking about that. "They'll tell us when they're ready."

"Let's hope that isn't too late," Angelica said. "Sorry . . . I was thinking aloud. Let's talk about the party."

Pez nodded. "No reason we can't do it right here."

"Sixteen?" Finn looked at Pez.

She nodded. "I'll make cutout number cookies. And if there's time, maybe a special batch of donuts."

"I'll get decorations at the dollar store. Birthday plates. Balloons. The whole shebang." Finn smiled. "Then *you'll* have enough time to bake donuts."

That made Pez smile. "I'll do what I can. I have something special for him. I just hope it arrives in time—and that he likes it."

Angelica raised her eyebrows, inviting her to say more. But whatever Pez had bought, she kept it to herself.

Honestly, after Uncle Ray's death, Angelica wasn't so sure Harley would appreciate the name plaque from *Deep Trouble*. The way he'd tossed his uncle's keys and wallet into the harbor? Maybe he'd do the same with the plaque. Then Danny Miller would find it—and sell it at the farmer's market a second time.

"I wish he still had Kemosabe," Ella said. "He'd be so proud to finally ride that motorcycle legally."

Harley just wasn't lucky that way. How many tough breaks could one guy stand? "Why do bad things happen to good people?" She wasn't really looking for an answer because she was pretty sure one didn't exist.

"Lots of good reasons," Pez said. "But it's still hard when they happen to someone as nice as Harley."

The truth? Besides Parker, Harley was the most decent guy Angelica knew. He hadn't always been that way . . . but he'd changed so much after all that he'd been through. The quarry. Uncle Ray's plot to kill him. Tangling with Clayton Kingman. But the real changes began when "Parker's God," as he used to call him, became his own.

"Some thought I was crazy to become a foster mom," Pez said. "Honestly, I had my share of doubts. But that boy . . ."

Angelica watched her face. Was she searching for just the right words—or was she too choked up to speak?

"I had no idea when he moved into the Crow's Nest . . . putting up all his signs and hanging those watercolors"—she smiled and reached for Ella's hand—"that he was doing so much more than decorating a room in my house."

Angelica waited for her to finish the thought, not daring to say a word for fear that it might break the spell. She silently urged her on. *Tell us, Pez. Tell us.*

Finn looked totally confused. "So . . . what was he *really* doing?"

"Decorating a room in my *heart*. A special place that's all his."

Okay, Ella definitely looked like she was about to lose it. "I know. I know. He *does* that, right?"

"I thank God for bringing Harley into my life." Pez said it with her eyes closed. Was she praying? "God, how I love that boy."

Ella nodded, swiping her tears. "And we're going to have one terrific party for him tomorrow night."

Angelica totally agreed. But they'd have to get him through the funeral first.

CHAPTER 60

ELLA SAT IN THE BACK SEAT, grateful Pez let her tag along to pick up KitKat. Parker rode up front. Harley was in the back with Ella, and the dog sat between them. Pez stopped at the bank on the way back to the coffee shop. It was a safe guess that she wasn't making a deposit.

A two-inch shaved spot with a neatly stitched cut on the top of Kit's head was the only evidence that the dog had tangled with the Strangler. She looked elated to be with Harley. She sat close. Actually, she leaned into him.

And Harley looked happier than she'd seen him in days. He turned Kit's nose his way with one finger. "No more chasing bad guys."

Ella wished Harley would take his own advice.

"I mean it, Kit."

She hated to think what might happen if KitKat met the guy again.

"From now on, we're keeping that leash clipped to that gorgeous collar of yours."

Ella laughed. "A garden hose collar can hardly be called gorgeous. I'd have picked something a *whole* lot more feminine for KitKat."

Pez ducked back into the car, beaming. "Well, I had quite a bit more in my balance than I'd thought."

Parker glanced back at Harley, the slightest smile on his face. Like there was an inside story there. Those two had more secrets than anybody Ella knew . . . except for herself and Jelly, of course.

Harley leaned forward. "We going to be okay?"

"Of course." Pez sounded confident. "God's got this."

Ella wished she could be half as sure about things as Pez.

"You all realize that KitKat here," Parker said, "has gotten closer to the Strangler than the police have? I'm going to keep an eye out for anyone with a limp." He turned to face the dog. "Did you get a chunk out of that bad guy, Kit? Did you draw blood?"

Kit let out a happy yip, like she understood exactly what Parker said.

Even the vet figured Kit took a piece of him with her.

Pez glanced at the rearview mirror. "I wish Kit could talk. She'd have a lot to tell."

Suddenly Harley grabbed Pez's headrest. "Wait a sec. I think Kit *did* give us a clue."

Okay, he totally had Ella's attention.

"We've got to go back to the vet."

CHAPTER 61

PARKER SQUATTED DOWN BESIDE HARLEY at the edge of the animal hospital parking lot. Harley examined the dried pile of Kit's vomit from the night before.

"You're acting weird, Mr. Lotitto." Ella held Kit's leash behind them.

Harley poked at something black, the size of a small jar lid. "I need a water bottle."

Pez handed him her own.

Harley doused the thing, then picked up one corner with his thumb and forefinger.

"Ew." Ella took a step back. "Harley, really. Enough playing junior CSI guy."

Too thick to be part of a sweatshirt. What was it?

"I'll be right back." Harley took off for the animal hospital entrance, still holding the mystery object.

"Too late to save it," Ella called after him. "I think it's dead."

Two minutes later he jogged back, smiling . . . his eyes on fire. He held his hand out with the mystery object on his palm. "All washed up now, Ella. Check it out."

She took a step back. "Still a big *ew* to me."

"You did good, Kit." Harley knelt down to show her. "Remember this?"

Her ears went flat against her head.

Parker took a closer look and whistled. "This makes so much sense. Good job, Kit!"

Ella and Pez pressed in now too. "Is that . . . a piece of rubber?"

Harley shook his head. "Neoprene. The Strangler was wearing a wet suit."

No wonder the cops at the roadblock kept coming up empty-handed. The Strangler wasn't getting onto the Neck by land at all.

CHAPTER 62

VINNY TORINO WAS NO FAN OF HARLEY LOTITTO. No wonder Ray hated the kid. At first, he'd seemed okay. He played by the rules. But he was up to something. Vinny stood on the dock in the South Basin. Skipped a stone across the harbor. Watched the Lotitto kid and his friend climb down the granite wall from T-wharf and join the girls checking the rocks and posts at the waterline. Obviously if he'd found Ray's evidence, he'd have called off the search party, right? So what was it he'd handed the detective?

Obviously the boy hadn't taken Vinny's note seriously. Did Lotitto think he could play games and get away with it? Or did he think the Strangler's threat wasn't real? He shouldn't have given the detective anything. The boy needed to be taught a hard lesson. Actually, the fact that he fed information to the detective—when the note clearly instructed him to keep the cops out—made Vinny's job that much easier. He was completely justified now. Whatever happened to the boy—and his friends—was his own fault.

Lochran had sources everywhere. He'd have someone in the Rockport PD find out exactly what Harley had handed him. Once Vinny got the word, he'd improvise from there. No biggie. And by Sunday night this would all be over. Evidence or no evidence, his instructions were the same.

Vinny turned the river rock in his hand until he found just the right spot. He bent low and threw it sidearm across the water. Seven. Eight. Nine skips before it disappeared. Clearly he hadn't lost his touch.

And he hadn't lost his touch dealing with problem people either. He'd make this one disappear . . . just like all the others.

CHAPTER 63

DAYLIGHT WAS SEEPING AWAY WITH THE TIDE, and Parker needed to make every minute count. He'd been checking under the buildings along the shoreline a good fifty yards from Harley. Jelly and Ella tagged along with Parker, even though he'd hinted they should fan out.

"Did Detective Greenwood feel the neoprene Kit upchucked was important?" Jelly's question sounded innocent enough. But Parker was pretty sure it was just a warmup to the real questions in her mind.

"Yeah, definitely excited. Pez, too. She's already started organizing shop owners for a new sort of neighborhood watch detail—starting tonight."

"There's one thing I don't understand," Jelly said.

Parker grinned. "Just one?"

"Ha-ha." She snagged his cap and slapped it on her head. "Ray is gone. It's too late to use the evidence as a bargaining chip to get him out of jail. So why are we pushing so hard to find it?"

"Ask Harley."

"We tried. Now we're asking you."

Parker nodded. "How about this. There's still a bad guy out there . . . and he needs to get locked up."

Jelly walked backward in front of him. "Has Detective Greenwood made you two junior deputies? Because this"—she swept her hand in a wide arc around the harbor—"feels like police work now."

"You're both sticking your necks out," Ella said. "Help us understand why."

Parker moved on to the next post. Checked the base for even the slightest bit of dry bag showing. Nothing, like every other one he'd checked. "Maybe it's the right—"

"Oh my goodness," Jelly said. "You can't just say it's the right thing to do—because El and I don't see it."

"I don't know what to say."

"Twenty questions." Jelly fell in step alongside him. Ella flanked him on the other side.

"I'm not going to—"

"If a question is too tough, let it pass," Jelly said. "Is there something El and I don't know?"

Parker smiled. "That'd be a pretty long list—"

"I'm serious."

"Okay, okay. Yes."

Jelly and El exchanged a look. "A reason why you two are still looking so hard?"

"Yes."

"And you think it's a good reason?"

"Yes."

Jelly's eyes got the slightest bit wider. "Do you think El and I would think it was a good reason—if we knew what it was?"

"Yes."

"Sheesh, Parker!" Jelly walked backward again. "I thought we were *done* with secrets."

"Almost."

"Why can't you tell us?"

He shook his head. "Yes or no questions, right?"

"Right. Okay. Okay. There's a reason you're still searching—but you can't say why. Has Detective Greenwood asked you not to tell us?"

"No."

"Pez?"

"No."

Jelly looked confused. She fell in step beside him again and glanced at El—like she was tossing her the ball.

"Okay," Ella said. "The lawyer?"

He was one of them. "Yes."

Jelly pumped her fist. "So maybe there's a legal reason you can't say more? But honestly, if Uncle Ray was killed because he had some evidence against Lochran, don't you think it might be a *teensy* bit dangerous to keep looking?"

He had to be honest. "Yes."

Jelly raised her eyebrows and stared at him for a long moment. "Will you keep searching for this—or is there a point when you'll stop?"

"I need a yes or no question."

"Right," Jelly said. "If you don't find this—by tomorrow night—will you stop?"

"No."

"But you'll break for Harley's party," Ella said. "Right?"

"Yes."

She looked relieved. "If you don't find it by Sunday night, will you stop?"

They *had* to find it by then. If not? "Yes. One last question. That's it."

Jelly held up her hand like she needed a minute to come up with something. She scooted over to Ella and whispered something in her ear. Ella said something back, and Jelly nodded.

"You admitted searching could be dangerous," Jelly said. "Do you believe something *worse* could happen if we don't find this—by Sunday night?"

Leave it to Jelly and Ella to finally come up with a really good question. Would he be saying too much to answer? They still wouldn't know anything about what the danger was.

El waved her hand in front of his eyes. "Are you going to answer?"

Parker locked eyes with Jelly for a moment . . . and she saw a shadow of fear there.

"He just did," Jelly said, concern all over her face. "Parker . . . please . . ."

"If we don't find it by tomorrow night, we'll tell you at the party."

"Everything?"

"I promise. Scout's honor."

Jelly smiled. "That'll make us both happy."

"Don't be so sure." It would scare the living daylights out of them.

"What do you mean?"

A text dinged in on Parker's phone. Relieved for the distraction, he whipped out his phone and smiled. "Wilson."

Jelly and Ella crowded in to read the text.

Need some help?

Look behind you.

Parker whirled around. Wilson stood on the sand at the base of the granite T-wharf wall. Backpack at his feet—with a machete handle sticking out the top.

"Wilson?!" Jelly and Ella screamed his name at the same time. They tore across the sand—straight for him. "What are you *doing* here?"

They nearly bowled him over. He laughed and regained his footing.

Harley and Kit hustled over to join the little reunion.

Wilson dropped onto one knee in front of the dog. "So this is Kit. Good-looking animal, that's for sure." He held out his hand for Kit to check him out.

"Why didn't you *tell* us you were coming?" Jelly slugged him in the arm.

"I texted Bucky."

Parker scrolled back through his texts and held up his phone. "Where?"

"Here." Wilson pointed. "My exact words. *I'm coming up with a plan.* And that's what I did. I came up—on the bus—with a plan."

Parker laughed. Clapped him on the back. Harley pulled him into a hug. "Thanks, bro."

"So." Jelly folded her arms—like she was trying to strike a tough-girl pose, but not quite pulling it off. "You have a plan for what? Finding the evidence? Stopping the Strangler?"

Wilson pointed at his machete. "We'll do it all. I'll use my Miccosukee tracking skills to find the evidence."

"And the Strangler?"

He grinned. "We'll put him in a choke hold. I'm calling it Operation Stranglehold."

Jelly groaned. "Are you hearing this insanity, Ella?" She circled her ear with one finger—then nodded toward the guys. "Boys. Thinking they can save the world."

"Nope." Wilson shrugged. "Just hoping to help my friends."

Ella pointed at Parker and Harley. "Well, if the friends you're referring to are *these* two bozos, they're hopeless."

Everyone laughed—except Parker. Ella was way closer to the truth than she knew. Things definitely were growing more hopeless by the minute. They had forty-eight hours to find the evidence. And if something didn't change drastically before then . . . things were going to get deadly.

CHAPTER 64

ANGELICA WAS THRILLED TO KNOW Wilson would be there for Harley's birthday party. The girls excused themselves for a washroom break—which was mostly to debrief about what they'd learned playing twenty questions.

When they got back to the boys, Wilson was different. He had that attack-mode, on-the-hunt look. There was only one logical explanation. The boys had told Wilson what they'd been hiding from the girls. Wilson's new focus said something about the seriousness of the secret . . . and it wasn't good. They searched until it got too dark to find a dry bag—unless it came with a flashing light.

Harley and Parker made plans for an early morning dive in Rockport Harbor to check under the docks—and every other underwater spot. They were stepping up the search—which did nothing to ease Angelica's concerns.

Wilson's "plan" for catching the Strangler was predictably simple. And the problem was, it was close enough to Pez's new plan that the thing looked like it was going to happen. Pez had explained to the shopkeepers the theory that the Strangler was coming in from the water. Maybe he had a skiff anchored out in the bay—or a partner in crime anchored a half block offshore. But the guy swam from a boat to the Neck, did his dirty work, and disappeared into Sandy Bay when he finished.

The theory made sense. Pez organized the shop owners in groups of no less than two or three. She assigned spots to keep watch every hundred feet or so along the Sandy Bay side of the Neck. They all felt the Strangler wouldn't risk entering from Rockport Harbor. That side was lit better, and the channel left him only one escape route. Starting tonight, from BayView Brew to the circle at the end of Bearskin Neck, groups would be keeping watch. And that's what it was—a neighborhood watch group. There was no law against that.

The fact that the boys were even allowed to be part of the shop-owners' watch detail was frustrating. But once the boys got wind that Pez was going to be out on the Neck herself, there was no stopping them.

Detective Greenwood wasn't wild about citizens crawling around the Neck after dark, but the police weren't about to enforce a curfew, either. There'd been too many burglaries . . . and the business owners of Rockport had reached powder-keg status. Restricting the shopkeepers in any way could very well be the spark that caused an explosive pushback. According to Pez, more and more shopkeepers were spending the night in their shops, but now they were armed. Some claimed that they hoped the Strangler *would* pay them a visit so they could stop him once and for all.

Wilson's Operation Stranglehold name caught on—which wasn't doing a thing to keep him humble.

Angelica's dad and Pez took a post near the coffee shop. Close by, Ella and Angelica had been assigned their place among the rocks. She was pretty sure Pez deliberately put them in the safest spot. Harley insisted the girls keep KitKat with them. With Kit's eyes, nose, and ears as sort of early warning devices, their spot would be even safer.

A group from the silversmith shop was next. Then a team from the Fish Shack stood guard over the entire west section of Old Harbor, including the Lumber and Middle Wharfs. Parker, Wilson, Harley, and

Finn had the east section of Old Harbor. Basically, they had the shoreline from the tip of White Wharf, along North Road, all the way to Doyle's Cove Road. The section was too big for them to watch from one vantage point, so they planned to have a roving patrol going.

Wilson carried his machete. Harley, his Louisville Slugger. Parker had Jimbo, his survival knife—and loaned Finn his famed Eddie Machete. Four guys carrying weapons and pumped full of adrenaline? *Sheesh*. It was a disaster waiting to happen.

Uncle Vaughn, along with a couple of guys from Roy Moore's, took the rugged section just beyond the boys. That was Angelica's only comfort. If something went wrong in the boys' zone, Uncle Vaughn would be close.

There were a couple more teams beyond Uncle Vaughn—not to mention the extra police and Vinnie Torino himself patrolling the Neck. Even harbormasters Eric and Maggie were out in *Alert 1*, cruising the harbor and out into Sandy Bay. A group text had been set up . . . so if one saw something fishy, everybody would be on the thread.

Ella promised Grams she'd keep her up to date every fifteen minutes. When she made her ten o'clock call, Angelica leaned close so she could listen in.

"I'm out on the porch, girls. There's no moon." Angelica looked skyward, and it was true. The moon was totally obscured—which added a heaviness to the dark surrounding them. "I'm sensing the Strangler is watching. Even now," Grams said. "Weighing the odds against him and getting a twisted thrill from the thought of striking tonight. I think you should come home."

Not unless the boys—and Pez—gave up on the stakeout. Right now, staying somewhere between the two groups put them in a safe spot. "We'll be careful, Grams. You know that."

"Ella, do you have your cross?"

El pulled it out from under her sweatshirt. "Always."

"You keep that close, Ella-girl. I fear there will be blood spilt tonight."

Angelica rubbed the goosebumps down on her arms. From Torino to the police to the shopkeepers . . . everybody wanted to see blood tonight. Honestly? Angelica kind of did too . . . as long as it was the Strangler's.

CHAPTER 65

VINNY TORINO CRUISED THE NECK with all windows down. The breeze off the ocean sailed through the cab, energizing him. Ray used to rib him about being afraid to take risks. But that wasn't it at all. Vinny was careful. He'd taken massive risks—countless times—but they were calculated. Before he moved forward, he'd always taken the time to find out where he might leave his flank open—and how to protect it.

Tonight was a perfect example. Neck security was insanely tight. Most guys would've pulled the plug on operations. Waited for a night with less risk. But if he did it right, the chances of getting caught were slim. And Vinny always did it right.

It was a matter of risk versus reward. Of course, pulling off a job tonight would be riskier. But the reward of burglarizing a place this heavily protected would be massive. He'd likely get more shopkeepers signing up for Cape Ann Angels Security, sure. But the big payoff was the almost superhuman status the Strangler would gain. If the Strangler could get past the net spread for him, there'd be a whole new level of fear at play.

Vinny had pulled the team together just after dark and put it up for a vote. Sal was all in for skippering the extraction boat. The Tres Diablos were itching for the challenge.

Vinny sketched the Neck, pinpointing the positions of each watch team. The darkest stretch was the one that Harley and the other boys were patrolling. Sure, it was the obvious spot to hit, but that's what made the best choice. While some *hoped* the Strangler would visit tonight, nobody really expected he would. The pure darkness of the night was their ally.

Jake would stay on the boat with Sal. Be an extra set of eyes and ears. Help with the extraction. Rocko and Eddie would share the same paddleboard. Go in for a quick hit—and get out.

If anything went wrong, all they had to do was run for the water. With the temp of Sandy Bay, who'd jump in after them? And with no moon lighting the water, they'd disappear soon enough. Sal would pick them up, keeping an eye out for the harbormasters. If Rocko or Eddie couldn't make it to water, Vinny would rendezvous with them himself. They'd hop in the second seat of the cab and lay on the floor covered with a tarp until he drove them off the Neck.

Vinny cruised down Doyle's Cove Road. Turned onto North. And sent the text to Sal to send in the team. They'd already chosen their target. He'd love to hit the coffee shop again tonight, but he could wait. Between Ironwing's dog and the ranger posted right there, it wasn't the right time.

It was going to be a fun night. And starting tomorrow, Lochran was going to keep him really busy all weekend. Basic bodyguard work at Ray's funeral. And then Sunday . . . the dirty work. The kind of stuff that separated the men from the boys. He wouldn't just beat those boys . . . he'd bury them.

CHAPTER 66

HARLEY MADE THE ROUNDS, walking alongside Parks. Wilson and Finn kept watch over their bit of coastline a good fifty yards ahead. The moment Wilson learned Finn brought Oreos, he'd claimed Finn as his patrol buddy.

Ella and Jelly had set up a text thread with the boys—separate from the larger one Pez had locked in. It seemed they found an excuse to text every five minutes. Harley saw right through that.

One dinged in from Ella like clockwork.

Wilson . . . is this what you hoped for when you hopped that Greyhound?

He wasted no time answering.

Hoping for a lot of things this trip.

Harley glanced at the text. "He's baiting her."

Such as?

Harley held the screen so Parker could see it. "And she takes the bait."

That SCARY Mastodon story you owe me.

Ella fired back a reply.

Masterson. Still not sure you boys can handle it.

Harley was enjoying this.

Afraid we'll die laughing?

VERY funny.

So the Mastodon story is VERY funny? Perfect. When this is over, I could use a good laugh.

"Oh yeah," Parks said. "The boys definitely won that little volley."

Harley climbed the wall running alongside White Wharf. The wind had raised whitecaps on the waves. The two of them searched the water's surface for any sign of the Strangler—or his boat. "There's no way he's swimming more than fifty yards—even with a wet suit."

"You wouldn't catch me swimming ten yards in the bay at night," Parker said.

"Great whites?"

Parker didn't say anything for a few moments. "They're here. Tagged ones have dinged the signal buoys."

Definitely a creepy thought.

They walked the wall. Climbed down the rocks to walk closer to the water. Found a spot to crouch in the shadows and keep a lookout.

"That Manhood 101 time with your grandpa?" He tried to sound completely casual. "You really find things to talk about every week?" Okay, so it wasn't the big question burning inside Harley, but his real question was a lot harder to ask.

Parker went on for five minutes straight about the latest secret of manhood his grandpa had shared. How the halfway principle didn't work. Instead, men needed to meet others all the way.

Is that what Parker had been doing for Harley? Searching for the evidence. Staying overnight at the coffee shop. Even now, sticking with him on patrol.

"Why don't you join us sometime?"

Bingo. *That's* what Harley wanted. He shrugged like he wasn't nearly as interested as he was. "Think your grandpa would mind?"

"You kidding?" Parker laughed. "He'd love it."

Harley's phone vibrated with a rapid-fire series of texts. "The girls are checking up on us again." But it was Wilson's picture on the screen—and a new text thread.

```
Found something.
Keep quiet.
Stay low.
Get here—FAST!
```

CHAPTER 67

HALF-CROUCHED, PARKER RAN BEHIND THE WALL separating Old Harbor from Sandy Bay. Harley kept pace, baseball bat with Kit's dried blood in hand. They veered away from Old Harbor Road, scrambling over a granite wall—and then a second.

The coastline running parallel to North Road morphed into the natural, weather-beaten rock that most tourists never saw.

Parker strained to see into the shadows. They raced high enough above the waterline to avoid running into a wet patch, but if his foot dropped into a crevice? He'd break something for sure.

Waves rumbled in from his left—masking all other sounds. Harley could have worn football spikes and nobody would've heard them coming.

Harley pulled ahead, like he'd run this very bit of Bearskin Neck every day. Just past Thurston Place, Harley slowed. He held up one hand and dropped on all fours. Parker followed his lead.

They had to be close, but they scanned for probably half a minute before Parker spotted Wilson. "There." He pointed to the spot where Wilson and Finn hunkered low among the rocks.

Parker gave the area a full 360 sweep before they made their way down to the others.

Even in the dim light, Wilson's excitement was impossible to miss. "Lookee what Oreo spotted." He pointed toward the water.

"All I see is rocks," Harley whispered.

Finn snickered. "Look closer."

A paddleboard, maybe twenty-five yards away, just above the high tide mark. The thing was tucked in tight—right in a crevice between the rocks. "How'd you even see that?"

"Oreos increase night vision," Finn said.

Parker needed to get those on the grocery list.

"Think it got washed in by the surf?" Harley's question was totally legit. The way it was wedged, maybe it was like the lobster buoys that break free and drift to shore.

"Maybe," Wilson said. "Or it's how the Strangler gets to a boat anchored farther out in the bay."

"We need to call this in." Parker dug out his phone. "But only to Detective Greenwood—not the group text." They didn't need every shop owner running to the spot.

"First we check it ourselves," Harley said.

"Harley's right," Wilson said. "We have to be sure. If we get him out here for a false alarm, he'd be leaving part of the Neck unprotected."

They weren't budging. The longer they waited to call, the greater the chance of the Strangler slipping away—if the paddleboard *was* his method of escape. "Okay—I'll go for a closer look." Staying in a crouch, Parker scurried over the rocks toward the waterline.

"I got your back." Wilson lit out behind him—and Harley followed. It was overkill, for sure, and increased their chances of being spotted. But this was no time to debate it.

The paddleboard had been spray-painted a flat, matte black. A perfect choice if the paddler wanted to move along the Neck in the dark, undetected.

Parker lifted one end. The thing moved easily . . . like it had been carefully placed—not wedged there by an angry wave.

"This is how he does it," Wilson whispered. "We got him!"

The paddleboard pointed to sea, making it a quick grab for the Strangler. He could scoop it up on the run—and launch without even having to turn the thing around.

"No paddle," Harley said.

Wilson did a swimming motion with his arms. "He stays low. Maneuvers it like a surfboard. Only it's bigger—and safer at night."

He was half right. How safe could it be paddling in the dark—especially with swells rolling in? And what about great whites?

"We've seen enough," Parker said. "Let's back away—and call it in." If the Strangler spotted them, he'd escape another way.

Finn held out a bag of Oreos the moment they got back. "Energy, anyone?"

"More like celebration." Wilson tucked a cookie inside his mouth.

Parker dimmed his screen and scrolled to Race Bannon's contact.

Wilson grabbed his arm. "Hold on, Bucky. There's four of us—and only one of him. I say we sit tight. Watch for him to show up. Nab him ourselves."

"And if he's armed?"

"With what, a speargun? He's not taking a Glock in saltwater. Look, we call the police, and they'll roar over with squealing tires and search-lights and sirens. They'll scare the guy away for sure."

"Wilson's right," Harley said. "And Greenwood will tell us to clear out immediately. The Strangler could slip away."

"I'm with Parker. Let's call the detective," Finn said. "The Strangler may not have a gun, but he'd have something. A knife?"

Wilson held up his machete. "We're armed too."

They absolutely couldn't sit on this intel. "We have to let someone know. Either I text my dad—or Greenwood," Parker said.

"Wait." Harley had his phone out. "A third option. Mr. Cape Ann Security himself. Vinny Torino will come in quiet—and if we help him catch the guy, I bet he'll keep an eye on the coffee shop even if Miss Lopez doesn't hire him."

Finn looked at him like he was crazy. "If the Strangler is caught, Miss Lopez won't *need* protection."

"Okay. You want the police. Harley and I want to do this ourselves. So let's meet halfway. The security guy." Wilson shrugged. "I say do it."

Harley immediately started a text.

For an instant, Parker thought of his Grandpa's latest talk with him. *A compromise was rarely a great choice.*

Harley added their exact coordinates before sending the text to Torino. "In the meantime, we've got to watch all points of the compass here." They divided the area around them like an imaginary pizza—with each of them watching their slice.

"Stay low, stay quiet, and stay still," Wilson whispered. "We don't want to scare the Strangler away."

Parker didn't figure a guy who'd managed to scare every shop owner on the Neck—and elude the police—would be that easy to spook. His phone vibrated—and apparently so did Wilson's and Harley's. It had to be the girls. Nobody made a move for their phone. *Not now, Jelly.*

They hadn't been in position for more than a few minutes before Parker saw movement. A shadowy figure climbing on the rocks some thirty yards away. Staying low—and hugging the shadows. Definitely coming from the direction of Bearskin Neck shops. Parker strained to see. "I got something."

He could sense the others looking over his shoulder. The man moved quickly—and directly toward the water. "Is it Torino?"

"Torino moves like a linebacker," Harley whispered. "This guy moves like a panther."

Every movement balanced. Catlike. But he was off his target. "He's going to miss the paddleboard if he stays on that trajectory."

"When he figures that out," Wilson pressed in, "he'll have to come our way."

"This is it, boys," Harley whispered. "I think we've finally got the Strangler."

CHAPTER 68

THE NIGHT WAS TOO QUIET, even with the waves. The only activity Ella had seen so far was Jelly on her phone.

Jelly let out a frustrated growl. "They're not answering my texts now." She looked down the coast like there was a chance of seeing the boys—which there wasn't. Not even in daylight.

"Maybe we overdid it." Actually, Ella was sure they did.

"So, what now? And if you say, 'Sit tight,' I'm going to scream."

"Let's be smart. And by that . . . I mean let's be *sneaky*."

Jelly smiled. "I can do sneaky." She thought for a moment, then tapped out a quick text with her thumbs. "They might stonewall *me* . . . but try doing that to your dad, Parker." She held the phone to show Ella the text.

Hey, Uncle Vaughn, just wanted to be sure my phone is okay. Suddenly not getting replies from texts to Parker or the others. Ella and I are fine. Is this text getting through?

"You sly devil. It's brilliant."

Jelly sent it off. "*Now* I'll sit tight."

The response came back immediately.

`I'll try him. Stand by.`

"That was easy." Jelly blew on her nails and buffed them on her shirt. "Sometimes we're sooo much smarter than those boys think we are."

Ella stared out over the bay. The swells seemed bigger since when they'd first planted themselves at their post. The theory—based on a scrap of rubber—that the Strangler swam to shore to burglarize stores? It was really beginning to sound like a desperate shot in the dark. "If he swims in from a boat, what about all his burglary tools? The boys probably didn't think of that. Can you imagine a guy swimming with a crowbar—or a sledgehammer?"

Jelly nodded. "The Strangler would have to be built like King Kong."

That made Ella smile. But it was obvious her friend was getting more anxious by the minute. Jelly's eyes were glued to the screen now.

Suddenly another one came in from Parker's dad.

"Finally!"

Ella leaned close so she could read.

`No response from Parker, Harley, or Wilson. Signal seems weak here. Is that the problem? Total blackout from both watch posts.`

`I texted Greenwood. Leaving my post to check. I'm close.`

Jelly's shoulders were tensed. She lifted Parker's cap off her head. Reseated it.

"You afraid we might've gotten him in trouble?"

Jelly shook her head. "Parker wouldn't ignore his dad's texts . . . unless he *couldn't* answer. She peered into the darkness. We aren't *getting* him in trouble. He's already in it."

CHAPTER 69

HARLEY VISUALLY TRACKED THE STRANGLER CLOSER and closer to the waterline. The Strangler crept from rock to rock, often staying absolutely still for what seemed like minutes. Slow. Careful. Watching, no doubt. Listening. No wonder he hadn't been caught. But he was still off target. He'd clearly miss the rendezvous with his paddleboard.

"We'll have him trapped," Harley whispered. "Sandy Bay in front of him—and no paddleboard."

"He'll have to come past us to get to his board," Wilson said, "and then we'll take him down."

Harley was still holding his phone. The thing vibrated, and Torino's picture showed on the dimmed screen.

`I'm here. Don't swing—or stab. From your 6:00.`

Vinny Torino crept out of the shadows, staying low. "Easy, fellas," he whispered. He crouched down beside them, clearly locking in on the figure nearing Sandy Bay.

"Thanks for the heads-up, gentlemen," Torino whispered. "I'm really gonna enjoy this."

Harley pointed at the paddleboard.

"Okay," Torino said. "Let's fan out a bit. When he comes for his board, we don't want to be in each other's way."

Slowly, they inched away from each other until they'd formed an impenetrable line blocking the route to his board behind them. Five against one. They had him.

The Strangler, still thirty yards away, moved straight toward the water, and parallel with their line—seemingly unaware of the ambush set for him. The guy had a full wet suit. Right down to booties, gloves, and a hood. Wearing the hood would definitely limit his hearing. Not smart, Strangler.

Red rover, red rover . . . let Strangler come over. Why that thought crossed Harley's mind, he had no idea. He eased into a set position. Ready to pounce.

The Strangler glanced up and down the coast. Looking for his paddleboard?

They could rush him now, but thirty yards wasn't nothing. The guy would have more of a lead on them than Harley liked. He could leap into the bay . . . and then what were they going to do? They had to wait until he walked into their trap.

The Strangler reached the last dry boulder—with nothing beyond it but the dark waters of Sandy Bay. He stood. Stretched. Seemed to be watching the waves.

What was he doing?

Suddenly the Strangler leaped into the water. Surfaced. Ducked under a wave, and struck out in a lazy breaststroke for open water—without his paddleboard?

"Guys!" Finn's voice. "There's two of them!"

While the five of them had been focused on Strangler One, his compadre had slipped behind their line and launched the paddleboard. Strangler Two stroked hard to rendezvous with the swimmer.

Shedding his hoodie, Wilson raced for the rock Strangler One had leaped from. Parks was close behind. Harley lit out after them—with Torino on his heels.

Wilson tossed his machete to the side. He sprung off the rock like an Olympic long jumper. He got swallowed instantly by the waves.

"Wilson!" Parks peeled off his sweatshirt. Kicked off his shoes. Jumped in after him.

Harley long-stepped to the top of that very rock. Searched the rough waters.

Torino came up behind him—grabbed Harley's shoulders. "Don't be stupid, Harley."

He spotted Wilson, power-stroking his way toward the Strangler. Likely the guy didn't think anybody was insane enough to follow him. Parker was a few strokes behind—gaining on both.

"What are they *doing*?"

"That's obvious," Torino said. "They're going to get themselves killed."

CHAPTER 70

PARKER'S BREATH CAME IN RAGGED, JERKY GASPS. He ducked under a wave to keep from being pushed into rocks—but regretted it instantly. The waters were a head-crushing cold.

Strangler One had rendezvoused with his double. He climbed onto the board with amazing speed now—like he'd just realized Wilson was practically on him. The man in front lay on his belly and stroked hard to distance themselves from shore.

If Wilson had still gripped his machete, likely he would've hacked the paddleboard in two. He grabbed Strangler One's ankle with both hands instead.

The Strangler spun around, gripping the sides of the paddleboard with both hands. He kicked to free himself from Wilson.

Almost there. Almost.

The heel of the Strangler's foot caught Wilson square in the face. His head snapped backward—and it worked like a switch—cutting the power circuit to his hands. The Strangler kicked again—but with both feet now—hitting Wilson like a battering ram. He slipped below the waves a half second before Parker got there.

"Wilson!" Parker yanked him to the surface and fought to keep his friend's face above the water. Blood streamed from his nose and a fresh cut on his cheek. His eyes were open—but only halfway. Parker scissors-kicked hard. Slipped his gimpy forearm under Wilson's arm and over his chest.

"I h-h-had him." Wilson's face dipped below the surface for an instant. "Lost him."

"Kick. Or we'll lose you, too."

Wilson seemed to be coming to. He kicked—and the waves helped drive them toward the black rocks. Torino was there. Harley. Reaching. Calling to them. Dad . . . pulling off his jacket.

A swell washed over him. Parker struggled to keep his head above water, but he felt he'd only get his head high enough to grab a shallow breath before being pulled under again. Wilson coughed and sputtered like he wasn't doing any better. "Help me, Wilson. Kick!"

Again he was under. But a strong hand on his arm gave him an assist. *Dad!*

"I got you. Swim, Parker!"

Torino swam up on his other side, prying Wilson out of Parker's grip. "Let go. I got him."

Parker obeyed immediately. The four of them fought their way to the rocks. Finn and Harley were there, motioning. Reaching. Urging them on.

Wilson was first. Finn and Harley each took a hand, boosted him to safety. Parker tried to climb the rocks himself, but his gimpy arm was sluggish. The rock slippery. And the swells smacked him against the granite like a pinball.

"Parks!" Harley reached low. "Hand!"

Parker reached. Harley practically yanked his arm from his socket, but he got him out of the water. *Thank you, Lord!*

Moments later Dad and Torino were out too. They sprawled out next to Wilson on the rocks just beyond the high-water line.

"Next time you boys decide to take a swim?" Torino smiled. "Try a pool instead."

Wilson sat up. "So close . . . I was so close!"

"To *drowning*," Torino said. "You got lucky."

Luck had nothing to do with it. God had bailed them out—again. Parker stared out into the bay. No sign of the paddleboard. The Stranglers had disappeared. Vanished like phantoms.

Detective Greenwood hustled down to them. "Thanks, Vaughn. Got your text." He glanced at Parker—which was just enough to make him kick himself for ignoring his gut. He should've contacted Greenwood when he first had the thought. If he had, the Stranglers might be in cuffs.

"I saw them disappear from up there." Greenwood jerked his thumb toward higher ground. "Called Eric and Maggie. *Alert 1* is on the way. Too late, I'm afraid."

And it was pretty much Parker's fault.

"Game over for the Stranglers, though," Finn said. "There'll be boats patrolling at night now."

Greenwood looked out over Sandy Bay. "The quarter ended, but not the game. They're not done."

A fresh chill tremored through Parker's body. And he was pretty sure it wasn't just because he was cold.

CHAPTER 71

ANGELICA WALKED THE FOOTPRINTS on the wall above the headboard. "Another day. Another disaster."

Ella laughed in that musical way. "Sometimes you have to ask yourself what those boys are thinking."

"They're *not* thinking. It's like the space between their ears is just that: space."

Now it was Grams's turn to laugh. "Men are highly complex creatures. More than we might imagine."

Angelica groaned. "Ah, well, there you go. You said *men*. I was talking about our boys."

"They're quickly becoming men," Grams said. "Men of character. Honor."

"Well, whatever they are, I feel what they did might've actually been more brave than stupid," Ella said. "They almost got the Strangler, right?"

The way Angelica saw it, Ella could find an upside to a landslide, but come *on*. "Wilson jumped into Sandy Bay—at night—in frigid April waters. He chased the criminal known as the Strangler—who happened to have a twin along. Parker followed—like Wilson was the Pied Piper. Should I go on?"

"Okay, okay." Ella laughed. "So maybe the line between stupid and brave is a fine one. But it all worked out. . . . Parker got to him in time."

Of *course* Parker got there. He'd do anything for a friend—unless it was Angelica asking him to pull back and play it safe for once. "He's getting worse, don't you think?"

Ella angled her head slightly. "Parker?"

Who else? "They both could have gone down. And with Wilson leaking blood . . . what if a great white came for a visit?"

"But none of that happened," Ella said. "Everything's okay."

"Is it?" The Strangler and clone hadn't been caught. "What's to stop them from targeting Parker—or Harley—for messing up their burglary operation?"

"Girls." Grams raised her hands. "Land sakes . . . you're both right. The boys were brave. And reckless. The Angel of Death came close enough to those young men tonight for them to hear its wings. This is a warning. A final sign."

That got Angelica turned around and sitting on the bed with her back to the headboard. Tonight was an example of what Grams had been saying all along. In an instant, the death count could go to three—or more—just because of a rash decision.

Grams stared out the window. "Those who stray from the path of understanding come to rest in the company of the dead."

"Still kind of a creepy thought, Grams, even if it's from the Bible." Angelica agreed.

"It's from the Holy Scriptures, girls." Grams nodded real slow, like she wanted the heaviness of that truth to sink deep into their souls.

"Are you saying . . ." Angelica hated to ask the question aloud, but she had to, didn't she? "Those who do dumb things—like the boys—will end up . . . you know." She drew one finger across her throat. She wasn't going to say the word out loud.

"I think the verse is talking about those who do evil. Deliberately straying from right paths. That's not our boys. But the Strangler—and whoever is part of this? They'll most certainly come face-to-face with the Reaper. And my fear?" She shook her head. "They'll drag one—or more—of our boys with them."

"Death comes in threes, and all within one week. That's what you keep telling us, Grams." Ella swung her feet off the bed. Sat on the edge. "We only need to keep those boys away from danger until the week has passed."

"So," Angelica said, "if Mr. Ironwing died in the wee hours of the morning Monday . . . we only have to make it two more days. Sunday night. But tonight just proves I can't protect them—and neither can you."

El seemed to be thinking about that. "They'd never do something too risky if we're *with* them, right? They wouldn't want *us* in danger."

Angelica smiled. "So we'll be Velcro. We'll stick with them."

Ella reached over and shook her hand. "We'll *vulcanize* ourselves to them if we have to."

Grams stood to leave. Her face not looking nearly as relieved as El's did right now. "The Angel of Death is greedy. A lot can happen in forty-eight hours."

Suddenly the breeze coming through Ella's open window seemed colder than it did minutes ago. Angelica hugged her knees and hoped it was just Grams's superstition talking . . . and not a premonition.

CHAPTER 72

HARLEY SAT AT THE COFFEE SHOP COUNTER. A hot shower had never felt so good. Wilson's nose still looked swollen, and the butterfly holding the slice on his cheek together had busted a wing. He'd have to ask Miss Lopez to give it another go.

Wilson was too busy chowing down on the plate of leftover pizza Miss Lopez left on the counter for them. "I can't believe I lost my machete."

If he hadn't dropped it before he leaped in the water, he may have lost more than his blade.

"Look for it tomorrow while we're gearing up for the dive," Parker said. "And if you don't find it, maybe we can all look before leaving for . . ."

The way he caught himself, Harley knew exactly what Parks almost said. "Before my uncle's funeral? I don't even want to go." As much as he couldn't stand the guy, Harley would be saying goodbye to the only other member of his family that he knew of. He wished he could skip the day somehow. Hop in a time travel machine and skip to Sunday.

"I can't wait to go," Wilson said. "I finally get to meet the moron."

Harley wasn't going to defend his uncle's honor. He didn't have any.

"We'll grab lunch afterward," Parker said. "Search the harbor if we don't find the evidence in the morning. And then there's your birthday party. Don't forget that."

Harley wasn't looking forward to that, either. Birthday parties were a family thing . . . and a reminder that Harley didn't have one. Instinctively he reached for Kemosabe's key around his neck. And he knew he had to get away—even if only for a few minutes. Pull himself together until Parks and Wilson got talking about something Harley could handle. "Be right back."

He left the two in the good company of the pizza. Told Kit to stay and hold his place for him. He took the stairs two at a time, his bare feet soundless on the stairs.

Miss Lopez's door was open—but the room was empty. Okay, maybe she was in the kitchen. He took the last flight of stairs—and heard something—or some*one* in the Crow's Nest. He slowed. Tiptoed up the last few steps. Pressed his face close to the wall, and peered around the doorjamb.

Miss Lopez was kneeling in front of his piggy tank . . . her back to him. She'd unscrewed the valve and set it on the floor beside her. She hummed some tune he didn't recognize, but he wanted to. Wanted to know the words. She rolled a ten- and twenty-dollar bill together and tapped them through the opening at the top of the tank. She reached for the valve and bowed her head before screwing it back in place.

"Father . . . take these loaves and fish and multiply them. And thank you, thank you, thank you for—"

He couldn't watch anymore. And it sure didn't feel right to listen. He used the dual railings like parallel bars and swooped to the first floor in three silent swings. Instead of going back to the coffee counter, he whistled for Kit and slipped out the back door the moment she bounded over. He found a spot in the shadows and sat with his back to a rock wall. His knees hiked up. Forearms crossed over them. Buried his face there.

Now he knew why the numbers were higher when he'd brought his savings to the bank. This wasn't the first time Miss Lopez had made a secret donation to his motorcycle fund. And here she was—with the extra expenses from Kit's injury, and without money coming in from the coffee shop—making sure his motorcycle fund was growing. He thought he'd been doing *her* a favor, but it turned out she'd been helping him all along.

Uncle Ray stole from him if he didn't hide his money. When he'd lived with the Gundersons, his foster dad accused Harley of stealing. Except for when he'd temporarily stayed with the Buckmans, nobody had treated him like family since his dad was gone.

Until now.

"Dear God . . . Lord Jesus . . . I haven't felt like I was part of a real family in a really long time. It scares me, you know? Is this going to end too?"

Kit nuzzled him under his arm. Like she wanted to get to his face. Wanted to remind him she was family too.

He worked his fingers under her collar and scratched gently. "Yeah, girl. You're mine now. We're together, you and me. Family."

The back door opened, and Wilson and Parks stepped outside. "Harley?"

He ran a backhand across his eyes and stood.

"What are you doing out here?" Wilson zeroed in on his eyes. "Were you *crying*?"

"Me?" He strode for the back door like he didn't have a care in the world.

"You were crying."

He didn't turn, but raised one hand. "Guilty. But hey . . . maybe I'm just that happy you made it up here. Can you blame me?"

Wilson laughed and caught up. "Perfectly understandable. And don't let anyone give you a hard time about it. Jelly and Ella are probably bawling their eyes out right now in total gratitude. The whole group of you is going to totally fall apart when I have to go back home." He grinned. "Unless, of course, we don't live that long."

CHAPTER 73

VINNY TORINO PULLED INTO HIS DRIVEWAY and locked his truck. After what just happened on the Neck, nobody figured the Strangler—or Stranglers—would be back tonight. He could abort his patrol routine early without worry of anyone growing suspicious.

There was a tiny bit of him that felt like that park ranger's kid—and Harley—had beaten him somehow. They caused him to change plans earlier than he'd banked on, anyway. Vinny didn't like anyone getting the upper hand. Which is why he especially liked the task Lochran was asking him to take on. Find the evidence, if possible. And eliminate Ray's nephew—whether he found the evidence or not. Lochran was actually going to pay him to do a job that Vinny would have done for free.

Vinny stepped inside and locked the front door behind him. He kept his Hellcat in the concealed carry waistband holster—and didn't turn on the lights. He knew his way around the house, and he liked to give the place a quick check before making himself an easy target. *Look alive. Stay alive.* Which is why he was still kicking—and so many of his old adversaries weren't.

He was careful about everything. He never wanted to give the police a reason to question him—or to get a search warrant for his house. There was too much squirreled away in the basement—and the oversize garage out back.

There'd been times he'd been hired to snatch something from one of the homes out near Eastern Point. He'd never left those homes without taking a little something extra for himself. He wasn't the kind of sicko who kept souvenirs from past jobs. That was all about ego and keeping score—and a great way to get caught someday. Guys like that kept mementos in spots where they could pull them out easily and gloat. Honestly, they needed their heads examined. Vinny wasn't into that kind of ego-stroking stupidity.

But there were some things too valuable to pass up. Guns. Collectibles. High-end antiques. He'd snagged enough coin collections to open his own coin shop. If he sold the contraband off a bit at a time, he'd live like a king for years. More than once he'd found a vehicle in a victim's garage that he couldn't pass up. A 1953 Ford F100 pickup had just called out to him . . . *Take me home.* And he did. It was worth some money, but what he really wanted was to keep it for himself. He'd move west in a few years. Have it repainted and use it for a daily driver.

The Corvettes were no-brainers. But the crown jewel was the 1970 Chevy Chevelle SS with the 454 and the LS6 upgrade. The four-barrel Holley carb fueled the big V8 that boasted over 500 horsepower. It was tough not to take that thing out and smoke the tires . . . but he wasn't that stupid. The thing was an absolute head-turner. Fire engine red with dual racing stripes running down the hood and over the cowl induction. The Chevelle had originally sold for $4,500 back in the day, but he'd seen one sell at auction in the last year for over two hundred big ones. The fact that he didn't have the pink slip would be an issue when it came time to sell, but there were plenty of private collectors who would get in line to buy that sweetheart, papers or no papers.

All these things—and more—should've been left behind at the crime scene. But Vinny knew he had what it took to avoid getting caught. He was careful. He had the smarts—and patience. That meant he didn't sell a thing. Not yet. And not here. Some guys had their fancy retirement accounts. Well, Vinny was building for his future—in his own way.

When it was time to pull up stakes and leave Cape Ann, he'd arrange for a car carrier to do an after-dark pickup. He'd rent a big ol' U-Haul and load it up at night with the rest of the trophies. He'd take his stash with him and disappear. Live on Easy Street. He just needed to make a little more moola, and he'd be gone.

Ray Lotitto had been stupid. Lochran wasn't the kind of guy he should've done business with—much less crossed. But Lochran was also the kind of boss who rewarded loyalty. Lochran would help Vinny hit his personal money goals way sooner than he would've otherwise.

But first, Vinny would make Lochran's problems disappear—and he'd enjoy every minute of it. In the process of messing up Vinny's plans tonight, the boys had given him the idea he'd use to mess them up permanently. Those boys managed to get stuck in Vinny's craw, but they were going to have an accident. In less than forty-eight hours.

CHAPTER 74

Saturday, April 22

Ella should have woken with a sense of excitement. Tonight was Harley's birthday party. But everything leading up to it filled her with dread.

Like the desperate search for the missing evidence. Powerful enough to put Lochran away for good—and get Uncle Ray killed. Would Lochran just sit around hoping Harley didn't find it? Not likely. But Parker made it clear that walking away from the search was more dangerous than staying on the hunt. How?

And then there was the funeral. Nobody would blame Harley for not attending. But he probably believed that being there was the right thing to do. So she would go as well. He needed to know his friends cared. And she needed to stick to the plan of staying close to the boys—until the threat of the "death comes in threes" week was over.

Was Harley dreading the funeral? How could he not? Maybe that was one good thing about him searching for the dry bag in Rockport Harbor this morning. At least it would keep his mind off seeing his uncle's body.

CHAPTER 75

PARKER ZIPPED HIS WET SUIT, doing his best to keep up with Harley. If the guy moved this fast underwater, he'd suck his tank dry in twenty minutes.

Diving was taboo in the harbor, but Dad got it cleared with the harbormasters. The lobster boats were out to sea, so traffic would be light. Harley and Parker promised to stay clear of the lanes anyway. They'd be diving under the docks, along the support poles propping up the yacht club, and checking the crevices between the granite blocks making up the retaining walls. Dad and Wilson would stay topside, keeping an eye peeled for boat traffic. Wilson had already found his machete and was back to T-wharf in record time.

Harley still seemed like he was on another planet. Totally dialed in to another wavelength. KitKat nuzzled his hand, but even then, Harley only seemed half there when he stroked her head.

Parker's dad was laser-focused on T-wharf. Like he expected

Lochran—or maybe Uncle Ray's lawyer—to visit. He had that wide stance thing going. Hands on hips. Looking more like he was on guard duty than spotting them for the dive.

Wilson paced the dock with his machete in hand, watching Harley and Parker gear up.

Parker jutted his chin toward the weapon. "Expecting trouble?"

"When I'm with you?" Wilson grinned. "Always. You sure no great whites come in the harbor?"

"Positive. They'd need a permit from the harbormaster." Honestly, the man-eating shark was something Parker hoped he'd never see. "But if one slips in, I'll let you take care of it."

Wilson waved the machete side to side. "I'll whittle him down into a little dogfish. That work for you?"

If only it were that easy.

Wilson scanned T-wharf. "After all Jelly's big talk about the need to cheer you two on—and she doesn't even show? Where is she?"

Parker had no idea. She'd texted early to find out what time they were starting.

"Bucky." Wilson pointed to T-wharf. Jelly—wearing a wet suit *and* her tank while riding her bike. He sheathed the machete and cupped his hands around his mouth. "Hey, crazy girl! Why aren't you wearing your fins, too? And your mask?"

Jelly spun her head his way just long enough to glare. She wobbled her way to the ramp, looking like she might roll off the edge into the harbor at any moment. She propped her bike against the rail and slid off the seat. Ella rode up behind her with Jelly's fins sticking out of her backpack.

"Jelly's *diving*?" Harley snapped out of whatever black hole he'd dropped into. "I thought she said she wouldn't dive until June."

Jelly wasn't a fan of the cold water, for sure. "Another set of eyes. We'll take 'em," Parker said. This would be her first real dive since her checkout dives in February. She'd taken a weekend course while down in Florida with her dad. She'd gotten her open-water certification—but hadn't been diving since.

Kit bounded over to meet the girls. Jelly tousled Kit's ears, then made her way down the ramp, both hands on the rails, like she wasn't sure the thing would hold the weight of her tank. "Wilson, are you just planning to watch—or would you be helpful for a change? Give Ella a hand with my gear."

Laughing, Wilson hustled down the dock and leaped for the granite-block wall. Spiderman couldn't have climbed it faster. He had the dive bag from El by the time Jelly reached the bottom of the ramp.

Harley sat on the edge of the dock next to Parker. Pulled on his fins. Glanced at Jelly as she sat beside them. "Here to make sure Parks and I don't swim into some danger zone?"

She shook her head. "You're already in it. I just can't stand seeing you boys in there alone."

Something about the way she said it rang true to Parker. She'd been fighting her tendency to be their guardian angel ever since the face-off with Clayton Kingman last fall.

Harley outlined his plans for checking the docks, supports, and granite walls in South Basin—all on one tank of air. "Then we surface. Grab a second tank—and do the North Basin if we don't find the dry bag here."

"You're doing back-to-backs? I only have the one tank," Jelly said.

Parker had his dad's. Harley had rented a backup when he'd gotten the fill.

"Itty-bitty lungs like yours?" Harley gave a half smile. "Your tank will go the distance."

"And then some," she said. But she didn't look nearly as confident as her voice sounded.

Parker caught her eye and held up his spare regulator on the extra-long air hose. He'd share his second tank with her when it got to that point.

Thanks. She mouthed the word.

The three of them slid off the edge of the dock. Immediately the water worked its icy fingers inside the wet suit. For a moment it looked like Kit was going to join them.

"Stay," Harley said. "I'll be back. Promise."

Kit whined. She dropped on her belly and leaned over the edge of the dock, sniffing the air as if she could tell his words carried the scent of truth. Was she remembering the moment her former owner went in the water—but didn't come back?

Dad dropped on one knee at the dock's edge and prayed for God to give them success. "Okay, boys—and Angelica. Dive safe." He checked his watch. "Get busy. You've got two dives ahead of you—and one funeral."

Wilson pointed their way with his machete. "And don't worry. I'm here to make sure the funeral isn't for one of you."

CHAPTER 76

THIS DIVE WAS WAY MORE INTENSE than all Angelica's checkout dives combined. The boys moved too fast. The water was too cold. And the leg that had taken the bullet last October wasn't quite as strong as she'd thought.

After thirty minutes, every muscle seemed on the verge of locking up. Even the muscles in her jaw were cramping from biting so hard on the regulator mouthpiece. When this was over, she'd head straight home. She'd put fresh jeans and her hoodie in the dryer while she showered, so they'd be nice and toasty after she drained the hot-water tank.

They'd mapped out a quick route to cover the network of floating docks and slips. Harley swam like his fins were motorized. Parker seemed more cautious, like he didn't want to second-guess himself later . . . wondering if he'd missed the dry bag.

The tide was still coming in, which she found comforting. If she did turn into a block of ice, at least the current wouldn't send her out to open sea. She'd wash up on shore—and the boys could pry the regulator out of her mouth and get her some blankets.

The docks were clear underneath. No real surprise there. A dry bag would have been easy to spot from fifteen feet away. The submerged portion of the granite-block wall leading to the yacht club was clear too. The three of them worked the wall together like a three-tiered layer cake. Parker up top. Harley on bottom. And Angelica like the cream filling between. They checked every space between the granite blocks big enough to hide a lobster—or a dry bag.

They pulled out flashlights under the yacht club. It felt like a basement closet for how dark it was. The morgue-like water temperature combined with the shadowy wall and beams holding up the club above them made her more than a little jumpy. She constantly checked to be sure Parker was directly overhead. Harley's bubbles from below sometimes blocked her view. But she didn't mind. She just liked knowing he was there. It took everything she had to keep her breathing slow and steady. She was going to stretch the air in her tank to the limits. She didn't want Parker cutting his dive shorter just because he had to share with her.

When Harley motioned that he was deep in the red zone and needed to surface, she checked her own gauge level. Nearly twelve hundred pounds of pressure left . . . almost half a tank. Under different circumstances she might have ribbed Harley about it, but not today.

Kit was waiting when they surfaced at the floating platform at the end of T-wharf. Clearly, she'd been tracking their bubbles just like the others. Angelica spit out her mouthpiece and gave Ella a weak wave. She didn't climb onto the platform—as much as she wanted to. If she did, the water would drain from her wet suit. Her body had warmed it some, even though it didn't feel like it. There was no way she wanted to take in a fresh batch of ice water for the second dive. And the colder she was, the quicker she'd use her air. No thanks. She'd wait for the boys in the water.

Uncle Vaughn and Wilson were ready with the two fresh tanks. Neither asked if they'd found the dry bag. One look at Harley's face was likely all the answer they'd needed. They helped swap out Parker's and Harley's tanks in record time.

"North Basin," Harley said. They'd check the granite blocks making up the front of T-wharf. Scan under the floating pier. "Cut to the north wall, and check it all the way around Bradley Wharf—and Tuna Wharf—if our air holds. We good?"

Kit sniffed at his gloved hand gripping the edge of the dock. She gave it a lick—but Harley didn't seem to notice.

Harley didn't even ask how Jelly's air was—which proved how consumed he was with finding Uncle Ray's evidence. He reseated his mask, slipped below the surface.

Parker caught her eye and tapped two fingers against his forearm. At least *somebody* wanted to know if she had enough air to dive again. She held up her computer gauge for him to see. He raised his eyebrows like he was truly impressed. He held up his spare regulator. "It's yours when you need it."

They descended together. It was a whole lot brighter now that they weren't under the yacht club, but a different kind of eerie feeling crept over her. She found herself glancing toward deeper water almost as much as she scanned the wall. Would a great white venture into the harbor?

By the time they'd crossed to the north wall of the basin, she'd brought her own tank pressure deep into the red zone. They hadn't made it to Bradley Wharf and Motif Number 1 before she signaled for Parker's regulator.

Her hopes of finding the bag had dropped right along with her tank pressure. Even before she took the first dive, had she really even believed they'd find it?

No.

And now the search was over . . . something the boys just didn't realize yet.

Soon Harley would have to raise the white flag on the search-and-recovery strategy—which meant Parker would too. There was only one thing niggling her, though. Might Lochran believe Harley knew where the evidence was hidden?

Maybe.

But if he did, he'd have had one of his goons watching Harley. By now they'd know Harley had no idea where it was. Lochran could rest easy knowing he was in the clear. Any decent man could see Harley deserved a break. Any decent man would just leave Harley alone. The only problem? Deep down, she knew Lochran wasn't a decent man.

CHAPTER 77

PARKER, HARLEY, AND JELLY PILED their gear aboard *Wings*. Dad and Wilson offered to rinse and stow everything while the divers left for hot showers.

"Your face is blue, Jelly," Wilson said. "I need a picture before you leave."

Mike Ironwing's face ghosted out of the room he haunted in Parker's memory—even though he'd done his best to lock that door and board the windows shut.

Parker broke a speed record getting showered and dressed. Black jeans. Button-down shirt—tucked in. The cleanest pair of shoes he owned. It wasn't until he'd stepped into the kitchen that he realized the shirt was the same one he'd worn to Devin's funeral a year ago.

Mom was in the kitchen, dropping a PB and J in a sandwich bag.

"You think I should change my shirt—or throw on one of dad's ties?"

Mom shook her head and handed him the plastic bag. "You look fine. Just hungry. This will hold you over until we get some real food in you. Before you go, there's some things you need to know about Quinn Lochran—and the funeral."

Mom was using her investigative reporting skills? Parker shouldn't have been surprised. She gave him a quick rundown of what she'd learned—which *did* surprise him. She hugged him when she'd finished. "I think Harley needs to know."

Parker nodded. "Before he walks into that funeral home." But first, he needed to get a quick call in to Grandpa. And he'd do it from *Wings*.

He hotfooted it to T-wharf—passing Wilson and Dad going the other way.

"We'll get cleaned up," Dad said, "and meet you at the funeral home."

Just the thought of the place made Parker's stomach do a backflip. He waved and kept moving. He took the last bite of the PB and J by the time he dropped into the captain's chair on *Wings*. Sometime after he'd left to hit the shower, the wind had shifted. It was coming in from the east now. *Wings* tugged at her lines like she wanted Parker to fire her up and skip across the top of the frantic little waves rushing toward the slip.

He dialed Grandpa and caught him up to speed. Relaying the facts was the easy part. Putting what he was feeling into words came a lot harder. "I'm trying, Grandpa. No compromising. I'm meeting Harley *all* the way. It's still not enough."

Grandpa was quiet for a moment. "Sometimes we just have to keep doing the right things—even when we don't think it's making a difference."

"Honestly? Searching Rockport Harbor was my only plan. I have no idea what the next right thing is now . . . much less how to meet him all the way. We're running out of time here. Harley has to come up with that evidence by tomorrow night."

"Sounds like that lawyer expects too much of Harley."

Parker couldn't agree more. "It's insane. The lawyer says Lochran isn't the kind of guy Harley should cross—as if Harley is dragging his feet on this." Parker stopped to take a breath. "It feels messed up."

"The world is a messed-up place, Parker. And dark."

Dark. Parker looked at the waters—especially how black they looked under the yacht club. "I'm feeling that darkness . . . like it's closing in. Going back to that funeral home again isn't helping either." He pictured the place the way he remembered it from last year. The line of students clinging to each other. Pictures of Devin everywhere. The sickening smell of dying flowers.

"Maybe you should stay home."

Grandpa's comment took Parker by surprise. "Harley needs me, Grandpa. I've got to be there. This isn't about me. I can't make it about me." And it was time he got moving.

"Mmmm. That's a man's answer, Parker. I'm proud of you."

Gulls circled overhead. Like they were searching for something they couldn't find either. "I just have to move on—and bury my own feelings on this or something, right?"

"Gravediggers bury things, Parker. Men deal with them. Now, I hear you. It feels dark because it *is* dark. But God will show you that next step if you ask him to."

He made it sound simple. But it wasn't. "All I know is I have to go to the funeral."

"See? You already know your next step."

"But what about after that?"

"One step at a time, Parker."

Easier said than done. "If we could just find that evidence, all this goes away."

"Or not." Grandpa hesitated for a moment. "Ray Lotitto was killed because he knew where the evidence was hidden. Now you and Harley are on the hunt. You may be in more danger when you find that evidence. Remember that."

"You're not helping me find a bright spot in all this, Grandpa." Ironwing's body. The Bearskin Neck Strangler. The murder of Harley's uncle. The missing evidence—and the need to find it by tomorrow night. Dark. Dark. Dark. And getting darker. "I'm feeling for the light switch, Grandpa, but I can't find it."

"You can *be* a light in a dark place," Grandpa said. "But you can't *make* light in a dark place. That's God's job."

"Well, then I hope *he* flips the switch soon." Parker hopped out of *Wings* and headed for the ramp going up onto T-wharf.

"There's a verse I keep on my desk. I'll text it to you. You just keep doing that next right thing . . . and you leave the lights to God, okay?"

"How about you ask him to send me a flashlight?" Parker was only half joking. "I see no light at the end of the tunnel, Grandpa. No hope that this will end—or can end well."

"Trust him to lead you, Parker. Even in darkness. He can bring light when you least expect it. He'll meet you where you're at. He'll show you how to be there for Harley. God is the *king* of meeting all the way."

Parker checked the time and broke into a jog for BayView. "Gotta go, Grandpa."

"I'll send you that text. And, Parker . . ."

He pressed the phone closer to his ear.

"You watch your back."

CHAPTER 78

VINNY TORINO STOOD AT THE RAMP just above the waterline. He threw a skipping stone sidearm into the North Basin. Clearly the boys—and their little girl friend from the coffee shop—didn't find what they were prospecting for. Their body language made that clear. Vaughn Buckman and the wild-looking new kid who'd stayed behind to clean the mess confirmed it. They wouldn't have looked so glum if the divers had struck gold. The stone clipped the crown of a wave far out in the harbor and kamikazed into another one a second later.

Who was that new kid? He'd never gotten a formal introduction last night, but the way he'd jumped in the bay chasing Rocko? It was like he had no fear. Or no sense. Either was dangerous. There was something about the way he'd moved that said the kid could handle himself in a clutch situation. Between that and his long hair, it looked like the guy had been brought up by wolves. He'd call him Mowgli for now. And what was the deal with the machete? Most guys his age would've been much more comfortable with a phone in their hand. Not Mowgli.

The Buckman kid phoned someone from his boat . . . but who? All dressed up for the funeral, but he stopped to make a phone call—in a spot where he couldn't possibly be overheard? It probably didn't matter—unless he was talking to the detective. The one thing Vinny was sure of? He wasn't going to underestimate Harley, Parker, Mowgli, *or* those girls. The way they were sticking together? He'd have to be ready to deal with all of them—as a group—when the time came. And it was coming soon.

Vinny didn't care about Ray's evidence. But his boss did. And Lochran would show his gratitude if Vinny delivered it to him. Lochran would think Vinny could walk on water by the time this was over. He chuckled to himself. Maybe he could.

What those boys needed was more motivation. Sure, they'd gotten the message that finding Ray's evidence was critically important. But did they *really* believe it was life and death? Doubtful.

But that would change.

They needed a gut message. Something that made the pit of their stomach twist with fear. A message that made them know that failing would be deadly.

Sending the right kind of message would be tricky now that the business owners felt they had the Bearskin Neck Strangler on the run. It would allow them to connect some dots. But it was worth the risk. If the message made them push harder—and they found Ray's evidence as a result? Vinny would be a hero in Lochran's eyes. And after a message like he had in mind, the boys wouldn't dare turn any evidence over to the police directly. They'd give it to Ray's lawyer. Vinny could work with that. Then the boys would drop their guard . . . which would make it easier to catch them flat-footed.

He slid his Walmart phone out of his pocket. The one that couldn't be traced to him. He made a call to Sal. Outlined his plan. Sal would take it from there. He'd get the crew together and do it right. His only question was when.

"During the funeral. But you won't have much time."

"I'm on it." Sal laughed. "I'm thinking that funeral home is going to be busy over the next few days. But I'm a big fan of supporting local business."

Vinny smiled. "That's what I love about you, Sal. Always willing to help with the dirty work."

"You mean the *fun* stuff, right?"

This time Vinny laughed. "You and I think so much alike, it's scary." Which was only a figure of speech—because he wasn't scared a bit. But before the day was over, Ray's nephew sure would be.

CHAPTER 79

HARLEY HATED TYING KIT'S LEASH to the porch railing outside the funeral home, but it beat leaving her at the coffee shop. "Maybe she'd pass for one of those comfort dogs—and I can bring her in."

"Better yet," Parker said, "let's send Kit in, and we'll wait here."

After what Parker told him about Lochran, Harley wished he could.

Parker's phone dinged, and he checked the text. "From Grandpa." He held the phone for Harley to read the screen.

"Even in darkness light dawns for the upright, for those who are gracious and compassionate and righteous." Psalm 112:4

Darkness. Harley's whole world seemed dark right now. Or maybe he was fighting some unseen darkness. Harley reread it. "So we just keep doing the right thing—and trust God will bring some light?"

Parks nodded. "But something tells me we aren't going to see any light in this place."

Harley had no doubts Lochran ordered Uncle Ray's murder—even though that would be impossible to prove. And now to learn that Lochran paid for the funeral—likely just to send a message to anybody who might be tempted to cross him? The guy was even more twisted than Harley imagined. Totally demented. Harley eyed the front doors of the place. No wonder Parks wanted to tell him before they went inside. "You think he's in there, don't you."

Parker's eyes said it all.

What would Harley do when he faced the man who'd had Uncle Ray murdered—then paid to have his body put on display?

"We can stall," Parks said. "Wait for the others?"

How would that look to Mr. Buckman? And to Miss Lopez? He shook his head. "Let's just get this over with."

He dropped on one knee and held Kit's face between his hands. "Wait right here for me, okay? Ella and Miss Lopez are on their way. Tell them I'm inside—and send them in pronto." He kissed Kit's forehead. "If you need me, bark your head off. Deal?" Kit's tail fanned the air like crazy.

Harley stood, brushed off his pants, and pulled open the door. The place reeked of death. Not like an actual odor, but more like the *feel* of the place. Dim light. Carpet that looked like it had taken as much grief as it had seen. Drapes that overpowered the windows . . . making it look like it was six o'clock instead of three. And the smell of roses. Like Devin's funeral all over again. It should have reminded him of his dad's funeral . . . but there hadn't been any flowers. *Waste of good money*, according to Uncle Ray. Had Lochran kicked in for flowers, too . . . or was it some kind of aerosol spray funeral homes used?

A black felt menu board directed them to Parlor C. Harley had the sudden urge to run. Why did he come? To pay his respects for a guy he didn't respect?

There was no good reason to be here . . . except that somehow it seemed like the right thing to do. Something a real man would do—no matter how much he didn't want to. Why was it that sometimes the easiest things to run from were actually the right things to do?

"This way." Parks took the lead.

Did he sense that Harley had choked? Parker looked back once just as they reached the arched entrance to the room—as if to be sure he was still following.

Harley caught up and walked in alongside him. They hadn't gone far enough to get a first down before they stopped like they'd been hit by an invisible linebacker. Lochran wasn't just sitting in the back row. He stood at the head of the casket. Like he was a family member—or a psycho.

Even more shocking? Mr. Torino—the owner of Cape Ann Security—stood nearby, hands behind his back, like some kind of Secret Service agent. All he was missing was the earpiece. What was going on?

Parks leaned close. "He *works* for Lochran?"

What else could it be? "Funeral homes don't hire bouncers."

Lochran motioned Harley up front like he'd been waiting for him.

"Sheesh, Parks. This feels deranged."

"Because that's what Lochran is. I'm going with." Parks fell in a half step behind.

The casket was the cheapest-looking thing Harley had ever seen. A pine box—with three rope handles on the side. No stain. No paint. Just plain, white pine. It looked like it came from a Western movie prop closet.

He was halfway up the aisle before he saw that Uncle Ray wore his prison jumpsuit. If Lochran paid for the funeral, he also dictated what Uncle Ray would wear. Was this to show would-be traitors that Lochran could get at anybody—anywhere . . . even if they were locked up tight in a secure prison? *This is crazy.*

Lochran smiled like he was greeting an old friend. "Young Mr. Lotitto. Thank you for coming. He looks *good*, doesn't he?"

Why did people always say stupid things like that? How could anybody stretched out in a casket actually look good? "He's *dead*."

Lochran winked. "Maybe that's why he looks so good."

For the second time since he'd stepped into Parlor C, Harley felt like he'd been hit. But this time he wanted to hit back. Instinctively he closed his fists.

Vinny Torino strode his way, like he knew Harley wanted to knock Lochran's teeth out.

"Harley, come here for a sec." Parks steered him away from the casket.

"Lemme go, Parks. He had him killed. He's rubbing my nose in it." Harley had no love for his uncle, but right now he wanted to rip Lochran's head off—*after* he knocked his teeth out.

Parks put himself between Harley and Lochran. "That was calculated. He's not stupid."

"No. He's insane."

"He's baiting you—God only knows why." Parks had his hand flat on Harley's chest now. "Keep your head."

"And Torino there—he knows us. Why would he take a job with that guy?"

"Doesn't matter. Let's go."

Harley stretched to look past Parks. Mr. Cape Ann Security stood next to Lochran now, like he was ready for a fight if it came to that. "This isn't right. How can God let Lochran get away with murder?" No wonder the loan shark needed a bodyguard.

"Who says he will?" Parks blocked his line of vision. "Ask God to help you—right now. That's how this works."

He knew that. But *still*. "You pray, Parks. I'm not closing my eyes with that slimeball around."

Parks prayed—but didn't close his eyes either. He asked God to deal with Lochran—and whoever did his dirty work. He asked God to give Harley the self-control he needed. A change of heart.

It wasn't like Harley got some massive urge to buy Lochran a cheese-and-sausage pizza or anything. And if Harley *did* have a pizza in his hands right now? He'd be tempted to shove it right up the guy's nose until it was packed tight with sausage chunks. But a sliver of change opened in Harley's dark thoughts. A ray of light. A way of escape. Like a tackle had pushed back a defender and opened a hole for him. Harley could ignore it. Or he could plow right through that opening before it closed again. "Let's check Kit."

"Right behind you."

Lochran smiled . . . like he was the guy behind the curtain, working all the controls. And in that instant Harley knew. Lochran hadn't arranged for Uncle Ray's funeral just to warn people about crossing him in the future. This was about sending *Harley* a message. To remind Harley that this wasn't over until Harley delivered Uncle Ray's evidence. A sick feeling twisted Harley's gut. What if the dry bag couldn't be found?

CHAPTER 80

ELLA LOCKED ELBOWS WITH JELLY and strode toward Parlor C. Maybe if she kept the pace up, she wouldn't turn and run like she wanted to. "Harley did not look good."

"Parker was with him. And he had that give-us-a-sec look on his face. Harley will be okay."

And Miss Lopez was only half a block away—together with Grams, the Buckmans, and Detective Greenwood. If Harley needed anything, they'd be there.

"We're doing this for Harley," Ella said. "Let's just go in for ten seconds and whisk right back outside." With Harley outside it seemed pointless to be inside now anyway. The word was out—thanks to a call from Parker's mom—about who paid for the funeral. Lochran . . . what a pig.

Parlor C was empty, except for Lochran—and Mr. Torino? Clearly, they were together. "Something stinks here."

Jelly slowed her pace. "Like rotten tuna."

Vinny Torino nodded at them—like he had nothing to hide. The head of Cape Ann Security—bodyguarding for a deadly loan shark?

Mr. Lochran wore a dark suit, complete with a blood-red rose pinned to his lapel. If he noticed the girls, he didn't show it.

Something inside Ella *screamed* for her not to step closer to the men. She stopped abruptly by the visitor guest book. There wasn't another name written there. She reached for the silver cross around her neck. "Something's off here . . . like seriously wrong."

Jelly squeezed her arm like she agreed.

Lochran leaned in close to the body of Ray Lotitto.

"He's *talking* to him?" Ella was staring now, but Lochran didn't make any effort to hide what he was doing. His lips were close enough to brush Uncle Ray's ear as he spoke. "Speaking to the dead? That's necromancy." Grams would have something to say about that.

Lochran stroked Uncle Ray's hand as he spoke to him.

"This is totally creeping me out." Ella dropped the guest registry pen. There was no way she'd write her name and address in the book now. She didn't want Lochran knowing where she lived.

"He's way beyond sick," Jelly whispered—as if they needed more evidence of that fact. "We should go."

But Ella was still mesmerized. It was like she'd been unplugged. She couldn't talk . . . swallow . . . blink.

Lochran gave Uncle Ray's hand a final pat and straightened. He reached for the flower pinned to his own suit lapel—and pulled the extra-long pin like he was arming a grenade. Lochran tucked the flower stem between the stiff fingers of Uncle Ray's clasped hands.

"This is getting weirder and weirder," Jelly whispered.

Mr. Lochran held the three-inch pin up to the light, inspecting the thing.

"What's he do—?"

With a sudden thrust, Lochran drove the pin deep into Uncle Ray's throat—like, all the way to his fingertips.

Ella gasped—and Jelly lurched backward like *she'd* been stabbed.

Lochran pulled the pin from Uncle Ray's neck and checked it like the thing was a cake tester. He wiped the needle clean between his thumb and forefinger, then licked the tips of both.

"I'm going to puke." Jelly clung tighter. "We have to get out . . ."

Ella took a step back, pulling Jelly with her. Lochran looked directly at them—with an incredibly eerie smile on his face. But his eyes . . . his *eyes* . . .

Both girls turned and ran from Parlor C.

"He knew we were here the whole time," Jelly said. "He *wanted* us to see that—but I *sooo* wish I hadn't."

Ella agreed, but the damage was done. They couldn't unsee what they'd just witnessed . . . and they'd already seen way too much.

CHAPTER 81

VINNY TORINO HAD WORKED WITH—and for—all kinds of sickos in the past. And he'd launched some pretty vile customers out of the bar. Alcohol had a way of unlocking dark basement doors inside some people. Doors that should be sealed shut with heavy iron plating and a welding torch. Honestly, he'd seen some pretty psycho stuff. Rocko Spinelli held the dubious honor of having the most demented criminal mind of anyone he'd ever known.

Until now.

He stood behind his employer and watched his depraved ritual. Part of him wanted to stop Lochran. But what good would that do? Ray had made his own mess, and it was too late to come to his rescue anyway.

Vinny had to look out for himself now. The wires in Lochran's brain were beyond twisted. They were tangled. But the man paid well—and often. Vinny would do Lochran's dirty work for now. But only until he'd built up a nice cash stash to disappear some night with his moving truck. He'd establish a new identity, vanish from the grid . . . and live like a king.

His mind drifted to Lochran's former right-hand man. If Vinny hadn't taken Ironwing out, he had no doubt Lochran would've made it happen. Which is why Vinny would never give Quinn Lochran a reason to doubt his loyalty. Questioning Lochran might lead to a stickpin in Vinny's throat. No thanks.

"The girls ran like a couple of scared rabbits," Lochran said. "They won't forget that little show anytime soon."

Neither would Vinny.

Lochran slid the pin into Ray's Adam's apple like it was a pin cushion. He didn't stop until the head of the pin sat like a cherry on top. He stepped back, as if admiring the addition. "You really shouldn't have messed with me, Ray. Such a stupid, stupid man."

Actually, Vinny couldn't disagree. He'd warned Ray not to borrow money from Lochran, hadn't he? But Ray thought he was smart enough to handle Lochran—and get his nephew to fork over money too. Things didn't exactly turn out the way Ray had predicted.

"Well, I think we're done here." Lochran strode for the door. "I do have a little unfinished business with Ray's nephew, though."

Vinny smiled. Lochran wasn't the only one.

CHAPTER 82

ANGELICA WOULD NEVER LOOK at a straight pin without seeing Lochran's bizarre ritual. Not for the rest of her life.

She stood at the front-porch railing of the funeral home, breathing in deep breaths of the salty sea air, wishing she'd never come.

Harley leaned back against the corner where the two porch railings met—deep in conversation with Parker and Wilson. Kit sat at his feet. Angelica wanted to join them. Wanted to tell them what she and Ella had seen. But clearly this wasn't the time.

Pez must have sensed that Harley needed space as well. She stood on the front steps of the porch, looking at Harley for a long moment, as if wanting to make sure he was okay before going in herself. Apparently satisfied, she followed Uncle Vaughn and the others inside.

Seconds later, Vinny Torino exited the funeral home and held the door for Mr. Lochran. The loan shark strolled over to Harley as casually as if he were walking up to an ice cream truck.

He brushed past Wilson and Parker and didn't stop until he stood way too close for Harley to maneuver. For the moment, he looked trapped. Kit went on a ferocious barking rampage, lunging at Vinny Torino like she would bury her fangs deep in his flesh if given the chance. Harley held her leash with both hands.

"Should we do something?" Ella's question was totally legit.

It took everything Angelica had in her not to drop into her old protector mode. "The boys can handle themselves. Let's give them some space."

Ella glanced at her. "Sometimes I think I liked the old Jelly better."

Kit was still going crazy. Maybe that was a way Angelica could help without looking over-protective. She hustled over and unwrapped the leash from around Harley's hand. "I got her."

KitKat fought Angelica all the way. She strained at the leash and clawed at the porch deck. Ella ran to help. It took both of them working together to get KitKat to the far end of the porch.

"I'm telling you," Torino said. "You've got a terrific sled dog there."

"Easy, girl. Harley's right there," Ella said. "He's okay."

Angelica wasn't so sure about that.

Mr. Torino struck up a conversation with Parker and Wilson—effectively steering them a few feet away from Harley. The men had the boys separated—and likely right where they wanted them.

Lochran leaned in close to Harley—speaking just inches from his ear. "Ella . . . are you *seeing* this?"

Harley's eyes widened—like he was fighting back panic. He shook his head . . . and then again.

A low growl rumbled up from deep inside Kit. The hair on her neck rose.

"What do we *do*?" Ella's voice—desperate. "We have to help him."

But how? Angelica looked at the doors to the funeral home, hoping her dad, or Pez, or Detective Greenwood would be coming out about now.

"Jelly!" Ella gripped her arm tight enough to bruise. "Look."

Lochran stroked Harley's forearm as he spoke—just like he'd done to Uncle Ray's hand minutes earlier.

"I'm going to be sick." Angelica wasn't exaggerating.

Lochran patted Harley's hand, turned, and strode down the porch steps at a crisp pace. Mr. Torino broke free from Parker and Wilson to follow.

KitKat tugged and pulled Angelica with more power than she imagined possible. Ella got her hands on the leash and looped the free end around a porch support to keep Kit from charging.

Harley spun around, leaned low over the railing and hurled. Spit. Then wiped his mouth with the back of his hand. He turned to face Parker and Wilson, but she saw just enough of his face to suck in her breath. Deathly pale.

Ella turned away—like she didn't want Harley to catch her staring. "What do you think he said to scare him so bad?"

Angelica shook her head. "But we're going to find out."

CHAPTER 83

PARKER HAD BEEN PLAYED BY VINNY TORINO. Wilson, too. He'd kept both of them busy so Lochran had a wide-open shot at Harley.

"Get me out of here, guys." Harley's eyes . . . haunted. "I'm serious."

Parker led the way off the porch—right past Jelly and Ella. By the questioning look in their eyes, they'd seen enough of what had just happened to be just as alarmed as he was.

Wilson grabbed Kit's leash, and the dog trotted happily alongside him.

Ella hurried to catch up, clutching her cross necklace in one hand. "Harley?"

But he was on the run—at least in his head. Parker had seen him like this before. When he'd learned Kemosabe was gone. When Ella and Jelly accused Harley of stealing Scorza's Wrangler. And when he'd insisted on meeting Scorza at the Salvages—which turned out to be a trap.

Harley stepped up his pace—and Ella fell behind, gripping her necklace with both hands now. Harley steamed ahead of Wilson, putting even more distance between Parker and himself.

"Parker." Jelly grabbed his arm. "He's in Lone Ranger mode. Stop him. He's going someplace *bad*."

He pried Jelly's fingers off his arm as gently as he could. "He's already *gone*. I just have to keep up."

She bit her lip. Nodded. "He needs you. What do I tell Pez—and your parents?"

"Ask them to pray."

"Parker!" Her voice, more of a quiet, desperate wail. "He's in a dark place again. What will you do?"

"Pray hard. And meet Harley where he's at. All the way."

"Even in darkness?"

He looked her square in the eyes. Was she going back to old habits, trying to control the situation? But all he saw on her face was concern—and tears. A line from a book he'd read popped into his mind. "Sometimes rescuing a friend from darkness . . . means going in after them."

CHAPTER 84

PARKER HOTFOOTED AFTER HARLEY, WILSON, AND KIT—now a quarter block ahead.

Jelly called after him. He turned back for a sec. She stood in the center of the sidewalk. She put her fist to her cheek with her pinky and thumb extended. "Call me?"

Parker waved, then burned up the pavement to catch his friends—clearly heading for T-wharf.

Wings. It had always helped clear Parker's head. Maybe Harley was hoping it would do the same for him.

He caught them on the ramp down to the docks.

Harley didn't stop until he'd swung aboard the Boston Whaler and Kit jumped in beside him. He sat hunkered over, pulling his head down to his knees with both hands. He rocked back and forth. Kit nuzzled him, looking for a way to his cheek.

Wilson locked eyes with Parker for a moment, then untied the dock lines without a word. Parker fired up the motor and backed her out of the slip. Rockport Harbor was as still as the air inside the funeral home.

Parker wheeled around the yacht club and into Outer Harbor, praying the whole time. Harley pulled Kit close. He wasn't holding his own head anymore. Now he cradled Kit's. Progress.

Once through the channel, Parker steered north. He stood at the console. Throttled forward—and let *Wings* fly.

Salt air. The breeze. The powerful roar of the boat's big motor. And the prayer. All of them were in play, and within minutes Harley's head was up. Eyes closed. Face into the wind. His lips were moving too—and Parker's spirit soared right along with *Wings*. So . . . Harley wasn't trying to do this all on his own after all.

They raced past Front Beach. Back Beach. Rowe Point. It wasn't until they'd passed Granite Pier that Harley met his eyes—and motioned for Parker to stop. "We have to talk."

Parker eased back on the throttle until he'd locked it in neutral. He cut the engine but left the key in the ignition. The boat pitched and rolled with the waves.

"Lochran wants that evidence," Harley said. "I told him we'd tried. Couldn't find it."

"I think your dear Uncle Ray was trying to pull a fast one on the cops . . . on all of us," Wilson said. "Claiming he hid some rock-solid evidence—hoping he'd use it as a get-out-of-jail card. I say it doesn't exist. Never did."

"You may be right," Harley said. "But all that matters is what Lochran believes. And he thinks I'm not trying hard enough."

Parker looked back toward Rockport. "We've checked every logical spot in the harbor."

"I'll call Uncle Ray's lawyer," Harley said. "Maybe he can talk to Lochran." He already had the phone out, scrolling through the contacts.

"First," Wilson said, "tell us exactly what the swamp rat said."

Harley tapped Kilbro's number on his phone. "Find it—or it wouldn't be my neck in the noose."

"Wouldn't?"

"Would *not*. But he said I'd wish it was."

Harley's phone connected. He tapped the speaker and held it up so they all could hear.

Sebastian Kilbro seemed relieved to hear Harley's voice. "You have it?"

Harley explained everything. "We have no idea where that evidence is—or if it even exists. We don't know what to do."

"Find it. That's what you do." The lawyer hesitated. "Look, if your uncle was blowing smoke, I'd have known. He had something—enough to take Lochran down."

"But I got *nothing*," Harley said. "Can't you talk to Lochran? Make him believe me?"

"Tell me you're not that naive."

"That bag of gator manure threatened Harley," Wilson leaned in close to the phone. "So they can bust him now, right? I mean, maybe that's all the evidence the cops really need."

"Tell me you have a witness," Kilbro said. "Anybody that can testify that they heard him threaten you?"

Harley's shoulders slumped. "Nobody."

"So it's your word against his." Kilbro swore. "Calling the police is a dead end."

Parker was pretty sure they'd all known that even before the lawyer answered.

"You get your heads together. Read that clue sheet again. And again. And again. Figure it out," Kilbro said. "It's the only way to stop him."

"We find it—and we get it to the police, right?" Harley looked from Wilson to Parker. "And as soon as the police get their hands on it, they'll arrest him, and we're safe. Is that it?"

"Not quite," Kilbro said. "You get that evidence to *me*. You don't tell a soul, you understand? You don't think this guy has people loyal to him in the PD? You give it to the wrong person, and that evidence disappears. Middle of the night—or middle of the day. You call me when you find it. We'll meet. I'll make backup copies before turning it in to the police.

I'll contact Mr. Lochran myself. Once he knows the police have it, you won't be a threat to him anymore. He'll be too busy talking to his *own* lawyer to bother with you."

"You really think so?"

"I do. But you've *got* to find that evidence. Until that's been found, nobody is safe. To Lochran, this is a war, Harley. He has no intention of becoming a POW. You have no idea what he's capable of. Do you understand me?"

Harley nodded. "Got it."

Parker couldn't get the idea of this being a war out of his head. "Mr. Kilbro, this is Parker Buckman. If we don't find the evidence, why wouldn't Lochran just drop it? As long as there's no evidence, he's safe."

"And how does he know Harley won't stumble onto it six months from now—and turn it in to the police? For Lochran, this is do or die."

Wilson leaned closer to the phone. "Meaning, either Lochran gets the evidence in his hands, or the creep knows he's dead, right? I say he's running scared right now."

For a long moment Kilbro didn't answer. "You're not listening to me. Lochran won't rest until he has the evidence—or is sure Harley will *never* find it. Do I really have to spell it out for you boys?" He sighed. "For Lochran it's do or die. Meaning . . . *you* do this . . . or *you* die."

CHAPTER 85

PARKER DIDN'T MOVE AFTER HARLEY POCKETED his phone. None of them did. It was like they were on the edge of a dark abyss, and the wrong word or movement would surely send them over the edge. "We're going to pray."

"Do it, Parks." Harley shook his head. "I'm not sure I've got the words."

Parker prayed for their safety. For strength. For courage. That God would help them solve the clues and find the evidence—before it was too late. And that somehow he'd lead them out of this darkness that had surrounded them.

"We have to get back," Harley said the instant Parker finished.

Wilson made a show of doing a full 360 scan. "Maybe we should stay out here. You're safe. We'll see a boat approaching from miles away—and Bucky will outrun them."

Harley was looking back toward shore now. "No . . . we've been away too long. I don't know what I was thinking. I'm not the one in danger." Harley looked more anxious by the second. "He said it *wouldn't* be my neck in a noose. If we don't find that evidence, he'll take it out on some-one else. Fire it up, Parks. Get me home."

Parker's phone rang at that instant. Jelly's picture was on the screen. He held it up for Harley to see. "Answer—or get moving. Your call."

"Answer." Harley motioned him to hurry. "Put her on speaker."

Jelly talked so fast she stumbled over her own words. They'd all talked outside the funeral home for a while, then walked together back to BayView Brew to set up for Harley's party. Jelly broke into tears. "Just get here."

Harley stood. "Miss Lopez?"

"She's fine. But not okay. I've got to go. Detective Greenwood just pulled up."

Harley pulled the phone close. "Miss Lopez—she got hurt?"

"Just shook up. Get here. Fast."

Parker fired up *Wings* and jammed the throttle forward. He kept to a straight line and didn't slow for anything. Wilson and Harley hung on for dear life, but neither complained about the speed or sea spray.

By the time he pulled into the slip, all of them were half-soaked. Kit shook, adding one more deluge of saltwater before jumping onto the pier.

Wilson secured the bow line. "I'll get the stern. You go. I'll catch you."

Parker pocketed the keys and ran two steps behind Harley and Kit. He heard Wilson pounding down the dock behind him seconds later.

Wilson skipped the ramp and leaped for the granite wall, reaching the top as Harley and Kit passed.

Jelly and Ella were on the sidewalk outside BayView Brew—watching for them.

The three of them didn't stop until they practically ran the girls over. Wilson rested his hands on his knees, gulping in air. "This better be good, Jelly. Or honestly—"

"Not good. It's all bad."

Harley tried to go inside, but Ella blocked the door. He stretched to look in the window.

"I'm not sure Pez wants you to come in yet," Ella said. "Maybe you should give her a minute." Clearly she wasn't going to move.

Without a word, Harley picked Ella up and hefted her over his shoulder like she weighed no more than a six-year-old.

"Harley!"

He pulled open the door and stepped inside. Parker and the rest followed. Harley didn't set Ella down until he was ten feet into the eating area.

Dad. Mom. Uncle Sammy. Pez. Grams. Detective Greenwood. They were all there—and staring at Mr. Bones. The coffee company skeleton hung from a noose secured to a rafter in the center of the room—wrists and ankles secured with nylon zip ties. The chalkboard of daily specials had been propped directly below it. The specials had been erased, and a new chalk message had been written in its place.

Give me what I want in 24 hours.
Don't leave me hanging—or I'll return the favor.

There was nothing obvious to prove Lochran was behind it, and it was a sure bet they'd find no proof no matter how hard forensics might search.

Harley swung a chair in place and stood on it. He tugged at the rope over Mr. Bones's head. "Somebody get me a knife."

Greenwood took charge—and talked Harley down from the chair. "We need pictures first, Harley. I'll take it down myself when we're done." The moment Harley's shoes touched the floor, Greenwood slid the chair out of reach.

The activity set Mr. Bones in motion. He did a lazy turn to face Parker. His Bones Coffee apron was gone, and he wore a BayView Brew one instead. Obviously snagged from one of the clothes hooks in the kitchen.

Why would somebody take the time to change Mr. Bones's apron?

"No." Harley stared at the thing, ashen-faced.

Parker followed his gaze. But it wasn't Harley's name embroidered on the apron like Parker expected.

Wilson read the name aloud. "Pez."

CHAPTER 86

HOW GRAMS CONVINCED EVERYONE to come to her place, Ella had no idea. The police wanted everyone cleared out to take pictures and check for prints. And there was a birthday party they needed to have for Harley, even though nobody felt like celebrating. But Grams was right. There was nothing they could do. She told Harley to bring the poem, and Pez to bring the presents. They'd all work on Uncle Ray's poem again, and then they'd stop and have a birthday party. It sounded ridiculous and genius all at the same time.

Harley's reaction to the message hanging from the rafters told Ella everything she needed to know. It was the answer they'd been looking for with the twenty questions game. And it all made sense. Harley's frantic search for the evidence was about protecting Pez.

Harley unfolded a new copy of the poem—but this time he let them read the letter from his Uncle Ray too—and the note he'd found in his bed. If Ella had any doubts about Harley's motivation, the letter wiped them all away. He'd been trying to look after Pez—and Ella and Jelly, too.

Ella read the poem aloud.

They gathered around the kitchen table. Tossed plenty of ideas out, but none of them stuck. Honestly, everything kept pointing to the obvious. The evidence, if it still existed, had been hidden in Rockport Harbor—and they'd already scoured all the likely hiding spots. Nobody saw the point of searching there again.

Parker's dad led the entire group in prayer. For God's protection mostly. And for a breakthrough on the poem. When he'd finished, they kicked the thing around awhile longer, but without any new revelations.

It was a dead end, and Ella was sure everyone sensed it.

"We need to set our minds on brighter things," Grams said. "And maybe things won't seem so dark after we do." She pulled out both Blueberry Ghost Pies she'd made for the event. She insisted Harley take Grandpa's favorite chair in the living room. A small pile of presents had been stacked on the coffee table next to it. One by one, all of them sat or stood in the living room to watch.

Cash from the Buckmans—and Jelly's dad. "For your motorcycle fund," Mrs. Buckman explained.

Wilson gave him a key. "For my trailer. When you come to visit, you'll have a place to stay."

"Harley's smarter than that," Jelly said. "You'll never convince him to go to the Everglades—just to sleep in a nice trailer."

"We'll see." Harley still looked pale, but he smiled like he knew something the girls didn't.

Pez had two presents for him. The first was a simple brass dog tag. Round, with *KitKat* in bold type on one side, Harley's name and the coffee shop address on the other. "If she ever leaves your side and gets lost—"

"Which isn't likely," Ella said. "Kit adores him—although we can't imagine why."

Pez laughed. "Well, if she does get lost, we want everyone to know where our home is."

Harley looked at her for a moment. There was something in his eyes Ella couldn't decipher any more than she could Ray's poem. He looked down like he was afraid someone might read his thoughts. He patted his leg, and Kit was at his side. He held KitKat's tag up to the garden hose collar and gave an approving nod. "Looks like we'll need pliers, girl. We'll get this on soon enough." He closed his fist around the new tag and drove it deep in his pocket.

Harley seemed to loosen up by the minute. Maybe it was the roomful of family and friends that made the difference, but the troubles—and dangers—seemed to fade. Each gift made Harley smile, and there was no doubt it was genuine.

A manila envelope sat with the other gifts, but Pez slipped it off the table. "Not the right time," she said. "We'll do this gift another day."

Which made Ella totally second-guess the present she and Jelly had for Harley. She'd hoped the salvaged nameplate would be a reminder of God's faithfulness or something. But what if it only reminded Harley of how awful Uncle Ray had been to him? Ray had been alive when they'd bought the thing. Now that he was dead, the nameplate sounded like a horrible idea. Ella should have trusted her earlier doubts—and left it in her room. She caught Jelly's eyes—who must have been thinking the same thing.

Jelly reached and slowly slid the present off the edge of the table.

"Hold on, Jelly." Wilson gripped her forearm and slipped the gift out of her hand. "That's Harley's name on the gift tag."

She shook her head. "But it's from Ella and me—so we have the right to take it back. It's a bad idea. We'll get him something else."

"First Miss Lopez takes back a present—and now you and Ella want to do the same? What kind of birthday is this?" Wilson handed the package off to Harley. Before Ella or Jelly could stop him, he'd ripped off the paper and pulled back the bubble wrap covering the front of the plaque. He stopped. A stunned look on his face. "Is this . . . ?"

Ella shrugged her apology. "I'm sorry. We bought it before your uncle

. . ." What had they been thinking? They should have tossed it in the garbage the moment they'd heard Uncle Ray had been murdered.

"We're both sorry." Jelly was on her feet, standing next to Harley with her hands out. "We'll make this disappear and find you something much better, okay?" She reached to take it, but Harley pulled it back.

He tore off the rest of the bubble wrap, holding it high for everyone to see. "You found *Deep Trouble*?" He looked at Parker, like maybe he'd been the one who'd discovered the wreck.

Jelly explained about the find at the farmer's market booth.

"Actually," Harley said, "I think I love this. A reminder, you know? About a man who made selfish choices all his life—and this is where it got him. *Deep Trouble*. And about my God who pulled Parks and me out of deep trouble."

The room was quiet for a long moment. Grams mopped tears from her cheeks. Pez hugged Parker's mom. Jelly looked like she'd wanted to hug someone but caught herself.

Harley was on his feet now, and he joined Parker, Wilson, and the two men. They examined the plaque, talking over each other the entire time.

Ella and Jelly exchanged a relieved look. Oh, yeah. That plaque was definitely a hit. Uncle Ray's poem sat on the table by the opened gifts. The last thing Ella wanted was for Harley to see that thing. It would ruin the moment.

She slipped out of her chair, bent over to pet Kit, and swiped the poem in one smooth move. Harley was still looking at the plaque with the others when she slipped back to the ring of chairs. He hadn't even noticed what she'd done. She'd give it back to him later. But not yet. She wanted him to forget and enjoy—at least for a little bit longer.

Uncle Ray and all his rules. Every one of them a proof of his selfish heart. And the fact that he put the clues for the missing evidence in a cryptic poem showed that he trusted nobody. Not his friends. Not his lawyer. Not a soul. When it came down to it, it was only Harley and Parker that he believed he could trust.

It was nothing less than a tragedy that he'd been killed before giving Harley the info he needed to find the evidence.

Jelly drifted over, and they both squeezed into Grandpa's recliner now that Harley had abandoned it.

Ella read the poem again and stopped midway. She stared. Reread the beginning with new eyes—a new perspective. Read all the way to the end again. It couldn't be, could it?

"Jelly," she spoke so soft that there was no chance of anyone else hearing. "I just noticed something about the poem I never did before. Tell me if you see it too . . . or tell me I'm crazy."

Jelly reached to steady Ella's hand. "I can't read it if you keep shaking the paper like that."

Ella definitely wasn't doing it on purpose. She watched Jelly speed-read the poem, but when she looked up, it was clear she hadn't seen anything new.

"I was looking at the boys with the plaque, and then I read the poem. Here, where it says *soon you'll be in trouble deep* . . . what if he was hinting at it being in *Deep Trouble*?

Jelly's eyes opened wide. She scanned the poem again. "*Watch your time, there's not a heap.* Of course . . . they'd be diving with a tank. It's all about time."

"*Below the place where some might crash.* This isn't about an intersection or a car accident. What do you say when you're dog-tired and you're going to go to bed?"

Jelly sucked in her breath. "I'm going to crash."

"There was a cabin in that boat. A bed, too. The evidence is in a dry bag stashed under the bunk in *Deep Trouble*." Now Jelly was shaking, too.

Jelly stood. Held the poem over her head and waved it like a white flag. "Everybody—listen up—Ella just solved Uncle Ray's poem!"

CHAPTER 87

ONE LOOK AT ELLA, AND HARLEY KNEW she'd figured out the mystery—or totally believed she had. Which was enough for him. He held both arms up to quiet everyone so Ella could talk.

The moment she made the connection with *Deep Trouble*, his pulse must have doubled. She was right. She had to be.

Everyone crowded around the poem again. Harley didn't need to. He'd memorized the thing days ago.

> Within earshot of the old bell,
> but only if you're feeling swell.
> Watch your time, 'cause there's not a heap,
> Soon you'll both be in trouble deep.
> Below the place where some might crash,
> in a bag never meant for trash.
> You'll find it's all there, nice and dry,

Evidence to make Lochran fry.
The place is dark, when it's not night.
So use your head, and bring a light.
Watch for Lochran, and Mr. White,
both have a nasty appetite.
They'll take your life, they'll take your soul,
They swallow careless dummies whole.

"Within earshot of the bell." Parker practically shouted the line from the poem. "The marker buoy. That's where they picked up Ray after *Deep Trouble* sank, right? And the bell would only be ringing if the waves—the *swells* were big enough. The boat went down within earshot of that buoy."

Which could still be a massive search area. "We have to find that salvage diver—and get him to lead us to *Deep Trouble*."

Ella had an incredibly determined look on her face. "We'll get on it."

"And this investigative reporter"—Mrs. Buckman raised her hand—"will help."

"Me, too," Miss Lopez rushed to Harley and hugged him. Hard.

It was the best birthday party Harley'd had since before his dad died. He got more than presents. He'd been given hope. He locked eyes with Ella. Smiled and shook his head. She looked like she'd scored a touchdown.

She pointed at him. Used both hands to form a circle. Pointed back at herself. Then spread her hands wide.

"I . . . owe . . . you . . . big?"

She smiled. "I'm glad we agree on that point, Mr. Lotitto. You'll be paying me back for the rest of your life—which will be a lot longer once we find that evidence."

The whole room burst into laughter.

God had answered prayer, hadn't he? Didn't Parks's dad pray for the real meaning of the poem not thirty minutes ago? *God—you are amazing. My end zone!* It had seemed like the game was over . . . but God had just put time on the clock—and given him a first down.

Even Ray's letter was loaded with clues he hadn't seen before. Harley read a couple of lines aloud. "I had the evidence—everything all set to come out on top . . . but *hit* an obstacle and I couldn't *bail* fast enough. I was *going down* and couldn't do a thing about it. I was glad I'd hidden the evidence where I did. You can *salvage* this situation."

"He hit an *obstacle*," Parker said. "Little Salvages. And he literally couldn't bail fast enough—and the bilge pumps couldn't keep up either. He was sinking. And saying we can *salvage* the situation? How come we didn't see this before?"

No wonder Uncle Ray said Harley would need Parks. They'd need *Wings*. Harley would need a dive buddy.

Everything made sense now. Except one thing. "So, who's this Mr. White?" Harley asked. "If he's as dangerous as Lochran, we'd better be on the lookout, right?"

The room got quiet.

Finally, Miss Lopez spoke. "I think I've got it. But I don't like it."

All eyes were fixed on her.

"The seal population. They're out there at the Salvages—right where *Deep Trouble* went down. And the seals bring the what?" She just let the question hang out there.

"Great whites," Grams whispered. "Lord Almighty . . . your uncle was warning you that man-eating sharks patrol the area."

CHAPTER 88

HARLEY SLIPPED OUT GRAMS'S FRONT DOOR. Gripped the porch rail and leaned toward the sea. The waves were giving the Headlands a pounding.

The sound of war.

A battle was coming—and there wasn't a thing Harley could do to stop it—or even slow it. There'd be no retreat. It truly was do or die. But now he had a fighting chance.

Kit leaned against his leg, like she wanted to remind him she was his. That she'd be there for him.

The rest were still inside. Making plans for how they'd find the salvage diver who'd found *Deep Trouble*. Just knowing they were on it was enough for Harley.

They still faced a massive challenge. He wasn't sure what would be worse to face—Quinn Lochran or a great white. A shark would come out of the shadows. Materialize right out of the endless nothingness of the ocean where visibility dropped off. A great white was fast. Silent.

And certainly deadly. There would be only one place of safety . . . and it would be bobbing somewhere sixty feet above him while he searched for *Deep Trouble*.

Escaping Lochran's noose might prove to be a greater challenge. That little stunt with Mr. Bones proved Lochran could get at Harley—or at those he loved—whenever he wanted. Maybe he'd send hired muscle to do the deed. Is that what Mr. Torino really was? Or maybe Lochran liked to do that kind of work himself. Clearly, walls couldn't stop Lochran from getting at Harley. The man could get anyplace a ghost could.

Uncle Ray, the self-proclaimed survivor, the guy who always landed on his feet, the guy who bragged he could cheat Death himself? Even he couldn't save himself from Lochran's reach—despite being surrounded by armed guards. Once Lochran believed someone had crossed him, the guy was a dead man. It was as if Ray had received the dreaded black spot of pirate lore.

And now Lochran had threatened Miss Lopez with the black spot.

Harley squatted and pulled Kit close. Buried his face in her neck. "We've got trouble, Kit. Big trouble." He pulled back, and she sniffed the air like she was testing his words, desperately wanting to understand what he was saying. He liked her collar, but it definitely didn't look right with no name tag. "I'll get that new tag on soon, girl. You're mine, though. I'm not leaving you."

Mike Ironwing. Only the fish knew whatever secrets Ironwing had intended to share. And right now, the fish were guarding Uncle Ray's evidence too.

Harley pulled out his phone and set a countdown timer for twenty-four hours, when the evidence had to be delivered. Pressed the Start button. Immediately the seconds slipped away, reminding him that the job was getting more impossible with every moment he lost. Already he had less than a day to locate the diver, find the wreck, elude the sharks, grab the evidence, and deliver the goods. *God, help me. God . . . help me.*

So many good things had come together for Harley. Miss Lopez. The Crow's Nest. Good friends. Even KitKat now. "God . . . please . . . don't let Lochran take this from me. Don't let him hurt Miss Lopez. He's too strong for me—and he knows that. But I have *you*. So give me strength. Give me success. Strengthen me . . . my faith . . . may I be more like Jesus—and Parks. Give me the right reactions . . . and quick reaction time. Give me the slingstones to take down this Goliath."

Miss Lopez would be staying with Grams and Ella tonight. Jelly and Mrs. Buckman would be there too. Wilson and Harley would stay with Parks. It was the strength-in-numbers kind of thing. But Harley held no illusions. He knew exactly where his strength came from.

"I'm your man forever. No matter what happens." Harley raised his face heavenward. "You know that, right?"

"I guess maybe I did." Ella's voice.

Harley froze for a second, then turned slowly to face her. "I didn't know you were—"

"*Shh-sh-shhh.*" She put a finger to her lips. "Don't say another word. Let's pretend I never heard that."

If only that were really true.

"We'll find the diver—and get the location of that boat. It's too late to make calls tonight, but first thing tomorrow we'll be all over it."

Ella stood close, probably so she could read his eyes. She was crazy good at that. She reached for Kit and drew slow, swirly patterns with one finger around the stitches on the crown of her head. "And Parker's dad—along with Jelly's—will get the tanks filled . . . and rent extras from the dive shop in Gloucester tomorrow."

The shop didn't open until noon. If all went well, they'd be on the water by one thirty. Underwater by two. That gave them enough time for two dives to find the boat—and the evidence hidden aboard.

"You're still going to church tomorrow, aren't you?"

Harley nodded. "I'm asking God for the moon. Seems like skipping church would be kind of dumb, you know?"

"I thought you'd say something like that." She smiled.

"I guess you think you know me pretty good."

This time she laughed. "Oh, Harley . . . you're easy. And you're getting more and more predictable. I know the kinds of things you'd do—and a whole lot of things you'd never do . . . not in a million years."

Predictable was the last thing he was feeling right now. He had no idea what he'd do if he didn't find the evidence. Ella was wrong. Harley was completely *un*predictable. And he was pretty sure there was absolutely *nothing* he wouldn't do . . . to keep Miss Lopez safe.

CHAPTER 89

VINNY TORINO PULLED THE CREW TOGETHER for a rare face-to-face meeting. They'd executed their jobs flawlessly up until this point, and he expected nothing less than a strong—if not perfect—finish.

Tomorrow night was the deadline—in every sense of the word. Whether Ray's nephew found the evidence or not, the book would have the same ending. It wasn't exactly going to be a happily-ever-after kind of story for Harley—and the ranger's kid, if he was with him when Vinny pulled his plug. Mowgli, too. "We have to expect that all three boys will be there—and armed with knives or machetes, at least. The girls may be there too."

The way Vinny saw it? Harley was supposed to be dead months ago. When Ray sliced that boat in half, the game was over for Harley. Somehow, he'd ended up in sudden-death overtime instead.

The crew went over every detail. Worked out the kinks. Hammered out a solid backup plan. By the time they'd finished, Vinny couldn't have been more confident.

Every one of the crew members would be packing, but that was only to keep Harley and friends from attempting to run. Firing a gun would only be a last resort. The end of the line for Harley—the way Vinny had it all planned—would be seen as an accident. Tragic. Terrible. And most definitely deadly.

CHAPTER 90

Sunday, April 23

Parker kept one hand on each knee, trying to keep them from going back into that bouncing thing they did. He felt more than a little weird that he was the only one from his family not doing something to help in the effort to find the salvage diver—or prep for the dive itself.

Harley looked just as restless next to him in the pew. He'd been determined to go to the church service, but Parker was pretty sure he was wrestling inside too. Wilson stayed with the others, insisting his machete needed sharpening.

Harley took notes all throughout the sermon—more than ever before. He rarely looked up. Just kept writing. Honestly, Parker tried to focus on what the pastor said, but his mind kept drifting to the dive.

Suddenly Harley pulled his phone from his pocket and held the screen so Parker could see it. *Miss Lopez.*

Harley leaned close. "I gotta take this. Be right back." He pressed the button to connect and hustled down the aisle toward the foyer like the place was on fire.

Harley's Bible and notes sat right there on the pew . . . like right in Parker's line of sight. He found himself reading before fully thinking through if he should.

Help me, God. Make me strong. Give me success. Don't let me mess up. Miss Lopez needs me . . . and you know how much I need her. Put me exactly where I should be— exactly when I should be there. Right time, right place, and give me the right stuff. I know you love me. I know you won't leave me. I know you care. Without you I can't win. With you I can't lose. You've rescued me before. I need your rescue again.

Parker stopped reading. Harley hadn't heard any more of the sermon than Parker had. He'd been prepping for what was coming next just as hard as Dad, Uncle Sammy, Mom, Pez, and the rest. He'd been doing the work of bringing this to the King—and strengthening himself in the Lord.

Parker needed to do a little more of that himself. It was exactly how he needed to prep for the last-ditch search. The best way to meet Harley all the way. His knees started bouncing again, but he didn't even try stopping them this time. Right now, there were more important things to focus on. He bowed his head . . . and got to work.

CHAPTER 91

GRAMS'S HOUSE HAD BECOME the mission control center. Or maybe just calling it a mission center was more accurate. To Ella, nothing felt controlled at all. Locating *Deep Trouble*—or rather the diver who'd found it—had proved more difficult than she'd hoped.

But thanks largely to Parker's mom, they had a phone number and address long before the boys got out of church. Unfortunately, getting the diver to pick up the phone was a different matter. Mr. Buckman and Jelly's dad had even gone to the man's address in Gloucester before hitting the dive shop. Nobody answered the doorbell—and the guy's truck wasn't in the driveway.

The dads came back with lots of filled tanks but no idea where to dive with them. They headed for T-wharf to outfit *Wings*, knowing that with every minute that passed, the chances of them diving at all were getting slimmer.

It was nearly 2 p.m. before Danny Miller, salvage diver and instructor, returned Ella's desperate messages. As it turned out, he was on vacation in Fort Myers and had tried ignoring the phone calls for hours. But Ella kept the phone vibrating, and apparently the salvage diver couldn't stand it any longer.

Ella put the phone on speaker as soon as his name came up on the screen. Grams, Jelly, Mrs. Buckman, and Pez all crowded around.

The news of Ray Lotitto's murder had already reached him. He didn't exactly sound busted up about it. The instant he heard what she wanted, he gave her the rundown on how he'd found *Deep Trouble*. Normally, he didn't reveal the exact location of any wrecks that he'd discovered. It allowed him to strip the boats of anything salvageable—anything that might make him some bucks online or at the outdoor markets.

Most wrecks he'd found had been picked clean of anything valuable by other divers. So when he'd found *Deep Trouble*—untouched since the moment it settled on the bottom of Sandy Bay—it had been a salvage diver's paradise. And because he despised Ray Lotitto the way he did, he had no intention of revealing the location until he'd unscrewed, unbolted, cut loose, or crowbarred free every single thing he could sell or trade.

None of that mattered to Ella. "We need the location. It's important."

"After I'm done with it," Danny said finally. "Besides, I can't help you even if I wanted to. I don't have my notebook with the exact coordinates with me."

"We're looking for a phone, nothing more," Ella said.

"You'd make a lousy salvage diver." Danny Miller laughed. "You're not going to get any money for a phone that's been underwater for months."

Should Ella say more? She looked at Pez, who gave her a nod.

"This isn't about salvaging pieces of the boat to sell, Mr. Miller. There was evidence on that phone. Recordings that Ray had held back from the police. We need to find it . . . and fast. Give me the location, and we won't take a barnacle off the boat—except that phone. The boat is yours to salvage."

"Tell you what. I'm back from vacay in a week. I'll go down myself and bring you the phone. How's that?"

"No good. We absolutely need that phone . . . today. We're not the only ones looking for it. A very bad man wants to make that evidence disappear forever—and he means business."

"So more than one party wants the wreck's location? Sounds like I may have a bidding war," Danny said. "What's your best offer?"

Grams's face clouded over, and she reached for the phone. Ella pulled back and held up one finger.

"Okay, Mr. Miller. Let me get this straight." Ella gave an exaggerated sigh. "Ray Lotitto was murdered because he was the *only* one who knew where the phone was hidden. And now *you* want to be the *only* living soul who knows where to find it? You're a brave man."

There was a long silence on the line. Pez leaned close and planted a kiss on Ella's head.

Danny Miller gave a frustrated growl. "Grab a pencil and paper. I'll give you some basic directions. All I can do is get you in the ballpark, but without my notebook, you're still going to have a devil of a time finding it."

And the devil to pay if they didn't.

CHAPTER 92

HARLEY HAD NEVER SEEN SO MANY scuba tanks lined up since he'd worked for his uncle at Rockport Dive Company. Parker's dad said everything was in place for two more boats to join them—complete with crews, and even a couple more divers. They were due any minute.

Parker secured four tanks aboard *Wings*. Harley added two more—just in case.

Parker's dad—together with Jelly's—worked like crazy alongside the boys to get *Wings* ready. Uncle Ray would've never helped Harley like those men did. But it was exactly the type of thing Harley's dad would've done if he were here. It was moments like this that made him ache for a family more than ever.

Focus, Harley. This wasn't the time to think about that kind of stuff. They were going into battle now, and it was time to batten down the hatches. Besides, he'd asked God for enough things, hadn't he? What if he'd already asked for too much—and God tossed out Harley's entire list?

That didn't sound like the kind of thing God would do, but this was no time to take chances. *God . . . just keep Miss Lopez safe. Please . . . help us find that evidence so nothing bad happens to her. This is what I really need. Take everything else I've asked for off the list, okay?* He hesitated for a moment. *Including finding a motorcycle someday like the one I lost. Forget I ever asked.*

Wilson helped Parks pull on his wet suit. Harley would get his on in a minute, but first he had a call to make. He pulled out his phone and dialed Uncle Ray's lawyer. Sebastian Kilbro must have had his phone in his hand because he answered before the second ring.

"Mr. Kilbro . . . we've figured out the clues—for real this time. The evidence was never in Rockport Harbor."

"So you have it?"

"Not yet, but we know where it is."

"Good work, Harley. I'm impressed. When will you have it in your hands?"

That was the big question, right? "It's on a boat. We're going to Sandy Bay right now to look for it."

There was a long pause. "If you're talking about the boat I *think* you're talking about, it sunk three miles offshore somewhere. I thought you said you knew where it is."

Harley swung out of *Wings* and walked to the end of the dock. "I *do* know where the evidence is—inside the boat. Now I just have to *locate* the boat. But we'll find it. You need to keep Miss Lopez safe."

"Listen, Harley," Kilbro said. "You're up against a very bad man. Finding the evidence is the only way to keep her safe. You know that. So find it. Put it right in my hands, and I'll take it from there. We're running out of time. I think you know that too."

Not what Harley wanted to hear.

"Call me the minute you get it. Got it?"

Oh yeah. Harley got it. He hustled back to *Wings*. Stepped aboard. Started pulling on his wet suit.

Wilson had his machete slung across his back. "Gas tank—and the spare—topped off."

Jelly's dad let out a whoop and pointed at two boats entering Outer Harbor. "We're in business."

Mr. Buckman gathered them around and went over the game plan. Jelly's dad would be aboard the lobster boat *Big Catch* with another National Park ranger as a dive buddy. The guy dove off Cape Ann all the time—and knew what he was doing. The captain was out of Gloucester—as good as they get.

Parker's dad would be aboard *Making Waves*, a 28-foot Boston Whaler with twin 250s on the transom. Harbormaster Eric had lined it up—and he'd be Mr. Buckman's dive buddy. The captain was a friend of Eric's.

Mr. Buckman had originally talked about diving with the boys—or dividing them onto other teams. But Harley and Parks had gone diving so many times together that they worked really well as a unit. That was a plus in the safety column. And Harley suspected Mr. Buckman wanted to treat them both like men. Whatever his reasons, Harley appreciated it.

The plan was simple. They'd follow Danny Miller's instructions to get them in the area. Since they didn't have exact coordinates, they'd anchor fifty yards or so apart, and do their best to dive a grid pattern so that one of the three teams would find *Deep Trouble*. Hopefully. The team that found the boat—and the bag—was to fire a flare, and the other boats would pull anchor and join them as soon as their divers surfaced—or meet back in Rockport Harbor.

"There's a fog bank moving in." Mr. Buckman shrugged like it was no big deal, but Harley could see the strain on the man's face. "We'll need to move fast—before the fog makes things too dangerous."

They'd have just enough time to squeeze in two dives . . . provided the weather held.

"One wreck to find," Dad said. "Two dives. Three boats on the hunt, and six divers."

"Seven!" Jelly trotted toward them, already wearing her wet suit, with a dive bag over her shoulder. "More eyes, more chances to find the boat."

"Or more chances to slow them down," Wilson said.

Actually, that didn't sound too far off. Harley was *not* liking the idea one bit. One look at Parks pretty well confirmed he felt the same way. Maybe they could get her to dive on her dad's team.

Miss Lopez and Parker's mom came to see them off. Actually, they were dressed like they'd hoped to ride along. But with Ella and Kit, *Wings* would be carrying six as it was—plus tons of gear. It was obvious that there really wasn't room, and Harley was pretty sure Miss Lopez wanted to give him space.

Miss Lopez handed Harley a bag. "Bananas. Bagels. Water. I grabbed what I could. I got to keep my boy fueled up."

My boy. MY boy.

"There's enough for all of you. You be careful, you hear?" She hugged Parker. Then Wilson. And when she hugged Harley, she didn't let go. She whispered close to his ear. "You come back to me in one piece, Harley. You hear me? Don't do anything crazy. I'll be bringing your name to the Throne."

He had no doubt of that. "You watch out for Lochran—and his Cape Ann *Angel*." He didn't even want to say the name Vinny Torino. The guy disgusted him now. And to think he'd thought the guy was some kind of superhero when he'd first met him.

"Okay, so I'll pray with my eyes open." Miss Lopez gave him a kiss on the cheek. "I'll watch out for Lochran—and you stay on the lookout for Mr. White."

CHAPTER 93

PARKER FOLLOWED THE OTHER TWO BOATS out the Rockport Harbor channel. Sandy Bay was a syrupy kind of flat. But weather changed fast along the coast, and anything could happen.

He opened *Wings* up and saw the man at the helm of *Making Waves* do the same. Dad and Harbormaster Eric were doing their best to suit up and ready their gear. *Big Catch* was already falling behind, and Uncle Sammy leaned out one side of the pilothouse like he was wishing he was in a boat with more get-up-and-go.

Little Salvages and Dry Salvages looked a whole lot farther from shore than just three miles. *Deep Trouble* had hit the rocks of Little Salvages and had gone down fast. The wind had been coming from the northeast that day, and from what Danny Miller had relayed to Ella, the boat was on the bottom approximately a hundred or hundred fifty yards west—give or take—of Little Salvages's southern tip. But that whole "give or take" factor still left them with an impossibly big area to comb.

Jelly worked her way back from her bow seat and stood beside him. "Are you and Harley mad at me?"

Mad was a pretty strong word. "Just concerned." He'd seen her limping after they'd finished diving in Rockport Harbor yesterday. Clearly her leg wasn't 100 percent yet. "The harbor was one thing. But out here with currents—and the pace Harley will set? You'll never keep up." Which meant they'd cover less ground—and could miss the wreck.

"Watch me."

"Just feeling like you're still seeing yourself as a protector."

She shook her head. "I'm trying so hard not to be. I just want to help. I've got two strong eyes."

"And one weak leg."

She touched his gimpy arm. "If you can do it . . ."

"Touché. But it's all legs out there."

"I won't slow you down."

"Jelly, you've had hardly any open-water experience. Maybe the best help would be if you just stayed—"

"If you finish that sentence, I'm going to slug you good. I'm *not* staying topside, just watching your bubbles."

Parker got it. He'd feel the same way if he was stuck in the boat while others went down. "We'll be pushing hard. There'll be no time for us to . . ." Maybe he was better off not finishing that sentence either.

"Babysit? I'll keep up. I'm quicker than you—and you know it." She snagged his cap and slapped it on her head as if to prove it. "And I'll use less air doing it—and you know that too."

He couldn't argue with her there. And with three divers, they'd swing a wider net for the wreck. "We can use all the help we can get."

She smiled—and returned his hat. She clamped her BCD to her tank, sprayed the inside of her mask with anti-fog, and pulled her hood over her head with determination.

Harley shot Parker a look like he wasn't so sure that Jelly would be a help at all.

Dad motioned for Parker to anchor, and he pulled the throttle back.

They were still, what? Three hundred yards from Little Salvages? He'd be nearest to the harbor if the fog moved in. It was the safest spot to be. Parker got that. But he wanted to get a lot closer to Little Salvages, like the two other boats. Could *Deep Trouble* have drifted this far before going down?

But God knew, right? "Lead us to the boat," Parker prayed out loud. "You showed Peter where to let down that net to catch the fish. Now You show us where to drop the anchor, okay?"

Wilson had the anchor in one hand with ten feet of heavy chain attached. He looped the 150-foot coil of ⅝-inch nylon anchor line in the other hand. He eyed Parker. "Praying again, Bucky?"

"I'm not talking to the gulls."

Wilson grinned. "I'm going to start calling you Preacher Boy if you keep that up."

Then Preacher Boy it was . . . because Parker sure wasn't going to stop praying.

"I'm liking this spot." Wilson dropped the anchor over the side, and together they made sure the thing held secure before cutting the motor.

A marker buoy gonged somewhere in the distance. "Hear that?" Parker pointed to his ear. "Within earshot of the bell."

"Which can be heard for a half mile in every direction." Wilson made a wide sweep with his machete. "You got a whole lot of bottom to cover."

Too much. *God, help us.*

Parker buckled his dive knife to his calf. Pulled on his hood. He shrugged into his BCD and secured the straps. Jelly and Harley were already sitting on the gunwales—fins on—seating their masks. Uncle Sammy waved as *Big Catch* passed. At that rate, it would likely be at least fifteen minutes before Uncle Sammy was in the water.

Making Waves circled a good fifty yards or more northeast of them, ready to drop anchor. Parker looked over the side into the black water. Finding *Deep Trouble* was worse than simply a shot in the dark. It was also a shot in the deep.

CHAPTER 94

ANGELICA HAD EXPECTED MORE PUSHBACK from the boys, but they were likely too focused on the job ahead. It was go time, and they were antsy to do what they came to do.

The boys wanted to be the first team in the water. First to the bottom. Like the boat would be right there, waiting for them. Ready to give up its secrets.

Kit looked jumpy—and stayed close to Harley.

Angelica added extra weight to her BCD pocket. With the thick neoprene of the cold-water wet suit, she'd need more weight to stay down. She'd come prepared and brought plenty. She'd show the boys she could pull her own weight too. Her goal? Not just keep up but stay ahead of them.

She was the first to roll backward off the gunwale. She didn't let out a peep when the icy water began its assault through the seams of her wet suit—even though she was screaming inside. She tapped her inflator to add a touch more air to her BCD. She achieved neutral buoyancy even as the boys splashed into Sandy Bay. She was ready and waiting. So far, so good.

Making Waves hadn't dropped anchor yet, but they looked close to doing exactly that. *Big Catch* was slowing up . . . now close to 150 yards away. Angelica guessed she'd be on the bottom with the boys long before either of the other two teams of divers.

Wilson had the signal gun out and loaded. "When you surface and tell me you found the boat, I'm sending up a flare."

Angelica was itching to see him do exactly that.

Parker went over last-minute instructions with Wilson—who'd taken his shirt off—even though it wasn't all that warm. He claimed the machete slung on his back was all the warmth he needed. Did Wilson expect there'd be trouble—or was he just hoping there would be? He looked like he was ready to fight off pirates.

Ella leaned over the gunwale. "You okay, Jelly?"

Angelica nodded. Maybe *okay* was overly optimistic, but she didn't want the boys getting any second thoughts about her.

"We follow the anchor line to the bottom," Parker said. "We get our bearings. Check our compass. Then we spread out no more than fifteen feet apart. We stay in a line. Don't lose sight of each other. We all come back safe. Am I missing anything?"

"Yeah," Harley said. "Let's find that boat."

"Jelly!" Ella was at the gunwale again, with Kit at her side. "Remember what Grams said." She drew her finger across her own throat and held up three fingers with her other hand."

Right. Death comes in threes. *Comforting thought.* She raised her BCD deflater hose and released a bit more air until she slipped below the surface. Parker took the lead with a feet-first descent alongside the anchor line. The bottom would be, what, forty feet below them? Sixty? The anchor line disappeared into the dark nothingness below—like there was no bottom at all.

Parker moved fast, like he had no fears of Mr. White suddenly showing up. Angelica stayed close, trying not to fall behind. Parker could equalize the pressure in his sinuses and his ears without having to squeeze his nose. Which simply allowed him to go faster.

Angelica had never mastered that technique, so she kept her fingers on her nosepiece as she descended, constantly working to release the pressure so it wouldn't slow her—or the boys.

Harley followed Angelica. Twice he got too close, brushing her with his fins. Maybe that was his way of pushing her. Still, it felt safer positioned between them—although if a great white showed up, they'd all be in trouble. Angelica was sure that's why Uncle Vaughn and her own dad took search positions closer to Little Salvages. The closer to the rocks, the more seals. The more seals, the greater the chance of running into Mr. White.

Stop thinking about sharks, Angelica.

If only it were that easy.

CHAPTER 95

HARLEY DID A 360-DEGREE SCAN the moment the bottom loomed into view. The visibility was good. Plenty of rock, but no wreck.

Parks checked his compass, pointed in the direction of shore, and motioned for them to fan out. Parks on the north end. Harley south. Jelly on the equator.

Harley power-stroked ahead. The faster he went, the more bottom they'd cover, right? And that would up their chances of finding *Deep Trouble.*

He stayed a good fifteen feet off the bottom. He would use less air than being deeper, and he wanted to see as far into the distance as possible. Parks seemed to have the same idea. Jelly stayed so close to the bottom that her fins kicked up puffs of sand now and then. Maybe she thought a great white wouldn't scoot so close to the bottom to pick her off. Or maybe she figured she was faster this way. She grabbed handholds on rocks at times to pull herself along while she kicked. Good. She needed to keep up.

Parks flashed him an okay sign, and Harley signaled back. Without being obvious, he angled off a bit so their search would take in a wider section of the bottom. Parks was still in sight, but getting hazy.

Help us, God. Help us. Sometimes a simple prayer said it all. He pictured Mr. Bones wearing Pez's apron. Would Lochran really hurt her? Doggone right he would.

Fifteen minutes. Maybe twenty. Harley kept his eyes on the bottom, not the clock. Parker would watch the time. They covered ground fast, but stroke after stroke, they found no evidence of a wreck. No debris. Nothing.

He gave Parks a side glance. It was as if he'd been waiting for Harley to look his way. Parks tapped two fingers on his own forearm.

Busted. He'd been drawing hard on his tank, and he'd purposely not looked at his pressure reading.

Jelly signaled back her remaining pressure. How she didn't use more air was a mystery. If they could swap tanks, he'd be able to go a whole lot farther.

Parker tapped his forearm again.

Reluctantly, Harley checked his gauge, and signaled back his air pressure reading. They were basically doing a drift dive here so they wouldn't have to backtrack to find the boat. The boat would come to them when they surfaced. But still, Harley's tank pressure was lower than the others. Ultra-safe diving meant starting your ascent when your tank still had plenty of pressure for the return. There would be the safety stop at a depth of fifteen feet for three minutes, and it was stupid to push the limits—which Harley was already doing. It left no room for the unforeseen. The unexpected. And diving was all about preparing for the unexpected, wasn't it?

Harley pointed at an imaginary watch on his wrist. Held up five fingers. Maybe with five more minutes they'd find the boat.

Parker shook his head and jerked his thumb toward the surface.

Parker rounded up Jelly and power-stroked to Harley. Once more he tapped his forearm with two fingers—as if he didn't believe Harley's tank pressure was as low as he'd signaled.

Harley held his pressure gauge so Parker could read it. Immediately Parker unclipped his marker buoy. Filled it with air. He released a thumb-spool of nylon line, allowing the inflatable to soar for the surface, signaling Wilson where to pick them up.

Jelly's eyes were wide, like she'd seen a ghost. Maybe it was the shadows. The cold. That feeling that you're all alone in a world where you'd die without the tank strapped to your back.

All that could mess with anybody's head. And right now, Jelly's head was on a swivel. Looking to one side, then the other. Checking behind them. The girl was on the edge, losing her nerve—like she was the one with the low air in her tank instead of Harley. She'd kept up. He had to give her that. But he was pretty sure she'd had enough and wouldn't be joining them on dive two.

Yeah, it was time to go up. To stay longer was downright risky. But if they didn't find *Deep Trouble*? Honestly, that seemed a whole lot more dangerous.

CHAPTER 96

"THERE!" ELLA POINTED at the orange marker buoy that broke the surface a good seventy-five yards away. The words *DIVER BELOW* ran the entire length of the six-foot signal buoy. "Maybe they found the boat, right?"

Wilson checked the time. "Doubtful. Likely they're low on air and they're coming up."

"Wow, aren't you Johnny Raincloud today."

"I just don't want to get carried away by emotions," Wilson said.

"You'd need to actually *have* emotions before you could get carried away by them."

Wilson pointed toward the Salvages. "Maybe you haven't noticed the fog is on the prowl."

Or as Grams would have said, *on the hunt*. Ella had been so focused on watching the surface of the water with Kit that she hadn't noticed the fog creeping in like a stalker. Little Salvages had been swallowed up completely. And with it, *Big Catch*. The lobster boat was nowhere to be seen. *Making Waves* was more of a fuzzy silhouette in a darkening sky.

"Finding the boat was a long shot," Wilson said.

"Parker never said that. And neither did Harley."

Wilson fired up the motor and let it idle. "They didn't have to. We all knew." He pulled up the anchor line, hand over hand, stopping every few seconds to coil it. "And now with the fog, the chances of a second dive are going way down."

What he said made sense, even though Ella wasn't quite ready to admit it. "We *have* to find the boat."

The moment Wilson had the anchor on board, he stood at the console and spun the wheel toward the inflatable.

Ella held on to the console and studied *Making Waves*. The captain was the only one on board, so Mr. Buckman and his ranger friend were still down. No marker buoys had been sent up. And no red flares, either.

Ella shifted her focus back to the inflatable signal marker, standing straight up like maybe someone was pulling on the line from below. She shaded her eyes to block out the lowering sun. She had an urge to call Grams. She'd seemed so uneasy when Ella left. "Death comes in threes, Ella-girl. One to go . . . and I fear today is the day. Take no chances, you hear me? Keep your cross close."

Ella reached for her necklace. What if they didn't take a second dive? They'd be safe that way, right? But if they didn't find the boat, Pez's risk skyrocketed. Either way, someone was at risk of becoming the third victim.

"Shouldn't they have surfaced by now?"

Wilson didn't answer. Maybe he was wondering the same thing.

"The inflatable . . . could it mean they need help?"

Wilson avoided her question for a moment. "They're okay."

"Is that a blood-brother thing . . . like you can sense somehow that they're not in trouble?"

Wilson shook his head. "Just before we anchored, Parker prayed."

Ella should have been praying more herself. "Prayer is good."

"It works for Bucky. I've seen it."

She had too. But prayer wasn't a guarantee that everything would be okay. She'd seen that, too. Had Mike Ironwing shot a prayer heavenward when he realized he was in danger? He might have. Kind of an instinct thing. And what about Uncle Ray? That instant he'd realized an inmate was bringing a deadly message from Lochran, might he have prayed? Entirely possible. Prayer didn't always change things. God was God . . . not a three-wish genie.

Wilson approached the inflatable marker slowly. A cauldron of bubbles boiled around the thing. "They're likely all together, waiting out their three minutes at fifteen feet. But keep a weather eye out for bubbles anyplace outside the group. I'd rather not clip someone on their ascent."

Suddenly a head broke the surface. Then two more. Kit yipped and wagged her tail. Ella took a deep breath, not realizing until that moment that she'd been holding it—or for how long.

"Chalk one up for prayer." Ella motioned like she was adding a hashmark to an invisible scoreboard. "Looks like everything is okay."

Wilson set the anchor and cut the engine. "Let's hope that doesn't change as quick as the weather does around here."

CHAPTER 97

PARKER ADDED A SHOT OF AIR TO HIS BCD. Wilson hustled to the stern to help them aboard. Treading water on the surface was the worst. He hated not seeing what might be below him. Closing in. He couldn't shake the gut feeling that they needed to get out of the water—*fast*.

Harley motioned Jelly onto the swim platform to one side of the motor. Which was good. Something had spooked her, and as much as Parker wanted to get in the boat himself, he felt a definite bit of relief when Jelly climbed aboard.

Harley boosted himself onto the swim platform on one side of the motor, and Parker did the same on the other—although his gimpy arm slowed him a bit.

Jelly had already shimmied out of her BCD and reached for Parker. "C'mon, c'mon." She motioned with both hands—but didn't meet his eyes. She scanned the surface instead. "Get your feet out of the water, okay?"

He handed her his fins. Wilson grabbed one shoulder of Parker's vest and lifted. What was with the assist? Had Parker missed something?

Kit greeted Harley with squirms and wiggles.

The instant Parker climbed aboard, he glanced back at the waters he'd just left. They looked darker somehow. If something had been there, he'd have never seen it until too late.

"Jelly—what did you see?"

She shook her head. "Nothing." But she still kept her focus on the surface. "I mean, I thought I saw something—just on the edge of our sight line."

He stared at her, waiting for more.

"Jelly?" Wilson waved his hand in front of her eyes. "Are you going to tell us, or what?"

"There's nothing to tell. I just had a funny feeling when we grouped up on the bottom."

"Funny, as in, you thought up a hilarious joke?" Wilson smiled. "Because if you did, we could all use a laugh."

"I had the sense we were being watched—and the feeling didn't let up all through our safety stop. Then we'd just started our final ascent . . . and I thought I saw a shadow—within a shadow. I tried to signal you." Jelly looked right at Parker now. "But you were a couple strokes ahead. When I looked back, the shadow was gone."

Okay, that was creepy.

"It was stupid." Jelly dropped into the bow seat. "I probably imagined the whole thing."

"Stupid," Wilson said. He pulled a T-shirt over his head. "Let's go with that."

"Or not." Ella handed Jelly a towel and sat beside her. "What did you *think* you saw?"

Her eyes begged Ella to drop it.

"You heard her. She imagined it." Wilson raised one hand like he was taking an oath in a courtroom. "If there were any *real* danger, my Miccosukee Early Warning System would've kicked in." He held his forearm out for everyone to see. "No goosebumps. No hair standing up straight. So no danger."

Sure, Jelly had gotten herself all worked up about things in the past. Disasters that had never happened. But who hadn't? She also had a sense about things—a way of knowing danger was near long before Parker did. And the truth was, even he'd felt *something* while he waited his turn to climb into the boat, right?

"Not so fast, straight arrow," Ella said. "I sensed some kind of danger for you all while I was in the boat. Now we hear Jelly felt it too. What do you call that?"

"Predictable. Par for the course. Or it might be the fact that you two have the MH gene." Wilson shrugged. "Take your pick."

"MH." Jelly glared at him. "This is when I'm supposed to take your bait—and ask you what it means, right?"

Wilson smiled. "Since you asked . . . MH . . . the Mass Hysteria gene."

"Ha-ha, Wilson." Ella hugged Jelly. "You make fun of what you don't understand. Maybe, when this is all over, we'll tell you the story of the Masterson house, and see if you boys don't suddenly develop the MH gene yourselves."

They all laughed, but it was short-lived.

"The real question is what we do about the second dive." Wilson nodded his head toward the fogbank. "By the time you give yourselves some surface time, I think the game is over."

The thing was so much bigger—or closer—than when they'd gone down. Neither of the other two boats were visible. Normally they'd wait an hour between dives. To let their bodies warm up, for sure. More importantly, every minute on the surface allowed them to shed nitrogen that naturally built up inside them with the compressed air they'd been breathing. "Wilson's right," Parker said. "In an hour we'll be totally socked in. Wilson and Ella won't see us surface." Which could prove disastrous.

"So we dive sooner," Harley had already removed his regulator and

BCD from his spent tank. "We got time on the clock for one more play." He slipped his BCD onto a fresh tank and clamped it in place.

Even the suggestion made Parker's heart pump faster. They could do it, sure. But it wasn't the most cautious route. And when they started shortcutting, they were asking for trouble, weren't they? "Let's give ourselves thirty minutes of surface time—then see."

Harley screwed his regulator on the new tank. "Fifteen."

Just enough time to swap out tanks and gear back up. Rushing a second dive was reckless. It wasn't a matter of Parker meeting Harley all the way . . . this was about staying safe. "Harley—"

"We wait thirty, and the fog will be worse—and we'll have to call the game."

If the fog wrapped them in its wings, they'd be insane to go down again. Without direct sunlight, the bottom would be a whole lot darker too. Sunset was set for 7:32, but between it being low in the sky—and filtered out by fog? Sunset would feel a whole lot earlier than that.

"Look," Harley said. "We've still got a window." He nodded toward the fogbank. "But it's closing fast. Just a quick dive. The way I'm chugging the air, it won't be a long one anyway. Twenty minutes. Let me run the ball one more time."

Parker turned off his air, released the purge valve, and unscrewed his regulator from his spent tank. Jelly watched him—like she wasn't sure if he was packing things up or switching to a second tank himself. Even Kit seemed confused. Ears flat back against her head.

"We can do this," Harley said. "We have to." He picked up his phone and stared at the screen. "It's five thirty. We have ninety minutes to come up with the evidence."

"We have until 9 p.m.," Jelly said.

Harley shook his head. "We have to get it to shore—to the lawyer—so he can deal with Lochran before it's too late." He held up his phone. "I've got no signal. I don't even know if Kilbro got Miss Lopez someplace safe." He thumped his forehead with his fist. "Why didn't I have her come with?"

That last bit was all Parker needed to hear. He released the clamp holding his tank to his BCD. He slid the buoyancy-compensating vest over the top and onto the spare tank.

Relief swept over Harley's face. "Let's do this." His hands were practically a blur. He cranked the air valve open on his regulator. Shrugged on his BCD. Buckled it. His hood was still in place. Now he stretched his mask over it but left it in a raised position over his forehead.

Jelly started the process of swapping tanks without a word. But her face said plenty, especially the way her mouth formed a straight, tight line. Wilson took the thumb spool and began reeling in the line for the marker buoy. Even he looked uneasy.

"Hold on." Ella gripped her cross necklace. "Guys, let's use our heads—not just our hearts."

"I'm using both." Harley drove his feet into his fins but didn't pull the heel straps in place. "My head says I can do this. My heart says I have to. If we wait—even thirty minutes—what if the weather gets worse? What if the other boats abort their second dive—and signal us to do the same?"

"Listen to me." Ella put her hands on Harley's shoulders. "Just stop and hear me out. Sit. *Please.*"

Harley sat on the gunwale of *Wings*, reached for Kit, and looked at her face.

"Grams was really uneasy when we left. I know you think she's just superstitious. But death comes in threes—and we've already had two." Ella didn't break eye contact. "Jelly sensed something bad just before surfacing. And I had a really bad feeling at about the same time. Can't you see what's happening?"

"My uncle was a bad man . . . and maybe some of that clung to his boat. Maybe you sensed something bad because we're so close to *Deep Trouble*. We have to finish, El."

"What if it was a great white that was close?" Ella took Harley's face between both hands. "Because that's what my heart was telling me."

Harley shook his head. "It was the boat. *Deep Trouble.*"

"Death happens in threes. Harley, come *on*!"

"What if you're right . . . and number three is Miss Lopez?" Harley squeezed his eyes shut like he was trying to break free of Ella's spell. "This is my last chance to stop it. Right here. Right now."

"But what if the third person is Parker—or Jelly? You'd risk *them*?"

Harley's shoulders slumped. He locked eyes with Parker for a moment. Gave a deep sigh. "Not in a million years."

"You think there's still time on the clock. But I think the game is over, Harley. I'm so sorry." And Ella really sounded sorry too.

He stared at the fog bank. Looked down into the water for a few long moments. "Okay, Parks. Jelly. Take thirty minutes—then you call it . . . dive or no dive. I won't risk either of you."

Ella hugged him. "Thank you! I knew you were bigger than that."

"Bigger?" Harley shook his head. "I never felt smaller."

CHAPTER 98

ANGELICA WASN'T READY TO DO CARTWHEELS. Not yet. Something felt off. Had Harley given up too easily—or was she overanalyzing him?

Clearly El didn't share her sense of foreboding. If the boat were big enough, she'd probably be skipping from one end to the other. Parker's shoulders looked relaxed, too, like he believed they were done. He started readying his gear for another dive, but slowly. Even she could tell he was just going through the motions. She'd follow his lead.

Maybe what Angelica had seen below—or thought she'd seen—was messing with her ability to think rationally. But what if she was right?

She secured her fresh tank to her BCD. Switched her regulator over. Turned on the air—all while keeping an eye on Harley.

Harley felt for the heel strap of one fin and slid it in place. Casual and slow, like he didn't want to draw any attention to what he was doing.

Dread swept over Angelica. She'd been right. Ella hadn't talked Harley out of anything. But he wasn't going to risk Parker or Jelly's safety either. He was going down . . . *alone*.

Part of her wanted to scream to Wilson to pull Harley off the side of the boat. Keep him from doing something absolutely stupid. But wouldn't that be just falling right back into her protector mode . . . the one that usually got her in trouble?

Death comes in threes. What if Harley was the third death that Grams had warned about? Stopping him was for his own good. How could that be wrong? But if she kept him from doing what he believed he had to do . . . how could that be right? Might her attempt to save his life . . . end up hurting him terribly? If something happened to Pez, he'd never forgive himself . . . or her.

God, what do I do? She'd been all about finding her own way for so long, and where had it gotten her?

Show me, God. Maybe she needed to play this more like Parker. He seemed to know what Harley needed—and met him where he was at.

But right now, Parker seemed clueless as to what was really happening. He'd swapped out his spent tank for the new one, but the thing was still sitting on the deck, propped between his knees. She caught his eyes. Did her very best to speak to him—without saying a word. Hoped he'd catch what she was trying to say. She deliberately looked down at her own hand—glancing back to make sure he followed her gaze. The instant he did, she made a couple of quick circles with her index finger. *Speed it up, Parker. Gear up—fast.* She darted her eyes toward Harley— hoping he'd get the hint to do the same.

Harley eased the second heel strap in place. Pulled Kit close. Whispered something in her ear. Kit's ears went back—like he'd told her exactly what he planned to do.

Maybe it was Angelica's imagination, but Parker seemed to pale just a bit. He nodded, and quietly began readying his gear faster. Okay, he got it.

Angelica reached for her fins and stacked them at her feet. Parker was maybe sixty seconds from being fully geared up. Angelica would be ready the instant he was.

Wilson finished reeling in the *DIVER BELOW* buoy and pulled it aboard—but didn't deflate it.

Ella was still flying high—relief all over her face. "I say we go back right now and make sure Miss Lopez is safe." She smiled, like she thought Harley would be all over that.

"She won't be safe without that evidence." Harley looked at the fog-bank. "I get it. The game's over—for all of you. But I'm going into overtime." Harley seated his mask over his face, slapped his mouthpiece in place, and did a perfect backward roll off the gunwale.

"Harley—no!" Ella leaned over the side—staring at the frenzy of bubbles and foam where Harley had disappeared. Kit leaped in after him.

Parker clipped into his BCD. "Jelly—stay. I'll be faster without you."

She shook her head. "The way he gulps air—he'll need to share with me to make it back. I'll catch up. Go!"

Parker pulled on his fins. "We follow his bubbles. We'll get a visual on him before he levels off at the bottom if we hurry."

"Please—go!" She motioned toward the water and seated her mask.

Kit yipped, swimming in a tight circle over Harley's bubbles.

Parker looked torn. "I can't lose you while I chase him."

Wilson jammed the thumb spool into Parker's gloved hand. "Play out the line as you go down. I'll follow the float the whole time so I won't lose you if the fog gets worse. Jelly will follow your line to catch you. Move it, Preacher Boy!"

Parker glanced at Jelly for a second—and she gave a quick nod. He seated his mask and rolled over the side.

"What have I done?" Ella wailed—looking half-dazed. "Something terrible will happen!"

"Jelly." Wilson grabbed both of her wrists.

Did he feel her pulse pounding, even through the wet suit?

"You ready?"

Geared up—yes. Ready? Not remotely.

"Bucky will catch him. Nobody gets to the bottom quicker." He brought her mouthpiece to her lips. "Follow that buoy line—that's all you need to do. It'll lead right to Bucky. I'll get the dog back in the boat. Go!"

She rolled backward—barely missing Kit. She splashed below the surface and bobbed back up again. The *DIVER BELOW* buoy twenty feet away, trembling like it feared this whole thing would end badly. Angelica swam on the surface, chasing hard after the buoy.

Diving alone—hoping to catch the boys? Terrifying. But waiting it out in the boat scared her more. She couldn't protect the boys. But she could help them. She reached Parker's buoy. Closed her hand around the towline. Looked back. Ella still looked stunned. Wilson flashed her an okay sign, like this was a casual dive to the bottom of a pool instead of Sandy Bay.

God—help me! She released the air in her BCD and slid below the surface.

She hadn't dropped ten feet before turning and piking for a headfirst descent. It would be faster—and meant less time alone. She pushed herself. One hand gripping her nose to equalize, one hand circling the lifeline leading her to Parker—and hopefully Harley.

The thin nylon line vanished just feet in front of her—much quicker than the anchor line had disappeared. No bubbles . . . just green-black nothingness. *Parker, where are you?*

Based on the angle of the line, Parker was way ahead. His bubbles must have risen too far in front of her to see. She pumped hard—already feeling the weakness in her thigh. Despite that, her fins propelled her deeper—at a faster rate than she'd ever gone before. She had nothing to prove by conserving air this time. She just had to get to the boys—fast.

What had she sensed when she'd been down before? She'd seen a shadow—or was it her imagination? *Dear God . . . help me, help me. Don't let me see a great white. I'm begging you, God!* This was the time she was supposed to make God some kind of promise, right? *If you do this for me—I promise to . . . what?* But what could she promise him? What could she offer him that would make him jump to answer her prayer? Nothing. Not a thing. She wasn't the kind of Christian Parker was. She never had been. Maybe she'd been working so hard to control things, she'd never fully surrendered to the one who was truly in control.

I'm scared, God. I just need you. I have for a long time . . . I just didn't know it.

The nylon cord was taut, like Parker was going so fast that the reel couldn't let line out quick enough. What if it snapped?

She counted strokes. *I'll see him in twenty strokes. Twenty really, really hard strokes.* When she hit twenty, she did it again—but upped it to fifty this time.

God. Please.

That profound sense of doom was back. The great white? She scanned a full 180 degrees but didn't slow to look behind her. A predator was near—and she was the prey. She'd prayed she wouldn't see a great white. She should've been more specific. *Sensing* the shark was near but not *seeing* it was worse. *God, I need to amend my prayer. Keep the sharks away!*

Twenty more strokes. Angelica spotted the silvery wobble of rising bubbles. She tapped into an energy-reserves locker she didn't know she had. Moments later she saw his silhouette. Parker was swimming parallel to Harley, but upside down, watching for her. Motioning her toward him. *Thank you, God!*

Parker tapped Harley, and the two of them waited for her to catch up.

If it weren't for all the gear, she would have wrapped them both in her arms and never let go.

Only when she was between them did she let free of the line to the *DIVER BELOW* buoy. And the boys didn't fan out. They stayed way closer to her than on the first dive. Were they doing it for her sake—or did they feel that eerie presence too?

The boys stayed a good twenty-five feet off the bottom. She could see farther than she had on dive one. But she also felt more exposed. If a shark closed in, there'd be no rock to duck behind. She'd be shark bait. They all would. Great whites were always on the hunt. And likely the three of them had been detected the moment they splashed into Sandy Bay.

Angelica had the growing dread that a predator was silently gaining on them. Ready to pick off a straggler. But she didn't dare look back. It would slow her momentarily—which would be a mistake. It took everything she had just to keep up with the boys—and the idea of falling behind them, even a few feet, was all the incentive she needed to drive her forward.

Parker checked his air. Seemed satisfied. Checked the compass and pointed to course correct. They were headed directly west, toward shore. The normally controlled, even comforting sound of her regulator had gone AWOL on this dive. The hiss of sucking air and gentle rumble of exhaled bubbles came at a much more desperate rate this time. She'd been in survival mode, hadn't cared how fast she emptied her tank. Judging by the bubbles tumbling from the boys, they were gulping air a lot faster than they normally did too. *Easy, Angelica. Steady that breathing.*

They pumped ahead. Five minutes. Maybe ten. Rock. Sand. Kelpy seaweed. Over and over and over.

Parker's head didn't move side-to-side. He focused straight ahead, probably relying on his peripheral vision to pick up any sign of the wreck. Harley had the same laser-focus thing going. Like he thought the key to finding *Deep Trouble* was getting more yardage. The boys crept ahead of her. Just a few feet. Had they forgotten she was there?

Angelica kept her head moving left to right for a wide visual sweep. Another long five minutes passed. It seemed like it anyway. And then . . . and then there was a shadow at the edges of her visibility to the south. Dark as a rock, but the lines weren't right. The shape seemed undeniable.

Neither of the boys noticed. They would've pointed—and immediately veered that way. *Stop them, Angelica!* But they were out of reach—and she didn't dare take her eyes off the wreck. It was barely visible as it was.

There's a way to shout into a mouthpiece without letting in a drip of water. She'd done it before—and had seen firsthand how nearby divers can actually hear it. Angelica filled her lungs—and screamed. Long. Hard. And she didn't let up.

Immediately both boys whirled around—their masks showcasing the alarm in their eyes.

She pointed frantically. They followed her finger to the dark hulk that had the unmistakable lines of a lobster boat. And in that instant, the boys each let out screams that could've been heard on the surface.

CHAPTER 99

PARKER'S LITTLE PLAN FOR THE THREE OF THEM to stay close together went right out the porthole. It was a race to the wreck, and Harley had pulled ahead. There was barely any break in the stream of bubbles rising from his friend. Like Harley was chugging so hard he might hyperventilate if he kept it up.

He glanced back. Jelly had fallen a full body length behind. She motioned for him to keep going.

The murky wreck took on shape and detail. The size was right. White, just like Uncle Ray's. And by the level of growth on the hull—or lack of it—the thing clearly hadn't been on the bottom for a year. Parker had cleaned hulls that hadn't been touched in twelve months, and they looked way worse.

The three of them approached from the starboard side, where a massive hole and gash had been punched into the hull below the waterline—in roughly the shape of an old-fashioned keyhole. The damage was definitely consistent with the type of fatal wound *Deep Trouble* had received from Little Salvages.

This has to be it. Thank you, God! This is it, right?

Harley angled downward on a final descent. Parker held up for a couple of seconds to let Jelly pass, then followed just far enough behind her fin tips not to get his mask knocked off.

Harley swung around the transom and instantly raised both hands in the air like he'd just scored a touchdown. Jelly and Parker joined him. Sure enough, *Deep Trouble* was painted along the width of the stern.

The three of them gathered in a group hug that Parker could only describe as joyous—and he was pretty sure he'd never used that word before in his life.

Deep Trouble had come to rest on its port side, exposing most of the keel, the entire rudder, and the propeller. No wonder the salvage diver didn't want to give the location. There was plenty left to scavenge.

Parker tied his signal-marker line to a cleat on the starboard gunwale. He checked his pressure gauge—and practically swallowed his regulator. He'd gulped down over sixty percent of his tank. Technically, he should have started his ascent before they'd even spotted the wreck.

He tapped two fingers against his forearm. Jelly signaled back: 1600 pounds of pressure. She still had a solid half tank left. Harley tapped out his answer: 800 pounds.

Not good.

Parker pointed to the surface with his thumb. At the rate he'd been using air, if Harley didn't go up—like right now—he might run out before they finished their three-minute safety stop at fifteen feet. They'd leave the buoy tied to *Deep Trouble* and signal the other boats once they got to the surface. If they hadn't taken their second dive, they'd have fresh tanks, right?

Harley tossed his gauge aside and pointed at the pilot house. Without hesitation, he pulled himself over the transom and raced for the gaping black hole leading to the cabin hold below.

Parker and Jelly followed. The hold was dark as sin. Why that expression went through his mind, Parker had no idea. But honestly, it looked darker than a basement closet—and twice as creepy. Wearing a tank, only one of them would be able to squeeze through the opening into the cabin. But there was no time even for that. Not for Harley, anyway. And clearly, he had no intention of aborting the mission. *Even in darkness. God, help us . . . even in darkness.*

Harley fumbled with the flashlight clipped to his BCD. Parker grabbed his arm to stop him. Jerked his thumb to the surface. They had to go up. Unless . . .

Parker pointed at Harley, then at the line leading to the surface and the *DIVER BELOW* buoy. *Follow it up, Harley.* It would break their safety code to split up, but with the line tied to the cleat, they would still be connected. Sort of.

Parker pointed to himself and Jelly—then to the black space below deck.

The desperation in Harley's eyes showed he understood. He had to surface—and trust Jelly and Parker would find the hidden dry bag. He squeezed his eyes shut in agony. That was clear enough for Parker to read. To be this close . . . and not finish the job? Parker knew his friend well enough. Harley needed to see the mission through. But that was impossible now. And there was no backup tank aboard *Wings*. Harley's dive was over.

Or was it? Maybe there was still a chance to meet Harley all the way.

CHAPTER 100

ELLA STUDIED HOW THE BUOY RODE in the water. It was standing upright like it was at attention now. "They've stopped."

Even Kit stared at the surface, unblinking, like she knew Harley was connected to it somehow.

Wilson stood at the gunwale and watched it for a few moments. "Agreed."

"You think they found it?" Ella could hear the doubt in her own voice.

Wilson didn't look all that hopeful. "Based on the clock? They're on their way up. Likely at the three-minute safety stop."

Ella checked the time. "They've already been down longer than their first dive."

Wilson started the motor, and crept close to the buoy. "We tried."

But they'd failed. A loneliness closed in as deep and thick as the fog that blocked the other boats—and now even land—from view.

She pictured Mr. Bones. Wearing Pez's apron. She'd been so worried about her friends taking this second dive—especially with Grams's warning in mind. *Death comes in threes.* But what if it wasn't them at all? What if Harley's fears were right? Without the evidence, it was Pez who was in the greatest danger.

Ella checked her phone. Still no signal. She had the desperate urge to call Pez. To tell her to hide. Lay low somewhere until this blew over. They had to get back to shore . . . like now. With no land in sight, it felt like they were in the middle of the Atlantic.

She stared at the water surrounding the buoy, willing the three of them to surface. But there wasn't a bit of surface disturbance. Which was odd. The three of them, sucking air just fifteen feet below? The surface should be bubbling like a Jacuzzi.

The boat's name plaque caught her eye: *Wings of the Dawn.* And that verse that had inspired Parker was engraved in a smaller font just below it: *"If I rise on the wings of the dawn, if I settle on the far side of the sea, even there your hand will guide me, your right hand will hold me fast."*

Was God guiding Parker even now—at the *bottom* of the sea? Would God hold him tight?

The water around the buoy remained still. "If they were at the safety stop, shouldn't we see bubbles?"

Wilson stood on the gunwale for a better angle, using one hand to steady himself against the hard-top roof over the driving console. "Okay . . . so they're still on the bottom—but staying put. Which means one of two things. Maybe three."

One was obvious. "They found the boat?"

"Could be." But he sounded doubtful. "Or somebody got separated, and the other two are waiting to surface—hoping they'll find them."

Ella fought a sense of panic. "And the third option?"

Wilson slid his machete from its sheath. "Something has them pinned down—and they don't feel it's safe to surface."

Tears blurred her vision. Grams's voice was in Ella's head again—but this time she couldn't push it away.

CHAPTER 101

HARLEY STARED AT PARKS. He'd slipped off his BCD and tank rig, and shook it in front of Harley. Parks still had the regulator in his mouth. He shook the pack again, and his meaning was clear. Jelly watched, wide-eyed. Parker always used less air than Harley . . . and a simple swap would even things out. Harley could stay down longer—and Parker could make Harley's tank stretch.

Parker reached for Harley's BCD release clips, and the motion spurred Harley back into action.

In seconds Harley was free of his vest and shrugging into Parker's. He loosened the straps some, then clipped the buckles. Only then did Parker remove his regulator and hand it to Harley. Harley did the same with his.

Parker handed Harley his flashlight—and motioned toward the dark hold. Instantly Harley ducked through the hatch leading below deck.

The cabin was absolute chaos. Tools. Foul weather gear. Coiled nylon ropes. An anchor line free and covering the floor and low side of the bulkhead. Lobster scooted on spiky legs to avoid the beam.

Below the place where some might crash,
in a bag not meant for trash.

The mattress was half off, now the bed for dozens of barnacles. He scooted the mattress back in place, revealing a series of latched doors in the cabinet below.

Harley flipped a lever, pulled open the compartment door, and trained the light inside. Junk mostly. No dry bag.

The second was the same. Parks had another flashlight out—and from his spot just outside the scuttle, he kept a beam on the wall of compartments.

Harley hit pay dirt on the third try. He stared at the royal blue waterproof bag floating against the roof of the cubbyhole. The fact that it was still buoyant proved no water had forced its way in. *Thank you, God!*

He grabbed the bag and held it up for Parks to see. Harley couldn't help but stare at it for a long moment. Whatever was inside got Uncle Ray killed. Miss Lopez could die too—if he didn't get it back quick enough.

Watch your time, there's not a heap,
soon you'll be in trouble deep.

Parker's air had to be dangerously low. *Move, Harley, get out of here!*

Turning around inside the tiny cabin proved to be trickier than he thought—especially with all the debris his fins kicked up. A rope coiled around his leg like a boa constrictor. The more furiously he shook his fin, the more snarled his foot got. Holding the bag and flashlight was bad enough, but trying to unravel the mess with one gloved hand? Impossible.

Keeping his legs still, he pulled himself out of the hold. Parker spotted the problem immediately. He unsheathed his knife—and went to work.

Jelly had that worried look going on. She tapped her forearm with two fingers. Harley checked the gauge and signaled back. He was okay. Not great, but okay. Parker had sawed through a rope—and was trying to slide the rest over Harley's fin—which wasn't cooperating.

Harley tapped Parks hard—and signed for his air pressure reading.

Parker held up the gauge. Harley's heart hammered out a warning as soon as he saw how deep in the red the air was. Harley peeled the heel strap down and kicked his fin off, freeing himself from the last of the coils tethering him to *Deep Trouble*. The fin dropped to the deck, sending up a cloud of silt. Even here gravity took over, and the fin slid down the sloping deck to where it met the gunwale.

Parker looked like he was about to chase the fin down, but Harley motioned frantically toward the surface with his thumb. They'd already pushed it way too long. He could buy new fins.

Harley signaled Jelly to begin their ascent. She shook her head furiously, eyes wide. She glanced at the deck like she'd seen something there. Immediately she studied the waters overhead, then looked back at the deck.

Now Parker was doing the same, like he was trying to figure out what had Jelly so spooked. He held up his pressure gauge and pointed to the surface.

Jelly held up both hands, palms toward them. She pointed at her eyes. Pointed at the deck. Okay . . . she saw something?

And then Harley saw it. Just the hint of a shadow passed over *Deep Trouble*'s deck. Like maybe Wilson had pulled up overhead in *Wings*. Waiting for them to surface.

But they were in nearly sixty feet of water. Too deep to see the shadow of the boat on the surface, even on a sunny day. No . . . what had passed overhead was big—but a lot closer than the surface.

He looked up at Jelly. She had one hand on her head symbolizing a dorsal fin. Whether she'd actually seen it, or just its shadow . . . he knew she was right.

> Watch out for Lochran, and Mr. White,
> both have a nasty appetite.
> They'll take your life, they'll take your soul,
> They swallow careless dummies whole.

Of all the times for Uncle Ray to be right. Wilson and Ella weren't the only ones waiting for them to surface. Mr. White was on the hunt.

CHAPTER 102

STILL NO BUBBLES. Ella stared at the water surrounding the *DIVER BELOW* marker. "What if the line got tangled on something? What if Parker just left the buoy there and they're already on the surface—but lost in the fog?"

"We'd hear him whistle. But Parker wouldn't ditch the buoy. It's dangerous."

"So is stretching their tank limits." She checked the time. "Harley practically sucked his first tank dry—and they've been down longer this dive."

Wilson didn't answer. He held his machete like a club. How did he expect to help them with that?

KitKat stretched over the gunwale. Sniffed at the water. Yipped.

Suddenly the marker buoy jetted away from them so fast the thing threw a wake. The bottom two feet got dragged below the surface—and the top of the buoy leaned at a forty-five-degree angle with the speed and force of whatever was on the other end of that line.

"Jelly was holding that line," Wilson said. "And that buoy was clipped to Parker!"

No human could swim at a fraction of that speed. "No!" Ella cried out.

Wilson stood beside her, machete in hand. "Hello, Mr. White," he whispered.

Suddenly the buoy stopped, bobbed once, then dropped on its side in the water. Clearly there was no tension on the line. It had been cut— or bitten through.

Grams was right. Death came in threes. And now death had swallowed its third victim.

CHAPTER 103

PARKER'S TANK COULD'VE BEEN EMPTY—but it wouldn't have mattered. He was still holding his breath. The great white had passed no more than twenty feet overhead. Close enough to see its teeth, gills pulsing like giant baffles, and eyes that looked as dead as the death they brought.

The monster swam right into the marker-buoy line, snapping it like a length of dental floss—even as part of it got stuck between its teeth. The moment the line touched the corner of its mouth, the thing took off with a burst of speed that rivaled the fastest quick-draw gator attack Parker had ever seen. The monster melted into the blue-green dark and disappeared.

But it wasn't gone. *Even in darkness light dawns . . . God . . . we need some light.*

Jelly clung to his arm, still staring in the direction the shark had disappeared. Harley stared too, but at least he was breathing. Harley piked and scooped his fin off the bottom and slipped it back on.

The last thing Parker wanted to do was surface. They'd be sitting ducks—and outside of a gator attack, he couldn't think of anything worse than being taken by a shark. If only they could stay right aboard *Deep Trouble* until somebody phoned for Uber Submarine Service. The pilothouse doubled nicely as a shark cage . . . or a crypt if they actually stayed. He checked his gauge. It confirmed what he already knew. If he didn't head for the surface, like right now, it wouldn't be a sub picking him up. It'd be a search-and-recovery team.

He jerked his thumb toward the surface. Harley looked scared but nodded. Terror haunted Jelly's eyes. She gripped his arm tighter.

Parker folded his hands together in front of him—reminding them to pray. Harley flashed him an okay sign, then clipped the dry bag to his BCD and pointed his thumb straight up. With one last look in the direction the great white had disappeared, they pushed off.

Jelly stayed between them, holding on to Harley with one hand and Parker with the other. With every stroke, they rose farther from the safety of the *Deep Trouble* pilothouse and deeper into the killing fields of the great white.

God, help us. God, help us. Parker's prayer wasn't flashy, but it was the best he could do. *You made every creature, even that man-eater. Keep him away, Lord. Keep him away.*

Parker sucked hard for every breath now, like he was breathing through a straw. His gauge showed what he already knew. He'd never make it through the three-minute safety stop. Drown or get eaten by a shark . . . two nightmare ways to die. Surface too fast, and he'd be asking for decompression sickness. Another deadly option.

Jelly must have seen his gauge. She let go of him only long enough to hand him her extra regulator on the octopus; then she grabbed him tighter than ever.

He drew in a couple of deep, grateful, breaths from her tank. At twenty feet his computer kicked in, starting the three-minute safety stop. Honestly? If he saw even a shadow of that great white, he'd claw for the surface with his two friends—whether the time was up or not.

Harley kept scanning. Jelly motioned for the surface. Parker worked his fins slowly to stay at depth. He held up two fingers. Two minutes to go.

Mr. White could be anywhere. *Oh, God. Oh, God. Help us.* They'd come so far. Had pretty much done the impossible—all thanks to God. He watched the gauge count down the seconds.

Thirty seconds to go. Twenty. Ten. Close enough. Parker started the ascent with Harley and Jelly keeping pace. The surface—in sight. The shadow of *Wings*—right there. Now might be the worst part. Surfacing, bobbing on the waves until they got in the boat. And wondering if Mr. White was racing up from the depths . . . to satisfy his nasty appetite.

CHAPTER 104

ANGELICA SURFACED NOT TEN FEET FROM *WINGS*. Instantly, she inflated her BCD with a shot of air.

Wilson stood at the transom alongside Ella, motioning her over, faces drawn with fear. "About time. Where's—?"

"Great white!" Angelica struck out for the boat.

Harley and Parker rose from a cauldron of bubbles—surfacing on either side of Jelly. They grabbed the bottom of her tank and propelled her to *Wings*.

Wilson leaned far over the side, stretching for her. "Move it, move it, move it!"

"Hurry, Jelly!" Ella scanned the surface of the water.

Parker clawed at the heel straps of Jelly's fins and winged them into the boat.

She grasped the edge of the swim platform. Wilson and Ella pulled while the other two boosted her out of the water. She clambered over the side and dropped to the deck in a heap.

"Bucky, Harley, let's go!" Immediately, Wilson was leaning over the transom again.

With Ella's help, Angelica scooted clear on all fours. She ditched her gear even as Wilson gave Parker a hand, and he tumbled into the boat.

Parker shed his BCD and scrambled to assist Wilson tugging Harley over the transom. The three of them dropped onto the deck in a tangled mass of arms and legs and scuba gear.

For a moment, none of them moved. Angelica actually held her breath, expecting Mr. White to crash through the boat in some frenzied vendetta to get at them.

Kit was all over Harley. Nuzzling. Play-biting. Tail fanning fast enough to fill a sail if the boat had one. Harley pulled her close and roughed her up a bit. "I'm back, girl. I told you, right?"

Angelica was pretty sure even KitKat realized how close they'd come to not making it at all.

Harley held up the dry bag. "Well, that was fun."

"Shark!" Ella pointed at a dorsal fin neatly slicing through the water—heading right for the starboard side of *Wings*. "He just passed under the boat!"

Wings seemed way too small. Angelica crawled to the other side and peered over the gunwale, but Mr. White was gone. "Get us out of here."

Parker stood, staring in the direction that the great white had disappeared. "This is his territory. I think he just warned us not to come back."

"No worries there," Angelica said. "If I want to play in the water, I'll sit under my sprinkler."

"What *happened* down there?" Ella stayed low, like she feared the shark might circle back, leap out of the water, and take her.

"Storytime later," Wilson said. "Right now, we need a decision." He pointed at the fog. "Do we look for the other two boats to tell them we got the goods—or find our way back to the harbor?"

Angelica checked her phone. No signal.

"It's after six." Harley stared into the fog. "We have to make sure Miss Lopez is okay—and get this to the lawyer."

Parker nodded. "We stick to the plan. Shoot up a couple flares. Hopefully they'll see it and know we headed back. But driving toward Little Salvages to search for them in this fog? We'd be asking for trouble."

Angelica had seen enough trouble already. "Just get to the harbor."

Wilson fired up the motor. Checked the compass. He hustled to the bow and held the flare gun high and over the side of the boat. He sent out two flares to the east, then dropped the gun and raced to the console. He checked the compass again and steered. "We'll take it slow until we get some decent visibility."

Totally uncharacteristic of Wilson to take safety precautions. But Angelica was relieved. And the slower pace made it a lot easier to shed wet suits.

Harley laid his tank and BCD on the deck. Actually, it was Parker's gear. Harley stared at the pressure gauge for a long moment. He nodded at Jelly's gauge. "How much?"

She held it up so he could see. With Parker drawing on the octopus, she'd dropped well into the danger zone herself—for the first time ever.

He nodded. Like he'd done the math in his head. If Parker hadn't followed Harley in, likely Harley wouldn't have made it. And if she hadn't joined them, Parker and Harley could have run out of air before they'd finished the three-minute safety stop. "If we hadn't played musical chairs with the air supply like we did . . ." He just let the thought hang there.

Sharing air exactly the way they did was the only reason Harley—and Parker—hadn't ended up looking like Mike Ironwing.

"Looks like I owe you big." Harley thumped his chest with his fist and pointed at Angelica. She had a feeling he'd never tease her again about how little air she used on a dive. She closed her eyes. Nodded back. Normally she might have teased him back. But not this time. She had her own thanks to offer . . . and she was pretty sure she'd never get over what she'd just learned. What if she'd had her way . . . and she'd somehow sabotaged Harley's effort to make one more dive? What if she'd stayed topside and not joined the boys? *Dear God . . . you are amazing to me.*

Each of them peeled out of their wet suits, toweled off, and threw on jeans and sweatshirts over their swimsuits as Wilson steered. How he could trust the GPS with this fog, Angelica didn't know. There was no shoreline in sight. She was just glad to be moving—and didn't care if they were headed for the harbor or not, as long as it was away from Mr. White.

"I got a signal!" Harley hit the favorites and tapped the picture of Pez. "C'mon, c'mon, c'mon." He sat on the very edge of the bow seat, his knee tapping out its own SOS. He glanced up . . . looking like a much younger version of himself. "Where *is* she?"

"Call that lawyer, Harley." Ella sidestepped tanks and fins and knelt in front of him. "We deliver that evidence, right? Then she's safe." Harley's eyes lost that wild, panicky look. The girl still had that mojo she could work on Harley.

Harley nodded. "Right." He reeled through the contacts on his phone. Found Sebastian Kilbro. Tapped speakerphone.

"Do you have it, Harley?"

The guy wasted no time.

"I can't get ahold of Miss Lopez. I have to know if—"

"She's safe, Harley. I got her a hotel room after we talked—made her turn off her phone so she can't be tracked. But I can't protect her long. Did you find it?"

"You're sure she's okay?"

"Stood outside the hotel room door until I heard her double-lock it."

Harley's face—relief.

"Did you *find* it?"

Harley opened Uncle Ray's dry bag and turned it upside down. A phone dropped out. "Oh, yeah." He smiled. "We got it."

Which meant they got Lochran.

"Who knows you have it?"

"Just my friends—here on the boat. We just got our signal back—and you're the only call that got through."

"Good. *Good.* Keep it that way, Harley. Hear me? How many friends?"

"Myself. Parks. Ella. Jelly. Wilson."

"Okay. Now, here's what I need you to do. All of you." Over the next two minutes Sebastian Kilbro outlined his plan. Harley was to meet him—and put the evidence in his hands. Once the lawyer put word out to Lochran that *he* held the evidence—the danger to Harley and Pez was over.

But Kilbro didn't want it to look obvious that he'd gotten the evidence from Harley. Lochran would know Harley had put an end run on him, and the chances of him seeking revenge went off the charts.

"Meet me at the Headlands," Kilbro said. "The whole group of you—stay together. Don't run. Don't act like you've discovered buried treasure. If Lochran's boys are watching, he may guess you've found the evidence. Pretend you're just a bunch of kids going to the Headlands to party."

"What about the police?" Ella leaned closer to the phone. "Why don't we just phone the police?"

It was a good question. Uncle Ray wanted the evidence to go through his lawyer so he could use it as a bargaining chip to get out of prison himself. But he was dead now . . . so why not give it directly to the police?

"Exactly what I'll do," Kilbro said. "But this is a dance, and it has to be choreographed just right. Nobody needs to know you found the phone, and keeping that secret is the only way to keep you—and Miss Lopez—safe. It puts all the focus on me—and you're off the hook. I'll bring it to my office and call the police from there. I'll tell them I found it. If there's an informant on the force, they won't hear a word about me getting it from you."

That made sense.

"Actually, all of you being here—at the same time—is essential," the lawyer said. "I'll go over instructions moving forward when you all get here. We all have to be on the same page. This is the best way to do that."

The breakwater materialized out of the fog. Just a silhouette, but the profile was unmistakable.

"Oh, yeah." Wilson grinned and steered for the channel. "Miccosukee instincts save the day again."

Angelica smiled too. On the inside, anyway. Her cheeks were still too cold to move.

"Where are you now—and how long before you get to the Headlands?" There was a definite urgency in Kilbro's voice.

Harley looked at Parker, who held up both hands and wiggled his fingers.

"Ten minutes. Fifteen at most."

"I'll be waiting. Close to the water." Kilbro hesitated. "We're not out of the woods yet. You understand? Don't talk to a soul. Don't text anyone. Got it? Do not pass Go. Do not collect $200. You keep what you've got and where you're going a secret and bring that evidence straight to me."

Compared to all they'd just gone through, walking the evidence to Canada would've been easy, if that's what Kilbro needed them to do. Keeping this secret—and getting to the Headlands—was nothing.

"Tell me you got that, Harley—and all your friends, too. This has to be executed perfectly, you understand?"

"I had you on speaker." Harley scanned the group and nodded. "We got it."

Parker and Wilson looked dead serious—and totally fired up—like delivering the evidence was some kind of black-ops mission. But it was almost over now, thank God.

"What about Mr. Lochran?" Angelica had to ask the question. "Aren't you even a tiny bit worried he'll go after *you*?"

"You let me worry about Lochran," Sabastian Kilbro said. "I know exactly how to deal with him."

CHAPTER 105

VINNY TORINO LOVED TO AMAZE PEOPLE. His former boss at the bar had been blown away with how Vinny handled rough situations. And tonight he'd elevate his status in Lochran's eyes to a level of wonder.

"Mr. Lochran will swear Vinny Torino can perform miracles," Vinny whispered. He stood on the boulders and looked out over fogbound Sandy Bay. Sal already had *Sea Monster* in position a couple hundred yards offshore, waiting at anchor. The fog kept the boat hidden—which was perfect.

Vinny was taking no chances that some resident or dog walker might spot him—or one of his crew—leaving the Headlands by land. They'd leave the Headlands the same way they'd arrived—in the inflatable dory from *Sea Monster*. He and the crew had been dropped off, and Sal steered the dory back to the lobster boat. An inflatable pulled up onto shore might mean a quicker getaway, but it might also be something a passerby could spot. At Vinny's signal, Sal would motor the inflatable boat back to shore to pick him and the crew up. Unless Vinny chose to walk on water, of course. He chuckled at his own joke.

In any case, it ensured a clean getaway . . . especially since they'd cruise all the way to Gloucester before docking. There'd be nothing to connect him to the scene here.

He fished a smooth stone from his pocket and threw the thing sidearm low over the water. It skipped lightly across the surface and disappeared into the fog—just like Vinny would once this was over.

Vinny hated anything that caught him unprepared. So over the last few hours, he'd worked hard to make sure he'd factored in every possible what-if scenario and had a backup plan for each. He was ready. The crew was well hidden—and knew the game plan.

Astonishing people was what Vinny did best. He'd sure caught Mike Ironwing napping. Totally off guard. The flabbergasted expression on his face the instant Ironwing knew he was finished? Priceless. A real Kodak moment.

His phone vibrated, and he smiled the moment he read the text. The ball was in play. The plan in motion. And Vinny was ready. He skipped one last stone out into the bay.

One regret popped into his head. Vinny really should have hired a photographer. There were going to be a lot more picture-worthy moments tonight.

CHAPTER 106

PARKER WAS THANKING GOD—and marveling at how things had worked out. They'd found the boat, retrieved the evidence, and evaded a great white—with barely enough air to fill a balloon by the time they'd finished. What were the odds that all that happened by chance? God might be invisible . . . but his fingerprints were all over this. They'd parked the boat, secured the lines, and left all their gear piled inside. Once the evidence was delivered, there'd be plenty of time to rinse and stow everything.

Harley took point position with Wilson at his side, machete in hand. This hardly seemed like a time for weapons, but Parker got it. He'd strapped his dive knife to his calf after shedding his wet suit. He liked the man-on-a-mission feel of it. He'd wear his knife to church if he could get away with it.

The four in front of him chattered away—which was good. It gave Parker a chance to work through one little thing that gnawed at him.

Parker was all about respecting authority—but when Sebastian Kilbro insisted they not tell a soul about what they were doing? Something about it didn't sit right with him, and in the blocks they'd walked since leaving T-wharf, he'd grown even more uneasy. He could hear Grandpa's voice in his head. Something he'd told Parker during one of their early M101 sessions. *"When someone tells you to do something—but insists you keep it a secret? Red flag, my boy. They're not out to do you any favors."*

Harley was all about doing exactly what Kilbro said . . . and Parker totally got that. But that didn't mean Parker shouldn't think for himself.

Parker took the rear of the single-file line as they entered the short, wooded path to the Headlands. He slipped his phone out of his pocket and whipped out a short group text without breaking his stride—to just five people. Dad and Uncle Sammy would get the message as soon as they neared shore enough to get a signal. Mom would get it sooner, of course. But maybe she was worried about Pez, and at least he could ease her mind on that one too. Grandpa would appreciate the update. And Race Bannon. He'd probably be disappointed they weren't giving the evidence to him directly instead of through Kilbro. But at least Parker would be keeping Greenwood in the loop.

`Found Deep Trouble, and cargo. Delivering to Kilbro now @ Headlands. He hid Pez to keep her safe. He says once we give him the dry bag, he'll keep us all safe from Lochran. He'll turn evidence over to the police personally-after making copies.`

It was short but said it all. Or almost everything. Something told him he needed to add that one more detail.

`He insisted we all keep our find and our meeting secret-even from you. And all five of us from the boat have to deliver the evidence together. Thought you should know. Felt off keeping a secret from you.`

Maybe he was seeing shadows where there were none, but he felt a tiny bit better knowing the others were in the loop. He'd barely pocketed his phone when they stepped out onto the windswept rocks of the Headlands.

Harley took off at a run over the rise and toward the water, with Kit bounding on a leash alongside him. Wilson followed a few steps behind, keeping pace with the girls. Parker hung back a bit and kept the shoulder-check thing going. He was the rear guard, right? And he wasn't going to do a half-baked job of it—even though this whole thing would likely be over in a few minutes. The instant Harley gave the evidence to the lawyer, the problem was out of their hands—for good.

The sun would be setting in thirty minutes, but fog had a way of making the sky seem a whole lot darker than 7 p.m. They'd gotten out of the water just in time. It would have been so shadowy at the bottom, the chances of them even finding *Deep Trouble* would have vanished.

Jelly dropped back to walk beside him. She grabbed his cap and slapped it on her head. "Why aren't you smiling, Parker Buckman? We're home free."

He shrugged. How was he supposed to explain what he was feeling—especially since he wasn't quite sure himself? She'd probably think he was being paranoid. "Maybe I won't believe this is over until we're back aboard *Wings*. Cleaning up."

She studied his face. "You think something's wrong?"

"It's not that something's *wrong*. Something doesn't feel *right*."

The tide was nearly at its lowest point. The rocks near the water's edge, and for twenty feet inland, were overgrown with black, mossy slime. Uncle Ray's lawyer stood waiting in a spot that was low and secluded between a couple of high boulders. The rock where he'd planted himself sloped to the water's edge as if it was a natural ramp into the bay. He stood just above slimy black growth marking the high-tide line. Kilbro motioned them closer like he couldn't wait to get this exchange over with either.

Harley and Wilson long-stepped their way to him. Sebastian Kilbro shook their hands. Clapped them on the backs. Job-well-done kind of stuff.

The dry bag was still in Harley's hand, Kit's leash in the other. He waved the bag, motioning Parker and Jelly to hurry, like he wasn't about to turn it over until they got there.

"Relax, Parker," Jelly said. "Enjoy the moment, okay? It's over."

He nodded, but it didn't *feel* over.

Jelly trotted the rest of the way, and Parker hustled to catch up.

"Looks like the gang is all here," Kilbro said.

Harley opened the bag, fished out the phone, and placed it in the lawyer's hands. "It's totally dead, but dry. All it should need is a recharging."

Sebastian Kilbro looked downright relieved.

"Did you tell Miss Lopez we found it—and that she's going to be safe now?"

He shook his head. "But it will be at the top of my list once I leave here."

Suddenly Wilson stared at his own forearm. Touched it lightly—and gave Parker a curious look. "Tingling."

Wilson's Miccosukee Early Warning System? The last time Parker had seen the hair rise on his arms like that, they'd been in the Everglades—and disaster followed.

Wilson's expression . . . confused. "Why now?" He scanned the fog-bound bay, as if expecting to see the ugly, black head of a gator surfacing nearby.

Jelly leaned in close. "We need to leave. Right now." Her face—dead serious. She stepped back. "You're right, Parker. Something feels off."

Harley dropped on one knee and pulled Kit close. "What happens to Lochran now?"

"I can answer that." Quinn Lochran stepped out from behind the large boulder—with Vinny Torino at his side.

Kit exploded in vicious, snarling barks. She lunged for Torino, and it took all Harley had to hold her back.

Sebastian Kilbro smiled apologetically. "Did you *really* think I'd go up against Mr. Lochran? And for free? Your uncle certainly wasn't going to pay. Live and learn, kids. Or maybe in this case . . . just learn."

"Remember me, pup?" Torino grinned. "Want Uncle Vinny to take you for another swim? You're *such* a good swimmer. So much better than your first owner was."

Torino murdered Mike Ironwing?

Jelly squeezed Parker's arm tighter, like she'd just put it together too.

"But to answer your question . . . what's going to happen to

Mr. Quinn Lochran now?" The man himself strode closer, Vinny Torino still at his side. "Absolutely nothing."

Wilson drew his machete. Took a wide stance like he expected Torino to attack.

Lochran laughed. "Easy, tiger. Look around before you get all Jim Bowie on me."

Three men had materialized from behind them—all carrying handguns and blocking their escape route.

The owner of Cape Ann Angels moved his hand in a sweeping motion. "Meet the Bearskin Neck Strangler's crew—most of them anyway. They're known as the Tres Diablos. Eddie. Jake. Rocko." Each of the men nodded or raised a hand when their name was called. Why would Torino offer their names?

Why else?

Torino pointed into the fog. "Sal is out there, just in case one of you Einsteins thinks of swimming to freedom. So let's all stay calm here, okay? And keep a tight rein on your sled dog."

Harley still struggled to keep Kit from breaking free. Parker had never heard such ferocious and frustrated snarling. It seemed Kit couldn't understand why Harley didn't let her go so she could protect them.

"Let's see everybody's hands," Rocko said. "Anybody reaching for a phone won't live long enough to call dial-a-prayer."

God, help us. Jesus . . . we need a rescue.

Lochran held out his palm, and the lawyer placed Ray's phone in his hand. Lochran bounced it a couple of times. "The way I heard it, the weight of evidence Ray had against me was *substantial*. But it doesn't feel all that weighty to me." He dropped the phone onto the rock and stomped it with his heel until the glass screen shattered.

"That isn't right," Ella whispered.

Lochran picked up the phone and placed it back in Torino's hand. "Take care of this, would you?"

Had Detective Greenwood gotten his text? Parker had to stall things so the police could get here.

"Miss Lopez." Harley's face—furious. "Where is she?"

The lawyer shrugged. "No idea. Probably wondering where *you* are."

"I *trusted* you."

"And I did exactly as you wanted," Kilbro said. "You were all about keeping Miss Lopez safe. And now that you found the evidence, she'll stay that way."

Harley shook his head. "You're a snake. You were never going to work out a deal for my Uncle Ray, were you?"

The lawyer smiled like he thought Harley was naive. "Your uncle thought he knew how life worked, but he totally missed the fine print on this one."

They all had. *God, help us. God, help us.* There was no way the five of them could go up against even one gun.

"So, Mr. Kilbro," Ella said, "why get Harley involved at all? Ray Lotitto trusted you with the clue sheet—so he trusted you with the evidence. All you had to do was destroy it."

The lawyer looked to Lochran, as if to see if it was okay to answer.

Lochran swept his hand toward the lawyer and gave a little bow. "By all means."

"We couldn't make the evidence disappear until we'd actually *found* it. Believe me, we tried cracking that stupid poem. Ray was a little paranoid and wouldn't even tell *me* where he'd hidden it. The only one he fully trusted was Harley."

"Now you have the phone," Harley said. "You got what you wanted. Just let us go."

Lochran shook his head. "And have all *five* of you telling the police we took it from you at gunpoint? Sounds like I'd be jumping out of the frying pan and into the fire, don't you think?"

"I would've been better off not finding the thing at all," Harley said.

"Not true. We couldn't take a chance you'd find it someday." Lochran smiled. "And now, thanks to *all* of you, no one will."

"It was at the bottom of Sandy Bay," Harley said. "Who would've ever found it?"

"You did," Kilbro said. "It was a loose end, and I don't like them any more than I do a loophole."

Kit still had the growling thing going on, but she wasn't pulling at the leash anymore. Which was good. Rocko looked more than willing to put a bullet in her if Lochran or Torino gave the nod.

God, help us. Do something, Lord!

"And now, I'll leave you to your fun." Lochran smiled. "I'm afraid I have more funerals to plan. Busy, busy, busy."

He gave a single nod to Vinny Torino, like it was a signal to do whatever he'd been instructed to do. Without a word, Lochran strode inland, Sebastian Kilbro at his side.

God . . . what do we do? What do we do? Help us, Lord—my strength. Grandpa's verse flashed through his mind again. *Even in darkness light dawns.* Yeah, he could use a little light right now. But it was getting darker by the second, and dawn was still a long way off.

"Okay, Mowgli," Vinny Torino motioned to Wilson. "Set the jungle knife on the ground."

If he'd noticed Parker's knife strapped to his calf, he wasn't concerned. Maybe he just figured he could unload a couple of bullets before Parker got it out of the sheath.

"Everybody got a mobile phone in their pocket?" Torino smiled like he knew the answer. "You keep it right there."

Okay, that made no sense. Why not make them hand them over?

"Here's what's going to happen." Torino motioned his crew to move in. "The five of you—and the pup—are going to take a little walk." He pointed to the slime-covered rock sloping down to the water's edge. "Right there. Everybody on the slip 'n slide."

Which is exactly what the rock would be like. Ella obeyed immediately—locking arms with Jelly as she did. Harley, Kit, Parker—and finally Wilson stepped onto the black slime. All of them spread their arms wide for balance—making those crazy gyrations to keep from falling. Each of them was reduced to having the abilities of a toddler. They took halting, jerky steps, trying not to lose their footing.

A genius strategy on Torino's part. None of them would be able to make any sudden moves. There was no risk of any of them jumping Torino or his crew—even if they were dumb enough to try. Kit was the only one who didn't seem to have traction problems.

"Life is war, kids," Torino said. "And if that doesn't come as a shock to you, I know something else that will."

"Switch to stun?" Rocko holstered the Glock and pulled a yellow-and-black taser from under his hoodie.

Torino nodded, and the others drew tasers of their own.

"Ladies first." Rocko swung the taser at Ella. He fired, and Ella lurched backward, landing hard on the slime ramp—taking Jelly down with her.

Parker reached for Jelly. Missed. Lost his balance and dropped to his hands and knees.

Both girls slid toward the water's edge, Jelly fighting it all the way. Somehow Jelly found a grip and kept them both from going in.

"Now you." Rocko picked Jelly off, and both girls tumbled into the water—disappearing below the surface.

Harley dropped Kit's leash and skated down the slope a half step ahead of Parker. There'd be no kneeling on the rocks, reaching for the girls. Likely neither of them had the ability to reach back. Harley and Parker leaped into the frigid bay.

Parker found Jelly and held her head above the surface. Harley was doing the same with Ella. Parker kicked hard, trying to keep from going under himself. Jelly coughed like she was having a choking fit. Seawater gurgled out of her mouth. Eyes wide. Panicky.

"Everybody in the pool!" Torino tasered Wilson—catching him at point-blank range.

Wilson dropped—but got hung up just before sliding fully into the water. Kit stood her ground, growling, like she was unsure what to do.

"How tragic," Torino said. "A bunch of teenagers hanging out at the Headlands. One slips into the cold April waters. Others try to help. Next thing you know, we've got five kids on ice . . . singing the blues. A freaky accident . . . but hey, accidents happen, right?"

Now Parker understood why Torino and his crew hadn't confiscated their mobile phones. If their bodies were found without them? That would look suspicious. Police would dig deeper. The tasers would lock them up long enough to drown—but without leaving obvious telltale marks. *God, don't let them get away with this!*

Jelly's eyes—still wild. Like she knew exactly how this would end. Her body, still rigid.

"I won't let you go. I got you." But for how long? If taser-guy took a bead on Parker, he'd go down—right along with Jelly.

"I did everything I was t-told," Harley shouted. "You got the evidence. Let us out, man!"

"God must love stupid people," Torino said. "He made so many of them. You're all loose ends—and I don't do sloppy work."

"Rocko." Torino motioned toward Wilson. "Help Mowgli into the pool."

The big guy with the taser inched his way down the slimy rock. If he pushed Wilson in, there was no way Harley or Parker could hold him up—*and* the girls.

"God—Lord Jesus—help us!" Parker cried out. "Stop them!"

Rocko pasted a look of mock terror on his face. "I better speed things along—in case the Almighty heard you." He swung wide of Kit—who seemed laser-focused on Torino anyway.

Wilson was still flat on his back, rigid and shaking. Rocko dropped into a crab-walk stance, edged closer—feet first—like he intended to kick Wilson into the water.

Jelly was coming out of it. She made shaky figure eights with both arms and didn't need quite so much effort from Parker to keep her nose above the surface.

"Mr. Torino." Parker took in water. Spit it out. "Let's deal."

The head of Cape Ann Security seemed to think that was funny. "You're not in any position for dealing, boy."

"Let us walk away. And I'll ask God to go easy on you." It was the best Parker could do.

Torino laughed—right along with the rest of his crew. He cupped a hand behind his ear. "No thunder." He made an exaggerated show of scanning the fogbound horizon. "And I sure don't see any lightning. I think I'll take my chances." He gave Rocko a nod. "Finish this, and I'll call in the inflatable."

Rocko kicked at Wilson—catching him in the shoulder. "Déjà vu, right? Me kicking you into the bay again." Wilson slid closer to the water. Rocko repositioned and kicked again. This time Wilson was ready. Somehow, he grabbed the guy's boot—and held on. Rocko kicked the side of Wilson's face with his other foot until Wilson lost his grip.

The guy backed just out of Wilson's reach, and tasered him again. Wilson lurched violently—and slid into the bay just two feet away from Parker.

Jelly grabbed fistfuls of the kelpy growth swaying from the edge of the boulders. "I'll h-hold on. Get W-Wilson!"

Parker ducked below the surface, grabbed a fistful of Wilson's T-shirt, and yanked him to the sruface. He did his best to keep Wilson's head out of the water—but he was a lot heavier than Jelly.

Ella grabbed the seaweed like Jelly did, and Harley got on Wilson's other side.

"You boys are next." Rocko inched his way down the slope, taser aimed right at Parker and Harley. "Say hi to Mr. Ironwing."

Tasered—while in the *water*? Would they be electrocuted—or just lose all ability to control their muscles? Either way, they'd be dead in less than two minutes—and Wilson would go down with them.

A growl rumbled up from deep inside Kit again. She took a slow, stalking step closer to Torino.

The Cape Ann Angels Security owner ignored the dog. He held Uncle Ray's phone high. "Say bye-bye." Was he talking about the phone . . . or them? Torino held the shattered phone like he intended to skip it across Sandy Bay.

Kit took another step closer.

Torino turned to face the water. He bent low and cocked his come-and-get-it arm way back.

Kit accepted the invitation. She lunged—teeth bared.

The chocolate lab sank her chompers deep into his tattooed arm. The phone clattered across the boulders. It spun and skittered, lodging against a rock covered with the black bay slime. Kit was in shredder mode. She twisted her head, ripping and tearing, but didn't release his arm.

Torino wheeled around with amazing speed and slammed the butt of his pistol on Kit's skull—opening her wound again. The dog dropped. Rocko scooted toward the dog like he wanted to make sure Kit wouldn't be able to attack again.

"Kit!" Harley let go of Wilson and dug at the sea growth—but there was no way he was climbing that slimy rock.

Wilson thrashed, like he was trying to get some kind of control back.

"Easy, Wilson—I got you!"

Torino stared in disbelief at his mauled arm. All that remained read-able of the ink was *Come*. The rest of the tattoo was a random assortment of partial words and letters—like bloody Scrabble pieces stuck to his arm.

Cradling his mangled arm, he eased his way across the kelpy growth to where the shattered phone lay. The instant he got there, he stuffed his gun in his waistband and picked up Uncle Ray's phone. The damage to his right arm was enough to make him throw lefty—and when he did—he lost his balance completely. The phone splashed into the bay barely thirty feet from shore, and Torino tobogganed into the water himself.

The Tres Diablos sprang to his aid—slip-sliding all the way.

Parker's heart spiked. This was their chance.

Wilson managed to get a handhold on the rocks. "I'm back. I just need a sec."

Jelly seemed 100 percent. She clawed at the rock. Parker ducked underwater, found her feet, planted his on the bottom, and gave her a boost. She was halfway on shore when he surfaced. She struggled to swing a leg up, but the slime wasn't allowing that.

Kit was on her feet again. She shook, seemingly unfazed except for the busted stitches on her head. She trotted down to Harley, tail wagging like she wanted to make sure he saw that Torino was in the water too. The fact that she didn't skitter at all was amazing.

"Kit!" Parker grabbed her leash and wrapped it around Jelly's hand. "Pull, girl. Pull!"

Kit dug in and tore up the rock like a sled dog, snapping the leash tight, pulling Jelly as she did. With Parker on one leg, and Harley on the other, they pushed with all their might—and Jelly was gone. Like she was caught in an alien tractor beam.

The instant Jelly hit dry rock, she sent Kit back to the water's edge.

"Run, Jelly!" Parker motioned to her. "Get help!"

Torino thrashed in the water not more than ten yards away. Getting a grip on the slimy rock proved impossible—especially with his wounded arm. Rocko came in too hot—and now there were two of them in the water. Jake and Eddie inched closer to help but seemed wary as they got near the water's edge.

Harley was already wrapping the leash around Ella's hand. Wilson had way more function back—and was there to assist. Moments later, Ella stood on dry rock and ran after Jelly.

Parker surfaced. Torino's man Eddie seemed to forget all about his boss in the water. He crouched low, pointing his 9mm at Parker. "Don't move! All three of you—freeze!"

Instinctively, Parker raised his hands, kicking harder to keep from going under. Could the guy miss from thirty feet away? He'd hit one of them for sure. Wilson and Harley treaded water beside him.

Eddie wiped his hand on his shirt and took a fresh grip on his Glock.

Torino held Jake's ankle now, struggling to pull himself out of the water while Rocko pushed from behind. "Jake—keep the boys covered. Eddie—find the girls—then call Sal in!"

CHAPTER 107

THE RUN UP THE HEADLANDS was uphill all the way—and the soggy jeans and hoodie weren't helping. Angelica needed more speed. A better leg. And a minor miracle.

Footsteps—behind her. She chanced a shoulder check.

"Don't stop!" Ella waved her on. "He's coming!"

Both girls left a wet trail to follow. "The boys?"

"Still in the bay."

Ella was right on her tail by the time Angelica hit the woods path. The instant they broke out into the clear on the other side, she saw Dad—and Uncle Vaughn—swinging out of the pickup. Detective Greenwood hustling from his SUV. Two more police cars roaring up the road.

"Straight to the water!" Angelica pointed, gulping in air.

"Hurry!" Ella wailed. "They've got guns—they're going to shoot them!"

Greenwood—gun out of its holster—sprinted down the trail. Mr. Buckman was right behind him.

"Lock yourselves in the truck," Dad said. "Stay low." He bolted after the other two men.

Angelica stared after them for a moment, intermittently gasping for breath—then holding it to listen.

"Threes." Ella held up three fingers . . . her eyes haunted. "Death comes in threes."

Exactly Angelica's thoughts. "What if it's not a *third* death today—but all three at one time?"

CRACK. A gunshot echoed through the fog. *CRACK. CRACK.*

"NO!" Angelica clamped her hands over her ears. Squeezed her eyes so tight that she blocked out all traces of light. Or maybe the whole world had gone dark. Her world definitely had.

CHAPTER 108

GUNSHOTS—AND NEARBY. Parker froze. Even Jake hesitated—gun still aimed their way. Like suddenly he wasn't so sure of his next move.

Detective Greenwood appeared over the rise, to the shock of Eddie—who'd holstered his weapon to crawl to the edge of the slimy rock. Greenwood held his pistol in a two-handed grip. "Drop it!"

Greenwood shortened the gap between him and Torino's men, ensuring his shot would be just as deadly as the look on his face. "Hands where I can see them!"

Torino released his grip on Eddie's ankle and ducked underwater. Jake dropped his gun and raised both arms high. Eddie stayed on all fours—not moving an inch. Rocko raised one hand—and used the other to tread water, a look of total disbelief on his face.

Torino's head broke the surface a good thirty feet from shore—just long enough to grab a breath. He ducked under again, his feet swirling the surface of the water for an instant before disappearing again.

"Parker!" Dad was there, easing his way down the slimy rock. "Any of you hurt?"

He and Uncle Sammy pulled the three boys out of the drink while Kit pranced around them. Jumping. Whining. Fanning her tail. Parker would've joined her if he wasn't so cold and waterlogged.

He climbed to dry rock on all fours alongside Wilson and Harley. Greenwood already had Eddie cuffed and lying belly-down on the bare rock.

Harley didn't look like he was ready to celebrate anything just yet. "Miss Lopez?"

"Called her just before we docked," Uncle Sammy said. "She's with Parker's mom—and Grams."

"Wait—the lawyer said—"

"He lied, Harley."

Harley nodded. "From the very beginning."

Water drained off the boys—but Parker didn't even feel cold anymore. The three of them looked at each other for a long moment. Wilson reached inside his sweatshirt and pulled out his gator-tooth necklace—along with the key to Kemosabe. Harley did the same, and Parker fished his out from under his wet clothes.

"Brothers—to the end." Wilson grinned.

Parker was pretty sure the three of them wouldn't stop smiling for a long time.

Greenwood left Rocko in the water until backup arrived. Even after the police hauled the Tres Diablos away, Greenwood stayed behind.

There were hugs. Congratulations. Claps on the back. And then Dad prayed while the six of them stood in a circle. To anyone observing from a distance, it was just a group of guys standing on the rocks of the Headlands. But for those *in* the circle, there was no question that they were standing in the throne room . . . in the very presence of Almighty

God. There were lots and lots of thanks—with a sense of awe. Detective Greenwood capped it off with prayer himself.

There was something else Parker felt as they prayed. And by the look on Harley's face when they'd finished—and even Wilson's—he was pretty sure he wasn't alone. Right there on the Headlands, they'd taken another step toward manhood. Something inside Parker soared to be in the presence of Dad. Uncle Sammy. Detective Greenwood. Real men. The boys were part of a bigger brotherhood now.

"Parker!" Jelly flew over the rise—with Ella beside her. Cheeks wet. Eyes red. "We heard shots. We couldn't wait any longer!"

Detective Greenwood raised one hand. "Guilty as charged. I'm not one to fire warning shots . . . but I had the sense I needed to let them know the police were there—and the game was over."

"And if he hadn't done that—right when he did?" Parker shuddered to think of it. "Eddie would have pulled that trigger."

Jelly and Ella practically mobbed Detective Greenwood. Hugging him. Thanking him.

"We saw Vinny Torino's crew in cuffs," Jelly said. "What about the Bearskin Neck Strangler himself?" She scanned the area, looking suddenly on edge.

Greenwood pointed toward the fogbank hulking in Sandy Bay. "Last seen heading that way."

"He talked of a boat—part of his crew," El said. "So . . . he just gets away?"

"We'll get him," Greenwood said. "If he goes to port anywhere between Rhode Island and Boston, we'll be waiting for him. It's Lochran I want right now." He looked from Harley to Parker. "That evidence you found—the stuff Ray collected?"

Harley pointed to the bay. "Gone."

Greenwood nodded like he'd expected that. He held up his pointer finger and thumb—with barely enough space between them to squeeze a toothpick. "We were that close. Mike Ironwing had enough on Lochran to put him away for several lifetimes. Whatever he had is gone. Now

Ray's evidence has been swallowed by Sandy Bay. Again. Lochran is more slippery than sea moss."

"Are we still in danger?" Parker asked the question that all of them were probably thinking. "Will Lochran retaliate somehow—against one of us?"

Greenwood was quiet for a long moment. "This is the man who pays for funerals of people he's whacked, just to make a statement."

A chill shuddered through Parker. And the sky seemed so much darker than it had just minutes ago.

"I'll promise you this," Greenwood said. "I'll stay on it. I'll find a new witness. Gather new evidence. Something. It may take years. But with God as my guide, we *will* put that monster in a cage."

Parker looked at him and knew that somehow God would help him do exactly that.

Kit nuzzled Harley, like she'd waited long enough for his attention. He knelt and carefully inspected the broken stitches on her head. "It's not too bad, right?"

To look at the happy expression on Kit's face, you'd think the blood was fake. But she'd bled enough for the blood to mat her fur from the crown of her head to her shoulder. He unclipped the leash. "You did good, girl. You know that? Real good."

"She seems to have adjusted to her new owner just fine," Greenwood said.

She definitely had.

Harley tried slipping the garden hose collar over her head, but Kit pulled away with a tiny yip. "Sorry, girl. Don't want to hurt you. Just need to get a better look at what that mean man did to you."

He went to work on the hose connection, and by the way he strained to unscrew it, the thing must have been cranked on really tight.

Kit squirmed a bit, like she didn't like the idea of the collar coming off.

"I like the thing, too, girl," Harley said. "I'll put your necklace right back on. Promise. If I can get it off, that is."

"Dry your hands, son." Uncle Sammy pointed at his own pants. "Right here. Try again."

Harley wiped his hands dry—and regripped the fittings. This time the seal loosened. Harley unscrewed the hose—and the instant he separated the two ends, something dropped out of the hosing and clattered to the granite boulder below.

A thumb drive.

All of them just stared at the thing. Nobody had to ask what it was—or what it was doing hidden in Kit's waterproof collar. They knew. That evidence Mike Ironwing had been gathering. The proof he'd claimed to have—the stuff that would put Lochran away for good . . . was right under their noses the entire time. Under Kit's nose, anyway.

Detective Greenwood stooped down. Picked it up. Bounced it in his palm a couple of times, laughing as he did. "Oh, Kit . . . you just made my job soooo much easier." He closed his hand around it and held his fist up to the sky. Bowed his head. "*That* was quick."

Greenwood turned to Parker. "Ask me that question again. The one about the chances of Lochran retaliating against you."

"Are we still in danger?"

Greenwood held up the thumb drive and smiled. "Not anymore."

CHAPTER 109

Spring break was over. School was back in session. It had been five days since the showdown at the Headlands. To Parker, the days had raced by in a whirlwind of extremes. Extreme high points. Joy. Relief. Hope for the future. Plans for Wilson's next visit. A heightened sense of God's presence that came from knowing he'd rescued them—when they couldn't save themselves.

Since the Bearskin Neck Strangler threat was gone, BayView Brew opened for business as usual that past Monday morning. That was a definite high point. Ella and Jelly sat Mr. Bones right up on the counter, holding the BayView Brew specials board. They had added the highly caffeinated Bogeyman Brew and Strangler Special for the reopening. Both were guaranteed to "keep you up at night."

Whether they had been on the schedule or not, Jelly and Ella had shown up at the coffee shop every day after school. Which meant Wilson, Harley, and Parker hung out there too. None of them had replaced their ruined phones until today—and there had definitely been benefits to that. Especially the amount of teasing they'd been able to give Jelly—since it was the third phone she'd lost to seawater in a year.

They'd commandeered a table that gave a killer view of Front Beach and Sandy Bay. Finn became more and more of a regular, and the six of them went through more Oreos than seemed humanly possible. They didn't even mind Bryce Scorza's visit with exaggerated tales of his favorite person in the whole world: himself. Jelly and Ella agreed it was the brush with death that gave them the strength to put up with anything . . . even Scorza. Finn insisted it was the Oreos.

But there had been low points. Like all day Monday. Sitting in classes . . . knowing Vinny Torino had escaped—and could be anywhere.

They didn't see Detective Greenwood at all Monday. Parker hoped he was hot on Vinny Torino's trail—and closing in.

"He's busy with that thumb drive," Jelly said. "Compiling all that evidence Kit was safeguarding. And when he's not doing that, he's interrogating Torino's crew."

She had sounded so sure—like she'd been getting updates from Greenwood directly.

"You know this?" Wilson asked. "Or are you guessing?"

Jelly raised her chin slightly. "Women's intuition."

"Ahhhh." Wilson raised his fingertips to his temples. "Using those wonderful and *mysterious* gifts you have that we *limited* males can't begin to understand."

"Got that right, buster."

"People make fun of things they don't understand." Ella nodded like it was a well-accepted fact. "Like artificial intelligence. The truth is, AI is so advanced that it's absolutely scary. And it's unstoppable. AI is soooo similar to women's intuition, or WI."

"Because they're both artificial?"

That comment had earned Wilson slugs in the arm by both girls.

As it turned out, it was Tuesday—after school—before they'd seen Detective Greenwood again. Ella, Jelly, Wilson, Harley, and Parker were back at their table in the coffee shop when Greenwood walked through the front door. His face made it pretty clear he wasn't stopping by for a donut. Parker replayed the whole scene in his head.

Pez led him to their table in the back—and he urged her to stay.

"Tell me you're bringing good news," Harley said.

"We picked up Vinny Torino." Detective Greenwood stated it without a shred of emotion. Like, dead serious.

"Where?"

"When?"

"Did he come peacefully?"

The questions came too fast for any human to answer.

Greenwood pointed out the window. "Front Beach. This morning. And he didn't put up a fight, if that's what you mean."

Pez's eyes narrowed. She cocked her head slightly and exchanged a glance with Ella. Parker had no idea what that was all about.

"I wish I'd looked out the Crow's Nest window to see you cuff him," Harley said.

"No need for cuffs. I didn't arrest him."

Pez closed her eyes in a knowing way.

"Tell me he's not getting off on some technicality," Jelly said.

Ella bolted from her seat. "That's *not* right."

"Oh, he'll still stand before the judge, trust me." Greenwood gave Pez a sideways glance. "A lot sooner than he figured, I'm sure. But it turns out this is totally out of my jurisdiction."

"You have to do *something*," Ella said.

Greenwood glanced at Pez again. "You want to tell them?"

"I think what Detective Greenwood is trying to say is that Vinny Torino is dead. They found him at the beach—and *picked* him up?"

Okay . . . *that* brought another barrage of questions. Greenwood raised both arms to quiet them down. "I'll tell you the basics. Most of it will come out today anyway. Yeah. He was dead."

Ella gripped Jelly's arm. "Death comes in threes. Grams was right."

Mike Ironwing. Ray Lotitto. And now Vinny Torino. There was no way anybody would talk Ella out of believing Grams's *death comes in threes* superstitions. Parker pictured Torino swimming out into the fog to meet the extraction boat. Except for the semi-mangled forearm, he'd looked strong. Like he could swim until morning. "He drowned?"

"The coroner hasn't submitted his official report, but personally? I'd say he bled out from some savage bite wounds." Greenwood glanced at KitKat.

"Torino and his crew drew first blood." Harley pulled Kit close. "She was only protecting us."

Wilson grinned. "I gotta get me a dog like that. Torino had that *Come and Get It* tattoo, right? Well, Kit came and got it, all right!"

"Kit is no killer. She only did what she had to do." Ella patted her leg, and Kit trotted over. "Torino was losing blood, sure . . . but fast enough to pass out before he got to his boat? I don't think so."

"But he *was* putting blood in the water, right?" Greenwood let the words hang there. He raised his eyebrows and shrugged. "Point is, we picked him up. What was left."

Jelly clamped her hands over her ears. "Mr. White!"

"Looks like."

Instantly Parker's mind replayed the scene from the bottom of Sandy Bay. When the great white passed over the wreck of *Deep Trouble*. The terror he'd fought back—especially on the ascent.

"Based on his crew's confessions, Torino masterminded the Bearskin Neck burglaries. From what I understand, Torino had a habit of collecting things from the jobs he did."

"Like . . . souvenirs?" Jelly hugged herself. "Sick trophies from his kills?"

Detective Greenwood shook his head. "According to his crew, Torino was way smarter than that. But if he saw something of *value*, he squirreled it away. More than once they helped him move things to his house. Even when he was hired to do a job, he found things to take as an added personal bonus."

"Jewelry?" Ella reached for the cross around her neck.

"And antiques. Art. One of his cohorts claims Torino swiped a Corvette from a place he did a job. I got a feeling we're going to find things in his house that will link him to plenty of burglaries. I just picked up the search warrant for his house."

"So if he was selling hot merchandise," Wilson said, "how come this guy never got caught before?"

Greenwood shrugged. "From the testimony I got? He'd never sold a thing. He planned to rent a moving truck someday. Move across the country and sell things quietly. Get enough cash to disappear. It was his retirement plan."

"He wasn't planning to retire this early, I'll bet."

Greenwood turned to Pez. "Anything missing from the shop here— maybe something you didn't notice at first?"

Pez shrugged. "Little things, sure. But nothing of real value. And last I checked? *My* collector Corvette is still back in the shed—right next to my collector rake and shovel."

Everyone laughed. Parker would never forget that day. Or the next one.

Because by Wednesday, Quinn Lochran had been arrested . . . without bond. Another high point. Jelly claimed that there was so much evidence against him that he'd never get out of prison . . . not in a million years. And Sebastian Kilbro was going to be needing a lawyer himself. Jelly wouldn't confirm who her source was, but Parker had a pretty good idea. Bryce Scorza had dropped by the coffee shop to talk to the girls a couple of times.

And just yesterday, Harley and Wilson joined Parker on *Wings* for his M101 session with Grandpa. Wilson seemed more interested in the GPS/depth gauge mounted on the console than in the depth of what Grandpa was saying. Harley seemed to pretty much hang on every word. And when Harley asked if he could be a regular part of their time? The only one who was happier than Parker was probably Grandpa.

But today—Friday—was going to be the best day of the week so far. The girls—along with Miss Lopez and Parker's mom—had planned a party at BayView Brew after closing. Mostly to celebrate—and to thank God for the ways he'd rescued them. Again. And Pez still had that one last present to give Harley for his birthday.

All five of them squeezed into their regular booth while Parker's mom and dad, Uncle Sammy, Pez, and Grams sat closer to the coffee counter. Detective Greenwood dropped in too. But this time he was all smiles.

"I've got one request before I step on the bus Sunday morning," Wilson said. "Tomorrow night we have some Smore'y Time with Ella. Out at the Headlands. I want to hear your story of that murder-suicide house."

"The Mastersons." Ella looked at Jelly. "A *terrifying* story. You think the boys are ready?"

Jelly looked doubtful.

"Hey," Wilson said. "We've seen—and lived through—plenty of scary things. Monster gators. An escaped convict. Being pinned in a sunken wreck by a great white—while running low on air. Not to mention being held at gunpoint by a murderer's gang? Oh, yeah . . . we've seen plenty of scarier things than an old house."

"*Haunted* house, Wilson," Ella said. "And there's nothing scarier than a haunted house. You'll see."

"So that means you'll tell us the story?" Wilson held out his hand to seal the deal.

Ella shook it, even as the adults left their table and walked over.

Pez held the manila envelope that she'd held off giving Harley the night they'd had his birthday party. She placed it in Harley's hands. "Your birthday card."

"Big card." Harley opened the flap and slid out a neat stack of papers. He stared at them for a moment—while Ella and Jelly stretched for a better view.

"Miss Lopez . . ." Harley hadn't flipped a page yet. "Is this for real?"

Parker stood to see.

Jelly beat him to it. "You want to *adopt* Harley?"

"With all my heart. But only if that's what he wants."

Harley dropped the papers on the table, bolted from his seat, and wrapped his arms around Pez. Lifted her off her feet. Buried his head at the base of her neck. He just held her there, his shoulders shaking in quiet sobs.

"I think Pez has her answer," Grams said.

Pez beamed. "You were mine from the first night you stayed in the Crow's Nest," she said. "And now I'm legally yours."

Who started the clapping, Parker wasn't sure. But everybody joined in. Cheering and whistling came naturally. Wilson pounded his fists on the table in a thundering drum roll.

The moment Harley set Pez down, others moved in to clap them on the back and exchange hugs.

Harley pulled Parker into a bear hug. "I've got a real home again, Parks. I'm finally home."

"Hold on," Ella said. "Does this mean Harley Davidson Lotitto is going to be Harley Davidson Lopez now?"

Pez shook her head. "Harley needs to keep his name. To honor his dad. But I'd like *my* name changed—if it's okay with Harley."

Okay, for the second time in the last couple of minutes Pez shocked Parker. This one might have been even bigger than the adoption papers.

Harley seemed to be in that same state of disbelief. "You want me to call you Miss *Lotitto*?"

"No," Pez whispered. "I was hoping you'd call me *Mom*."

Again, the cheers and whistles.

Harley looked at her. "Mom." He grinned. "Yeah. I can do that."

That's when it hit Parker. Harley hadn't even known his bio mom. In all his sixteen years, he'd never been able to call anybody *Mom*—until now.

"Well, I hate to interrupt this terrific family reunion," Detective Greenwood said. "But I wonder if I could interest you all in taking a little field trip with me."

Parker, Harley, Wilson. All three of them were up for whatever Greenwood had in mind. Jelly and Ella didn't look so sure until after he'd explained. In the police search process at Vinny Torino's house and garage, he'd found something that he believed belonged at BayView Brew. All he needed was a positive ID, and he could attach the right name with it. Yes, it would officially be catalogued as part of the evidence for the case, but eventually it would be returned.

"All of you know the shop—whether you work here or come for donuts and coffee like I do," Greenwood said. "Which is to say, if it belongs here like I believe it does, I think every one of you will recognize it. I'll put you all down as witnesses to testify to that fact, and it may expedite the process of getting it back here."

"Going to the Strangler's place?" Wilson raised his hand. "Count me in."

They all were—100 percent. Only Grams bowed out, and they dropped her at Beulah before driving to Torino's home in Gloucester.

"His basement is packed. That'll take some major excavating to see what all we have. But the garage is where we're headed." Greenwood went over the ground rules before he took them inside. "Touch nothing. Take nothing. Stay together."

"So basically you should handcuff us," Ella said.

"Just keep your hands in your pockets."

Greenwood led them around behind the two-story house to a huge garage that crouched in the shadows. No windows, with an overhead door at either end. Handy for parking collector cars—or slipping them away in the middle of the night.

Greenwood used his flashlight to get them inside. Only after he'd closed the overhead door did he flip on the lights.

"Whoa." Parker's dad was the first to speak.

Tarps covered four different vehicles. Clearly one was an old pickup. The others were low-profiled enough to be the rumored Chevys. "Is the collector Corvette here?" Parker wished they could lift the tarps.

"Obviously our source was misinformed. Mr. Torino had two very collectible Corvettes—and a really sweet Chevelle. Probably over a quarter million right there in his retirement fund."

"Hokey smokies," Wilson whispered. "I seem to remember one of *those* missing from the coffee shop. Oh yeah . . . and it was mine."

Boxes were stacked in neat rows—and nearly up to the rafters in some places. All of them sealed tight and labeled with letters and numbers that made absolutely no sense. Obviously a code. The guy was organized.

Jelly's hand was out of her pocket. She let one finger slide along the length of one box as she passed. "What's in the boxes?"

Greenwood led the parade, stepping wide around the cars. "Still have to go through most of them. But he boosted some really, really big coin and stamp collections. Pretty hard to trace those. He was smart that way. From what I've seen, he had a good eye for value. He knew what to keep. He should have retired a long time ago. He could have lived like a king."

"Now he'll have to answer to the King of kings," Pez said.

"Got that right." Greenwood held up one hand to stop the parade. He took a shaky breath. Smiled. "You ready, Pez?"

All Parker saw were sealed boxes. What was Greenwood so excited about?

"You really think you have something that belongs to me?" Pez didn't look convinced.

"I have no doubt it belongs at BayView Brew." Greenwood took a deep breath. Blew it out. "But the true owner is your son." Greenwood stepped to one side. Just enough to see the tail end of a tarp covering something that looked an awful lot like a motorcycle.

Harley rushed from behind Parker, then stopped abruptly. "You're not messing with me, Detective. Tell me you're not messing with me."

Greenwood picked up one corner of the tarp. "See for yourself."

Harley glanced back at Parker and jerked his head for him to follow. Wilson came too. The three of them lifted the tarp with a reverence befitting a flag draping the coffin of a fallen soldier.

Ella and Jelly both screamed when the tarp rose high enough to reveal the name *Kemosabe* on the gas tank. Pez was smiling, filming the whole thing—just like any other mom would've been doing.

"Oh, my goodness. *Oh, my goodness.*" Harley didn't bother hiding the tears running down his cheeks. "I thought it'd been dumped in the bay."

"Apparently Torino thought it was too valuable. He added it to his retirement stash." Greenwood put his arm around Harley's shoulders. "My guess? Your uncle never knew."

Harley reached inside his shirt. Pulled out his lanyard with the gator tooth—and the motorcycle key. He slid it into the ignition slot. Turned it. The battery was dead, but clearly it was the right key.

"I call that a positive ID," Greenwood said. "It'll take some time for processing—especially this being considered evidence. But I'll get Kemosabe back in your hands by summer. How's that?"

Harley nodded. Parker was pretty sure he couldn't have gotten a word out anyway.

"I've got a good friend who works in a Chicago suburb. His name is Jeff Aiello. He's a motorcycle cop. He's gone to the Top Gun equivalent of motorcycle training, and he's an instructor himself now. That guy really *knows* how to handle a bike. He'll be coming east for a visit soon. Maybe I'll have him give you some special training. Make sure you stay safe on the road. Would you be open to that?"

Harley nodded, still unable to talk.

"Definitely yes," Ella said. "He owes me a ride—and I want to make sure he knows what he's doing."

The garage of stolen goods was filled with laughter now.

"Hey," Wilson pulled his lanyard out from under his shirt. "I got a key too. I'll make another visit when Kemosabe comes home. And if Harley won't give you a ride—"

"I will *never* ride on the back if you're driving—even if Officer Aiello gives you private lessons for a month."

Parker's dad knelt beside Kemosabe. "Think we could push-start this—just to see if we can get it going?"

Greenwood shrugged. "As long as we raise the garage door for ventilation. And stay inside."

Harley swung a leg over Kemosabe, tapped it into neutral. Wrapped his hands around the grips.

Wilson stood on one side. Parker the other. Dad and Uncle Sammy got directly behind the bike. They pushed the thing right down the center aisle of the garage.

Harley squeezed the clutch, dropped the bike into third gear, and let the clutch out again. Immediately the engine turned over while Harley goosed the gas.

The rich, deep rumble of the straight pipes echoed throughout the garage.

Harley braked to a stop, his feet touching the floor on either side of the bike. He bowed his head, revved a few times, then finally cut the engine. For a moment, the garage seemed extra quiet.

"It's like your dad was looking out for you," Wilson said. "He gave you the bike a second time."

"The first time? Yeah, that was my dad. But this time?" Harley smiled. "It's a gift from my Father."

Dad slung his arm around Parker's shoulder. They locked eyes for a moment—and Parker saw the pride there. No, that wasn't it. It was something more. Respect. For just an instant he thought of Grandpa—and how he'd urged him to meet Harley all the way. Would they be here now if Parker had just settled for some kind of "meet you halfway" strategy?

Harley slipped the key back around his neck. Tapped his chest a couple of times with a closed fist—and pointed at Detective Greenwood. "I got no words. Thanks doesn't nearly cover this."

He kissed two fingers—and touched the gas cap. He swung off Kemosabe and marched right over to Pez. "What do you say, Mom? Think we can squeeze this thing in your shed?"

"It's *our* shed, Harley. We may have to move my collector Corvette over a bit, but we'll get Kemosabe in."

Oh yeah. It was a week of extremes. And tonight had been the best of the best. Just days ago, things had looked so dark—with no sign of dawn. But the Lord had a way of bringing unexpected light—even in darkness. Even when there hadn't been any hope or hint of light. Clearly God had been meeting Parker—and Harley—all the way. Which shouldn't have surprised Parker as much as it did. After all, God had invented the concept.

EPILOGUE

Saturday, April 29

Saturday night, Parker, Harley, and Wilson met the girls for S'morey Time. S'mores over a small shore fire at the Headlands, to be followed by Ella's story—which by now had reached some kind of legendary status. Kit stayed with Pez—who was visiting Grams.

For maximum effect, Ella insisted they leave the Headlands and follow her to the Masterson house so she could tell the story there. It was one of those three-story homes built for sea captains back in the day. Completely dark and shrouded by towering trees that had been hiding its secrets for nearly a hundred years.

Parker stood at the six-foot iron fence that guarded the property. Gripped a pair of the heavy spires. "Total overkill. Nobody in their right mind would step inside that place."

"You think that fence is there to stop unwanted visitors from going inside?" El shook her head. "It's about keeping what's inside from getting *out*."

Wilson snickered.

"It's haunted." Ella stated it like a scientific fact. "You all know that, right?"

Nobody answered. They just stood along the fence, taking in the sight of the creepy place.

"There's nothing scarier than a haunted house," Ella said. "Nothing."

"Except alligators," Wilson said. "Sharks. Serial Killers. Cat 5 hurricanes. Diving sixty feet from the surface and knowing you don't have enough air to make it back. Being on the wrong end of a taser—when you're up to your neck in water. Take your pick. Any of those are *way* scarier than a haunted house. To me, this old firetrap doesn't even make the 'kinda scary' list."

"We'll see." She was quiet for several moments. "It was incredibly dark—just like tonight. The kind of dark that clings to you—and won't let go. It was as if the long, bony fingers of the night pressed and probed, searching for a way inside, into your very soul."

"And on that very night—the night before Halloween, 1938— Jedidiah and Eliza Masterson met their untimely deaths. Here."

She paused, as if knowing they'd all be staring at the place.

"The bizarre set of falling dominoes that led to the dual demise started, strangely enough, with Orson Welles—and a dramatic radio program describing an alien invasion in real time. He wasn't just reading some script. He weaved the story so convincingly that listeners believed the invasion was really happening. His infamous *War of the Worlds* broadcast toppled the first domino."

She paused for a second. "When it came to describing a Martian invasion, Welles served up a regular three-course dinner—and Jedidiah swallowed every bite. Jedidiah and Eliza hunkered over the radio with the dial tuned to CBS. They'd snuffed out every lamp in the house. They feared the invading aliens would see the lights and incinerate them with a Martian heat ray.

"Convinced the world was doomed, Jedidiah scrawled out a note— and stuck it to the organ with a wad of Juicy Fruit gum. Jedidiah and his pretty wife, Eliza, would rather die than fall into alien hands. His note ended with these four words: *They'll never get us.*"

Ella looked Parker in the eyes, as if she wanted to make sure he hadn't missed a word. Then she zeroed in on Harley, and Parker couldn't help but do the same. Honestly, Harley's mouth must have gone dirt dry. His Adam's apple was working like he was having an awful time swallowing. Wilson didn't look any better.

Ella pointed to a silhouetted gable rising high on the dark roofline. "That's the organ loft—where a Wurlitzer pipe organ still sits. Jedidiah pushed his sweet Eliza from that open third-story window—proving him right about one thing, anyway." She paused long enough for Parker to picture the woman falling. Screaming. "The aliens never got his dear wife . . . but the Reaper sure did."

Parker rubbed down goosebumps rising on his arms—but caught himself. The slightest smile turned up one corner of Ella's mouth. *Terrific.* Busted.

"Jedidiah slung a noose over a rafter high above the old organ . . . and hung himself. The theory goes that the dead weight caused the rope to stretch. Or maybe it was his neck. But either way, it was just enough for his big toe to settle on one of the keys—A-sharp, to be precise."

Ella cocked her head slightly and paused—like she could actually hear it.

"That one eerie note—ghosting out the open window—eventually led to the discovery of the bodies. Neighbors heard the incessant, mournful tone—and called the police to investigate."

Parker rested his forehead against the cold iron of the fencing now. Wilson's smirk had vanished. He stared at the place—like he could see Jedidiah Masterson . . . stiff with rigor mortis. That big toe . . . holding down the key.

"For years afterward, neighbors claimed they heard the organ on especially dark nights—and definitely on the anniversary of the murder-suicide. Unable to stand it any longer, one brave fisherman vowed to break into the house and disassemble that demon pipe organ so it would never play again."

"A stick of dynamite would do the job," Wilson said.

Ella stared at him. He raised both hands in apology and motioned for her to continue.

"The fisherman went in with his toolbox. He removed every one of the pipes—and stacked them beside the Wurlitzer. Essentially, he'd removed the organ's voice box. But something happened just as he finished—he never would say what. He flew out of the house like a bat out of a very dark cave—leaving the tools and organ pipes behind. The man never went back for them either. He lost his voice in a way too—because he never spoke about it again."

"That's *total* baloney," Wilson said. His voice cracked when he said it, which made him sound a whole lot less convincing. "You promised us a *scary* story. This doesn't even rate. It's just an empty house. Probably isn't a harmonica inside, much less an organ."

"That's easy to say on *this* side of the fence, Wilson." Ella locked elbows with Jelly and turned to face him. "But I'll bet you wouldn't talk quite so tough if you were on the *other* side."

Wilson seemed to be sizing up the house. "I'll prove just how unscary that place is."

"*Un*scary?" Jelly shook her head. "I don't think that's a word, Wilson."

"Whatever." He waved her off. "I'll go inside the fence. No—inside the *house*. With Bucky and Harley. I got my new phone here. We'll go to the third floor and take a group selfie with that make-believe organ—or the stack of pipes. Will that be enough to prove just how *unscary* we see this place?"

Parker absolutely believed Wilson was bluffing. Maybe the girls would guess that too. But would they take that chance? Not if the house was as dangerous as they made it sound. They'd back down before Wilson did something stupid just to prove his point—and dragged Parker and Harley with.

Jelly pointed to a barely visible line of graffiti painted above the front doors of the place. "*Welcome to Hotel California.* Did you read that, Wilson—or are you still sounding it out?"

"What?" By the confused look on his face, he missed the shout-out to the old song.

"You can check in anytime you want," Parker quoted.

Jelly looked happy that one of them got the reference. "But you can *never* leave."

"This is soooo bogus." Wilson shook the bars like he was testing them. "Third floor. Selfie. Us three men. We're doing this. You with us, girls?"

Ella shook her head. "Not even a little bit."

"Girls." Wilson circled his ear with his finger and pointed at them. "They talk tough, but the truth? Hot air. Cold feet."

For an instant, it looked like Jelly was going to let him have it. Instead, she set her jaw in that way she did when she'd made her mind up about something.

"We go in. Climb to the organ loft." Wilson nodded like it was as simple as ordering a pizza. "We take a selfie. And we're heroes. Local legends."

"You still have to get back *out*," Ella said.

Wilson snickered. "Easy-peasy. Right, amigos?"

Parker wasn't quite as gung ho as Wilson. Even Harley looked perfectly happy to stay outside the fence.

Maybe Wilson took their silence as agreement. "And as a bonus, we'll bring you back one of those organ pipes as a souvenir—*if* they exist."

Jelly's eyes narrowed. "I don't doubt you're stupid enough to go in—but you *really* think you boys can get out of there without wetting your pants?"

Okay, if Parker was on the fence, he was off it after that comment. "We'll be just fine, right, guys?" They'd squeeze in one more adventure before Wilson got on the bus in the morning.

Jelly checked her replacement phone. "If you're going in, might as well go big. We want a picture of you three—with the organ behind you—after ten o'clock. I'd rather have you do it at midnight, but that isn't going to fly at home."

After ten *did* sound scarier than going now—even though it only meant waiting another twenty minutes. "Done. You girls going to be all right out here, all *alone* without us?"

"Don't you boys worry about us."

"Trust me," Wilson said. "We're not."

Parker agreed. In fact, a tiny bit of him hoped Jelly and Ella would get totally spooked while the guys went inside. He pictured it. The three of them climbing back over the iron fence—carrying one of those organ pipes. The girls running to them—cheeks terror-streaked with tears. Shaking. Clinging to the boys like they'd never let them go. Oh, yeah . . . this was going to be good.

Ella eyed the boarded windows of the Masterson house. "Last chance, boys. How about you give this up."

"Nooo thanks," Wilson said. "You'll hold it over our heads forever. Do we look like we've got the heebie-jeebies, Ella?"

"No . . . but you should," she whispered. "There is nothing scarier than a haunted house. Why can't you admit that?"

The boys laughed. Loud. It sounded a little forced to Parker, but hopefully the volume made up for it.

The girls didn't seem amused. "Ten o'clock. Take pictures. We'll be waiting for you at Grams's house—on the front porch."

Parker smiled. The girls were too afraid to even wait outside the Masterson house alone? That figured.

"If you're not on my porch by ten thirty, I'm making a phone call." Ella backed away.

Wilson made an exaggerated show of looking over his shoulder. "Who you gonna call?"

She smiled and hummed a few bars from *Ghostbusters*—another song from another era.

Wilson had walked right into it—but seemed clueless. "You're such a girl."

"Says the *brave* boy who hasn't even gone inside the haunted house yet—or climbed to the third floor."

"We'll see you, girls"—Parker checked the time—"in less than an hour . . . ten thirty. On your front porch."

"With"—Wilson got all in Jelly's face—"dry pants."

Jelly smiled. "Lord willing." She locked elbows with Ella and walked along the iron fence. They turned the corner, and with one final wave, they were gone.

Not twenty minutes later, at the stroke of ten, Parker, Wilson, and Harley scaled the fence and worked their way to the back of the house. They found a broken window with a couple of boards missing. All three of them flipped on their flashlight apps and swung them around inside the opening. Parker wished he'd brought a real flashlight. And Jimbo.

"We going in?" Wilson held his light under his chin, forming scary shadows on his face. "Or are we too afraid of what's inside?"

Turning back wasn't an option. Squeezing through was tight, but Parker did it.

Wilson pulled one more board free before going inside. "It'll be easier for me this way. And quicker for us to get out, right?"

Parker expected the house to be dead quiet. But it wasn't. He looked at the other two to see if they heard the creaks overhead. "Mice?"

"Rats."

Whatever it was, Parker hoped they'd crawl back into the dark hole they'd come from. And then? All creaking stopped. *Creepy.* "Either we go up to the loft—or we get out. But let's not stay here."

Wilson led the way, but even as they climbed the stairs, Parker couldn't shake the uneasy sense they were being watched. Cobwebs clung to Parker's face—and he clawed them free.

They found the loft—and the massive organ was actually there. The vintage Wurlitzer hunkered next to the window—where Eliza had gotten her push to the promised land. Parker froze. Stacked to one side stood piles of metal organ pipes—just like Ella said. Big ones. Small ones. The pipes actually *had* been removed from the organ?

"Holy Toledo," Harley whispered. "Hol—eee . . . To-leeedo."

The keyboard was covered with dust. Parker stared. One key was depressed as if an invisible finger held it down. Or was it a big toe?

Wilson picked at what looked like a marble-sized dab of putty stuck to one side of the keyboard. His eyes went wide. "Juicy Fruit?"

Parker wouldn't bet against it. The sense that they should vamoose got stronger. "We've already been here too long."

"Let's get the picture," Harley said, "grab one of those organ pipes from the stack—and skedaddle out of here."

Wilson swiped his phone onto the camera app. "We'll show those girls what real men are all about—and that we aren't afraid of a haunted house."

Parker gave him a sideways look. "Except we don't *actually* think it's haunted."

Wilson held his phone just below his chin so the flashlight app created creepy shadows under his eyes again. "Oh, I totally believe the house is haunted. Murder? Suicide? I mean, look at the place. There's something way off here. I'm just saying *we* aren't afraid—even though the place *is* haunted."

"Sheesh, Wilson," Parker said. "I can't believe you swallowed Ella's story."

"And I can't believe *you* can't accept the obvious." Wilson slid the organ bench to the wall opposite where the organ stood and propped his phone on top. "I want as much of the organ in this shot as we can get. You two get ready."

Parker knelt in front of the big old Wurlitzer, and Harley took a knee too. Parker wasn't wild about having his back to the thing—and Harley kept glancing over his shoulder, like he expected the thing to reach out and grab them.

Wilson set the timer for ten seconds—and pushed the button. He hustled over and knelt right beside Harley and Parker. "Big smiles, gentlemen! Say Jelly!"

The seconds reeled by. *Seven. Six. Five.*

A slow, steady note rose from behind them—from the Wurlitzer organ—even though every pipe had been disconnected.

Wilson screamed bloody murder—his voice rising octaves higher than the pipe wailing. Parker and Harley joined his choir. The camera flashed—blinding Parker for an instant.

Still—the pipe wailed. Louder. *Louder.* And closer!

Survival instinct kicked in. Raw. Primitive. Parker found his legs and scrambled for the door—right behind Wilson and Harley. They pounded down the stairs and tore down the hallway.

Wilson kicked more boards off the first-floor window and dove through, doing a tuck-and-roll thing on the black soil. Harley and Parker followed.

Parker hit the iron fence and clawed his way to the top, vaulting over to the other side right behind Wilson and Harley. His T-shirt snagged the spear-tip end topping a spire, but he ripped free.

Harley's running back abilities burst out of hibernation, and he pulled ahead. Parker ran shoulder to shoulder with Wilson. Over a rock wall, through a yard, down a driveway—and right down the middle of the street.

Harley ran three blocks before stopping. He planted his hands on the trunk of an ancient tree and leaned into it. Parker pounded to a stop and rested his hands on his knees, sucking wind. Wilson dropped in beside him, breathing heavy, pacing, hands on hips and eyes on the stars above.

Parker kept his eyes peeled—fighting back the ridiculous thought that whatever they'd encountered in the organ loft was following their scent.

"Okay," Harley said. "*What* just happened back there?"

Wilson stopped pacing but didn't turn his back on the Masterson place. "You *know* what happened. We just encountered the other side, man. And don't you say ghosts aren't real, Bucky. You were there."

Parker couldn't argue. Not that he agreed with Wilson, but he hadn't caught his breath enough to speak.

"We don't believe in ghosts," Harley said. "Right, Parks?"

Parker nodded.

"Yeah? Well, we stepped into the twilight zone—the supernatural," Wilson said. "Ghosts. Zombies. Evil spirits. Phantom presence. The undead. Call it whatever you want . . . but *something* was there."

"Ghosts don't exist," Parker said, finally. "But demons do."

"Like that's any better?" Wilson stared at him, wide-eyed. "So we're in agreement. We all survived a brush with demons—or *something* from the other side."

"What do we tell the girls?" Harley's question was legit. "We talked a big game before they left."

"We tell them nothing," Wilson said. "Or we'll never hear the end of it. We aren't due until ten thirty. We stall here for a bit. Catch our breath. Walk up to Grams's place slow and easy—like nothing happened."

The girls would see right through them, wouldn't they? "What do we do when they ask to see the picture?"

"Hold on." Wilson patted his pocket and groaned. "I left my new phone on the organ bench."

Parker checked the time. "There's still time to go back—if we hustle."

"Are you *totally* loose?" Wilson held his head with both hands. "We just faced off against the supernatural—and lived to keep our mouths shut about it. I'm not going back."

"We were supposed to get one of those organ pipes, too," Harley said.

Wilson stared down the block in the direction of the Masterson house. "We're *not* going back."

"No picture. No pipe." Harley looked from Parker to Wilson. "We got no proof we even went in."

"Maybe we should forget meeting the girls tonight." Even as Parker said it, he knew it wouldn't fly. To not show was worse than showing up empty-handed.

"We *have* to go," Wilson said. "But we say nothing about the music. They'll think we've lost it—like . . . we've completely gone off the rails."

They were still disagreeing about exactly what to say when they approached Grams's porch. Jelly and Ella were there, sitting on the swing with a blanket across their laps, smiling and chattering about something. Kit sat on the porch beside them, head on Ella's lap. She ran to meet Harley, bowling right into him.

"Right on time." Ella waved and motioned them over.

"Let me handle this, gentlemen," Wilson said. He took the lead and strode up the porch steps.

"Well, if it isn't our three fearless heroes," Jelly said. "Looks like your pants are dry. Where's the organ pipe?"

"You should've been there," Wilson said. "Creepy place. But cool, you know? We saw the organ."

"Let's see the pictures."

"Yeah, well, we seem to have lost my phone. Crazy, right?"

"Or convenient." Jelly pointed at Parker's ripped T-shirt. "Looks like a phone isn't the only thing you boys lost. But you got a picture, right? A shot to show our three brave heroes in action?"

She could drill down all she wanted, but Wilson looked determined not to tell them what really happened in the organ loft. "I saw the flash. So I guess there's a picture. I never checked, but I'm sure it's good. If we find the phone—"

Ella pulled her phone out from under the blanket. "Somebody actually sent a photo to *my* phone—from yours." She had her phone open to the photo gallery. "Looks like you caught a picture in the organ loft all right . . . and you're right . . . it's really, *really* good." She angled the screen to give the boys a better view.

It definitely was the picture taken with the self-timer. Mouths gaping. Eyes panicked. All three of them in motion, clearly trying to escape. Parker stared at the screen.

"How on *earth* . . . ?" Harley looked equally confused.

Wilson grabbed Parker by his ripped T-shirt—and pulled him aside. "I don't know how they got that, but we're out of here. C'mon, Harley."

"Looks like the boys are on the run *again*," Ella said. "But just not in such a panic this time."

"Don't even look at them." Wilson marched down the porch steps. "We're *not* giving them the satisfaction. Until we figure out how they got that picture—"

Suddenly Parker heard it. That same mournful note they'd heard in the organ loft. All three of them stopped dead. Parker whirled around.

Jelly stood there, her mouth on the narrow end of a pipe from that Wurlitzer . . . no more than twenty inches long. "Sound familiar, boys? And it happens to be A-sharp."

"You two . . . were there?" Wilson looked stunned. "You went in—ahead of us?"

Parker was just as blown away. The girls fought all their fears of the place—just for the joy of pranking the three of them? That was incredibly . . . *amazing*.

"How do you think we got this?" Ella held up Wilson's phone. "We were squeezed in tight behind the organ. You might have checked there . . . but you all were too busy scrambling to get out of the room—and screaming."

Jelly looked way too proud of herself. "I'd say Wilson's was more of a prepubescent shriek."

"That was my Miccosukee war cry."

"Well, whatever you call that, it was terrifying." Ella sat on the porch railing. "Admit it boys. Gators. Sharks. Crazed killers. All of them absolutely scary stuff. But there's nothing scarier—not even for you three *brave* heroes—than a haunted house. And we've got the picture to prove it."

"Okay. Okay." Wilson held both hands up. "I'll admit . . ." He paused for a few moments while they all waited. "Actually . . . I'll admit nothing." He grinned. "And that's all I've got to say."

The girls broke out laughing. They hugged each other like they'd won some major victory. Maybe they had. But in that moment, Parker knew—more than ever before—that this bond they had, the five of them, wasn't something that would break. Not ever. Wilson would be back to visit. There'd be lots more adventures—for sure.

"Actually?" Harley raked the hair off his forehead with one hand. "I can think of one thing that's scarier than gators, sharks, bad guys—and yeah . . . even a haunted house. And I think all three of us agree on this." He looked directly at Parker like he wanted to be sure they were on the same wavelength.

Parker was pretty sure they were. "The one thing scarier than a haunted house? That's easy." He slung his arms around Wilson and Harley. "Girls."

Jelly and Ella shrieked in what could only be described as total delight. Jelly snagged Parker's cap and slapped it on her head. "And don't you boys *ever* forget that!"

Parker smiled. "Forgetting would be absolutely impossible." He believed that with all his heart.

The girls would never let them.

NOTE FROM THE AUTHOR

HAVE YOU EVER WATCHED A MOVIE and loved it, but then found the sequel disappointing? That sometimes happens with books, too. But I didn't want it to happen with the High Water series. I prayed that somehow God would make each book better than the last, and I believe he answered my prayers. *Even in Darkness* is probably my favorite book of the series!

I love how Parker—and Harley, too—are growing into Christian young men of character and integrity. In this book, Parker learned something important about relationships, about meeting others all the way—not just halfway. It's something I've personally been working on for a long time and have found to be life-changing.

I also love how our friends faced the darkness growing around them. Maybe you've experienced times when there's no light at the end of the tunnel—none that you could see, anyway. But God can bring light when it seems like there is no hope. He can transform a dark situation and bring light into our lives, even if we can't imagine how. I've seen it again and again. Recall the Bible verse that Grandpa gave Parker: "Even in darkness light dawns for the upright, for those who are gracious and compassionate and righteous" (Psalm 112:4).

As you've experienced the adventures of Parker, Angelica, Harley, Ella, and Wilson, I hope they have helped you gain wisdom that will make a difference in your life in powerful ways. That's one of the things

I was praying for as I wrote. And I pray you'll cling tight to God and His love and mercy. I've found Him to be so faithful—I'd be lost without Him.

I've loved writing this series, and I would love to hear from you. Contact me through my website: TimShoemaker.com. Tell me what you liked about the stories. And then go online and post a review for each book—it makes a big difference!

What's next for me? By God's grace, more stories like the ones you've enjoyed. By the time you read this, I'll be working hard on the first story of a new series. I'm also working on a book for young men. The proposed title is *The Way This Works . . . Becoming the Man God Designed You to Be*. Watch for it.

Thanks for reading, my friend!

Writing by God's grace, and for His Glory. For my good—and for yours!
Tim Shoemaker

SPECIAL THANKS TO . . .

Jim Olsen: My dive buddy, brother-in-law, and good friend, thank you for encouraging me to take the advanced scuba classes with you—and for planning the dives in the Florida Keys. The extra experience gained definitely helped with making the diving scenes in *Even in Darkness* that much more real!

Rockport Harbormasters Scott Story and Rosemarie Lesch: For again going above and beyond the call of duty. I loved sitting in your office and hearing stories from both of you. Remember when I said I'd heard there were no sharks in the area? I laughed as you straightened me out and talked about the great white sharks nearby. Learning that the seal population draws the sharks made a nice addition to this story. And thank you for the tour of *Alert 1* and the ride out into the harbor. I got so much more than great input from you, and I have two new friends.

Dave and Cyndi Darsch: For finding ways to provide a great place for me to write whenever I visited Florida. Your idea this past February may just have been your most creative one yet!

The Team at Dunkin: When I needed a change of pace to write, you provided a great spot. Tina, Palak, Sheetal, Raksha, Sara, Arpita, Sudheer, and Arpita S., thank you for your hospitality. You greet me by name and with a smile, often anticipating my order before I even get the words out. I may be racking up loyalty points every time I visit, but you all are a big reason why I keep coming back!

Carlos, Iris, Adolfo, Alex, and the crew at Culver's: Thank you for a great place to write when I wanted a comfy booth and an order of french fries or a shake. You know your customers, and I always feel like you're happy I stopped in. Thank you for making your restaurant a nice atmosphere for me to work in.

Matt, Giancarlo, Emily, and the crew at Blackwood BBQ: The moment I step out of my truck and inhale that classic barbecue aroma, I'm already smiling. That's a great way to start my work time. The tall tables with the stools, the music, the mood of the place, and your friendliness all combine to make this one of my favorite places to visit. Thanks for that!

Nancy Rue: Thank you to my mentor, friend, and encourager. It seems each book is so different in the challenges it brings. As I finished this one, you gave me valuable advice about taking time off that proved to be exactly what I needed.

Larry Weeden and Danny Huerta: I'm so grateful for your support! Dear brothers, you completely understand the readers we're seeking to reach and impact. It is such an encouragement to know we're on the same page—and the same team.

Vance Fry: Thank you for your steady editing and the terrific job you did in making the story stronger. Your bits of encouragement have meant a ton to me throughout the series, especially on *Even in Darkness*.

Cheryl: I'm so grateful for a wife who supports and encourages me the way you do. You're the first one to read everything I write—you've been such a huge help to me! You gave me a key piece of feedback for *The Deep End*—which changed the ending completely. And there were ripple effects that impacted *The Second Storm*—and massively came into play with how *Even in Darkness* ended. Your input was right on target, and this book is absolutely better for it. I love you, Babe!

My Lord and God: You deserve all my thanks. The things You've brought me through as we wrote the High Water series . . . the things You've taught me . . . absolutely amazing! Through every struggle, every fear, every triumph . . . You were there. And if someone reads carefully, they'll see You in the story too. Between the lines. You are the heart of the story. Thanks again for the joy of writing this series with You. I am Your man . . . forever!

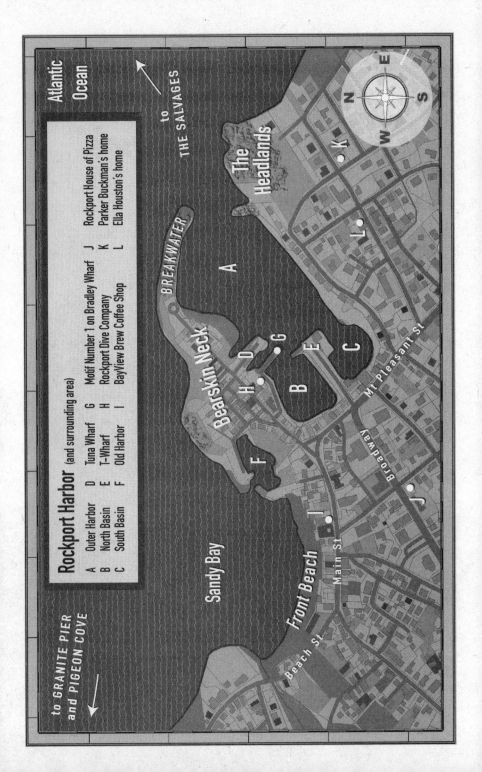

Rockport Harbor (and surrounding area)

A Outer Harbor
B North Basin
C South Basin
D Tuna Wharf
E T-Wharf
F Old Harbor
G Motif Number 1 on Bradley Wharf
H Rockport Dive Company
I BayView Brew Coffee Shop
J Rockport House of Pizza
K Parker Buckman's home
L Ella Houston's home

Atlantic Ocean

to THE SALVAGES

to GRANITE PIER and PIGEON COVE

Sandy Bay

Front Beach

BREAKWATER

Bearskin Neck

The Headlands

Beach St

Main St

Broadway

Mt Pleasant St

N E S W

More from Tim Shoemaker!

Check out these suspenseful adventures in the
High Water™ novel series.

Whether he's facing down alligators in Florida or ghosts in Massachusetts, Parker Buckman keeps finding himself right in the middle of a mystery ... **and danger!**

Join Parker as he risks everything to help his friends and learns to trust in God's perfect timing.

Keep an eye out for more books to come!

Read *Easy Target*, another great novel by Tim Shoemaker!

Taking on bullies comes with hidden danger ... becoming one yourself. Ex-homeschooler Hudson Sutton is thrust into public school his eighth-grade year. He's an outsider—and an easy target. When he sticks up for "Pancake" he makes two allies—and plenty of enemies.

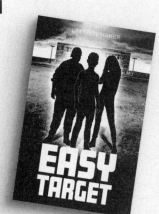

Get these books, and more, at:
FocusOnTheFamily.com/HighWater